OUTER PERIMETER

ALSO BY KEN GODDARD

First Evidence
Balefire
The Alchemist
Prey
Wildfire
Cheater
Double Blind

BANTAM BOOKS

NEW YORK TORONTO LONDON

SYDNEY AUCKLAND

OUTER PERIMETER

KEN GODDARD

OUTER PERIMETER
A Bantam Book / February 2001

Library of Congress Cataloging-in-Publication Data

Goddard, Kenneth W. (Kenneth William)
Outer perimeter / Ken Goddard.
p.   cm.
ISBN 0-553-10883-2
1. Government investigators—Fiction. 2. Indians of North America—Fiction.
3. Human-alien encounters—Fiction. 4. Oregon—Fiction. I. Title.

PS3557.O285 O98 2001
813'.54—dc21   00-064232

Published simultaneously in the United States and Canada

PRINTED IN THE UNITED STATES OF AMERICA

BVG   10   9   8   7   6   5   4   3   2   1

This book is dedicated to Terry, my treasured brother-in-law, who faced and fought the outer perimeter with courage and humor and good faith . . . in a manner that can only be described as heroic.

ACKNOWLEDGMENTS

My sincere thanks to Bob, Naomi, Jody, and Terry, who continued to provide the critical inspiration for this ongoing story. And to Gena, Michelle, Ed, Elliott, Bucky, Judy, and Gina, who checked facts, figures, context, fantasy, and spelling with unfaltering good humor. And, last, but certainly not least, to Anne Groell, my dear editor, who worked the final manuscript into much better shape, and was trusting and patient beyond belief.

AUTHOR'S NOTE

For the folks who don't happen to reside in the beautiful and infinitely variable state of Oregon, and therefore might be curious, as well as skeptical: There is no Bancoo Indian tribe, living inside or out of the equally fictitious county of Jasper, Oregon. Both are simply artifacts of my imagination . . . and the latter a place where I can create havoc with my characters amongst the local authorities and politicians without risking a felony traffic stop or subpoena.

In this same regard, I have no reason to think my real-life special agent buddy, Bob Dawson, is actually flying Apache helicopters for any federal agency, or that the NSA has been busy constructing extraterrestrial research centers in or around ethereal Jasper County landscape— which, if it did exist, would probably be tucked away, in some clever space-time-warp fold, just a little north of Jackson, Josephine, and Klamath counties . . . and perhaps just a bit south of Douglas and Deschutes. Which is pretty much where you'd also find the Twelfth Circuit Court.

But as for the Kray-Sacs themselves, and their army of fervent believers . . . well, it is a big universe out there . . . and this is, after all, Oregon.

—Ken Goddard

"HALLUCINATION: AN EXTREMELY RARE PHENOMENON, IN WHICH A COMPLETELY CONVINCING REALITY SURROUNDS A PERSON, WITH HIS EYES OPEN, A REALITY THAT HE ALONE CAN EXPERIENCE AND INTERACT WITH."

—Alexander Shulgin and Ann Shulgin, *Tihkal*
—*Places in the Mind,* Transform Press, 1997.

EXCERPTS FROM THE FIELD NOTEBOOK
OF OSP DETECTIVE-SERGEANT COLIN CELLARS

STATE OF OREGON
Twelfth Circuit Court:

Hon. David W. MacMullen, Circuit Court Judge

Oregon State Patrol
OSP (Salem) Headquarters:

Alice Hightower	Major, Internal Affairs Commander Acting Region 9 Commander

Region 9 Office:

Rodney Hawkins	Captain, Regional Commander (status: missing . . . assumed dead)
Don Talbert	Captain (provisional) (status: on leave . . . injured on duty)
Tom Bauer	Patrol Sergeant, Acting Watch Commander
Colin Cellars	Detective-Sergeant, CSI
Alex Espinoza	Detective-Sergeant, Major Crimes
Dick Waldrip	Patrol Sergeant
Michael Lee	Trooper, CSI
Ruth Wilkinson	Front Desk Clerk

OSP (Medford) Crime Laboratory:

Jack Wilson	Supervising Serologist

JASPER COUNTY, OREGON
Jasper County Coroner's Office

Morgue:

Dr. Elliott Sutta	Chief Pathologist
Kathy Buckhouse	Lab Assistant

US FISH AND WILDLIFE SERVICE
Division of Law Enforcement

Jasper County Resident Agent Office:

Wilbur Boggs	Special Agent

National Fish and Wildlife Forensics Laboratory:

Dr. Jody Catlin	Senior Forensic Scientist (DNA)
Melissa Washington	Forensic Scientist (DNA)

US DRUG ENFORCEMENT ADMINISTRATION
Internal Affairs Division

Western Regional Office:

Elizabeth Mardeaux	Supervisory Special Agent

US NATIONAL SECURITY AGENCY
Office of Technical Support

Waycross Laser Research Center:

Bernard Lackman	Project Director
Dr. Malcolm Byzor	Deputy Project Director/Chief Scientist
Dr. Eric Marston	Senior Research Associate
Arkaminus Gregorias	Special Agent in Charge, Security
Dr. Jason Cohan	Chief Programmer
Dr. Bill Dobres	Design Engineer
Valerie Sandersohn	Laboratory Technician

US ARMY
Special Operations

Eighth Delta Forces Detachment:

Mike Montgomery	Captain, Detachment Commander
John Kessler	Lieutenant, Team Leader
Ed Dombrowski	Staff Sergeant

THE BANCOOS:

Rascoos Rain-Song	The old man
Lonecoos Sun-Chaser	The younger man
Lastcoos Sun-Chaser	The youngest man
Cascadia Rain-Song	The old man's daughter
Kray-Sacs	Mythical creatures from Bancoo legends

MISCELLANEOUS PLAYERS:

Bob Dawson	Friend of Colin Cellars
Patrick Bergéone	Photojournalist
Claire-Anne Leduc	Journalist Friend of Patrick Bergéone
Yvie Byzor	Wife of Malcolm Byzor
Eleanor Patterson	President of the Alliance of Believers
Allesandra	Friend of Bob Dawson
Dr. H. Milhaus Pleausant	Psychiatrist

PROLOGUE

"I'M SORRY, SIR," THE DISPATCHER SAID IN A PROFESSIONALLY patient voice, "but we never release the home phone numbers or duty schedules of our officers. If you'd like to leave a message, I'll be happy to transfer you to his voice mail."

"But I've already done that, many—" Patrick Bergéone started to say in an exasperated voice, then shook his head. "Yes, please."

Bergéone waited for the automated message system to wind through its routine, then spoke carefully into the mouthpiece.

"Hello? Detective-Sergeant Colin Cellars? This is Patrick Bergéone calling once again, and I am hoping you will be able to call me back very soon. It is most important that I speak with you. It is Saturday now, and the time is"—he glanced down at his wristwatch—"almost ten o'clock in the morning. I am here in Jasper Springs, at the Wind Shelter Lodge. Please call me here, or on my cell phone, as soon as you can."

He recited the phone numbers, hung up the phone, then turned his attention back to the screen of the small television on his motel-room dresser.

It had been threatening rain all morning, and the predictions were getting worse. Four to five inches now, with plenty of thunder and lightning to make things interesting, according to the weatherman, who stood next to a wall-size satellite map with a glum look on his face. The colorful graphics showed why. Another massive cold front dropping down fast out of British Columbia, bringing with it a typical Canadian mix of sleet, snow, and negative temperatures. Within twenty-four to thirty-six hours, according to the weatherman, the rain- and ground-water would start turning into ice and slush, thereby making life miserable for anyone unfortunate enough to be out on the roadways.

Bergéone got up from the thinly padded motel-room chair, pulled back the drapes to stare out at the darkening thunderheads, sighed deeply, then went back to his chair. He used the remote to scan through the available channels, finally settling on an old black-and-white Western.

By 10:30 A.M., the sidewalks around the small town of Jasper Springs, Oregon, were almost completely deserted as the local residents remained indoors, waiting patiently for the predicted downpour to begin.

At 11:00 A.M., the winds began to pick up . . . and by 11:15, the ionic concentrations in the air had become more noticeable.

But still no rain . . . and still no response from Detective-Sergeant Cellars.

Finally, around 11:30, when he could no longer tolerate the movie's stilted dialogue, or his persistently silent telephone, Patrick Bergéone grabbed his raincoat and headed for the door. There was always the chance that the United States weathermen were no better at predicting the weather than their European counterparts.

Thus, when the deluge finally did begin, a few minutes before noon, the sudden pressure drop was almost jarring.

Bergéone was several blocks away from his motel, crossing in front of a dark, gloomy, single-story building bearing an old, hand-painted wooden sign that read THE LONG SHOT SALOON when he felt the air go still. He ducked under an awning just as heavy raindrops began to descend.

As the intensity of the rainfall increased, Bergéone realized his light raincoat was completely inadequate. He would never get back to his motel room without being thoroughly drenched. So he looked around at his available options, and decided that a saloon—even a dark and gloomy one—might be an excellent place to wait out the storm.

He saw them as soon as he stepped through the open doorway: three rough-looking, knife-scarred, and moderately sober Native Americans with dark eyes, shoulder-length black hair, and reddish bronze skin. They were huddled together around a crude table fashioned from an overturned fiber-optic cable spool in the darkened corner opposite the six-stool bar.

Bergéone hesitated.

Finding himself in a potentially dangerous situation was not a new experience. As an aggressive French photojournalist who traveled all over the world on his assignments, such occurrences had long since become a way of life. Which meant he was always prepared to make a quick and discreet exit . . . ideally before he became the focus of attention.

But the three men in the corner barely glanced in his direction. And the rain was coming down even harder now, which narrowed his options considerably. An investigative reporter on the TV set over the bar was describing the first in a mysterious series of cathedral desecrations in the Loire Valley of France. So he walked in, sat at the barstool farthest from the open doorway—which turned out to be the one closest to their table—ordered a beer, and made a halfhearted effort to focus his attention on the familiar images.

Which was how he happened to be close enough to hear those first intriguing words.

I won't take you there.

To Bergéone, who'd had few contacts with Native Americans over the course of his travels in the US, the two younger men looked like they might have been in their mid-twenties. And the older one, who wore a faded headband over his tied-back locks, could have been forty or even sixty. He really couldn't tell. Nor did he have any idea as to their possible tribal origins, much less of their current problems in life.

It was an unfortunate gap in his knowledge of American history and culture that Patrick Bergéone would later regret. For had he spent a little more time researching the history of Jasper County, Oregon, Bergéone might have immediately recognized the obsidian amulets around the necks of these three men as being characteristic of a small and isolated tribe of Native Americans known as the Ah-Ree-Ban-Coo-Taks.

Or, more simply, the Bancoos.

And that being the case, he might have recalled the recent series of local newspaper articles describing, in some detail, the suspicious circumstances surrounding the disappearance of a young Bancoo woman named Cascadia. A young woman who, according to the reporter, had been the last purebred, fertile, and unmarried female of the tribe . . . or, at least, the last one willing to acknowledge her reproductive status and Bancoo ancestry.

Which, in turn, might have caused him to remember the reporter's vivid description of the seething hatred the few remaining Bancoo men held for their white brethren. That is, the "thieving, bastard white-eyes" who'd been luring their women away for generations with whispered dreams of fancy clothes and pretty jewelry . . . and now, with even more tempting promises of VCRs, shopping malls, and maid service. Thus setting the stage for the rapidly impending demise of the Bancoo tribe.

Had he known all that, and had there been no other factors involved, Bergéone would simply have relocated to a more distant stool without a second thought. Or, better still, to an even more distant table on the other side of the bar, thereby allowing the din of the incessant downpour to completely mask all traces of what was intended to be a private conversation.

But there were other factors involved.

First, and foremost, he had come to Oregon in search of stories about the lesser-known haunts of the American West that he would sell to a small, select cadre of well-paying European magazines. Stories about rumored wilderness hideaways where creatures from other worlds supposedly came together for purposes too chilling and gruesome to imagine. Such was the international reputation of southern Oregon. Or, at least, among the devoted fans of such nonsense. Which explained why there existed a small, select cadre of European magazine publishers who were perfectly willing to advance funds to satisfy the cravings of their insatiable readers. And if the rumors he'd heard about Detective-Sergeant Colin Cellars of the Oregon State Patrol were even partially true, he stood to make a small fortune.

Secondly, he was taking advantage of this publisher-paid trip to follow up on an even more intriguing story that might pay off equally well . . . if the much-better-funded investigative reporters from France2 and the German Broadcasting Corporation didn't get there first.

But most importantly, the slurred words of these three men were simply too intriguing to ignore.

Accordingly, he remained in place, sipping his beer and staring out the open doorway at the torrential rain as he tried to block out the sounds of the tin roof and the water pouring off the overwhelmed gutters. His ears were tuned to their voices, listening for the words that had first caught his attention.

I'm telling you, it's a terrible place. An evil place. I won't take you there.

There were other things being said now, most of it sounding like native slang mixed in with distinctly Anglo curses. But those eight slurred words continued to stand out from all the others. Eight words that the older one insistently muttered over and over.

An evil place. I won't take you there.

Finally, and in the face of every cautionary instinct he possessed, Bergéone decided to approach these men. The problem was how to do it safely.

The bartender provided the opportunity.

"That's sacrilegious," the beefy man muttered in response to a close-up image of freshly sheared stone where an ancient gargoyle had once stared outward with fearsome—and supposedly protective—eyes from the eight-hundred-year-old north wall of the Chartres Cathedral. An inset in the upper right-hand corner showed what the missing gargoyle had looked like. The investigative reporter was speculating how the thief could have scaled the high wall, and then gotten away without detection. Truly a fascinating mystery.

Bergéone suddenly realized that the bartender was speaking to him. "Pardon?"

"Eight cathedrals desecrated," the bartender muttered, polishing shot glasses with the white towel tucked under his apron as he stared up at the TV. "How can a person do something like that, and live with themselves?"

"Many more than eight, I'm afraid," Bergéone replied.

"What?" The bartender stopped polishing the glass in his hand and turned away from the TV to stare at the newcomer.

"It has been going on for six months now," Bergéone said. "In France, in Germany, and now in the US, too, I'm told. Gargoyles broken off of Gothic structures. Icons and statues chipped or wrenched loose from walls and altars. Even a thousand-year-old statue of the Mother herself stolen from the Loire, of all places."

"Are you saying it's the same people that's doing this . . . all over the world?" The bartender looked incredulous.

"Perhaps . . . or maybe just opportunistic thieves, how do you say it, copycatting each other?" Bergéone suggested.

"But why?"

"Probably for the money such a relic would bring in the underground markets. Or perhaps just for a personal trophy. Who can say?" Bergéone brought his shoulders up in a Gallic shrug.

"A terrible thing," the bartender muttered.

"And I'm even told such things have happened to the religious sites of your Native Americans," Bergéone suggested cautiously.

"Really? Where did you hear that?" The bartender looked curious.

"It is something I am researching . . . for a story," Bergéone explained. He made a quick gesture over his shoulder. "Do you think those men would know anything about such happenings?"

"Who, those three?" The bartender gave them a brief, reappraising glance. "I doubt it."

Bergéone sighed. "Yes, you are probably right. But who knows what stories they might have heard. And besides"—he turned his head to stare out at the open doorway—"it's a bad day to be outside."

"It is that," the bartender conceded.

"So, could you tell me the tab, please?"

"Your tab? Two beers. Five dollars."

"No, not mine." Bergéone turned his head in the general direction of the corner table. "Theirs."

The bartender hesitated, suddenly alert and wary. "That's none of your concern," he finally said.

"I understand that. But I am a friend. Will this cover it?" He removed a folded-over fifty from his shirt pocket and placed it on the bar.

The bartender ignored the money. "What do you want?"

"An introduction, *mon ami*. Just that; nothing more."

The bartender's eyes narrowed. In the past six months, he'd broken up seven Bancoo knife fights, the last with a cut-down, double-barreled shotgun he'd almost been forced to use . . . and he had no intention of putting his life on the line again for some stupid tourist. The Bancoos were dangerous and unpredictable. Everybody who lived around here knew that, and kept their distance. Even the other Oregonian native tribe members made no secret of their distaste for their supposed Indian brothers. Very dangerous and very unpredictable. Always had been, and probably always would be . . . until they went the way of the dinosaurs and the dodo birds. Which couldn't happen too soon, as far as the bartender was concerned.

"I am a friend," Bergéone insisted, putting everything he had into his best earnest expression. "A very good friend. They just don't know it yet."

It was a risky move at best, and the bartender said so . . . emphatically, and among several other things. But Bergéone had a well-deserved reputation for being foolishly brave, with a nose for a good story. And so he persisted until finally the bartender gave in.

Moments later, he placed three chilled bottles of the most expensive local microbrew on the scarred surface of the cable-spool table, bent down, whispered something to the three men, then motioned with his head in the direction of the newcomer.

The three Bancoos turned and stared at Bergéone, their dark eyes glistening with resentment . . . and something else. Hatred, perhaps? Bergéone couldn't tell. It did occur to him, however, that the bartender might be right. Perhaps he should leave now, while he still could.

But Bergéone was not a coward in any meaningful sense. So he forced himself to remain seated, determined not to show fear—just as he would have done in the wild, in the presence of any dangerous predator.

It's the only way, he told himself as he met their stare. *There is nothing else I can do.*

Finally, the older of the three turned away, stared at the rain for almost a full minute . . . then motioned for Bergéone to come over to the table.

———

Two fresh rounds later, the older one with the headband, whose name was Rascoos Rain-Song, began to speak in a flat monotone.

"We think it's possible that she may have gone to a sacred place, hidden away far in the mountains . . . built inside a deep cave . . . at a high cliff junction between the Klamath National Forest and our tribal land. It's an ancient place, once known only to the medicine man of our tribe, and very difficult to find, even if you know where you're going. But the last medicine man died very young, in an accident, many years ago. And there was no one prepared to follow in his footsteps, so the sacred place was lost for many years. It was my father—their great-uncle"—he motioned with his head at the other, younger men—"who rediscovered it when I was a child. And for a long time, he kept its location secret. And it remained that way, a secret place known only to him . . . until the day I began to follow him on his treks. I was very patient—leaving before him and placing myself where I could learn a new piece of his route each morning—until, finally, I was able to watch him stand before the entrance to the cave. That was the day I learned about the signs. And the day my father . . . had his accident."

He stopped talking then, and turned to stare out at the falling rain.

"An accident? What kind of accident?" Bergéone whispered.

The old man ignored him.

Bergéone was almost afraid to breathe, much less speak, but he couldn't let it end there. Not now.

"What signs did you learn about?" he tried again in a gentle voice.

Rascoos Rain-Song remained silent, his watery eyes still fixed on the open doorway.

Bergéone began to wonder if he hadn't pushed it too far.

"The shaman signs . . . the carvings on the rock face," the older man finally said, blinking the glassy wetness from his eyes. "The warnings to stay away."

"Away from what?"

"I don't know."

"It's the money—the gold—it has to be," Lastcoos Sun-Chaser, the youngest of the three Bancoo men, muttered. "All of the treasures the medicine men were keeping for themselves . . . and protecting with their stupid superstitions."

"Perhaps." The older man shrugged, as if to say he didn't wish to reignite a long-standing tribal argument in front of this white-eyed stranger.

"Not perhaps, Uncle, absolutely true," Lonecoos Sun-Chaser, Lastcoos's older brother, broke in. "But your father, our great-uncle, wasn't afraid of the Kray-Sacs. He told us that many times."

"Kray-Sacs?" Bergéone turned to face the old man.

"The evil ones," the old man whispered.

Patrick Bergéone's eyes lit up. He could scarcely believe his luck. "Evil ones?"

The older man nodded slowly, but his watery eyes remained on the doorway.

"Who are they?" Bergéone pressed.

"You don't want to know."

The words were barely audible over the torrential rainfall. It was as if Rascoos Rain-Song had suddenly realized his voice might carry . . . to some distant place he didn't want to think about.

"You see," Lastcoos Sun-Chaser hissed, "he's doing it to you, too. Trying to scare you away with superstitious nonsense. He's just like all the others. He wants to keep it all for himself."

"Keep what?"

"Our wealth . . . our heritage . . . and perhaps even his own daughter," the young Bancoo muttered.

The older man's head snapped around, his black eyes turning deadly cold, and the younger man immediately brought his hands up in apology.

"No, I didn't mean it that way, Uncle. I just—"

"You just want to see for yourself," the older man suggested. "To see that these fabled treasures . . . and Cascadia . . . are not there."

"Yes."

The older man paused for a long moment as the anger drained out of him. Then, finally, he seemed to shudder . . . and dropped his head in apparent resignation.

"All right, yes, I will take you both . . . to see for yourselves," he said. "I owe you that much. And why not? What do any of us have to lose now?"

The two younger men were smiling, visibly delighted by their sudden good fortune. They signaled to the bartender for another round as Bergéone said: "But what about me?"

The three Bancoos turned their heads to stare at the journalist, their black eyes locked on his. And, for the first time, Bergéone was afraid.

The older one was the first to speak.

"Why should I take you? So you can try to steal from us, too? Like all the other thieving bastard white-eyes?" he demanded.

The idea seemed to amuse Lonecoos Sun-Chaser, who made a show of brushing his fingers across the leather-wrapped grip of the hunting knife at his belt.

"Never! I don't want any of your money," Bergéone insisted quickly. "I told you, I'm a photojournalist. I can tell your story. I can tell the world about the fate of the glorious Bancoo tribe, and how the greedy Americans stole it from you."

"But you're a white-eyes, too," Lastcoos Sun-Chaser pointed out.

"No, *mon ami,* I'm French. That's different. We have always been on your side. And besides, how can I possibly steal from you when you are three and I am one . . . and I have no weapons, only my camera?" he added reasonably.

He wouldn't tell them how. And with any luck at all, he thought, they would never know.

———

That had been yesterday.

Now, twenty-five hours later, Patrick Bergéone was somewhere in the southern Oregon wilderness, crouched down against a Douglas fir, chilled and shivering, and trying to keep from sliding back down the narrow, clay-mud-and-rock ravine that was almost vertical in some parts. It had taken them half an hour to make it this far. And he knew that if he lost his footing now, he might never make it this far again, even if his camera managed to survive the fall.

This was the third such ravine they had climbed in the past two hours, this one in almost total darkness, and it was all that Bergéone could do to keep his legs and arms moving.

A few feet in front of him, the three Bancoo men were crouched on a narrow ridge. The two younger ones shivered as they examined, under the dim light of Rascoos Rain-Song's pen flashlight, what might have been the remnants of a footprint. For reasons he wasn't about to voice, Bergéone found it satisfying that the younger Bancoos were clearly in as bad shape as he was.

Or worse, perhaps. At least I don't have a head threatening to burst from a hangover.

Which was clearly not the case with Lonecoos and Lastcoos Sun-Chaser. During the last six hours, the two younger men had complained vehemently at every break, accusing Rascoos Rain-Song of being lost . . . or deliberately taking them along an unnecessarily difficult path. Both had stopped to vomit . . . Lonecoos three times so far. But every time the elder Bancoo threatened to turn back, the youthful complainers grew silent and grudgingly resumed the climb.

"See, right there," Rascoos Rain-Song was saying as he pointed with the narrow beam of his small flashlight. "Someone has been here before us . . . and not so long ago."

From Bergéone's perspective, the dimly visible "footprint" was just a smear in the clay that could have been made by anyone—or anything. But he wasn't about to tell them.

"Was it Cascadia?" Lonecoos Sun-Chaser demanded in between gasps for breath.

Ever since Cascadia's disappearance, the older Lonecoos had been increasingly insistent that she had chosen him to carry on the tribal heritage. Although, from Bergéone's sense of things, it wasn't clear that the young woman had ever expressed any interest in or intention to marry either of these Bancoo warriors. A perfectly understandable decision on her part, as far as the photojournalist was concerned.

"I don't know," the older man said simply, and resumed his climb.

Wordlessly, the two younger Bancoos and Bergéone quickly followed, laboring to stay close. Rascoos Rain-Song had been adamant that no one other than himself would bring a flashlight. And he'd been equally insistent that Bergéone leave his cell phone and the strobe light for his camera in the trunk of the car as well.

They paused again, fifteen minutes later, on a wider ridge, to eat and drink from the rations in their packs . . . which gave Bergéone time to contemplate the conversation he'd had with Rascoos Rain-Song in the car while the younger ones were in the store buying provisions.

"What did your father and your grandfather do at this sacred place?" he'd asked.

"Leave offerings," Rascoos Rain-Song had answered vaguely.

"To the gods?"

"Yes."

"Were these offerings . . . accepted?"

The older one had shrugged.

"What does it look like inside?" Bergéone had pressed.

"There is a long, narrow, winding tunnel leading to an upper chamber that is very big . . . perhaps an acre in size; perhaps larger. It's difficult to tell because the darkness is so complete. There is only the glow of the minerals in the rock walls high overhead to help you find your way, and you must wait for your eyes to adjust so that you can see anything at all."

"But what about a flashlight?"

"No! I told you, any form of light inside the chambers is absolutely forbidden."

Bergéone wanted to press the issue, but Rascoos Rain-Song went on. "In the middle, there is a square stone altar where the offerings are left, and—" He hesitated. "Next to the altar, there is a crude stairway cut into the floor leading to the lower levels."

"What's down there?"

The old man had shrugged again. "I don't know. I've only been in the upper chamber. I have never attempted to go into the tombs."

"Tombs? Do you mean people are actually buried there?"

"Perhaps." His voice seemed to catch. "My father used that word. I asked my father if our ancestors were buried down there, but he said he didn't think so. 'Bancoos don't bury their dead in stone,' he told me. Only the Kray-Sacs."

"These Kray-Sacs . . . they bury their dead in stone graves?" Bergéone had pressed again, cautiously.

"I don't know," Rascoos Rain-Song repeated. "My father said no one in the Bancoo tribe knew who built the altar and the chambers, or why . . . not even the medicine men. He learned that when he was being considered for the teaching."

"The teaching to become a medicine man himself?"

Rascoos Rain-Song had glared at him for a long moment from the driver's seat. "Yes."

"What else did they tell him?"

"That, according to legend, the place had been built over a deep crypt with many layers and many chambers within each layer . . . but that no one really knows what lies below, because no one has ever entered the lower chambers and returned to tell the tale. Not even a medicine man."

"Was that the accident you spoke about?"

"Yes."

"So your father really was being trained as a medicine man?"

The old man had hesitated. "Yes."

"Why don't you tell Lonecoos and Lastcoos that?"

"Because my father also told me other things."

"Such as?"

The old man had sighed, visibly reluctant to reveal—or, perhaps, even to remember—the words.

"That day, he took me outside and told me to stay there until he returned. And he also told me that I should never enter the cave again. That it was an evil place. And if I ever went inside again, with or without him, the Kray-Sacs would reach out for my soul. But, in any case, no matter if I went inside or not, I must never do anything to attract their attention, because if I did, they would follow me . . . and I would never escape them."

"They?"

"Yes . . . they," he said emphatically.

"Who . . . are these Kray-Sacs?"

"I don't know. My father never told me."

"So, that day, you waited outside the cave . . . and your father went back inside?"

"Yes."

"And then what did he say to you when he came out?"

"He never came out," Rascoos Rain-Song whispered softly.

Bergéone blinked in shock. "Did you call for him?" he asked finally.

"Yes, of course, for many hours . . . or so it seemed."

"And?"

"He never answered. Finally, I went back inside again and searched the entire upper chamber—on my hands and knees, mostly, because I couldn't see very well—but he wasn't there. Then, I stood at the top of the stairway behind the altar, stared down into the darkness, and called for my father over and over, hearing my voice echo from the depths—from very far away, it seemed—but he never answered."

"And you didn't—?"

The old man shook his head wordlessly.

"And this is where—" Bergéone had hesitated, almost afraid to speak the words, "you think your daughter may have gone."

The old man had nodded silently, his dark eyes filling with tears.

They spoke no more until the younger ones returned.

———————

Those were the words echoing through Patrick Bergéone's head. Not *it's an evil place*. Or *I can't take you there*. But rather:

He never came out.

And:

He never answered.

The words still sent shivers down Bergéone's spine.

According to Rascoos Rain-Song, they were near the entrance of the cave. From the place where they last rested, it had only taken another fifteen minutes to make the final climb. It involved a very cautious traverse across a narrow ledge barely six inches wide. And a long drop—at least three hundred feet, according to the old man who had briefly waved his tiny flashlight into the empty darkness before being the first to cross—if they slipped or lost their grip. The goal was a larger plateau surrounded by ancient trees that had embedded their roots in the rock hundreds of years ago.

Like the two younger Bancoos, it had taken every bit of Bergéone's remaining strength and courage to make that crossing. Which made it perfectly understandable that he would collapse at the edge of the trees.

The older man had urged him on. "We're almost there. The entrance is about thirty yards away, in through the trees," he'd said, but Bergéone had shaken his head.

"No, I must rest for a moment . . . and then assemble my camera. You go on. I'll catch up. It will be easy for me to do. There is some moonlight now, and I'll be able to see your flashlight."

So they'd left him, and he'd watched the faint beam flicker through the black mass of the trees, waiting until he was sure they were gone before he removed one of what looked like a matched pair of miniature light meters from his camera bag.

It was, in fact, a functional light meter, but it had other less-obvious uses as well. Such as the ability to function as a remotely operated geopositional satellite transmitter/receiver if a pair of switches were set in the proper order. Bergéone hesitated.

The switches determined the means of activating and tracking the device, either by satellite relay or handheld tracker. But like any other electronic device, there was a trade-off between efficiency and power. The LOCAL—handheld tracker—settings were the most efficient in terms of power usage, but the range was limited. High mountains or even buildings could block or deflect the signals. If both switches were set to SAT—satellite relay—the small devices could be activated and tracked by computer from anywhere in the world. The AUTO activation setting allowed the device to be activated by either system.

The problem was distance and power. The energy needed to send pulsed locator signals back up to the satellite would quickly drain the device's two lithium batteries—which, in the best of circumstances, held about ten minutes of signaling power.

But it's very cold out here, Bergéone realized. *Which means the batteries won't last long anyway.*

Because he didn't know how long it would be until he could separate himself from his guides and return to the site, Bergéone decided to compromise. He set the activator switch to AUTO and the transmitter switch to LOCAL, and then placed the device in a rocky outcropping well above his head, in such a manner that the concealed antenna had a clear view of the western sky. If all went well, it would remain there, inert and therefore undetectable by even the most sensitive triangulation equipment, until he activated it with the concealed tracking system built into his camera . . . or until Claire-Anne Leduc sent the activation signal over the satellite. At that point, on the LOCAL setting, the device would transmit its location for precisely one minute, and then automatically shut off to save power for the next activation signal. The very expensive multipurpose light meters and camera system had been a gift from a friend in the French Security Bureau, and had proven their worth on many such assignments.

Then, having assured himself that he and Claire-Anne would be able to find this spot again, later—without the aid of potentially treacherous Bancoo guides—Bergéone quickly assembled his camera and began to work his way through the dense stand of ancient trees toward the distant light.

It was only as he approached the outer perimeter of the trees that he realized the flashlight beam wasn't moving. In fact, it was barely visible.

"Rascoos?" he whispered.

Nothing.

"Lonecoos? Lastcoos?"

Still nothing.

Perplexed, but not especially concerned, Bergéone stepped away from the trees, moved forward in slow, cautious steps, then reached down to retrieve the small flashlight from a jagged pile of rocks where it appeared to have fallen.

The beam had gone from a faint white to an even fainter yellow, which told Bergéone that the small batteries were nearly exhausted. A quick scan with the fading beam revealed that he was in a small clearing, about five meters wide and ten meters long, bordered by trees at his back and high rock walls on the other three sides.

But it was the rocky wall opposite the trees that drew his attention.

It was not what he'd been expecting at all.

Because it really wasn't a wall . . . or the entrance to a cave, as Rascoos Rain-Song had described. More like a huge version of one of the Chartres Cathedral gargoyles, two dark eyes hovering over an anguished and gaping mouth.

Even taking into account the silence, the isolation, the darkness, and the mysterious disappearance of his three companions, the sight of the cliff face was more chilling than Bergéone would have thought possible.

Equally chilling was the inescapable sense that he was being watched, from above or beyond, although every time he scanned up or around with the flashlight, he saw no one.

"Rascoos?" he hissed. "Lonecoos? Lastcoos?"

Nothing.

Only the sound of his voice echoing from somewhere deep inside the mountain.

As he moved closer, the dull glow of the flashlight beam revealed the presence of several grotesque carvings protruding from the cliff face around the cave entrance. But Bergéone paid them no mind, his attention completely focused on the dark, cavernous opening. As if he expected someone—or something—to come lunging out at him.

But there was no sound of movement, not from inside the cave or from without. In fact, there were no sounds at all—except for the faint rustling of tree branches overhead and his own labored breathing.

He stood there for almost a full minute, seemingly mesmerized by the gaping darkness, until his will to go forward finally overcame the increasingly shrill and insistent warnings emanating from the depths of his subconscious.

As Bergéone stepped into the rough-carved stone entranceway, he had an unnerving sense that the head-high tunnel had begun to narrow in response to his presence. He forced himself to ignore the sensation and continued to move forward . . . trying not to react as his shoulders continually brushed against the confining walls of the zigzagging tunnel. He made another sharp turn . . . and then, without warning, found himself inside a vast cavern that might not have any meaningful boundaries—or, at least, none meaningful to someone like himself. There was a faint glow from what might have been minerals embedded in the stone ceiling high overhead, but the light was much too faint to reveal any sense of size or structure . . . and the fading beam of his small flashlight was much too weak to offer any useful illumination.

Bergéone could feel his heart pounding in his chest.

But there is no reason to be frightened, he reminded himself. *No reason at all. You are in a dark and unknown place, and your mind will play tricks on you if you allow it to do so. You must be brave.*

He continued to move forward in slow, cautious increments—sliding his soft-soled shoes against the rough stone floor and sweeping the nearly useless flashlight beam in front of him. Then, suddenly, his left foot and then his knee struck a square chunk of stone that he determined with fumbling hands to be roughly three meters on each side and half that in height.

What is this? The altar Rascoos Rain-Song spoke of?

As he continued to run his hands over the roughly chiseled stone, seeking some kind of defining structure—or perhaps even an opening—he discovered that his eyes were, in fact, starting to adjust rapidly. He could almost make out another dark shape about ten or twelve meters away.

Another altar?

No, he realized as he moved forward. It was much too tall for that.

He moved closer, and with the faint beam of the flashlight, he was able to make out the rough, irregular shapes. There were hundreds of them—the heads of gargoyles, icons, statues—each embedded in a hollowed-out niche in a huge, sprawling structure that rose high into the darkness.

He started to reach for one of the statues—an ancient-looking relic that looked very much like the image of the missing Virgin Mary statue—when his acutely tuned ears heard . . . what?

The whispery sound of movement?

There! He heard it again, closer this time. Coming toward him?

Before he could even begin to contain the sudden rush of fear, Patrick Bergéone's survival instincts prompted him to turn and run.

———

Sometime later, he had no idea how long, Patrick Bergéone found himself standing outside the cave entrance, staring back at the gaping stone maw with his hand braced against the vaguely reassuring stability of his tripod-mounted camera as he waited for his heart to stop pounding.

His arms and shoulders still ached from their frequent collisions with the rough rock walls of the tunnel. And his hands still shook uncontrollably. But the tremors were less frequent now that he had more or less convinced himself he was truly alone.

Once he'd come out of the tunnel, scrambling frantically on his hands and knees, he had somehow forced himself to stop running. Instead, he hid in the trees, trembling against the rough bark of the huge trunks . . . and waited in abject terror . . . ready to lunge up at any moment to see who or what might emerge from the mouth of the cave. But though he waited, nothing appeared in the maw of the cliff face. And so, finally, he had managed to convince himself that the whispery sounds of movement had simply been phantom noises created by his fevered imagination. He could still remember how the frantic scrabbling of his soft-soled shoes against the rough stone had echoed far away into the hollow darkness . . . as if the imagined residents of those deeply hidden recesses were laughing at him.

That had been, what, fifteen minutes ago? A half hour? Somehow, he'd lost track of the time. He looked around.

Where are you, Rascoos?

Lonecoos?

Lastcoos?

But his former companions were nowhere to be seen . . . or heard. They had simply disappeared.

Almost like what Rascoos Rain-Song had said about his father, Bergéone realized.

He never came out.

He never answered.

And something else.

He told me not to go into the tomb. That it was an evil place. That if I did go inside, it would reach out for my soul. But in any case, no matter if I went inside or not, I must never do anything to attract their attention, because if I did, they would follow me . . . and I would never escape them.

Fearful words at best . . . but more chilling now that he'd been inside the cavern himself.

Still, Bergéone was determined not to give in to his fears, knowing how easily such a thing could paralyze him.

And besides, this is stupid, he reminded himself. *They're probably just playing with me. Hiding in the trees, waiting to see what I'll do. Laughing to themselves. Stupid, thieving, bastard white-eye, probably pissed his pants by now.*

He'd show them.

It occurred to Bergéone to wonder if Rascoos or one of the others had seen him plant the GPS transmitter. But he shook that idea off, too, knowing—or at least hoping—that, in the faint moonlight, it would have been impossible for them to see what he was doing.

No, he assured himself, *the transmitter is safe, and Claire-Anne will*

know where I am at, so there is no problem . . . even if I have to use it to sig-
nal for help.

And while he was here, he might as well do his job.

He held the second light meter against the face of the stone gargoyle, to measure the reflected light, and then blinked in confusion
when the tiny device registered zero. A quick reset of the switches produced the same reading.

No light reflection at all.

Nonsense, Bergéone muttered to himself.

He'd used the flashlight to focus the lens, but the faint beam wouldn't
provide enough light to paint the cave face. It would have to be a long
exposure. He was tempted to retrieve the other light meter, but there
were several reasons why he didn't want to do that. So he decided, instead, simply to bracket his exposures. He'd taken such time-lapse shots
before, in similar moonlight, so there wouldn't be a difficulty in getting
a useable negative. It was just a matter of patience.

He took one last look through the viewfinder, set the delay timer,
and stepped forward into the gaping maw of the entrance. Then he
reached up to place his bare hand on the cold, chiseled head of an especially fearsome-looking creature with the small stone in its mouth that
looked as if it was straining to wrench itself free of the rock wall. A deliberate act of defiance, so that he could reassure the world—and perhaps most importantly, himself—that there was nothing to fear from
the ancient stone . . . or the gaping black maw at his back.

Nothing at all.

And certainly no reason for his imagination to suddenly start voic-
ing the concern that the incredibly cold figure might be trying to draw
the heat away from his body, or—

CLICK!

Even though he'd been expecting it, the loud sound of the shutter
snapping open in the crisp night air was jarring, and almost caused him
to jerk his hand away from the fearsome carving. But he recovered
quickly, steadying himself against the open jaws of the ancient stone
gargoyle. And even managed a weak smile as he forced himself to remain immobile.

No reason to be startled, he reminded himself. *You could always depend on the shutter components of a modern f2.8 lens to make audible sounds when they slid against each other.*

It would be a classic time exposure . . . almost a minute in duration. Plenty of time for the proof to be permanently etched on the high-quality, ultrasensitive black-and-white film. The proof that, for whatever reason, he felt compelled to produce.

As directed, the shutter remained open for precisely fifty-six seconds, fully exposing the film to the faint rays of reflected moonlight . . . while, somewhere in the surrounding darkness, an increasingly faint and distant voice screamed out in horrified anguish.

Then, finally, with another loud click, the shutter snapped shut and began to wait with cold, mechanical indifference for the next opportunity to perform its precisely measured task.

But on this particular night, the camera would wait in vain because the man who would set the timer—the foolishly courageous Patrick Bergéone—was no longer there.

CHAPTER ONE

"BAD BIRD ONE, THIS IS MOTHER HEN, HOW DO YOU COPY?"

Colin Cellars thumbed the mike switch. "Bad Bird One, copy, five-by-five."

"Bad Bird One, be advised that, according to my radar, you are approaching the outer perimeter markers. Effect an immediate . . . oh shit!"

Colin Cellars blinked, grinned, then thumbed the mike switch again. "Bad Bird One to Mother Hen, please repeat that last transmission. Unable to copy."

The answer came back immediately.

"Mother Hen to Bad Birds One and Two, be advised, I've got a board full of reds and a smoking starboard engine. I'm shutting it down and returning to base."

"Bad Bird Two to Mother Hen, I've got your six."

"Copy that, Bad Bird Two. Bad Bird One, remain in the pattern and continue your sweeps."

"Bad Bird One, copy," Cellars spoke into his helmet mike . . . and smiled.

For almost twenty minutes, Cellars continued to fly the established sweep patterns, allowing the sophisticated ground radar electronically to paint then record the subtle variations in the surrounding foliage.

Then, at the far northeastern end of his sweep, after checking his watch and verifying—visually and by radar—that there were no other aircraft in the area, Cellars abruptly broke out of the pattern, dropped down to about fifty feet above treetop level, and sent the powerful attack helicopter surging forward on a northeasterly heading.

For almost five minutes, as the airspeed gauge steadied around 200 mph and the powerful turbine engines roared, Cellars kept the smoothly vibrating airship steady on the thirty-degree heading.

At the end of the five-minute run, he dropped back to a relatively slow 160 mph, briefly shifted his attention to the chronometer at the lower right corner of the instrument panel, and smiled in anticipation.

Any moment now.

He paused to shift his shoulders against the snug web harness and adjust his grip on the joystick. Then, with a sudden, backwards-snapping motion of his head, he flipped the helmet-mounted night-vision goggles out of the way. The bright green images instantly shifted to black and shades of gray. He blinked, quickly verified his three-dimensional position on the instrument panel, shifted the angle of the main rotor blades with a twist of his wrist, then brought the joystick around to the right in a smooth, deliberate motion.

Cellars felt the surge of the powerful turbines and the pull of gravity in every cell in his body as the Apache helicopter, responding with mechanical perfection, came around in a tight, due-easterly turn less than thirty feet above the treetops.

It all happened in the span of a few seconds.

As Cellars completed his turn, the panoramic view through the thick armored-glass windshield remained a monochromatic expanse of grayish black trees beneath a thin layer of black sky covered by dark gray clouds. Then, in a display of pure magic, the edge of a distant cloud began to glow a faint reddish orange.

At that moment, Cellars sensed rather than saw the grayish black blur as it streaked upward from a barely visible gap in the trees, right in front of his low-flying and rapidly accelerating helicopter . . . and then, in a seemingly desperate, indecisive—and aerodynamically impossible— move, came to a sudden stop.

The physical impact was just as stunning as the first moment of sunrise.

Cellars felt the undercarriage of the Apache rip away, and then, for a brief moment, catch on something that seemed to crumble inward . . . before some kind of incredible momentum wrenched the heavily armored combat helicopter to the right and down like a child's toy.

It was his often-practiced ability to fly by instruments alone, and his trained faith in the accuracy of his horizon indicator, that saved him in those first critical seconds as he fought to disengage and level the crippled airship. Or at least that's what Cellars thought saved him, because the other possibility—that whatever it was he'd hit was struggling desperately to keep both of them from crashing into those lethal treetops— made no sense at all.

But he didn't have time to think about that, because his instrument panel was now lit up like the reddish orange clouds, and the emergency Klaxons were ringing in his earphones, demanding that he do something, right now, because . . .

Ringing?

Colin Cellars wrenched himself upward, blinking in shock . . . until comprehension finally returned and he reached across the bed for the phone, only vaguely aware that his entire body was covered in sweat.

"Yes . . . hello?" he rasped. He was breathing so hard, he could barely get the words out.

"Sergeant Cellars?"

"Yes?"

Helicopter? What the hell . . . ?

"This is Trooper Lee, sir. Michael Lee, Region Nine CSI. Nine-Ida-Seven. I'm sorry to wake you, but I've got something out here I thought you might want to take a look at. I know you're not on duty right now, but—"

On duty? What time is it? Cellars had to work to focus his blurred eyes on the face of the alarm clock. *Almost midnight? Jesus.*

"It's not just that I'm off duty, Trooper," Cellars said, trying to control his breathing. "I'm still on administrative leave, pending a medical evaluation, which means I'm not supposed to be responding to any crime scenes."

"Yes, sir, I, uh, realize that . . . and I guess this really isn't an official call," the trooper said hesitantly. "It's just that I'm the only CSI officer on duty this evening, and I've never worked a major scene before on my own, and I sure could use a second opinion."

"What have you got?"

"A body. I—"

The call suddenly disconnected, leaving Cellars with a buzzing handset. He shook his head sleepily and returned the handset to the receiver.

Fifteen seconds later, the phone rang again.

"Cellars."

"Sorry about that, sir," the familiar voice said. "Kinda windy up here. Trees are swaying back and forth a lot. Must be getting in the way of the receivers."

"You said something about having a body?"

"Yes, sir. Or, at least, I thought I had one."

"You *thought* you had one?"

"Yes, sir."

"But you don't anymore?"

"No, sir. It's gone."

"What do you mean it's gone?"

"Well, it was draped over a big branch, about twenty-five feet up, in a big black oak. I spotted it from the road with my vehicle searchlight, but I was too far away to see anything other than a suspicious shape. So I got in closer with my flashlight, but a couple big branches were in the way, and I still couldn't see enough to be, you know, sure. I tried to get a picture with my electronic camera, but I was too far away to pick up anything useful. So I went back to the car for my thirty-five-millimeter, figuring I might be able to pick up something with a telephoto lens and a better flash. But when I got back to the tree—"

"It was gone."

"Yes, sir."

Cellars hesitated. He wasn't supposed to be out at homicide scenes, or at any scenes at all, for that matter. But he remembered Lee from the recent CSI school. A young, hardworking kid who listened carefully, asked pertinent questions, and took a lot of notes. Proud to be the first Korean-American on the OSP, and not the kind of officer you'd expect to call for help the first time a camera jammed or a plaster cast of a tire track failed to set. A suddenly missing body, however, was something else entirely.

"I thought, you know, it might be one of those missing people we've been looking for all this time," the young trooper added when Cellars remained silent. "The ones you were sent here to find."

"Is anybody there with you?" Cellars asked.

"No, sir. I'm out here by myself."

"Who's on call for homicides?"

"Uh, Detective-Sergeant Espinoza, sir. Nine-Delta-One. And I did call him first, like I'm supposed to, but he said he's been ordered to remain on call and not respond unless we've got a confirmed victim. Something about the regional overtime budget, and too many missing persons calls that turn out to be unfounded."

"What?"

"Yes, sir, that's what he said. It's a new policy, I guess."

"Since when?"

"According to Espinoza, since Hightower put it into effect last week."

"Major . . . Hightower? From Internal Affairs in Salem? She's down here?"

"Yes, sir. Apparently taking over the region until Lieutenant Talbert gets out of the hospital or they assign a new captain."

"Jesus, that's just what we need," Cellars whispered, mostly to himself.

"Uh, what was that, sir?" Lee asked hesitantly.

Cellars sighed, then shook his head in resignation as he reached for the pen and notepad on the nightstand.

"Never mind. Is it still raining out there?"

"No, sir, it stopped raining earlier this evening. But it's been snowing off and on the last couple of hours."

Wonderful. Cellars considered the lonely comforts of his still-warm bed, the fact that it would probably stay lonely if he didn't figure out how to regain the affections of Jody Catlin or some other substitute girlfriend, and the repercussions that were likely to follow if he responded to this call-out. "Where are you at, Lee?"

"Out on the Old Mill Road, about a half mile north of forest road one-one-seven-two, about fifty yards south of the Odane River culvert."

Cellars paused for a moment, trying to visualize the Region 9 map he'd been trying to memorize for the past couple of months. The location Lee described was in a mountainous area at the far northwest corner of the region.

The only saving grace, Cellars decided, was that his cabin was located about a third of the way between the station and the Odane River culvert. It could have been worse.

"Can you hang on for another forty-five minutes or so?"

"Yes, sir, no problem."

"Okay, stay put. I'll be there."

CHAPTER TWO

AT 0055 HOURS ON THE COLD AND SNOWY MORNING, COLIN CELLARS pulled his pickup truck to the side of the road, about twenty feet behind an empty white OSP scout car. He shut off his engine, rolled down his side window, and waited for CSI Officer Lee to appear and walk him to the scene.

Two minutes later, there was still no movement in or around the scout car. But the cold was starting to make Cellars's ears tingle, and it was starting to snow again.

Keeping his eyes on the scout car and the surrounding area illuminated by his headlights, Cellars reached into his glove compartment and pulled out a small, portable police radio. He hesitated briefly, then brought the radio up to the side of his mouth.

"Oregon-Nine-Echo-One to Oregon-Nine-Ida-Seven. What's your ninety-seven?"

Dead silence.

"Oregon-Nine-Echo-One to Oregon-Nine-Ida-Seven," he repeated. "Report your location."

Again, nothing.

Shit.

Leaning forward, Cellars pulled a heavy four-cell flashlight out from under his seat, slipped the portable radio into his jacket pocket, grabbed a black knit ski cap out of the glove compartment, and pulled it down over his ears. Then he shut off the truck headlights—causing the scout car virtually to disappear in the cloud-covered darkness—quietly opened the driver's side door, slid out of the truck, and gently pressed the door back against the frame with what he hoped was a minimum of noise.

Having done all that, he drew his .40-caliber SIG-Sauer semiautomatic from his shoulder holster, thumbed his flashlight on, quickly swept the narrow beam back and forth across the road, then slowly moved to the driver's side of the scout car.

The scout car was empty. Cellars frowned as he swept the flashlight beam across the dash and radio console, then quickly turned his attention to the surrounding area. There was a thermos bottle lying in the snow next to the left front tire; a thermos cup about ten feet away in the middle of the road; what looked like splattered and frozen coffee droplets down the left front panel and driver's side door of the vehicle; and two separate sets of matching boot prints. The first set, barely visible in the freshly fallen snow, went into the forest and came back again . . . at least twice, as best Cellars could tell. The second set went down the road, disappeared around a curve, and didn't return.

Cellars reached into his coat pocket for the police radio, to call for backup. But just as he started to make the call, he noticed something interesting about the pattern of coffee droplets. He knelt to examine the frozen streaks more closely, noted the positioning of the thermos and cup again, brushed the fallen snow off the thermos bottle, then stood and put the police radio back in his pocket.

He found Lee around the curve and about twenty yards up the road, standing next to the railing over the Odane River culvert with a 12-gauge Remington 870 pump shotgun in his hands, staring intently into the forest.

"You have something against carrying a radio with you when you leave your vehicle? Not to mention staying inside your vehicle and keeping warm?" Cellars inquired as he came up alongside the uniformed officer.

"Uh, no, sir, not usually," the young trooper replied in a distinctly edgy voice. Cellars noticed that his eyes never left the forest.

"So what's the problem?"

"There's something out there."

"Something? Not someone?" Cellars asked as he quickly turned his head and flashlight beam in the direction of the densely packed trees and underbrush.

"Definitely something," Lee replied. "I'm not sure about the 'someone' part."

"How do you know? Did you see something?"

"No, sir. Just heard it. Something moving through the trees."

"When was that?"

"The first time? Right after I called you on my cell phone. I remembered you told us at the last CSI class how important it was to establish a scene perimeter right away, so we don't screw things up during the search. So I walked back to my scout car to get some perimeter tape and my CSI kit. I got a roll of tape and the kit out of the trunk. Then I poured myself a cup of coffee, because it was going to be a while before you got here. I was still drinking the coffee when I heard something moving around out there . . . in the general direction of the tree where I found the body."

"So you tossed your cup, then knocked your thermos off the hood of the car?"

The young trooper blinked in surprise. "Yes, sir, that's right. I guess I did that when I went back into my vehicle for my shotgun . . . and a box of slug rounds."

"Understandable," Cellars commented as he continued to examine the trees and underbrush with his flashlight beam. "And the next time you heard movement was—?"

"About ten minutes before you got here, heading in this general direction. I figured that if I followed the noise, and stayed on the road, I ought to be able to hear or see something coming my way before it got too close."

"Sounds like a reasonable plan. But you didn't see or hear anything after that?"

"No, sir."

"And that was about twenty minutes ago?"

"Yes, sir, about that."

"Okay, then, why don't we assume that whatever it was is long gone . . . and head back to that black oak you told me about," Cellars suggested. "See if we can figure out what we've got here."

The young trooper seemed to hesitate, then nodded in agreement.

The two OSP officers made their way back down to the scout car and followed the first set of Lee's almost obliterated boot prints to the base of what looked to be a forty-foot black oak. The irregular trunk looked to be at least four to five feet in diameter.

"This it?" Cellars asked as he scanned the rough bark and bare branches with his flashlight beam.

"Yes, sir. That big branch up there, to the left." Lee indicated it with his own flashlight beam.

"So you were thinking what, a cougar, maybe?"

"A cougar?" Lee turned to face Cellars with an embarrassed look on his face.

"Otherwise known as a puma or mountain lion. Roughly, a hundred-pound cat. Perfectly capable of dragging a deer carcass of roughly equivalent weight up a big black oak—which would explain what looks like claw marks in the bark—but probably not capable of dragging a larger human carcass up that same tree. A kid, or small female, maybe, but probably not your average beer-gut human male."

"Yeah, I guess that's right," Lee said hesitantly.

"Which, I assume, is why you brought your thirty-five along? In case you got a chance for a nice wildlife shot while you were out searching for homicide suspects and victims?"

The young trooper looked guiltily at the strobe-flash-rigged thirty-five-millimeter camera dangling from the strap over his shoulder.

"And which could explain why you jury-rigged a mount for that camera on your dash? Only we're probably talking about the deer now, instead of the cougar, because you don't see too many cougars running across the road in front a scout car's headlights in the middle of the night. Mostly because they're a whole lot smarter than your average deer.

"But," Cellars went on when the young trooper remained silent, "that still doesn't explain what you were doing on a remote mountain road, shining your vehicle searchlight in tree branches some twenty-five feet off the ground when you're supposed to be patrolling a little closer to town, where most of your CSI calls are probably going to occur."

"Uh, well . . ."

"So tell me, Trooper Lee, what's the going price for genuine Oregon Bigfoot photos these days?"

The young trooper sighed and stared down at his boots.

"I guess maybe about fifty grand. Something in that range," he mumbled.

"Or a whole lot more if the photo's really sharp—like what you might get with a top-of-the-line thirty-five rigged with what looks like a thousand-dollar chunk of glass up front, fast film, and a half-megawatt strobe . . . or even full-megawatt headlight beams, if you really got lucky and caught the critter crossing a road. And we won't even discuss what a genuine Bigfoot footprint plaster cast made by a professional crime scene investigator might bring on the open market, much less a genuine Bigfoot carcass shot by that very same fellow. Which, I suppose, would explain the box of 12-gauge slug rounds, since CSI officers don't get called out to help extract a barricaded suspect very often. Not even in Jasper County, Oregon."

"I guess I called the wrong guy out, huh?" Lee whispered after a moment.

"No, all things considered, I'd say you called exactly the right guy."

"Really?" The young trooper's head came up. "Why's that?"

"Do you have any idea why I'm on administrative leave and facing a psych exam before I can go back on duty?" Cellars asked.

"Yes, sir, I guess I've heard a lot of the stories that are going around."

"About me and Lieutenant Talbert and Captain Hawkins? And some interesting creatures that I may or may not have seen, because I may or may not have had hallucinogenic drugs in my system at the time?"

"Uh, yes, sir. I guess I heard something about that, too."

"So, taking all of that into consideration, Trooper Lee, what do you think the chances are that I'm going to call the station and tell them that I deliberately violated a direct order, responded to a possible homicide scene in the middle of the night, and caught one of our brand-new CSI officers trying to catch or shoot a Sasquatch?"

Lee thought about that for a few seconds.

"I guess that wouldn't go over real good, would it?"

"No, I don't think so," Cellars said. "Not even with Lieutenant Talbert, much less Major Hightower, who, I'm told, doesn't have much of a sense of humor in the best of circumstances. So tell me, Lee, apart from everything else we talked about tonight, do you still think you saw a human body up this tree?"

The young trooper hesitated, looked down at his boots again, then back up at Cellars.

"Yes, sir, I do."

"Fair enough. Do you still have that can of green spray paint we issued to all the new CSI officers?"

"Yes, sir. Right in my kit." He held up the small briefcase.

"Good. So why don't you take it out, and mark the base of this tree so you can find it again, then mark the road by your scout car so you can come back here in the daylight to make a proper search of those tree branches and I can go home and get some sleep?"

"But . . ."

"Then," Cellars went on, "if it turns out the lab finds some human blood or even some interesting nonhuman hairs in those samples you're going to collect when you can actually see what you're doing, then maybe you and I can come back here on our off-duty hours and see what we can track down. How does that sound?"

The young trooper took one last look up at the darkened branches of the huge black oak, then quickly knelt and opened up his CSI kit.

"Fine by me, sir," he said with what Cellars interpreted as heartfelt relief. "Definitely fine by me."

CHAPTER THREE

IN THE PREDAWN DARKNESS, THREE FIGURES MOVED SLOWLY AND cautiously toward the edge of the dense, old-growth forest that formed a natural perimeter line around the five-acre clearing that contained Detective-Sergeant Colin Cellars's new, remote, and isolated log cabin.

They were less than a dozen feet from the clearing when a muted but persistent series of buzzing sounds suddenly echoed through the thick tree trunks and chilled night air.

The three figures—a young doe and her two fawns—immediately froze, their ears up and back legs tensed to flee.

But after a moment, the buzzing sounds stopped . . . and didn't resume. So it wasn't long before the young doe was on the move again, back to the critically important task of seeking out energy-rich sources of food . . . for herself and her two very-late-born young.

She knew, from past experience, that she would find enticing clumps of food in the middle of the clearing, close to the man-made structure. Mostly winter vegetables and bulb flowers planted by the human creature that had moved into the long-empty cabin fifty-some nights ago. But also, every now and then, small piles of sweet-tasting clover hay. Even better, there were no dogs at the cabin to spot their approach and give chase.

And better yet, the human creature who had been spending the last few weeks working around the cabin—digging holes and trenches, laying culverts and pipe, stringing wire, repairing old structures and building new ones—didn't seem to care that she and her fawns and the other nonhibernating herbivores continued to devour the young and tender plants almost as quickly as he set them in the ground.

So she continued to return, every morning before dawn for the last couple of weeks, growing bolder—and less fearful of the human—every day.

In point of fact, the human in question actually enjoyed their presence, and saw to it that the supply of young plants remained steady. He even put out small piles of hay when he ran short of seedlings. But these were simple creatures, who had no way of knowing—much less understanding—that their presence filled a need, and a critical gap, in his life.

The clearing was one of the few dependable sources of food left, now, and the unseasonably icy winter air offered little reassurance that warmer days would follow anytime soon. So it was tempting to leave the shelter of the dense old-growth trees to see what might be had.

Tempting, but at the same time extremely dangerous. Over the past two days, she had become increasingly aware that there were new and strange predators in this area, in addition to the human. Terrifying creatures that moved so quickly and soundlessly that—

She froze again, this time in response to something she sensed, rather than heard or saw.

The two late-born fawns froze in place also. But their reactions were still dangerously slow for this extended time of winter, when their

natural enemies—silently prowling cougars and the occasional aggressive bobcat—were increasingly active and determined to feed. A very
dangerous time to be tentatively fleet of foot but otherwise helpless in
the face of a clawed and hungry predator.

Normally, the doe would have admonished her fawns with a meaningful glare, but she was too busy for that now. Instead, she was moving
her head in tiny increments, trying desperately to focus her raised and
cupped ears—which were much more sensitive than her widened and
dilated eyes—on the tiniest of sounds that might tell her where—

There!

She started to whip her head around . . . then instinctively refocused
every bit of her muscular energy into a desperate lunge, because the
whispery sound—actually little more than the sound of displaced air—
was suddenly very close.

Much too close.

The fawns, still too young to do much more than react to their
mother's body language, heard nothing at all. Nothing, at least, until the
alarming sounds of hooves digging for purchase into the ice-hardened
ground, and of lungs desperately sucking in air, and of a muscular
throat being torn open by a flashing set of terribly sharp claws, hit their
smaller ears all at once.

It was only then that they reacted, instinctively, by lunging away
from the terrifying sounds . . . and right into a death that was no less
quick and brutal than their mother's.

Immediately, the surrounding forest fell silent, and remained that
way for almost a full minute as all of the smaller residents—on the
ground and in the trees—watched and waited in shared terror. But their
fear wouldn't last long, if only because violent death was an inevitable
and inescapable element of life in the old-growth forest. And so, one by
one, these smaller residents quietly resumed their nightly activities. But
they did so in a shaken manner, as if somehow aware that, this time,
their nightly brush with death had been different . . . and even more
frightening than usual.

They fed, these predatory newcomers, in a manner that spoke more of savage pleasure than of nutritional need. Their energy reserves were acceptable, and they could have waited—for days or weeks if necessary—had they chosen to do so.

But they preferred to be completely filled, honed, and ready.

For these were not predators as such—simplistic creatures activated by hunger and driven by instinct to find sources of food to satisfy an immediate need. These were retrievers. Highly evolved organisms, activated by complex biological sensors that had detected the loss of an entire exploratory team, and thus driven by duty and purpose to recover the lost evidence. The ones Allesandra had warned Cellars about. The ones that might come . . .

They fed quickly and efficiently, to maximize their reserves and to put a fine edge on their hunter/killer skills. Then, sated, they moved forward once again, to see what opportunity might present itself by this latest intrusion on their methodical and ultimately deadly surveillance.

CHAPTER FOUR

DETECTIVE-SERGEANT COLIN CELLARS HUNG UP THE PHONE, THEN turned his attention back to the twelve uniformed officers seated facing him in the briefing room.

"All right, ladies and gentlemen," he said, "good news for a change. We just received word from Salem that our request to expand Region Nine's CSI program has been approved, effective at 2000 hours this Friday evening, which is"—Cellars glanced down at his wristwatch—"about fifteen minutes from now. Just in time for the graveyard shift."

Cellars looked around at the expectant faces.

"They approved two CSI teams—designated Nine-Tango-Whiskey and Nine-Tango-Yankee—for ten-hour days, four days on and three off, with six officers assigned to each team. And even better, not that any of you are in this for the money"—Cellars smiled—"all assigned officers will receive senior detective pay during the duration of the assignment."

The briefing room erupted in celebratory cheers, whistles, and hand-slapping. Something they'd all been training for the past six weeks had finally come through.

Cellars waited until the ruckus died down.

"Okay, now for the bad news. I've been told we can expect another typical Jasper County winter evening tonight, which means intermittent moonlight, subzero temperatures, thick fog, and heavy rain . . . with a good chance that the rain will turn to snow."

He scanned the twelve faces, but no one seemed dismayed by the prospect. Which wasn't too surprising, he reminded himself, since every one of these newly appointed investigators had spent the better part of his or her adult life in the wide valleys formed by the Cascade and Siskiyou Mountain Ranges of southern Oregon.

If they're not used to a little bad weather by now, they never will be, Cellars told himself, making an effort to ignore the all-too-familiar faces in the back row as he considered the visibility issue once again.

Given the nature of the still-unidentified suspects, who were thought to have kidnapped or killed something in excess of fifty southern Oregon victims over the past year, visibility would be a crucial issue for the responding CSI teams. Everything Cellars knew—or thought he knew—about these serial predators suggested they would continue to strike out of the darkness, hit hard, and then disappear . . . most likely with their victims . . . and leaving little evidence of their crime.

Or, at least, very little that had been discovered so far.

But there had to be more evidence. Had to be. It was a basic precept of crime scene investigation . . . that it was impossible for a suspect, victim, and crime scene to come together without the creation or exchange of physical evidence. It was just a matter of taking the time to find it.

Which, as far as Cellars was concerned, simply meant that Region 9 CSI officers had to spend more time at the scenes.

But it was difficult to concentrate on a search for trace evidence when the suspects were targeting the crime scene investigators—as Cellars himself had been targeted a few weeks ago. And, in any case, there was no way that a CSI officer could safely work alone under such conditions.

Thus the concept of the six-officer CSI teams: two highly trained crime scene investigators working with their heads down, recording the details of the scene and searching for the relevant traces of physical evidence, while a communications expert continuously relayed digital copies of the rapidly accumulating data to headquarters. And all of this under the oversight of a team leader who would monitor and direct the progress of the crime scene investigation while two SWAT-trained marksmen provided close cover with military assault rifles and extremely lethal, liquid-Teflon-tipped ammunition.

It was a good, workable plan. But even so, the safety of the CSI officers would be completely dependent upon the covering officers having enough time to spot and sight on their targets. Which meant that if the visibility stayed at thirty to forty feet, like it was right now, there was a very real possibility that they could lose somebody tonight. Possibly even an entire team if things really went to shit. Like it had two months ago.

The thought made Cellars feel sick to his stomach.

"In approximately fifteen minutes," he went on, "you're going to be out on the roads, waiting for the calls to start coming in. It's a Friday evening, and we know from experience that our suspects like to hit on cold, rainy, and foggy Friday evenings, so you probably won't have to wait too long. Which means you all stay alert," Cellars added emphatically. "No daydreaming, no reminiscing about girlfriends or boyfriends, no beer talk. Body armor and helmets are to be on and secured at all times when you are out of the vehicle . . . and that specifically includes the search team members. I know the gear is heavy and cumbersome, that it gets in the way and slows you down, but that doesn't matter. You wear it. Does everybody understand that?"

Twelve heads nodded in unison.

"Communications officers," Cellars continued, "in between calls and during routine patrol, you will function as the primary CSI vehicle drivers. In doing so, you will maintain a random patrol pattern within your assigned sectors, but make sure you stay close to main access roads for a rapid response. At the same time, make sure you keep your communications lines open and monitor all personal and vehicle recorders on a routine basis. Team leaders will verify that all recorders are activated at the time of any call-out, and once again before any member of the team exits the CSI vehicle. Cover teams, keep your eyes on the side and rear quadrants until you arrive at the scene and exit the vehicle . . . then keep your eyes on the trees because they are the most likely point of attack. Does everybody understand what they're supposed to do?"

Cellars's eyes scanned the briefing room, flickering past the four all-too-familiar faces in the back row, but saw no indication that anyone was confused or uncertain about their assignments.

"Okay, good. Now let's walk through it from the point of arrival at the scene."

Cellars turned to face the flat-screen monitor that covered a five-foot-by-eight-foot portion of the wall behind the podium, and activated the laser pointer in his hand.

"Assume we have a man-down call in a warehouse complex that is surrounded on three sides by US Forest land. According to the informant, the body of the victim is located halfway between the tree line and this warehouse. Nine-Tango-Whiskey gets the call, responds to the scene, observes what appears to be the victim here—"

Cellars made an X with the red laser point.

"—and then parks its vehicle right here."

He made a second X a few inches away from the first.

"Tango-Whiskey leader, what do you do next?"

One of the four veteran CSI officers in the back row—a team leader, according to the patch on his uniform sleeve, whose face Cellars couldn't quite make out—responded immediately.

"I would verify with Malcolm that all vehicle and personal recorders are functioning properly, then call in our arrival and the fact that we've spotted the possible victim . . . and, ideally, also advise that no suspects are observed in the immediate area," he added with a half smile.

"Okay, then what?"

"Bobby and Terry immediately exit our vehicle and establish cover positions at the three o'clock and nine o'clock relative to our line of sight on the victim. Under current operating conditions, they will deploy with laser-equipped assault rifles instead of their normal shotguns."

"What are the colors of their lasers?"

The CSI team leader paused for only a moment.

"Bobby's is red and Terry's is green."

"Why is it important for you to know that?"

"An assault can come from several angles at the same time," the team leader replied. "In the event we are attacked, my secondary job is to step in and cover any exposed areas of our outer perimeter. As such, I need to know immediately if one of our protecting officers goes down, or if an angle of approach isn't being covered."

"Go on."

"One member of our search team—under most circumstances, that will be Melissa—will stay with the vehicle during our initial search of the crime scene. Her job is to watch our relative six o'clock position while Malcolm continues to make certain that all communications lines remain open and that all recorders are continuing to function properly. Once I verify that everyone is in place, and that all instruments and recorders are functioning properly, Jody and I approach the body . . . watching out for any possible suspects and/or booby traps as we go."

Cellars nodded approvingly, and the officer continued on.

"If the victim is still alive, I immediately call for the paramedics and monitor the immediate area, while Jody applies pressure to any bleeding wounds and monitors the victim's breathing—and conducts CPR if necessary—until the paramedics arrive."

"At this point, do you ask for assistance from any of your other team members?"

"Absolutely not. They all maintain their positions, no matter what."

"Go on."

"If the victim is dead, Jody finds a spot on a thigh—or any other large muscle mass—that looks to be free of blood or other physical evidence, then applies and activates a time-of-death vampire gauge. Once we've verified that the TOD device is operating properly, we retrace our steps back to the vehicle, discuss the situation with our other team members, then establish an outer scene perimeter."

"Why do you do that?"

The leader of Nine-Tango-Whiskey shrugged agreeably, as if to suggest that the answer was obvious to even the most inexperienced CSI officer. "Because we need to limit our search to the area where we're most likely to find evidence. And that, by logic and by definition, would be the area closest to the victim because that's where the suspects most likely interacted with our victim . . . and therefore most likely transferred some physical evidence."

"And what happens if you fail to set an appropriate outer scene perimeter?" Cellars asked, discomforted by the fact that he still couldn't quite make out the face of the team leader.

There are only two, he thought. *I ought to know them.*

"Too far out and we waste a lot of valuable time searching areas where nothing happened. Too close in and we end up never finding all of the crucial pieces of evidence," the officer responded matter-of-factly.

"That being the case, how do you know how far out from the victim to set your scene perimeter?" Cellars pressed.

"That's where the guesswork of crime scene investigation comes into play. Since we won't know for sure what really happened—or where it happened—until we finish our investigation and thoroughly assess all of the evidence, we work the odds. Look for obvious disturbances, obvious entry and escape points . . . keeping in mind that the suspect—if he or she had the time, and the opportunity—might have rigged the scene to throw us off."

"Or set you up," Cellars said.

"That's right. So we give ourselves plenty of room, set up the perimeter tape—or in this case, the electronic sensors," he amended— "and get to work, hoping that we didn't happen to park our vehicle on top of the most useful evidence when we arrived."

"Exactly." Cellars nodded approvingly. "And don't forget," he added, directing his comments to the other officers in the room, "the outer perimeter is your danger point—the place where you're most likely going to make a serious mistake—"

An alarm bell rang somewhere in the background.

"—because after the first three or four hours at the scene, you're going to start getting tired, and your mind will be trying to tell you that anything outside the perimeter you established at the onset of your investigation is not your problem, and that may not be the case at all."

Cellars glanced down at his watch again. Eighteen hundred hours sharp.

"Okay, it's time to get going, so one last time: Don't ever forget, whoever or whatever our suspects may be, they are extremely dangerous, and have no qualms whatsoever about killing or capturing a police officer. So stay alert out there and be careful, but do whatever you can to find the evidence. We need to put a stop to these kidnappings and killings right now. And the only way we can do that is to find the linking evidence."

A hand was raised in the front of the room.

"Yes?"

"What about you, Sergeant? Are they putting you back on duty?"

Cellars frowned and shook his head. "No, not yet. I've still got to pass that psych exam. But as soon as that's over, I'll be out there with you. Count on that."

"Yes, sir, we will." The young trooper smiled cheerfully.

Cellars remained standing at the podium as the twelve members of his two new CSI teams filed out of the briefing room, thinking: *That's right, go out there, do your job, and be careful, so I can get a decent night's sleep for a change. I'm getting tired of all this nonsense. Very, very tired.*

The leader of Nine-Tango-Whiskey walked past, and Cellars froze.

Like looking into a mirror, he thought as the team leader disappeared through the doorway. He turned away from the other three all-too-familiar faces as they exited the room. Something about the haunted expressions in their eyes bothered him.

———

More time passed. Minutes or hours, Colin Cellars had no idea. But the words were still echoing in his mind—

Stay alert.

Be careful.

Don't ever forget: Whoever or whatever our suspects may be, they are extremely dangerous and have no qualms whatsoever about killing or cap-turing a police officer.

—when the alarm bell rang again. An alert notification this time, prefacing the concerned voice of the OMARR-9 regional dispatcher coming out of the overhead speakers.

"OMARR-Nine to Oregon-Nine-Tango-Whiskey-One, be advised we are receiving a broken signal from your vehicle transmitters. Please verify your frequency and power settings."

No response.

"Oregon-Nine-Tango-Whiskey-One, do you copy?"

Again, no response.

"OMARR-Nine to any Nine-Tango-Whiskey officer," the dis-patcher repeated, "please respond immediately. We are receiving inter-mittent and broken signals from your—"

Then, in a suddenly much more tense voice: "Nine-Tango-Whiskey, we are now showing flat lines on three—no, all team monitors. Repeat, flat lines on all Tango-Whiskey monitors. Do you copy? Does anyone copy?"

Still no response.

The bell again, louder this time . . . alerting everyone on the Jasper County law enforcement frequencies that an emergency broadcast would follow immediately.

"OMARR-Nine to any officers in the vicinity of Route One-Twenty-Three and Lexington, we have a possible CSI-team-down situa-tion at the Katchell warehouse complex. Flat-lined monitors indicate all six Oregon-Nine-Tango-Whiskey officers are down. Repeat, we have a possible multiple-officer-down situation at—"

Cellars felt his mind and arms and shoulders start to go numb.

Jody? Bobby? Malcolm?

No. Can't be. Not Jody. Not—

Hey, wait a minute.

Bell?

What bell?

Colin Cellars's eyes snapped open, and he lunged upward . . . only to find himself sitting up in the middle of his bed again, his upper torso trembling and covered with sweat.

What the—where am I?

Then the alarm bell went off again, this time very long and loud. Almost like a doorbell.

Oh . . . yeah, right.

He closed his eyes in shaken relief, wondering as he did so if he was ever going to sleep like a normal person again.

CHAPTER FIVE

UNBEKNOWNST TO DETECTIVE-SERGEANT COLIN CELLARS, THE DIE
had been cast regarding his chances of getting a good night's sleep exactly four weeks and two days earlier. That was when Dr. Eric Marston,
near the end of his Thursday afternoon lecture on the mathematics of
wave theory, looked up from his lecture notes and noticed the raised
hand in the middle of the darkened lecture room.

He frowned for a moment. Most of the attendees of Marston's lectures were grad students who had been advised to do so in order to gain
some insight into the workings of the brilliant mind of the university's
latest adjunct faculty member. As such, and after the first two lectures,
they all knew better than to interrupt Marston with questions. He wasn't
that kind of an instructor.

"Yes?"

"Dr. Marston, I'm sorry, but I simply don't understand. How can you be so certain?"

Marston blinked in amazement, but not because of his questioner's audacity or her physical beauty. In point of fact, Marston didn't even realize there was an extremely attractive young woman in the lecture room. Given his generally poor eyesight, his reliance on slides to keep his lectures on track, and his tendency to wear his reading glasses rather than his more irritating bifocals, he only saw his students as darkened figures in a darkened room. It was her voice—rich in tone and deeply resonant—that drew and held his attention.

"Certain of what?" he asked unnecessarily. He understood the question perfectly. He simply wanted to hear that pure, throaty resonance again.

"That there is, beyond any doubt, intelligent life beyond Earth?"

Eric Marston cocked his head and then smiled. "Actually, I find it very easy to believe in mathematical certainties," he responded.

It was an honest answer to a perfectly reasonable question.

But it was also an evasive answer—a lie, in fact.

Moments later, the bell announcing the end of the lecture hour rang. And it might have ended there, the lie unresolved and perhaps even forgotten, if Marston had simply followed his normal routine of departing through the side door and hurrying out to the nearby parking lot where his driver should have been waiting.

But Marston's driver had called in sick that morning, and all the other drivers had been otherwise occupied, so Marston had elected to drive himself out to the university for this particular lecture. And the testing of a piece of equipment he needed for the next stage of his phased laser research wouldn't be completed until tomorrow morning, so there really wasn't any pressing reason why he had to hurry back to his primary place of employment.

He was still shuffling his papers at the podium, ignoring the animated background chatter of his departing class, when he realized that someone was standing next to him at the podium.

"Dr. Marston?"

Startled, Marston brought his head up . . . then blinked in shock.

The young woman standing before him had long, coal-black hair, smooth reddish-tanned skin, dark—almost black—eyes, and was absolutely beautiful. Stunningly beautiful, in fact. But Marston hardly noticed her physical attributes. Up close, her voice was even more vibrant and alluring, as if she'd tuned her vocal cords to a perfect alignment with some kind of biological antenna in his head. Which, in a sense, she had.

"Yes, can I help you?" he asked, having to force the words past suddenly dry lips. He could feel his heart start to pound in his chest and had to fight against a sudden urge to bolt toward the side door.

"Only if you promise not to lie to me again."

Marston felt his knees start to wobble, and he fought to regain some small portion of his professorial dignity.

"I beg your pardon?"

She didn't answer right away. Instead, she just stood there, staring at him with those black eyes. Then, finally, her lips parted as she repeated in a soft, resonant voice: "I have so many things to ask you, so many things I desperately want to understand. But before I do, you must promise that you won't lie to me again. Not ever."

"I—I can't do that."

This time it was her turn to blink. "Why not?"

Marston stared down at his shoes, his sense of intellectual confidence torn to shreds by a rush of conflicting emotions he couldn't even begin to comprehend, much less bring under control.

"I can't tell you," he finally whispered.

He was still staring down at his shoes, sickened by the realization that he was going to lose her—lose that wonderful voice—when he suddenly felt her hand against his wrist.

It wasn't that he wanted to lie to her. God forbid.

Not then, and certainly not later, as they sat side by side in the back of a darkened coffee shop, talking in soft tones and feeling the heat from each other's body. The moment when she made it perfectly clear that lying was the one unfaithful act that she could never forgive . . . or forget.

"I love sitting here next to you, and I love listening to your voice," she whispered, her lips brushing against his ear as her breast pressed tight against his unmoving arm.

"I feel the same way," he whispered, shaken to the very core of his being.

"But you have to understand," she went on as if he'd never spoken, "if you lie to me, you'll never see me again."

He believed her. One more lie and she would disappear out of his life forever, leaving a gaping hole that he knew—without the slightest doubt—would never be filled. So he promised himself that somehow, in some manner, he would never lie to her again.

But the problem was, how could he possibly tell her the truth?

How could he explain that lying—to her, as well as to virtually everyone else outside of his small circle of peers and supervisors—was one of the most important and crucial elements in his official job description?

———

After several days of increasingly desperate brainstorming, made worse by the nightly phone calls she made to his small and now increasingly lonely studio apartment, Dr. Eric Marston finally had an answer to his dilemma.

It all came down to one basic pair of conflicting problems that would have sounded depressingly familiar to almost any lovestruck schoolboy.

If he wanted to keep this incredible young woman from asking too many probing questions about his work that he simply couldn't answer, then he had to find some way to keep her distracted. But, at the same time, if he wanted to keep her for himself, then he had to find some way of keeping her attention focused on the incredibly absurd idea that he was interesting and important.

And that, from Dr. Eric Marston's perspective, was the most difficult and frustrating problem of all, because the only thing he could think of that made him the least bit interesting and important was his work.

The solution that he came up with was childishly simple, and actually—in the context of far more important things—very harmless. Although, as he faithfully recorded in his illicit diary, he was pretty sure that his small group of peers—and, certainly, the Research Center Directorate—would be dismayed and perhaps even horrified if they ever found out.

As it turned out, he was absolutely right.

CHAPTER SIX

IN SPITE OF FEELING DISORIENTED, CONFUSED, AND EXTREMELY tired, Colin Cellars still had the presence of mind to check the array of video and sensor monitors he and Malcolm Byzor had mounted on the wall near his bed before he walked downstairs and opened his front door.

One of the flat-screen monitors displayed, in bright blue dots, the one-second-interval-tracked movements of the delivery van parked in his driveway. Another series of red diamonds revealed the equivalent one-second-interval "footprint" track of a single individual who had walked from the driver's side door to Cellars's front porch. Two other monitor screens displayed front and side views of that individual. All of the other monitors showed no unusual activity in the five acres of clearing that surrounded his log cabin.

Nothing out of the ordinary, as far as Cellars could tell, other than the fact that the deer—a young mule deer and her fawns, who had become regular visitors over the past few weeks—hadn't shown up yet that morning. But he still took the precaution of sliding his .40-caliber SIG-Sauer semiautomatic pistol under the back waistband of his jeans before going downstairs, and checking the peephole before releasing the dead bolt.

Okay, Dawson, Cellars thought as he pulled open the heavy door, *wherever you are, I hope you're satisfied. I'm finally starting to act like a little old lady who's absolutely convinced that every creaking floorboard is an approaching robber, rapist, or ax murderer.*

In addition to looking annoyingly earnest, alert, and energetic at six o'clock in the morning, the slender young man standing on Cellars's front porch—wearing low-cut boots, brown pants, and a thick down jacket with the logo RELIABLE MESSENGER SERVICES embroidered in bright blue thread on the breast pocket—also seemed vaguely apologetic.

"I'm sorry I had to keep leaning on that buzzer, sir," he said as he watched Cellars sign the receipt, "but you live pretty far off the beaten path, and I had very specific instructions to stay here until I personally handed you that envelope. And it looks like it's about ready to start snowing or hailing again, any minute now, so I figured—"

"No problem, I had to get up pretty soon anyway," Cellars replied, instinctively taking in the surrounding scenery as he handed the receipt pad back to the messenger. He started to reach into his back pocket to pull out his wallet, then realized he'd left it on his dresser. "Hold on just a second and I'll get you—"

"That's okay, sir, it's already been taken care of," the messenger called over his shoulder as he ran back to his van.

Sir?

Already been taken care of?

Cellars stood there on his front porch and stared at the rapidly departing delivery van with a growing sense of unease. It could be the truck, he told himself, or the remnants of the second weird dream of the night that were still flickering somewhere in the depths of his subconscious.

Definitely weird. Have to remember to tell Pleausant, he thought as he tried to remember the context of the dream—the bizarre idea that Jody

Catlin, Bobby Dawson, and Malcolm Byzor, his treasured childhood friends, had been working crime scenes for the Oregon State Patrol under his direct supervision—without any appreciable success. He finally gave up the effort and turned his attention to the block printing on the letter-size manila envelope.

Very familiar block printing, in fact.

Dawson?

A sudden blast of cold air reminded Cellars that he was standing out on his front porch in nothing but jeans and a light pullover shirt . . . at six o'clock on what looked to be yet another cold, dark, and icy morning in Jasper County, Oregon. The messenger had been right, he realized. It did look like it was about to start to snow or hail at any moment.

"Wonderful," he muttered to himself as he went back inside and slammed the door shut.

———

They were intrigued by this latest development; so much so, that the dominant one immediately released her subordinate to follow the delivery van.

It was a good decision. Valuable information might be gleaned from the driver, and the timing was almost perfect. Even so, the less-experienced retriever's eyes glistened in a brief flash of amusement as she acknowledged the order.

It wasn't a question of priorities. Detective-Sergeant Colin Cellars—and his connection to Bobby Dawson—was the recognized key to any successful recovery, and it made sense to double the coverage on his movements. But the retrievers were expected to function independently, without the slightest concern or need for backup. Only when a project was in a critical stage—as this one most certainly was—was more than one retriever activated to pick up after a failed exploration. But the entire Exploratory Control System had been designed to be endlessly adaptable. That was the beauty of it . . . and the elegance.

In any case, two highly aggressive and experienced retrievers at a shared surveillance site were still considered an overkill by a factor of two . . . especially if they ever got in each other's way. Which had been known to happen when things got completely confused or out of control. But that wouldn't happen on this particular mission. The team leader would see to that. Any such possibilities—or at least the most likely ones—had been fully discussed during the initial planning stages. Given the circumstances, and the limited number of targets involved, there should be no significant surprises, or delays.

Which was not to say these retrievers took their quarry lightly. The humans were clever creatures, and dangerous, too, in terms of persistence, thoughtfulness, and logical progression—as well as a very limited technical sense. It spoke well of the inherent adaptability of the basic double-stranded helix model . . . and of the Greater Evolutionary Plan, the dominant one mused.

The Ancient Ones would be pleased.

But even so, it was much too early in their development for these humans to be finding evidence of other, far more advanced civilizations. That could be extremely dangerous . . . and had to be avoided at any cost. Even if it meant a full-scale retrieval and extermination, and a subsequent reseeding. All of which would be a terrible waste of time . . . and an even worse blot on the historical records of the recovery team.

But none of that would be necessary once the lost evidence was retrieved, the bodies recovered, and all records of their existence on this planet destroyed.

Which would happen . . . very soon now, the dominant one reminded herself, finding visceral comfort in the anticipation of events to come.

The urge to protect—and, if necessary, to recover—the young ones during their critical early explorations was deeply ingrained in the retrievers.

It wasn't just maternal.

It was organismic.

And the Deities save any lesser organism that had the misfortune to get in the way.

The mother of Allesandra smiled—a cold and vicious smile—as she allowed her eyes to focus briefly on the distant, closed door of Detective-Sergeant Colin Cellars.

CHAPTER SEVEN

TEN MINUTES LATER, AS CELLARS SAT IN HIS FAVORITE READING chair and stared at the bizarre contents of the manila envelope, the phone next to his chair rang loudly.

"Hello?"

"Hi, it's me."

Jody.

He recognized her distinctive voice immediately, even over the soft rock music in the background. And then felt the all-too-familiar pang in his chest as the image of Jody Catlin, with her shimmering blue eyes, flowing dark hair, and mischievous dimpled grin, appeared in his mind.

But then, as always, the face of Jody Catlin diffused into a slightly altered image: the face of a very similar but altogether different woman that he simply couldn't erase from his memories.

Allesandra.

"Did you get a special delivery from Bobby this morning?" Jody demanded before Cellars could respond.

No "good morning, how are you?" No "I had a nice time last Saturday. Let's do it again sometime soon." Just "hi, it's me." This was the way their relationship had been for the last couple of weeks, ever since that first night after her release from the observation ward.

Distant. Very distant.

Colin Cellars sighed.

"I'm looking at it right now," he said, unable to keep from yawning.

"Well?"

"Well, what?"

A pause, then, "Maybe I'm overreacting, but I think he's finally gone off the deep end this time."

"Oh, really? Why do you say that?"

In spite of the fact that he was virtually certain he recognized Bobby Dawson's characteristic block printing on the mysterious manila envelope, the unusual behavior of the messenger was still pinging at Cellars's subconscious. How many earnest and apologetic young deliverymen started their rounds at six o'clock in the morning, then didn't bother to hang around for a potential double tip? Not many, in Cellars's experience. Accordingly, he'd set the .40-caliber SIG-Sauer semiautomatic pistol down on the lamp table—within easy reach—and had then spent the last five minutes carefully feeling the thin envelope before finally shrugging off his sense of caution and breaking the seal.

He'd found a single eight-by-ten black-and-white photo, and another envelope containing an incomprehensible note, presumably written in French, and apparently from the Paris-based desk of a journalist named Claire-Anne Leduc.

"Why?" Jody Catlin squawked in disbelief. "Are you serious? Hockey Fans of the Seventeenth Century? With the Pope as the central figure, selling crucifixion dogs and beer to the Rolling Stones? And all these strange gargoyles and religious artifacts?"

Cellars's eyebrows furrowed in confusion.

"Jody, what the hell are you talking about?" he demanded.

"Aren't you looking at it?"

"I'm looking at a very gloomy and slightly blurry, black-and-white photograph of some guy I've never seen before leaning against some kind of really weird-looking stone carving. But I don't see any Popes, hockey fans, or any kind of hot dogs, much less any religious artifacts. What are you looking at?"

"A black-and-white photograph of Bobby's latest art project. And the Pope is definitely there in the stadium. No question about it."

"In a seventeenth-century hockey stadium, along with the Stones?"

"The Stones, the Three Musketeers, the Pep Boys—remember them? Manny, Moe, and Jack?—who seem to be sponsoring the opposing team with auto parts T-shirts, Rembrandt, Rubens, Caravaggio, and . . . if I'm reading the insert correctly . . . Elvis and the Holy Trinity of Blondes."

"All of whom—or at least the last three—undoubtedly have gargantuan bare breasts?" Cellars guessed, smiling slightly in spite of his confusion.

"Exactly. And then there's a second page with a cartoon sketch of Elmer Fudd surrounded by a bunch of what looks like gargoyles, icons, and other religious statues . . . one of which is labeled *Mother of the Loire*."

"Sounds like classic Dawson to me," Cellars commented. "And definitely way out there . . . which doesn't come as a tremendous surprise, seeing as how we all know our mutual buddy's been dancing around on the outer edge of sanity for pretty much his entire life." He tossed the photograph onto his lamp table. "But be that as it may, you're still avoiding the question."

"What question?"

"The one I asked you last Saturday."

Another, much longer pause.

"I don't remember."

Cellars sighed.

"Okay, let's try it one more time. Are you going back to Dr. Pleasant again—with me or without me, either way—yes or no?"

"If you're going to put it that way, the answer is no."

"Why the hell not?"

"Because I'm not about to let somebody like that peel back the top of my skull just so he can try to exorcise my demons."

"I don't think that's quite how the process works," Cellars pointed out.

"Oh, really? How would you know? Have you seen him yet?" the raspy voice on the other end of the line demanded.

"Briefly," Cellars acknowledged.

"So what did you talk about? Me?"

"The four of us, actually," Cellars responded. "You, me, Bobby, and Malcolm."

That seemed to catch Jody Catlin off guard. For about six seconds, the only thing that Cellars could hear was the sound of her breathing.

"That's strange," she finally said. "Why would Pleausant be interested in Malcolm?"

"I don't know. I suppose he wanted to have a sense of how the four of us were connected."

"And you told him?"

He could hear the accusation in her voice.

"I told him, briefly, about how we all got together in the first place, when we were kids . . . and how we managed to get twisted up and separated about ten years later . . . and how none of that mattered anymore. Or at least not to me," he added pointedly.

"And how did he respond to that?"

"He didn't, really," Cellars said. "Mostly, he just nodded and took notes. I got the impression he was saving his more probing questions for my session this afternoon."

"You're still going?" she asked, sounding incredulous.

"Sure, why not?"

And besides, what choice do I have? Cellars thought morosely.

"I told you before, Colin, you're out of your mind if you go there," Jody said flatly.

"Maybe so," Cellars acknowledged, "but that's exactly what the OSP's going to think if I don't go."

The voice at the other end of the line hesitated.

"Okay, fine . . . be my guest. Let that creepy bastard peel back the top of your skull and try to flush all those nasty demons of yours out. Then come back and tell me how good it felt. Maybe, if you're really convincing, I'll go back. But don't count on it."

"As I recall, the original idea was that the three of us would all go together," Cellars reminded her.

"Who? You, me, and Bobby?" Jody Catlin laughed derisively. "That'll be the day. Can you imagine a shrink like Pleausant trying to poke around in Bobby's psyche? Probably get that big, hairy hand of his bit right off," she added in a voice filled with what Cellars thought sounded like pleasant anticipation.

"That way," he went on patiently, trying—without much success—to ignore the mental imagery, "we might actually accomplish something." He wasn't going to mention that Dawson's unexpected arrival in Pleausant's office, and the altercation that followed, was the primary reason his initial session with Pleausant had been so brief.

"Such as?"

"I don't know. Figure out why we can't . . . why I couldn't—"

"Colin, you and I don't need some freaky, government-paid psychiatrist to help us figure out our problem," Jody Catlin interjected, not even trying to keep the pain and bitterness out of her voice. "It's her, plain and simple."

Colin Cellars closed his eyes and sighed once again.

"Well?"

"Look, Jody, we've been through this before. It's not like I'm in love with the bitch. She used me, just like she used Bobby. Like a chunk of raw meat that she chewed on for a while, then tossed aside. And besides, she's dead . . . or gone. Or . . . whatever." His voice drifted off uncertainly.

"But you were in love with her, damn it! You both were."

"It wasn't love. I don't know how to describe it. In fact, I'm not sure it's even describable. But it definitely wasn't love. Or at least not the way I understand the term. More like a fascination . . . or compulsion," he added hesitantly.

"Compulsion? Is that what you call it?" The familiar husky laugh again, but there was no humor in her voice at all. Only the anger and the pain . . . and something that, to Cellars, sounded very much like fear. "Come on, Colin, admit it. Every time we try to get together now—not that we even try that anymore," she added bitterly, "you're thinking about her. I know you are. I can see it in your eyes."

"Jody—"

"Damn it, Colin, even when we talk on the phone, you don't see my face. You see hers. You can't get her out of your head, can you?"

A long pause.

"No, I can't," he whispered.

"Why not?" Jody demanded. "I'm here, Colin. I'm real . . . and she's dead. Absolutely dead and gone. Bobby blew her head apart with that damned Sharps rifle, and then the two of you picked up all the rocks and pieces and turned them over to Malcolm. Don't you remember?"

"I know Allesandra is dead, and I know we killed her. But—"

"Oh, to hell with it. I can't even talk with you anymore."

"Jody—"

The phone went dead in Cellars's hand.

CHAPTER EIGHT

THE TAP INTO THE PHONE LINE WAS YIELDING NOTHING OF DIRECT value, only a steady stream of seemingly random data, back and forth. But, as unproductive as the tap was, the presence of a seemingly random data flow was useful information in and of itself.

It suggested, among many other things, that the phones on both ends of the conversation were encrypted at a relatively sophisticated level . . . thus implying high-level connections with one of their primary targets.

Given the time, and access to the necessary equipment, the dominant one could have easily broken the code. And even without the equipment, the rhythm of the data flow gave her the sense that the underlying matrices were relatively simple. But none of that relatively advanced—and normally forbidden—technology would be necessary here. The tap she had surreptitiously inserted through the outer walls of the cabin gave her half of the conversation.

And as it turned out, the half she needed.

I know Allesandra is dead, and I know we killed her.

Fateful words . . . and the ones she had been seeking.

Confirmation.

But even so, there was no hurry. Not now. Not when everything was in place.

Accordingly, she waited until the steady flow of data stopped before she sliced through the thin wires with an almost indifferent flick of her claws.

Then, having cut the phone line, she left the shelter of the trees and approached the cabin. Now that the decision had been made, she was determined to take him quickly, when he stepped outside to leave more food for the birds and before he could use his cell phone to raise an alarm. That would give her more time to extract critical information . . . and, later, to dispose of the body.

And once they had done so, she would go after the others, one at a time.

Coldly.

Methodically.

And without the slightest sense of mercy.

For she had none, this experienced retriever. Only a sense of mission . . . and urgency.

One of the Ancient Ones would be coming soon, to assess the status of the project, and she had to be ready.

CHAPTER NINE

CELLARS STARED AT THE HUMMING PHONE IN HIS HAND, FEELING his mind go numb as he realized that he might have let it go too far this time.

What was it that Dr. Pleausant had said?

It's okay to talk about what she remembers, but don't push her too hard. And don't even think about getting her to testify about her experiences at a hearing or in court. If you do that, she'll just retreat further . . . to the point that you could lose her for good.

Is that what I just did? Cellars agonized as he continued to stare down at the phone in his hand. *Lose her for good?*

It was a depressing thought.

But what else could I do? Lie to her? Tell her that I never think about her anymore? Tell her that I don't remember what happened, either?

Lost in the aftereffects of his latest argument with the woman who, over the past fifteen years, had never ceased to be the focus of what little romance he'd had in his life, Colin Cellars was barely aware of having dropped the handset back down on the receiver.

Which was why the sudden, shrill ringing startled him, and caused him to grab at the handset.

The phone was dead.

But before he had a chance to think about why, or how, his cell phone began to demand attention.

"Jody, I—"

Then he hesitated when he realized there was no music in the background this time.

"Hello?"

"How's it going, *compadre?*"

Dawson.

Cellars wanted to say something like "Where the hell have you been the past few weeks?" Or "Why did you wait so long to call?" But some cautionary sense warned him he might be better off if he didn't know.

"Well," he answered instead, "all things considered, I guess I've been better . . . and a hell of a lot worse."

"Yeah, that's what I hear," Dawson replied. "So I figured I'd better check in, see if I could cheer you up some."

"Good luck."

"Let me guess. You were just talking with Jody, and she's pissed off at you because she thinks you've still got Allesandra on the brain."

Cellars sighed heavily.

"Dawson," he finally said, "why do I get the feeling that I'm the only one of us who doesn't know—on at least an hourly basis—what everyone else is doing?"

"Hey, what can I tell you? Somebody's got to be the wascal wabbit in this little magic show. Can't see any reason why I should be the only one with a cottontail pinned to his ass all the time."

"What?"

"And speaking of which"—Bobby Dawson chuckled—"I understand

from our mutual buddy that you've been doing a real good job of burrowing yourself in."

"You call rigging a couple of security systems around my house 'burrowing myself in'?"

"Log house smack-dab in the middle of a clearing that's surrounded on three sides by a national forest; free-fire zone with a clear line of sight going out a couple hundred yards in all directions; sealed gun slits; three-dimensional laser trip wires; no interior walls downstairs except for the bathroom; a rifled 870 with an extended magazine and a bandolier of buckshot and sabot slugs mounted on each wall? Sounds like the Alamo mentality to me," Dawson replied.

"The . . . Alamo mentality?"

"Yep. Classic old-style military thinking, Colin. Find yourself a nice, secure hidey-hole; stock up on water, ammo, and groceries; nail the back door shut; and then dare the bastards to come in after you. Nice idea in theory, but not so good in practice. You might ask the good Colonel Travis about that. Unless, of course, all you want to do is make some noise and take a bunch of them with you."

"I don't have the advantage of being able to communicate with heroic ghosts," Cellars muttered. "And besides, wasn't that basically what you did up at your cabin, when Allesandra and her little shadow buddies were hunting for your ass?"

Dawson chuckled. "Not exactly. The smart rabbits always dig themselves at least one back door before they hunker down."

"I see," Cellars replied dubiously. "Does this mean you've got a better idea . . . as far as my welfare and mental health are concerned?"

"That I do."

"I'm all ears."

"Exactly what I'm worried about."

"What?"

"That in spite of the best efforts of Malcolm and yours truly, you just might end up being the primary free-range rabbit on this deal."

Cellars sighed heavily again.

"You know, Bobby, seeing as how you disappeared on me right after everything went to shit with Allesandra, popped up unexpectedly right in the middle of my psych evaluation, then disappeared again, I really would like to know where you're calling from. But that's probably a dumb question, right?"

"Nope. A perfectly good one," Bobby Dawson replied in his characteristically cheerful voice. "Fact is, my DEA buddies ask me that very same question every time I check in to see how they're doing. Poor bastards. Wouldn't you think, with all that expensive surveillance gear they keep spending my hard-earned tax dollars on, they'd be able to track back one simple little phone call? Especially when I make it a point to call in at pretty much the same time every day?"

"To tell you the truth, the thing I have trouble believing is that you actually pay your taxes. But, in any case, they probably could track you down if you didn't have Malcolm rigging the game in your favor," Cellars pointed out.

"Well, yeah, you're probably right," Dawson agreed. "Always nice to have a first-class electronics genius on your side when things start getting a little technical."

"So, tell me, why exactly are you picking on your DEA buddies these days? Just to piss them off? Or is it more along the line that guys like Pleausant and the NSA just aren't stimulating enough?"

Dawson chuckled. "No, I reckon there's a little more to it. But before we get into all that serious shit, I've got a question for you. What'd you think of it?"

"What did I think of what?"

"Didn't you get it?"

Cellars blinked in sudden realization. "You mean that photo?"

"That's not just a photograph, Colin, my man. If my guess is right, it may turn out to be a significant piece of the puzzle. Maybe even some sort of Bancoo connection. So keep it to yourself, and don't lose track of it."

"*Bancoo connection?* Puzzle? What—?"

"*The* puzzle, Colin, my man. The big question marks. Who, what, when, where, and why. We won't even bother to get into the 'how.' Probably enough to make my head hurt."

Cellars shook his head in confusion. "Bobby, honest to God, I have no idea what you're talking about."

"No, not yet, but you will . . . just as soon as I get you together with a very interesting new friend of mine."

"Oh, yeah? And who's that?"

"You'll see." Dawson chuckled again. "Hey, before I forget, what's the password on your alarm system out there, in case I need a hidey-hole to drop into real quick?"

"You remember the street address of the range you and I used to shoot at when we were kids?"

Dawson paused for a moment.

"Yep, my favorite calibers."

"There you go. Easy to remember."

"*Muchas gracias, amigo.* Hey, listen, I understand you managed to wrangle another appointment with my good buddy this afternoon."

"If you're talking about Pleasant, that's right. You planning on showing up again, see if you can get him to wet his pants two visits in a row?"

"Be delighted to, partner. But, to tell you the truth, I really don't think my messing around with the good doctor's sense of reality would do much for your law enforcement career right at the moment, so why don't we get together afterward?"

"I'm sure Pleasant would be eternally grateful," Cellars replied. "Any particular time and place?"

"Just hang loose, I'll let you know when . . . uh-oh, looks like my little friend finally showed up. Gotta go. Bye."

"Bobby, wait—!"

Click.

CHAPTER TEN

STILL TREMBLING FROM AFTEREFFECTS OF SHOCK, AS WELL AS THE icy wind, the young deliveryman stared in dismay at the pair of flat tires, the first of which had nearly gotten him killed.

And still might cost me my job, if I can't get a tow truck to respond to a radio pretty damned quick, he reminded himself as he stepped back from the disabled van to further examine his surroundings.

What little he was able to see in the thick fog turned out to be chilling.

Another fifteen feet and the heavy delivery van would have slid all the way off the road, across a narrow dirt embankment, in between two precariously positioned pines, and through a split-rail fence. And then—as he discovered when he braced himself against one of the flimsy fence posts and looked down—right over a steep cliff edge for a drop of God knew how far. Probably several hundred feet, he guessed.

"Damn, that was close," the young man whispered as he quickly moved to more secure ground.

In fact, it really had been a very near thing.

He'd been running very late . . . mostly because of the unauthorized delivery, but also because of a wrong turn he'd made after coming out of Colin Cellars's long and winding access road. So, in an effort to make up the lost time—and in violation of all company rules and regs to the contrary—he'd been traveling well over the safe speed limit for the prevailing road and weather conditions when the van's left rear tire suddenly ruptured.

A blowout on a narrow, downward-sloping icy road with blind curves, poor visibility even without the shifting fog, and another storm rapidly approaching, was a dicey situation at best—even for an experienced driver. But given the location of the blowout, and the inherent stability of the heavy, low-slung van, even a rookie should have been able to bring the situation under control. A couple of quick taps on the brakes, a little bit of panicky steering to compensate for the van's yaw and momentum, and the sturdy vehicle would have ground itself to a stop against the side of the mountain on the opposite side of the road. A bit worse for the wear and tear, no doubt; but van and driver would still have been in one piece.

The inherent stability of the van, however, was lost the moment that the back end began to swing out to the left and crossed over the center divider, whereupon the front tires hit a nearly invisible patch of black ice. At that point, the delivery van became, in essence, a large, heavy hockey puck.

It was heading straight for the fog-concealed, cliffside edge—completely out of control, as far as the helpless young driver was concerned—when, miracle of all miracles, the left front tire suddenly blew out.

Even more miraculous, the downward momentum of the second blowout occurred just at the right moment—sending the edge of the suddenly exposed front wheel rim deep into the frozen, but far less solid, dirt edge of the road, thereby causing the van to grind to a stop.

Now, as he staggered back to the van, it occurred to the driver that he might be able to work himself out of his dilemma by threatening to sue the company for installing cheap tires. No one would have to know that the second blowout had actually been a lifesaver. But when he knelt to examine the left front tire, hoping against all odds to find a cheap retread, the actual cause of his salvation became readily apparent.

"A goddamned nail . . . out here in the middle of nowhere? I don't believe it," the young deliveryman rasped hoarsely as he pulled himself up and reached into the van cab for the radio mike.

The saving nail head gleamed in silent reply amid the twisted and ice-encrusted tire treads.

The second offending nail head would have been visible, too, but the young deliveryman was much too busy fumbling with the frequency selector on the van's console radio to bother examining the rear tire.

"Come on, damn it! Isn't anybody out there?" he yelled into the mike. But no matter which frequency he used, all he got in return was static.

It was only then that the deliveryman paused to think about where he actually was on the all-too-familiar road.

"Oh shit," he whispered.

He realized, now, there was a very good reason why his radio wasn't picking up anything. And why it never would. Not out here.

Not out on Broken Back.

Had he not been distracted by the ultimately irresistible offer of a hundred dollars to make a quick, illicit delivery to Colin Cellars's remote cabin, the young driver would have realized that the diversion would take him through a stretch of roadway known to the locals as Broken Back. So named because, on a map, it looked like a long, thin snake that had its back broken in about a dozen places.

But, more to the point, Broken Back also happened to be one of the infamous dead zones so prevalent in the mountainous regions of Jasper County. A section where even the relatively wide and flexible radio waves in the AM band had difficulty penetrating the masses of rock and trees that surrounded and encapsulated the narrow, windy, backcountry road.

The driver realized, at that moment, that he would lose his job for sure, now. Because the only way he'd ever get a tow truck out here would be to hike out—a good three or four miles—in cold, gloomy, foggy weather that was threatening to get worse by the minute. Knowing, as he did so, that even if he did manage to contact a tow company and even if an extra tire for the van was readily available, it would be noon at least before he got back on his delivery rounds. Which meant there was absolutely no possibility that he'd make even half of his stops and pickups by the guaranteed arrival time.

Which, normally, wouldn't have been all that big a deal. Accidents happened, and the presence of a nail in a flat tire would have been enough in the way of evidence to keep the manager from taking the resulting penalties out of his paycheck. All he would have had to do was change the flat, finish his stops, and then deliver the blown tire—complete with nail—to the manager the next day.

But having two flats was a different story altogether. First of all, the van only carried one spare, so someone was going to have to make a run out to Broken Back with another tire, which meant—unless he could pay someone off—the manager was bound to see the charge slip and start asking questions. And if one of those questions ever touched on the nonexistent shipment that had sent him out on Broken Back in the first place, then his relatively high-paying job with Reliable Messenger Services would be finished.

It was such a distracting thought that the young man never heard or saw the dark, shadowy figure coming up behind him in the concealing fog.

Instead, it was the sharp report of a gunshot that brought his head up. And a high-pitched scream of surprise and pain—immediately followed by the sound of a heavy body crashing to the ground behind him—that caused the young deliveryman to spin around and stare across the hood of his disabled van into the gray, hazy mist.

He was starting to back away from the van, thinking that some kind of injured animal—a bear, maybe—was on the other side, when the shadowy form of some kind of creature rose up from behind the van hood.

The deliveryman's immediate reaction was one of relief, because he knew a bear didn't have a head like that. But that relief was immediately obliterated by his stunning realization that nothing else—or at least nothing he knew of—had a head like that, either.

Then, to his horror, he saw what looked like a big construction nail—at least a ten-penny job, with blue strips of plastic bunched up under the head—sticking out of the creature's forehead, just above the . . .

At that moment, the creature's eyes opened.

The young deliveryman stumbled backward, screaming, and slipped on the black ice just as a much louder gunshot echoed through the mountains.

He had a vague sense of something whipping past his head, and the terrible sound of an expanding-tip bullet exploding through hard tissue echoed in his ears. But he was much too busy screaming—and trying to regain his balance—to focus any attention on the completely unfamiliar sounds.

But then, mercifully, his head hit the ice hard, and all of his terror dissolved into nothingness.

———

High up in the tree line, and about 150 yards from the disabled delivery van, Bobby Dawson smoothly worked the bolt to eject a smoking brass cartridge casing and feed a second high-velocity, hollow-pointed .375-caliber round into the chamber of his heavy, scoped rifle.

The encrypted cell phone that Malcolm Byzor had given him several weeks ago, now a useless pile of broken chipboards and plastic, lay forgotten in the snow, the victim of his hasty effort to reposition himself for the critical second nail shot when he'd suddenly realized the delivery van was still sliding toward the cliff edge.

Then, after verifying his trusted .44 Magnum revolver was close at hand, Dawson settled back into his camouflaged position and waited with the easy patience of a professional hunter . . . and the pleasant anticipation of a cold-hearted killer.

To see if these alien creatures—who had been tracking and monitoring his friends over the past two days—had, in fact, been arrogant enough to split up and send only one of their kind to intercept and interrogate the unsuspecting youth about the package he'd just delivered to the remote cabin.

CHAPTER ELEVEN

SHE WAS INSIDE THE TRACTOR SHED NEXT TO COLIN CELLARS'S cabin now—waiting with predatory patience for the moment he left the shelter of the cabin, and listening at a tiny hole she'd carefully bored at the juncture between two of the cabin's thick wall logs—when she heard him speak two of the critical names.

Bobby.

Malcolm.

Alert now, the dominant one slid back into the shadows . . . to listen and to see what more she could glean from her auditory surveillance. There was no point in wasting a useful opportunity.

That was when she felt it.

The sensation of a sudden, chilling emptiness . . . as if, for a brief moment, she had come into physical contact with the void.

The sensation was elusive—the others were too far away for direct telepathic communication—but at the same time, all too familiar . . . and all too real.

In a barely measurable instant, the dominant one set aside her personal anger and began to focus on the problem at hand, concentrating now on her sensors.

The ethereal web that held them together was weaker now, by a measurable and significant amount. There was no doubt about it. One of the retrievers had just been destroyed.

Her immediate instinct was to bare her teeth and scream her outrage into the dark, clouded sky, thereby notifying these lesser creatures that they had transgressed . . . and would pay with their lives. But she held back, responding to a sudden sense of foreboding that, in essence, amounted to a fear of the unknown. And a more pertinent issue.

Which one did they lose?

It was an important question. And, in the greater scheme of things, far more important than the information that might be gleaned from the inquisition of a single human . . . even one as directly involved in the missing evidence as was this Colin Cellars.

The retrievers were not to be killed or destroyed. That was simply unacceptable. But the possibility that the recovery itself might have been put into jeopardy by the loss of a crucially placed retriever was worse . . . far worse. That was unthinkable.

The situation would have to be investigated immediately. There was no other option.

The personal rage was still there, but discernible only in the flickering glare of the dominant one's cold eyes as she drew back into the increasingly foggy shadows of the cold and gloomy dawn. Alert, as always, for the surveillance that they all sensed . . . but, as yet, hadn't located.

———

Colin Cellars shook his head in frustration as he folded up the cell phone.

He knew, instinctively, that he should be concentrating on other things—like what the strange phone call from Bobby Dawson was all about, or why his home phone had suddenly gone dead—but he couldn't get Jody Catlin's pleading voice out of his mind.

Don't you remember?

Yeah, right.

As if he could possibly forget about her . . . or Allesandra . . . or about all of the mind-numbing and gut-wrenching events that had occurred on that incredible afternoon out by Bobby Dawson's cabin almost two months ago.

Cellars shuddered.

Oh, yeah, Jody, I definitely remember every minute of it. Like it happened yesterday. The question is, do you?

That was the point—or at least one of the points—the two of them had been discussing for the last four weeks. First at her hospital room . . . then at Cellars's new house, the evening she'd been let out . . . and that disastrous next morning . . . then, ever since, over the phone, from wherever she was staying.

The question of what was real, and what wasn't.

But it was a circular argument, with no possible resolution, because they couldn't even begin to agree on what had actually taken place during that incredible and terrifying six-day period . . . much less prove any of it. Especially now that all of the relevant evidence was either missing, destroyed, or in the hands of the National Security Agency.

And especially when that supposed reality involves a couple dozen gunshots that I fired at a bunch of shadows . . . an erotic, horrifying, and nearly fatal contact with a mesmerizing alien femme fatale . . . and some incomprehensible DNA samples that supposedly possessed three sets of base pairs instead of the customary two . . . not to mention a couple of silicon atoms in that extra set of base pairs where there should have been carbons. All of which is described, in gory detail, in a police report that doesn't make any sense at all to me, either, and I wrote the damned thing, Cellars thought glumly as he glanced down at his wristwatch and realized he was running late.

And then, of course, the one piece of actual evidence that we still have: the confirmed presence of a hallucinogenic drug in the sample of my blood that I voluntarily provided to the Oregon State Patrol.

Cellars walked over to the bedroom portion of his new home and started to remove his work clothes—a pair of faded blue jeans, a thick flannel shirt, and low-cut hiking boots—from the closet.

But I didn't imagine any of it. I know I didn't, he tried to convince himself for perhaps the hundredth time as he got dressed, then secured the SIG-Sauer's leather holster over his left shoulder and his badge to his wide belt. *I couldn't have. And neither could she. But she won't admit it. Or can't.*

That was the other factor. The possibility that Jody Catlin, his childhood friend and would-be lover, had somehow managed to tuck it all away back in some deep, dark, and unreachable corner of her mind . . . where it wouldn't bother her anymore.

Selective awareness, the doctor had called it. The real memories are still there, and she might even acknowledge them every now and then. But at this stage, you can expect her to fight desperately against any effort to bring them back to the surface. And if you persist, she'll just wall herself off.

Which is exactly what happened, Cellars suddenly realized, as Jody's last words echoed through his mind.

I'm here, Colin. I'm real . . . and she's dead. Absolutely dead and gone. Bobby blew her head apart with that damned Sharps rifle, and then the two of you picked up all the rocks and pieces and turned them over to Malcolm. Don't you remember?

Selective awareness.

Cellars understood the term now because he knew for a fact that Jody Catlin hadn't seen anyone—much less he and Dawson—collect the stones and turn them over to Malcolm.

She couldn't have, because she was unconscious, in shock, and on the way to the hospital at the time. And I know that for a fact, because I was the one who was driving her there.

Cellars sighed as the solemn words of Dr. H. Milhaus Pleausant whispered through his mind again.

It's okay to talk about what she remembers, but don't push her too hard. And don't even think about getting her to testify about her experiences at a hearing or in court. If you do that, she'll just retreat further . . . to the point that you could lose her for good.

It was perfectly reasonable advice, and Cellars wasn't about to put his treasured friendship with Jody Catlin—or her sanity—at any more risk by doing so.

But that being the case, he was facing a very difficult problem. According to Sergeant Tom Bauer—who had been functioning as OSP Region 9's acting watch commander and station commander since Captain Hawkins's apparent death and the hospitalization of Lieutenant Talbert—the bizarre nature of some of Cellars's comments shortly after what was now being widely referred to in the OSP as the Dawson Incident had seriously jarred some of the brass up in Salem. So much so, it was very possible that Cellars might need a supportive eyewitness just to stay employed as an Oregon State Patrol officer.

Which was probably the primary reason headquarters sent the head of Internal Affairs down to oversee things in Region 9, Cellars realized.

But if Jody Catlin couldn't testify as to what she saw during those mind-numbing six days, then the only other person in the world who could possibly verify the details Cellars had so vividly described in his investigative report was Bobby Dawson.

Which was an unfortunate situation at best, because the reputation of ex–Special Agent Bobby Dawson was equally infamous in the annals of the federal Drug Enforcement Agency—Dawson's most recent employer—which very definitely wanted its helicopter and four missing agents back. Or, alternatively, a reasonable explanation as to why a five-ton Apache attack helicopter, a supposedly fiery crash site, and four members of the DEA's accident-investigating Internal Affairs team were still missing.

And how did I describe him . . . my long-lost buddy and Sharps-rifle-shooting savior, upon whom I'm going to have to depend to vouch for my *sanity? A person who—to quote my own investigative report—in his more lucid moments, considers himself to be some kind of reincarnation of Peter Pan, Wyatt Earp, and General George Armstrong Custer?*

Oh yeah, and who is now creating pen-and-ink sketches of the Pope selling hot dogs and beer to a stadium full of retrograded seventeenth-century hockey fans, and sending them out to his friends by courier at six o'clock in the morning, Cellars reminded himself. *All the while successfully avoiding the teams of DEA agents who are presumably doing their best to serve him with very explicit search and arrest warrants.*

Wonderful.

His cell phone rang again just as Cellars was reaching for his jacket.

"Hello?"

"What's wrong with your phone?"

Jody!

"I don't know. There's supposed to be another storm coming in. Probably a line down somewhere. It doesn't matter. I—"

"Look, I'm sorry . . . I just—"

She hesitated, seeming unable to go on.

"Jody, listen, what if I get Bobby to go there with us?"

"What? To see Pleausant? Are you serious?" she asked incredulously.

"Sure. Why not?"

"Think about what you're saying, Colin. Even if you knew where Bobby is right now—which I assume you don't, or the DEA and the NSA would have you in custody by now—how could you possibly convince him to do something like that?" Jody Catlin asked reasonably.

"First of all, I assume Malcolm knows how to find him. Or, at least, he always claims he does."

"So?"

"I'll get Malcolm to arrange a meeting, or a conference call, or whatever, then appeal to Bobby's pride."

"His pride?"

"It's a guy thing," Cellars tried to explain. "The only way to deal with fear is to—" He hesitated.

"My God," Jody Catlin whispered. "That's it, isn't it? You're still afraid of her. Even though she's dead."

Cellars remained silent.

"And Bobby is, too, isn't he?"

"I don't know," Cellars replied honestly. "It's not something we ever talked about. Tell you the truth, it's kind of a new concept, Bobby being afraid of something."

There was a long pause.

"Colin, she is dead, isn't she? Tell me that's not an issue here."

Cellars could hear the edge of pure, unadulterated terror working its way into her voice.

"No, it's not an issue," he said quickly. "She's dead, plain and simple. You and I were both there when Bobby's bullet caught her right between the eyes . . . and we both saw the result, remember?" Still, he wondered how deep those memories were buried.

"Then what are you and Bobby afraid of? That she could be—what?—put back together again? Regenerated? Reconstituted?"

Definite signs of panic in her voice now.

But she's acknowledging the critical part, Cellars suddenly realized. The fact that Allesandra really was—or had been—something other than human. Or, at least, the assumed fact, he reminded himself. There was still the little matter of evidence. But that was far less important, as far as Cellars was concerned, than the possibility that his friend was losing her grip on reality.

So that's all it is, he thought with a sense of relief. *She's not psychotic. Just scared. Which is perfectly understandable, because I am, too.*

"No, I didn't say that," he replied quickly. "There's no reason at all to believe those stones could be regenerated or restored, or whatever you want to call it, to any kind of life. It's . . . just an idea that Malcolm's been muttering about for the last couple of months."

"What? Using lasers to bring her back?"

"It's just a theory. Nothing to worry about," Cellars said hurriedly. "It's based on something Allesandra told me. She said they were capable of reverting into some kind of emergency standby state—essentially a rock, or something that looks and feels like a rock—when their metabolic systems get shut off. Look, I don't pretend to understand any of this. But you saw her holding those six rocks, and you saw Bobby's bullet hit her right between the eyes, and you saw her fall . . . and the next thing any of us know, there's seven rocks on the ground . . . and no Allesandra, right?"

He waited hopefully, but the line remained silent.

"And before that, when I accidentally exposed one of those rocks to the blue-green lasers in Malcolm's crime scene scanner, it moved all by itself . . . after it had been sealed into a manila evidence envelope.

Moved the whole damned envelope about two feet across the top of a desk. Or, at least, I think it did."

Still no response from the other end of the line.

Don't hang up, Jody, Cellars pleaded silently. *Please, not again.*

"But in spite of all of that," Cellars pressed on carefully, "given the nature of the drug the hospital lab supposedly found in the blood sample I provided, I'd be perfectly willing to shrug the whole six days off as some kind of extended hallucination. Even though I have no idea as to when, or how, or why I might have been drugged . . . or even if I really was, for that matter. But you and Bobby both saw some of it. And Malcolm was able to verify—from the computer files of my crime scene scanner—more movement by that same stone when I activated his scanning lasers twice within a matter of minutes inside Bobby's cabin basement. So—"

"They really are going to try it, aren't they? The regeneration?"

Her voice was catching almost continuously now . . . which was unnerving because it sounded to Cellars like she might be teetering on the edge of a complete nervous breakdown. Something that Dr. Pleausant had suggested was a very real possibility in the first two or three months after experiencing a severe traumatic shock. Which was why the medical staff had wanted to keep her at the clinic for at least a couple more weeks . . . if not a couple of months. But Jody had insisted on checking herself out, then refused to tell him where she was staying. Somewhere safe and far away, that was all she'd say on the subject. And Malcolm had reassured him she really was safe, so he hadn't tried to track the location of her calls . . . yet.

What was it, two weeks ago now?

"No, absolutely not," Cellars said emphatically. "Malcolm won't let them. Not now."

"But how could he possibly stop them? I mean, think about it, Colin. The military industrial complex . . . the advanced technology. How could they possibly not go for it?"

"Because, first, they have to get their hands on the stones . . . which they can't possibly do, because the stones are now in the possession of the National Security Agency. And we know, for a fact—or, at least, according to Malcolm—that the NSA doesn't answer to anyone except the president."

"But—"

"And the same goes for the military," Cellars reminded. "Civilian control all the way down the line, and more world-class weapons platforms than they can keep track of. So, unless some general is willing to risk life in prison just to see if a handful of stones might have any military use beyond slingshot ammo, I think we're safe." It occurred to Cellars to be thankful that Malcolm had insisted on installing encryption devices on all of his phones. He could only hope that his buddy had done the same thing at Jody's hideaway, wherever that was.

Either that, or anyone listening in on this conversation is really going to start worrying about our sanity, he thought ruefully, as Jody remained silent.

"Look, Malcolm is in charge of the assessment project," Cellars pressed on in what he hoped was an encouraging and supportive tone. "And you know Malcolm. There isn't a general or political appointee alive who's going to be able to outsmart him . . . or force him to do something incredibly stupid like that. Especially not until they're ready."

"Ready? What do you mean, ready?"

"It's a matter of containment . . . and common sense. The NSA is not about to try to regenerate those creatures until they're absolutely sure they know how to keep them contained . . . and controlled. They wouldn't dare."

"But how could they possibly know—?"

"That's just it, they don't," Cellars interrupted quickly . . . trying, as he did so, to ignore the tightening in his chest. "Right now, they don't have the first idea about how to contain these things. In fact, when you stop to think about it, they don't even know for sure that these creatures exist. Because the only people we know of who did see them in their adaptive state and lived to talk about it are the three of us. And right now, as far as I know, I'm the only one who's willing to admit that he did see them," he reminded her pointedly.

"What about your Lieutenant Talbert?"

It was an evasive response, at best, but Cellars let it pass. *At least she's still on the line, and acknowledging the topic,* he thought hopefully. It was a start.

"I'm not sure Talbert's going to be very helpful with any of this. I was able to talk with him, briefly, about two weeks ago, right after he came out of the coma. But as best I could tell, he has no independent memory of leaving me at the crash site on Timberline Road, or of dropping my blood sample off at Providence Hospital on his way to turning my CSI vehicle over to the OSP crime lab for processing. He seemed to have a vague recollection of someone or something ramming into the back of whatever vehicle he was driving about two miles from the hospital. After that, apparently, it's all one big blank . . . until he woke up on a respirator in the Providence Hospital intensive care ward six weeks later."

"Oh."

"My CSI vehicle," Cellars went on, "the one I know Talbert was in because I saw him drive it away from my crash site, has never been located; and a comprehensive DNA comparison verified that the blood sample he delivered to the hospital toxicology lab is mine. There are some interesting Polaroid photos in Talbert's hospital records that document some pretty incredible wounds—which are mostly healed scars now—he was in a coma for almost a month and a half before he finally came around—but there's nothing definitive as far as I could tell. Or at least nothing we can use as evidence."

"Great," she muttered sarcastically.

"By the way," Cellars added, "it's Captain Talbert now. Or at least it will be once the doctors ever clear him to come back to work. In the meantime, they made Sergeant Bauer acting station commander until Talbert's status is resolved."

Poor bastard, Cellars thought, as Catlin remained silent.

It occurred to him to wonder why Bauer had asked him to stop by the hospital this morning. *Probably looking for someone to help out with the paperwork. Christ, what a nightmare.*

Cellars tried to imagine what it must have been like for the amiable and previously free-roaming patrol sergeant suddenly to find himself saddled with two headache-generating Regional desk jobs; a missing OSP captain; and a suspended CSI detective-sergeant who claimed to have taken potshots at extraterrestrials.

Even more worrisome: In spite of Cellars's persistent albeit cautious inquiries, no one in the headquarters office professed to having any idea about what his next field assignment would be once he came back off his mandated two-month administrative leave.

Assuming, of course, that I actually get another field assignment, instead of an administrative desk job, Cellars thought morosely. He was all too aware that the OSP hadn't, as far as he knew, put together a hearing board on the Dawson Incident . . . a fact that could easily make the whole question of his going back into the field a moot point.

It occurred to Cellars that he might be a whole lot better off if he simply volunteered to help Bauer, up front, before someone in Salem came up with something much worse. The trouble was, at the moment, he really couldn't think of an assignment that would be much worse.

"Has anybody been able to talk with Talbert recently?" Jody asked hesitantly. "To see if he remembers what happened when they—"

Her voice dropped away, as if the memories of her own encounter with the visitors were still much too painful . . . or too terrifying.

"I don't think so," Cellars said. "According to Bauer, they've had him tucked away in the ICU ward ever since he came out of the coma. Something about the doctors trying to fight off some kind of respiratory infection that got out of control. I'm going to stop by the hospital this morning, see how he's doing, before I—"

"So, as far as you know, he never did see who it was who attacked him?" Jody interrupted.

"No, apparently not. Or, if he did, he isn't saying anything," Cellars added thoughtfully.

"Smart man," Jody muttered in a soft, but steadier voice.

"Maybe," Cellars acknowledged. "But, in any case, it leaves us exactly in the same position we were when this conversation started: with nothing in the way of supporting evidence."

"What about my DNA extracts?"

"What about them?"

"Melissa and I both worked on those tissue samples you sent over with Jack Wilson. All three of us were in sight of each other during the entire extraction process, and all three of us saw the data—especially the part about the silicon substitutions on the third set of base pairs. Melissa and Jack can both testify to all of that . . . and I'll bet they would. So what more does anyone want?"

"That's very fine, as far as it goes," Cellars agreed. "But when you stop to think about it, the only thing the three of you saw were images on a monitor. Just graphic interpretations of data generated by a computer program that was actually running the sequencer."

"So?"

"Every one of those sequence images could have been faked by a good computer programmer," Cellars pointed out. "It wouldn't have been all that hard to do, especially if at least one of you was in on the conspiracy."

"Melissa or Jack? Are you serious?"

"You and I know the likelihood of that is next to zero," Cellars agreed. "But that's because we know them . . . or think we do. But even so, no matter what the three of you might agree to, you still don't have copies of your data, your charts, or the extracts and tissue samples. Or any other piece of physical evidence to back up your statements, for that matter," he added, "because you turned all that over to someone you had good reason to believe was a Jasper County sheriff's deputy.

"And don't forget," Cellars went on when Jody didn't respond, "the NSA has written testimony from three highly regarded emeritus professors of organic chemistry who state emphatically that the silicon-carbon substitution on the extra set of base pairs you, Melissa, and Jack described is physically impossible to reproduce."

"With our existing technology."

"Or maybe impossible, period, which is certainly what they suggested in their report."

"So, where does that leave us?"

"At the same place we've been for the last two months. Keeping our heads down, and what we know—or, at least, what we think we know—to ourselves while we try to get on with our lives."

"Knowing full well that if we ever did say anything to anyone outside our immediate law enforcement group, we'd be branded as nutcases and probably forced to retire from our jobs," Jody Catlin finished. "After all, who's going to trust a nutcase to work with evidence?"

"Exactly," Cellars agreed. "But don't you see, that gives us an advantage?"

"No, I don't see that at all. Explain it to me."

"It gives us time. Time to try to make sense of what we know, and what we think we know. And, more importantly, time for Malcolm to work out the containment issues. Which means that as long as no one else—like the military—knows NSA has the rocks, then Malcolm and his genius buddies can take as much time as they need to work out all the safety factors before they even think about experimenting with the lasers."

"So how long are we talking about?"

"I don't know," Cellars confessed. "According to Malcolm, ten years at an absolute minimum. But I expect they'll probably wait twenty, just to be safe. I mean even the federal government wouldn't be crazy enough to let a bunch of NSA research scientists cut corners on a crucial step like that, no matter how badly they—or the military—might want the technology."

"Yeah, maybe—"

"And then there's the matter of energy levels," Cellars pressed on. "If Malcolm's estimates are even halfway close, I get the impression that we're years—maybe even decades—away from constructing phased blue-green lasers with that kind of focused power."

"But how would they know that? They're just guessing. They have to be," Jody protested. "I mean, no matter how smart Malcolm is—and I'll grant you he can be pretty damned brilliant when he puts his mind to it—or how many other off-the-chart-IQ geniuses he's got working with him, how can they possibly even estimate what it's going to take to regenerate one of these . . . creatures? Assuming that it's even possible in the first place," she added.

Cellars smiled. *Okay, that's more like it.*

"I think what it really comes down to is risk assessment," he suggested in a quiet voice. "Something we know that Malcolm's really good at. So I've got to believe—as long as he's in control of the project, or as long as he can influence whoever is in control—that he'll be able to keep the gung ho characters in the government from doing something really stupid. And with any luck, by the time they do figure out the containment problem, and start in on the laser experiments, the three of us will be old and gray and senile . . . and not even remember why we ever cared."

"But what if—?" She hesitated, and Cellars could hear the deep, desperate fear in her voice again.

"What if what?" he pressed gently.

"What if more of these creatures do come back for the stones—the evidence they left behind?"

She paused for a long moment.

"My God, that's it, isn't it?" she whispered hoarsely. "That's why you're isolating yourself out in the woods like that. You think they are coming back . . . or that they're already here."

There it was, finally out in the open, the crux of the issue. Not to mention the absolutely terrifying possibility that had been haunting Cellars's memories and dreams for the last two months.

If they did come back, or—as Allesandra had implied—were already here, what could he do about it? Or what could the OSP do about it, for that matter? Send out six-officer crime scene investigation teams and watch them get chewed up and spit out, one after the other? Only this time for real?

"I think it's a possibility," he admitted, trying to keep his voice steady for her sake as well as his own. "I don't think Malcolm is all that convinced, but—"

"But if they do come back for the stones, or they're already here, then we're the ones they'll come after first," Jody pointed out. "Not Malcolm."

"If they do come back, they'll come after Bobby and me, not you," Cellars said in what he hoped was a convincing voice. "We're the ones who caused them all the grief in the first place. We're the ones who killed Allesandra to get you back. And we're the ones who collected the stones and turned them over to the NSA. You didn't have anything to do with that."

You couldn't have, he thought. *You were in a catatonic state in a psychiatric observation ward when Bobby turned those stones over to Malcolm, so nobody's going to pay much attention if you start rambling about extraterrestrial visitors. You're out of it now. You've got to be.*

"But—"

"And that's only if these things really do exist, and they're not some kind of hallucinatory aberration," Cellars reminded her. "We don't know that for sure. Or, at least, I don't."

"What do you mean you don't?" Jody demanded, her voice rising in pitch. "You saw her. I know you did, because I was there, too! And you . . . you made love to her! You can't tell me—!"

Uh-oh.

"Jody, what I meant was—" Cellars tried, but once again, he found himself talking into a dead phone.

CHAPTER TWELVE

WHEN THE YOUNG DELIVERYMAN FINALLY REGAINED CONSCIOUS-
ness, he became aware of two things:

One, that the back of his head hurt terribly, right in the spot where
he could feel a big lump.

And two, that he was sprawled out in the back of his van, which was
almost completely empty, except for—

Two tires? What happened to all my packages? What the—?

Then he remembered.

The blown tire.

The uncontrollable slide.

And the second blown tire, which had resulted in—

Oh Jesus!

The huge, strange head coming up over the hood of his van. The head with . . . a construction nail stuck in the front? Was that really what he remembered? A big, bloody construction nail stuck right in the forehead, just above the—

Eyes.

For a long moment, the young deliveryman remained frozen in place on the floor of the van, paralyzed by the memory of those horrible eyes . . . that couldn't possibly be real.

Must have hit my head. Just don't remember.

But then, as he remained there on the cold metal floor of the van, he realized that something was wrong. How could any of that have possibly happened when the van was still upright, instead of being tilted at an angle like it had been with two flat—?

The idea caused him to lunge in the direction of the two tires, a move that made his headache much worse, and his left arm hurt, too . . . like someone had stabbed him with a sharp needle? But he didn't care about that because he was busy searching for—

There!

A big construction nail, buried all the way to the head, but clearly visible against the dirty rubber treads.

Thus inspired, it only took him a few seconds to find the nail in the other tire.

So what does that mean? That the whole thing—the accident and everything—was just some crazy dream?

But if that's the case, then where the hell are my packages?

It took the young deliveryman almost five minutes to work up his courage to the point that he was able to crawl forward to the front of the delivery van, stick his head up, and look out through the windows.

The surrounding scenery was just the way he remembered it . . . except that it had started to snow some time ago. The road was now covered with snow in both directions, but he could still see the two pines and the split-rail fence. What he couldn't see was any monstrous head . . . or any tracks of a creature that might possibly have a head like that. Or any tracks whatsoever, he realized. Not even his own. Which didn't make any sense at all.

So who changed the tires? And who brought a spare? And why does my arm hurt?

He didn't have an answer for those questions. Or at least none that made any sense.

So what do I do now? Go outside and look around?

Yeah, right.

Without even thinking about it, he quickly reached over and locked both doors. That was when he noticed his keys, dangling from the van's ignition switch . . . and the single brown-paper-wrapped package on the floor below the keys, with a block-printed note.

I'M COVERING FOR YOU, HOSS

ONLY ONE MORE PACKAGE TO DELIVER

THEN YOU'D BETTER MOVE TO HIGH GROUND

NEW JOB, NEW STATE,

MIGHT NOT BE SO LUCKY NEXT TIME.

Ten seconds later, the young deliveryman was maneuvering the heavy van down the lower section of Broken Back as quickly and as carefully as he possibly could . . . thinking, as he did so, that a new job in a new state was one hell of a good idea.

CHAPTER THIRTEEN

TEN MINUTES LATER, COLIN CELLARS WAS STANDING INSIDE HIS attached garage, in the process of activating his home security system with the thumbprint-activated keypad Malcolm Byzor had installed next to the door, when his cell phone started ringing again.

Now what?

He fumbled with his jacket pocket until he finally managed to extract the demanding instrument.

"Jody?"

But instead of the familiar soft music in the background, there was dead silence on the other end of a very hollow-sounding line.

"Jody, is that you?" Cellars tried again, and got more hollow-sounding silence.

"Having a bad morning, are we?"

He recognized the voice immediately. Malcolm Byzor. Longtime friend, electronics wizard, computer genius, genuine grade-A government spook . . . and apparently alive and well, in spite of the bizarre and chilling dream, Cellars realized with some relief.

"I've had better."

"Have you considered sleeping pills?" Byzor was aware that Cellars had been having trouble with the constantly recurring dreams.

"I'll be fine once I get myself adjusted to night-shift time again," Cellars said as he rubbed his eyes and tried, unsuccessfully, to stifle a yawn. "It's just been a while."

"So they're letting you go back on duty?"

"I think so. I should know today after my session with Pleausant."

"Great. Hey, sorry to wake you, but I was calling to see if you and Jody are still on for dinner tonight?"

Cellars hesitated, remembering the abruptly ended conversation. "Well, Jody might show up, but I'd say the chances of the two of us being entertaining company for the entire evening are pretty slim."

"Are you two still at it?"

"Yeah, afraid so," Cellars acknowledged. "Look, maybe it'd be better if I stayed away this time, came by some other night."

"You might be amazed at what Yvie and I find entertaining these days . . . especially when it involves our friends," Byzor replied cryptically. "So, what's the argument about this time? Same basic topic?"

"More or less. She still thinks I'm in love with a dead alien creature that may or may not have even existed in the first place."

"Which you are, of course," Byzor noted helpfully.

"That, and the fact that I've been trying to get her to go back to counseling with me, and she's not having any of it," Cellars added, ignoring his friend's half-teasing comment.

"You know, I always assumed Bobby was the designated nutcase of our little quartet . . . but you and Jody are really making a run for the title," Byzor said. "In fact, I'm starting to get the distinct impression that things were working out a whole lot better between the two of you when you weren't speaking to each other."

"Thank you, Doctor Ruth," Cellars replied sarcastically.

"On the other hand . . ." Byzor hesitated. "I wanted to talk with you about something, anyway, and it was going to be a little difficult if Jody was there."

"So talk."

"No, not on the phone."

"What do you mean? I thought you said this thing was protected with encryption?"

"Yes and no."

"Meaning?"

"Your home phone and your cell phone are both encrypted with the most powerful algorithm software I could use without violating a couple of pretty serious national-security regulations," Byzor explained. "But even highly complex algorithms can be broken if you have enough computing power at your disposal."

Cellars had the strange sensation that his survival instincts had suddenly perked their ears up. "Why do I get the feeling this is the part where the director cues the spooky music?" he asked uneasily.

"What? Oh . . . no, nothing like that," Byzor replied absentmindedly. "It's just . . . listen, do you think you could come by and pick me up this evening, say around six? I had to drop my car off at the shop this morning, and it's not ready like they promised. I was going to call Yvie and ask her to come pick me up, but I really hate to do that in weather like this."

Cellars blinked again as he looked across at the drawn curtains that concealed his bedroom window, suddenly disturbed by the feeling that something Byzor had just said didn't make any sense . . . even though he didn't know what or why.

"So what's the weather like?"

"Cold, wet, and gloomy, which seems to be the norm for this time of the year, according to my neighbors. Looks like we might get a few more inches of snow tonight or tomorrow morning."

"Wonderful."

"Actually, Yvie and I don't mind at all. At least we're not facing another Washington, DC, summer."

"Sounds like you two adjusted to the move just fine."

"Haven't got everything unpacked yet—too much going on at the office. Which reminds me," Byzor went on, "Yvie's going to have a hard time getting dinner ready if she has to stop everything to come get me."

"Keep her focused on the cooking," Cellars said emphatically. "I'll be happy to pick you up."

"That way," Byzor went on, "if Jody's there when we arrive, and you still don't think the evening's going to work out, you can always just drop me off and go home. I'll just tell them you got called out."

Then it occurred to him.

The shop?

This ought to be a really interesting conversation, Malcolm, my friend. Since when did you start trusting your car engine to a garage mechanic?

"Sounds like a plan to me," Cellars said with forced casualness. "So where do I pick you up? Same place?"

"No, actually, we closed down the assessment team office and moved into better quarters a couple weeks ago. Do you know how to find Sensabaugh Road?"

"Isn't that the new one that turns off Route Seven, out by the northeast corner of the university campus?" Cellars asked with a sinking sensation in his stomach.

Sensabaugh Road. Where dozens of covered flatbed haulers, tractor-trailers, and delivery vans had been disappearing behind increasingly secure fencing and twenty-four-hour-guarded gates for the past eight weeks. This according to OSP patrol officers and Jasper County sheriff's deputies who invariably found themselves blocked when they ignored the PRIVATE PROPERTY—RESTRICTED ACCESS signs and drove up to the gates.

The 160-acre site was definitely on university property, no question about that. But, according to the OSP officers Cellars had been meeting with for coffee every morning the last couple of weeks, even the university police had very limited access. Rumor had it that the university was getting to activate a long-vacant, state-of-the-art, computer sciences research facility, the innards of which had been donated by a wealthy alumnus who wanted to keep the whole thing under wraps until the ribbon cutting scheduled for sometime in the fall. Microsoft or Intel, everyone figured, but no one knew for sure. And given the amount of money involved—at least $400 million, someone claimed—no one in the administrative or computer sciences offices of the university wanted to risk losing the center by asking too many questions.

Those were the rumors, anyway.

"That's it," Byzor replied. "Take a left at the main intersection, then follow the road about a mile or so until you come to the first gate. The access code this month is bogus. B-O-G-U-S. Drive another couple of miles until you get to the guard shack. I'll meet you there, at the visitor's entrance, at six. Okay?"

"Yeah, sure, but—"

Sensabaugh Road is an NSA project? Jesus Christ, Malcolm, I thought you said—?

Click.

———

Colin Cellars stared at the inert cell phone in his hand for a long moment, muttered something impolite, closed the cover, got into his truck, shut the door . . . and waited.

As he expected, it didn't take long—less than three minutes—for the cell phone to ring again.

"Whoever this is, this time," he whispered in a barely controlled voice, "it had better be important, or at least relevant, because I'm about ready to heave this damned cell phone into the nearest trash can."

There was a long pause, then:

"I'll make it quick, then. One simple question. Kindly explain to me why I'm still in love with the two of you?"

Jody.

"I wouldn't even know how to begin to answer that question." Cellars had to force the words through a constricted throat. "Probably some kind of incurable genetic flaw. Nothing you can do about it. Either that, or Bobby and I were just born lucky."

Another long pause, and then—to Cellars's immense relief—she laughed. Just like she'd laughed a thousand times before. That distinctive, raspy-throated laugh that never failed to captivate his heart . . . and his imagination.

"I guess it's true, then. I really must be out of my mind."

"No, you're not," Cellars said quietly. "You're just scared. We all are."

"You and Bobby . . . and Malcolm, too?" The disbelief was evident in her voice.

"Oh, yeah, even Malcolm," Cellars said, remembering the uncharacteristic hesitancy in Malcolm Byzor's voice a few minutes ago. "We're just dealing with it differently."

"But you and Bobby, you're going to deal with it by confronting them when they come back, aren't you?"

"That's right . . . if they come back," he added.

"But how can you?"

"They're not invulnerable, Jody. We proved that. They're just smarter and faster and stronger than we are . . . and they can probably change their shapes to look like whatever they want, that's all."

"My God, isn't that enough?"

"It's a pretty decent advantage," Cellars conceded. "But even so, when you get right down to it, they're biological systems, just like us . . . which means they can be shut off. We just have to figure out where and how they're the most vulnerable. Either that, or it's going to be a pretty brief confrontation." He tried to joke, but it came off flat. It really wasn't funny, and they both knew it.

For about fifteen seconds, neither of them spoke.

"You know what scares me the most?" Jody finally whispered.

"No, what's that?" Cellars asked, not at all sure he wanted to know.

"All the time the four of us have been together, we've always faced things as a team, and we always came out on top. Because no matter what we came up against, at least one of us always had an idea . . . or an edge.

"But Malcolm said something to me a few days ago that really terrified me," Jody went on before Cellars could respond. "He said that, this time, the four of us have to stay apart . . . because if we try to fight these things together, back-to-back, like we've always done, then we don't stand a chance. Do you have any idea what he was talking about?"

"No, I don't," Cellars said, feeling a distinctive chill going up his spine.

"But, if we do that—stay apart, like he said—then what are we go-ing to do when these things come looking for us?"

"I don't know," Cellars confessed. "But if they do, we'll come up with something. We'll have to."

He could hear what sounded like her fingernails tapping against the phone—nervously, like she was trying to make up her mind about something important.

"Colin, the real reason I called back was, I have to ask you some-thing."

"Go ahead."

"What do you know about Dr. Pleausant? I mean *really* know?"

Cellars eyebrows furrowed in confusion. "Nothing in particular, I suppose. He's a psychiatrist—supposedly a good one, according to our personnel staff at headquarters—and he's part of a medical group the OSP has on contract for officer health and welfare issues."

"Are you sure about that?"

"You mean about the contract? Yeah, I know several officers who've gone to them for family counseling, alcoholism, things like that."

"No, I mean Pleausant. Do you know when he joined the firm? Where he came from? Anything like that?"

"No, not really. Just that he's a name on their letterhead."

There was another long pause.

"Colin, this is going to sound stupid." Her voice softer now, but the fear was definitely still there—and it made his heart ache.

"After what we've both been through . . . and seen . . . the last couple of months, I seriously doubt that," Cellars responded, feeling his heart start to beat faster even though he had no idea what she was about to say.

"This Dr. Pleausant—" She hesitated. "I don't know how else to say it, and I don't even know why I'm saying it. But I know it's true, and you've got to believe me. There's something not right about him."

"Jody—"

"Please, Colin, if you can possibly avoid it . . . don't go there."

CHAPTER FOURTEEN

THE PHONE JARRED DR. ERIC MARSTON OUT OF A GUILTY AND REST-
less daydream. Immediately alert, he reached for the handset with a
sense of dread.

*Oh God, they found out. What am I going to say? What am I going
to do?*

After weeks of worrying, and fretting, and pondering . . . weeks of
applying every aspect of his considerable intellect to what had become,
for him, an irresolvable and all-consuming quandary . . . he still had no
idea what he was going to do. Or say.

"Hello?" he whispered in a hoarse voice.

"Eric?"

The familiar voice struck at his heart like a ray of sunlight.

"Cascadia?"

Just saying her name made him feel like a schoolboy again, caught up in the mental turmoil of his first true love. Like the schoolboy he'd never been.

"Did I wake you?"

"No," he lied, and immediately felt guilty because she'd know. She always knew.

"I'm sorry, but I'm so excited, I just couldn't wait any longer. Did you—?"

So excited. Can't wait any longer. I love you.

The words ricocheted through his mind, triggering erotic memories of her soft full lips against his . . . and her full, firm breasts pressing against his hands. Her melodic voice whispering in his ear . . . and his mind being caught up in a huge swell of desire and fulfillment that surged forward, propelling him—

He shook his head, desperately fighting off the overwhelming sense of arousal as he realized that he hadn't heard what she said.

"What?" he asked in a tight voice, swallowing hard.

"Were you able to arrange it? For tonight? Like you promised?"

Tonight. Oh God.

He had to force the word past his constricted larynx . . . past the last desperate vestiges of his protective soul. He knew he was doomed, but he didn't care. He really didn't.

"Yes."

Committed.

"Oh, Eric, I can't wait. I'm so excited."

The memories burst forth again, and he could feel—actually feel—her body, hot and demanding, against his. It was as if she was there, in his bed, wrapping her arms and legs around him . . . extending every feverish cell of her incredible body and drawing him in. Exactly the way he'd dreamed it might be.

No, he corrected, would be. Absolutely would be.

Maybe even . . . tonight? he thought, and then shoved the idea aside because it was too much to hope for. Much too much.

"Eric," she whispered in that voice that he was absolutely helpless to resist, "you're so wonderful. I love you. I really do."

He smiled then, understanding, in a way he never had before, that he was truly and completely happy.

And caring not at all that, in the very same sense, he was also completely and irrevocably doomed.

CHAPTER FIFTEEN

"GOOD TO SEE YOU AGAIN, COLIN. AND, WITH ANY LUCK, UNDER less trying circumstances this time," Dr. Pleausant added as he motioned Cellars to a comfortable-looking chair opposite his own.

"I don't think Bobby will be joining us today," Cellars said as he sat down.

"That's certainly good to hear . . . although please let him know that I really would like to talk with him when he's in a more amiable mood," Pleausant added. "He could be the key to some of the issues that are bothering you . . . and Jody, too, of course."

"I'll be sure to let him know if he ever contacts me again."

"Yes, please do. I'm sure we can arrange a time and a place that would be mutually agreeable."

Somehow, Cellars didn't think the psychiatrist was being completely forthright, but he kept his thoughts to himself. Pleasant, for his part, seemed to be examining Cellars's face more closely.

"You look tired."

"I haven't been sleeping well lately," Cellars acknowledged as he settled back into what turned out to be a very comfortable chair.

"The dreams are continuing?"

"Yes."

"Do you still find them disturbing?"

"Yes. Very much so."

"Why is that?"

"A lot of reasons. I find myself in meetings with people who shouldn't be there . . . or in that situation. I find myself doing things that I don't know how to do, such as flying a helicopter or playing a twelve-string guitar. I find myself having sex with beautiful women whom I've never seen before. Or, even more bizarre, with a beautiful woman that I do know and have had sex with before . . . but in places and situations that we've never been in. Or at least I don't think we have."

"But you're not sure?"

"No, I'm not. Not anymore."

"But, in any case, these dreams still bother you?"

Cellars nodded. "I think it's because they seem so real, so vivid, so . . . detailed. Whatever the reason, I keep waking up in a cold sweat, two or three times every night, like I'm scared to death of something but I don't know what . . . or why."

"Dreams can be quite vivid, but they don't necessarily have any direct connection to reality," Pleasant reminded him. "Sometimes they're just bits and pieces of unrelated memories, and things people have said to you, all jumbled together in a seamless flow that seems to make sense at the time."

He was a tall, slender man with clean-shaven features and light gray hair. A gentle-looking man who seemed to emanate care and concern for all those in his presence.

Or, at least, that's the way he seemed at our first session, Cellars thought. Today, for whatever reason, Pleasant seemed far more cold and analytical . . . as if the unexpected incident with Bobby Dawson at the quickly terminated end of Cellars's earlier session had, somehow, re-defined their relationship as doctor and patient.

"In that case, I think I'd like to schedule myself for a complete brainwashing. Hot wax, the works."

Pleasant's eyes flickered in a brief smile. "Actually, I'm not sure the profession does much of that sort of thing anymore. Would you like something to drink?" He gestured to the selection of bottled water and fruit juice decanters, and a small coffeepot set on a wooden shelf on the opposite side of the small, gloomy room.

"No, thanks."

Pleasant paused and stared at Cellars for a long moment.

"You seem uncomfortable," he finally said. "Do you think it might have something to do with how you feel about being one of my patients?"

"There's probably a lot of truth to that," Cellars conceded. "I'm certainly not thrilled by the idea."

"About taking part in therapy?"

"About being sent to therapy," Cellars corrected.

"But you are here voluntarily. Isn't that true? I mean, no one's forced you to be here, have they?"

"Nobody forced me to be *here,* specifically," Cellars corrected. "But at the same time, I don't see this as a completely voluntary situation."

"Why is that?"

Cellars calmly met the psychiatrist's probing gaze. "As you know, a couple of months ago, I went through a fairly traumatic shooting incident . . . actually, a series of shooting incidents. And as a result of all that—and the report I filed shortly thereafter—I now need a medical clearance to continue to work in the field as a police officer, and to carry a badge and a gun for the state of Oregon. A psychiatric review is a mandatory part of that clearance process, and your medical group holds a state contract to provide such reviews. So, at the most basic level, that's why I'm here."

Pleasant nodded silently in understanding.

"But, apart from all that—and on a more personal level—I also have a problem that I need to resolve," Cellars went on calmly. "As far as problems go, it's a fairly simple one, and I really ought to be able to work it out myself. Or at least I think I should. But, so far, I haven't been very successful in doing that. And I'm running out of time, as far as the OSP is concerned, so I need help. You were highly recommended by the police officers' association, for some work you did up in Portland, and the rules of a medical assessment allow me to request a specific doctor. That's why I'm sitting here talking with you instead of one of your associates."

"Because you want me to help you resolve a closely related personal problem in addition to evaluating your fitness for duty with the OSP?"

"That's right."

Pleasant hesitated for a brief moment.

"Have you considered the possibility that, if I were to do so, I could find myself in an awkward conflict-of-interest situation . . . as to what I might be obligated to report back to your agency?"

"I would like you to evaluate my state of mind, Dr. Pleasant, with respect to both issues—my fitness for duty and my personal problem," Cellars said. "Unless it turns out that I'm schizophrenic, I have to assume that the two are closely linked. And that being the case, you're welcome to report to the OSP on either or both, separately or together, as you see fit."

"I see."

"And, in that same regard," Cellars added, "I would consider any potential conflict-of-interest situation to be your problem to resolve, not mine. If it became a significant issue, I assume you'd let me know."

"Yes, of course. The OSP has to be satisfied with your overall state of mind—as a general condition of your employment as a police officer—in any case. But let me ask you something, Colin. We've been talking about what the OSP wants, but where does *your* sense of satisfaction fit into all of this . . . with respect to your personal problem, that is?"

"In other words, what do I want?"

"Yes." Pleasant nodded.

"It's very simple. The OSP has a major investigation under way into the disappearance of approximately fifty Jackson County citizens and law enforcement officers . . . and the only way we're going to resolve those disappearances is to work the evidence. There are at least thirty-five to forty potential crime scenes—all of which are cold, and getting colder every day—but all of which need to be reexamined or reevaluated. To do that, we really need to put several fully trained crime scene investigators on the case. But the OSP is pretty light on fully trained CSI officers at the moment, so I'm the only one assigned to the investigation.

"All of which means," Cellars went on when Pleausant remained silent, "the OSP needs to decide, in a very short period of time, if it's safe and prudent to put me back out on the street with a gun and a badge and a CSI kit. And a part of that decision will certainly be based upon your evaluation of my sanity or my fitness for duty."

"Yes, I understand all of that," Pleausant nodded, "but—"

"As far as my personal problem is concerned," Cellars went on, "I'm not working under the same time restraints as the OSP. Or, at least, I don't think I am. So I'm not all that much in a hurry for you to walk me through the process."

"Really? Why is that?"

"As it happens, I'm reasonably confident that the resolution to my problem will come in due time . . . and I'm willing to be patient, if given the time."

"I see."

The room was silent for a good thirty seconds, as Pleausant seemed to be mulling over Cellars's comments.

"Does it bother you, that you couldn't . . . resolve this personal problem yourself?" he finally asked.

"Yes, of course it does."

Pleausant looked down at his hands for a moment, then nodded understandingly. "I don't mean this to sound condescending, Colin, but I must tell you that, in my view, your reaction to all of this seems perfectly reasonable."

"Really? Why?"

Pleausant quickly brought his head back up; and, if anything, his eyes seemed colder and more probing. "You're a detective-sergeant with nineteen years on the force. You hold a master's degree in forensic science. You're considered to be highly skilled in what I gather is the rather complex and demanding, and occasionally stressful, field of crime scene investigation. And I gather that not many officers possess the necessary patience and tenacity, along with the requisite technical skills, to perform such work successfully. Which is, I believe, the reason Lieutenant Talbert and Sergeant Bauer want very much to put you back out on the street as soon as possible."

"Not Major Hightower?"

"I suppose it's fair to say she's not convinced yet," Pleasant conceded.

He paused for a moment to readjust his lanky frame in the chair.

"According to your yearly evaluations," Pleasant went on, "your supervisors view you as a highly trained, highly motivated, and eminently self-confident CSI officer who takes pride in his work, and who is accustomed to overcoming difficult obstacles and accomplishing assigned tasks without assistance. You're also described as an officer who disdains the use of intimidation or physical force. I found it especially interesting that these comments were substantiated by a noticeable lack of citizen complaints in your file."

"There are complaints in my file," Cellars corrected. "Several, in fact."

"Yes, of course, routine ones. And, from what I saw, virtually all from people who strongly object to the idea of police officers interfering in their daily lives on principle. You just happened to be the officer who made the contact. But none were for the use of unnecessary force."

"No, nothing like that," Cellars agreed.

Pleasant looked down at his notes for a few seconds, then brought his head back up slowly. "That's an interesting word, 'disdains.'"

Cellars shrugged. "From my perspective, it's more like a philosophical point of view. I just don't see any point or purpose in trying to intimidate people, or beat the shit out of them, if I can sweet-talk them into being cooperative."

That seemed to get Pleasant's attention. His cold, probing eyes seemed to light up briefly . . . as if they'd come upon a particularly interesting piece of mental flotsam. "And how do you think your fellow officers feel about this philosophical point of view of yours?"

"I'd say most of them agree with it. Most probably try to live by it. But it isn't always easy."

"No, I suppose not." Pleausant looked down at his hands again. "In your opinion, why do you think *you're* able to live by it?"

"I don't know, maybe because I tend to be stubborn . . . and I don't like to lose."

Pleausant's head snapped back up. He seemed to fix Cellars in his gaze, and, for the first time, Cellars thought he saw something in the psychiatrist's eyes that actually looked formidable, if not necessarily menacing.

At that moment, a floorboard in an adjoining room creaked, and Pleausant's head snapped around.

"Excuse me a moment," he said as he came up out of the chair in a graceful and athletic motion, and then—before Cellars could respond—disappeared from the room.

CHAPTER SIXTEEN

TWO MINUTES LATER, PLEAUSANT CAME BACK INTO THE ROOM, looking agitated.

"Problems?" Cellars inquired.

The psychiatrist looked as if he was going to say something, then shook his head. "No, nothing significant. Now, then, where were we?"

"I think we were talking about my not liking to lose," Cellars said cautiously as he adjusted himself in the chair.

"Yes, of course. By losing, you mean finding yourself in a position where you might have to resort to the use of physical . . . or perhaps even lethal, force . . . when you'd prefer not to do so?"

"That's right."

"So, in that sense, is it fair to say that you view your stubbornness as a positive trait?"

"Not necessarily. There are times when forceful action, or even lethal force, is the logical and proper recourse . . . for the safety of the public at large, my fellow officers, or myself. By ignoring that logic and holding back too long, it's possible I could place a member of the public, or another officer, at unnecessary risk."

"And yourself as well."

"I suppose."

"It doesn't bother you that you could be hurt or killed in the performance of your duties as a police officer?"

"That's an inherent risk of the job. We all know that. But I don't see it as a significant risk."

"Is that so? Why not?"

"Simple. In most officer-suspect confrontations, we almost always have an overwhelming advantage," Cellars replied.

Pleausant's eyebrows furrowed. "I'm afraid my ignorance of your profession is starting to show. Would you mind expanding on that comment?"

"Sure. As police officers, we're trained to recognize and deal with an unexpected confrontation, we're equipped and proficient with a wide range of lethal and nonlethal weapons, and we're constantly prepared to back each other up under any circumstances. On the other hand, our typical suspects are usually surprised and distracted by the confrontation; they're almost always emotionally upset, or under the influence of drugs or alcohol; and, as a rule, they're almost always flying by the seat of their pants. In other words, operating without any kind of thought-out plan. If they have partners, or associates, they rarely trust each other. And they usually give each other up at the first opportunity to make a deal, so paranoia is a constant occupational handicap. And, if that weren't enough, these typical suspects tend to be inept or inexperienced with whatever weapons they may have in their possession, and rarely put much effort into keeping them clean or in good working condition. Thus, our overwhelming advantage."

"But things can go wrong. In fact, they often do," Pleasant pointed out. "Which is presumably why so many police officers get hurt or killed every year."

"Things can go wrong," Cellars agreed. "But as a general rule, when an officer gets hurt or killed, it's usually because he was either careless or unlucky."

"The idea of being hurt or killed as a result of bad luck . . . as opposed to an actual mistake on your part . . . doesn't concern you?"

Cellars shrugged. "Murphy's Law usually applies to both sides of the equation. And, in any case, tends to favor the person who's best prepared for the unexpected. So, here again, we usually have the advantage. But, to answer your question more directly: Sure, the idea of being caught off guard, or being unlucky, concerns me. That's why I try to stay alert and flexible when I'm out in the field. But I don't dwell on it."

"I gather your crime scene work places you in the field more often than not?"

Cellars nodded. "I'm in the field most of the time when I'm on duty. As the roving CSI officer for OSP Region Nine, which encompasses the southwestern portion of the state, my job is to respond to calls that involve the more serious crimes . . . usually homicide, robbery, or rape. Apart from my assigned investigation, if there's nothing going on, then I'm free to deal with less serious issues—such as traffic violations—as I see fit."

"You mentioned that one of your inherent advantages as a police officer is that you are constantly prepared to back each other up. Do you routinely call for a backup when you find yourself in one of these confrontational situations?"

"If the situation calls for it."

"Would you say you call for backup fairly frequently?"

"No, not really."

"Why not?"

"I try to assess the situation right away. If I feel I can handle it by myself, then there's no need to pull the backup officer away from someone who might need him or her more."

"But, in any case, would it be fair to say that, given the choice, you prefer to handle things yourself . . . to resolve your own problems, so to speak?"

"I suppose that's a fair assessment."

"You're aware that many of your supervisors have noted this in your yearly evaluations . . . both positively and negatively?"

"Yes."

"But, in any case, you don't seem to mind working alone?" Pleausant pressed.

"No, not at all."

"Do you carry a firearm with you on a routine basis?"

"Yes, of course."

"Are you carrying one with you now?"

"No."

"Really?" Pleausant's eyes flickered in surprise. "Not even a backup weapon?"

"No."

"Why not? I was under the impression Oregon State Patrol officers were expected to be armed and ready to perform their duties at all times."

"Most police officers set aside their weapons when they're trying to deal with personal problems," Cellars replied.

"Like going to see your friendly shrink?"

"Or going to the toilet. You can only take paranoia so far before it gets to be a problem."

"An all-too-appropriate analogy for the psychiatric profession, as well, I'm afraid." Pleausant's eyes seemed to almost glisten now, and Cellars decided he'd had enough.

"Dr. Pleausant, pardon me for being blunt, but I didn't come here to play word games with you. Maybe that's part of the process, and if it is, I apologize. But we seem to be wandering a bit . . . and that concerns me, because I came here to get help, and I don't have a great deal of time."

"Then let's get to it," Pleausant agreed. "So tell me, how would you describe this personal problem of yours, in your own words?"

"Well, apart from my dreams, I'm concerned that I may have seen things . . . that weren't real . . . during a recent investigation."

"I assume, based on my limited conversations with Lieutenant

Talbert and my more extensive ones with Sergeant Bauer, that we're talking about extraterrestrial creatures? Creatures not of this Earth, I believe is the way the phrase goes?"

"That's right."

"You believe you actually engaged with some of these creatures, physically . . . sexually, even . . . and, shall we say, in a violent and aggressive manner. You expressed this opinion to others, even in a signed investigative report, and now you're concerned about the fact that you did. Yet, I understand you recently gave a lecture in which you acknowledged the extremely high probability that some such creatures must exist outside of our small and remote solar system?"

"That's right," Cellars acknowledged.

"And do you believe that, as a forensic scientist and as a police investigator?"

"Yes, I do."

"So what is it that you find so difficult to believe about your own situation?" Pleausant asked. "That these creatures would, in fact, show up here, at this beautiful little spot . . . at precisely the point in time when you—Detective-Sergeant Colin Cellars—happen to be living and working and investigating?"

"Exactly."

"You don't want to believe these creatures exist. Yet, I'm told you fired, what was it, twenty-four rounds at these supposed beings over a period of several days?"

"That's right."

"But, you see, that's really the crux of my concern, Colin," Pleausant said quietly. "Because, given your record, your well-documented disdain for unnecessary violence, and the fact that, according to your file, you've never fired your weapon at any other suspect during your entire nineteen-year career, I can only assume you thought you were shooting at someone—or something—that was life-threatening."

"That's right."

"Were these creatures armed?"

Cellars hesitated. "I don't know."

"You don't know. But, yet, you found them sufficiently threatening to discharge your pistol at them twenty-four times . . . with the full intention to kill, every time you pulled the trigger, I assume?"

"Yes, of course."

A look of dismay crossed Pleausant's face. "You say that like you had no other choice."

"I don't think I did."

"So what you're telling me, in essence, is that these indistinct, shadowy, and possibly unarmed creatures were so threatening to you that you immediately resorted to lethal force, every time . . . instead of dropping back to a less lethal form of control."

"That's right."

"How do you explain that?"

"I don't have an explanation, Doctor. That's my problem. I just reacted to the situation."

"As you've been trained to do."

"We aren't trained to deal with extraterrestrials, so I assume I was responding to the cumulative effect of nineteen years of law enforcement training," Cellars corrected. "But, at the same time, I was certainly never trained to shoot at indistinct shadows . . . so I can hardly use my training as an excuse, or as a justification."

"Actually, though, I understand that you do have a possible excuse," Pleausant suggested.

"You mean the fact that a toxicology lab found drugs in a blood sample I provided to the OSP right after the incident?"

"Yes."

"Drugs could certainly be a factor in all of this," Cellars acknowledged.

"Did they tell you what drugs were involved?"

"Yes. It was a drug known as MDMA."

"MDMA is a very potent, and—to some degree—unpredictable hallucinogen, as I'm sure you know," Pleausant offered. "I trust you also have at least a general understanding of what that means?"

"From a scientific point of view, yes. But not as a user."

"It could certainly explain the shadows . . . and even your perception that everything else around you was going forward in a fairly normal manner," Pleasant suggested. "And the fact that you perceived yourself to be functioning in a normal manner isn't completely out of the question either, although—"

"I should have at least been aware of a transition period . . . either going under the influence or coming out?" Cellars suggested.

"Yes, that would be expected. But there are so many unknown variables . . . relating to both you and the drug. And psychiatry has such limited knowledge about these new compounds—"

"Because law enforcement officers tend to arrest the researchers?" Cellars smiled.

"A compelling irony, at the very least," Pleasant agreed. "But where does that leave you?"

"With an unresolved problem. The thing is, I really don't believe I was drugged. One, because I should be able to remember either being drugged or going through a transition, and I don't. And two, because everything that happened—or that I think happened—is very clear in my memory. On the other hand, some of those memories are pretty bizarre."

"Such as?"

Cellars shrugged. "How about an incredibly intense sexual relationship with a woman named Allesandra, who first seemed to melt into my brain when we were in bed together . . . and then transformed herself into some kind of terrifying alien creature when Bobby and I confronted her. And then into a stone when Bobby blew her head off, for starters?"

"Bobby being Bobby Dawson, our friend with the unfortunate sense of humor?" Pleasant asked in a quiet—and almost cold—voice.

"That's right."

"And this Allesandra . . . is she the one who looked remarkably like your friend, Jody Catlin . . . the young woman that both you and your friend Dawson were in love with?"

"Yes."

Pleasant nodded slowly for several seconds.

"Dr. Alexander Shulgin has an interesting definition of the hallucinogenic effect," the psychiatrist went on in a deep thoughtful voice, as if he was speaking more to himself than to Cellars. "He believes it's possible for a subject to find himself surrounded by a reality that is not only completely convincing in terms of what he believes he sees, but tangible as well. The implication being that you can actually engage and interact with that reality, and still not realize that it is anything but real."

"You're suggesting that Allesandra was nothing more than an illusion?"

"Given the issue of the MDMA in your bloodstream, I would think you'd want to consider that as a very real possibility."

That was blood sample, not bloodstream, Doctor, Cellars thought. *And besides, she was real. I know she was real. I held her in my arms. Felt the heat from her body. Felt her . . . felt us . . . merge into some kind of oneness that I can't even begin to describe, much less explain. And then saw her change back . . . into one of them . . . and then change again when she died.*

If she died.

"Then why do I still think otherwise, Doctor? After all that you've said here, why do I still really, truly, believe she was real . . . in every sense?"

"It's difficult to say. The traumatized mind reaching out, seeking comfort and solid ground? Or—certainly possible in your situation—a traumatized body overwhelming a stressed and exhausted but otherwise well-functioning mind? In any case, it's a healthy process, Sergeant. You really shouldn't fight it."

"I don't want to fight it. I just want to understand it. And that's exactly what I intend to do. But, in the meantime, where does that leave me?"

"You mean with respect to being allowed to function as a police officer?"

"Yes."

"The concern, of course—the one that Major Hightower, Lieutenant Talbert, Sergeant Bauer, and I face—is the possibility that you might be a danger to the public."

"If I were a danger to the public, taking into account the number of rounds I fired and vehicles I destroyed, you'd think that at least one member of the general public would have been injured in some manner," Cellars pointed out. "But, in fact, as it turned out, I was able to control the vehicles and my direction of fire in an appropriate manner . . . just as I've been trained to do . . . with the result that not one member of the general public was put at risk during those confrontations."

"Yes, from what I've been told by Sergeant Bauer, that seems to have been the case," Pleasant conceded. .

Cellars started to say something else, then frowned and reached for the pager on his belt.

Pleasant cocked his head curiously. "Duty calls?"

Cellars quickly scanned the words on the small pager screen, frowned again, then nodded. "I'm sorry, Doctor, but it looks like I have to go. Should we schedule another appointment?"

"I don't think that will be necessary," Pleasant said. "I think we've covered most of the relevant topics."

"Except for one," Cellars said as he got up out of the chair, walked over to the coat rack, and retrieved his jacket.

"Oh, really? What's that?"

"The matter of control."

"I'm afraid I don't understand."

"It's very simple, Doctor. Whoever—or whatever—these creatures are, they seem to have kidnapped or killed at least fifty Jasper County citizens and law enforcement officers. And if that's really the case, my job is to hunt them down, and bring them to justice. I can do that as a police officer, working under all of the controls and restrictions that are inherent to the job. Or I can do it on my own, like my friend Bobby, without any controls at all."

Cellars paused, as he slipped on his jacket, and locked his gaze on Pleasant's glistening eyes one last time.

"It seems to be your call, Doctor. Thank you for your time."

CHAPTER SEVENTEEN

THE SNOW HAD STARTED FALLING IN EARNEST BY THE TIME CELLARS pulled his truck into the parking lot at Providence Hospital. He took the elevator to the third floor, and found Oregon State Patrol Sergeant Tom Bauer and a middle-aged woman—about five-eight, one-twenty-five, with short-cropped gray hair and a matching business suit—standing outside the doorway to Captain Don Talbert's hospital room. The body language was all too easy to read.

So this is Major Hightower, Cellars thought. Something about her seemed oddly familiar, even though he was fairly certain that he'd never actually met or even seen her before.

Bauer, a tall, lean, native Oregonian with the perpetual tan of a veteran field officer, was still getting accustomed to the idea of acting like a watch commander. He stepped forward to greet Cellars with a welcoming smile and a firm handshake, just as he would have done a few weeks ago with any other peer sergeant.

Better watch yourself, Tom, Cellars thought. *Keep on being nice to the field troops like this and the brass will eat you alive.*

But if Bauer had any concerns in that regard, they didn't show.

"Good to see you again, Colin," Bauer said. "Thanks for stopping by."

"Sure, no problem."

"Major Hightower, this is Detective-Sergeant Colin Cellars," Bauer went on as he turned his attention back to Hightower. "Colin was the responding CSI officer at the Dawson cabin two months ago. He's just coming back off of extended administrative leave, so I asked him to check in with us on his way to the station this morning," he added, almost as an afterthought.

"Hello, Sergeant. Nice to finally meet you," Hightower said in a no-nonsense voice as she extended a hand that was surprisingly firm and muscular for a woman who had supposedly spent the last ten years behind a desk in Internal Affairs. It was a casual and almost indifferent response. Almost as if Hightower hadn't been aware of Cellars's role in the nightmarish events of the last two months, much less that Cellars might be stopping by the hospital at this particular time.

Immediately, warning bells began going off in the back of Cellars's head . . . because things weren't making any sense at all.

Like every other OSP officer in Region 9, Cellars was now aware that Hightower had come down from headquarters to investigate personally the bizarre series of events that had led to the presumed death of Station Commander Rodney Hawkins, and the near-fatal injuries to then Lieutenant/Watch Commander Don Talbert.

In doing so, it was fully expected that Hightower would also involve herself in some of the related issues, such as the abduction of a forensic scientist named Jody Catlin, from the nearby National Fish and Wildlife Forensics Laboratory; the destruction or disappearance of three OSP vehicles; a series of linked OSP-officer-involved shootings in which the suspects had simply vanished; a homicide victim named Bobby Dawson who was no longer dead; and approximately sixty items of missing evidence.

And if that wasn't enough to keep Hightower fully occupied during the next few weeks, word had it that she was also expected to oversee all Region 9 activities until Talbert was back on his feet and able to take charge of his new command . . . or until another captain was permanently assigned to the job.

Whether or not Hightower would actually investigate the persistent rumor that the entire episode was the work of extraterrestrial beings intent on retrieving their lost evidence was still a matter of conjecture. Probably because no one in the Salem Public Safety Building was willing to put that question to Hightower directly.

But in any case, Cellars knew for a fact that this was the first time he had actually met the head of Internal Affairs on a face-to-face basis . . . which was a little surprising, all by itself.

As the responding officer on the Dawson homicide crime scene—not to mention the only officer in the history of the Oregon State Patrol to discharge twenty-four rounds at fleeing suspects during a single twenty-four-hour period—Colin Cellars had expected to be the immediate focus of a fairly intense Internal Affairs interrogation. But it had been almost two months since the shootings, and, apparently, at least a week since Hightower's arrival at the Region 9 Station, and there had been no call for him to stand down from his mandated administrative leave and report to the station commander's office.

So, why no summons? Cellars wondered. *Not that I'm complaining, mind you,* he added as he reached out to shake the Internal Affairs commander's extended hand.

"Yes, ma'am, nice to meet you, too. Sorry it had to be under these circumstances."

"Understood," Hightower acknowledged with a brief nod.

Like Cellars, Tom Bauer was casually dressed in blue jeans, long-sleeved casual shirt, and low-cut hiking boots. But Cellars immediately noted the shoulder-holstered .40-caliber SIG-Sauer semiautomatic pistol and the body-armor vest under Bauer's field jacket, and the bulge of a similar vest and weapon under Hightower's more formal suit jacket. Interesting accessories for a pair of commanding officers whose primary duties supposedly involved bureaucratic decision making and the approval of incident reports.

But if anything, the presence of the heavy standard-issue weapons—as opposed to the much smaller and lighter backup-type firearms that most of the command officers normally carried—the vests, and the three very alert uniformed OSP officers in the hallway were reassuring to Cellars. They offered encouraging evidence that Bauer and Hightower were taking the Dawson Incident very seriously indeed.

Or at least the Hawkins and Talbert portions of the incident, Cellars reminded himself as he turned to Bauer. The other issues might turn out to be a different situation entirely.

"So how's Talbert doing?" he asked.

"A whole lot better than he was last week . . . which isn't necessarily saying a hell of a lot," Bauer added, the expression on his face turning grim. "Come on in and see for yourself."

The sight of Watch Commander Don Talbert propped there in the crisply white-sheeted hospital bed jarred Cellars. It had been almost two weeks since the severely injured watch commander had come out of his coma. The monitors and saline drips were gone now, and the hospital bed was raised to a semisitting position; but there was little about the pale, haggard face that reminded Cellars of his once-vibrant and physically commanding supervisor. Bandages still covered one side of Talbert's face and both of his hands and arms, and he looked like he'd lost at least fifty pounds.

In point of fact, Talbert looked like a man who had come very close to dying, and was still a long way from full recovery. Only his characteristic crew cut and one exposed eye appeared strong and defiant as he glared at the nurse who was taking his pulse and other vital signs.

"Try to keep it to a few minutes," the nurse advised, then shut the door behind her when Cellars, Bauer, and Hightower nodded agreeably.

"Hi, Captain, how are you feeling?" Cellars asked as he approached the bed.

"About the way I look," Talbert rasped. "Spare me the stupid questions, Cellars. Get in closer where I can see you clearly."

Closer, so you can see me? Jesus, Talbert, what the hell happened to you out there?

Cellars and Bauer moved over to the left side of the bed. Hightower remained at the door.

"Okay, that's better." Talbert's one exposed eye locked on Cellars's face. "Understand you're coming back on duty today."

"I'm hoping to start back to work this afternoon," Cellars acknowledged. "Getting tired of being out on forced leave when I don't feel sick . . . physically or mentally," he added for Hightower's benefit.

"After you clear your medical evaluation?" Talbert asked, although it wasn't really a question.

"I talked with Dr. Pleasant earlier this afternoon," Cellars acknowledged.

"So how do you feel about that?"

Talbert's voice still sounded raspy and weak, but his one eye seemed to be burning through Cellars's skull.

"You mean how do I feel about defending my supposed sanity in front of a department-hired shrink . . . and possibly an OSP review board if things don't go my way with the good doctor?"

"However you want to put it," Talbert said.

"I saw what I saw, and I described those observations in my CSI report," Cellars replied evenly. "That report stands as written. If the OSP doesn't like what they read there, they can tear it up or they can fire me. In the meantime, and as long as I'm allowed to, I plan on doing my job."

"Which is?"

Cellars hesitated, caught off guard by the direction of the question.

"As far as I know, I'm still assigned to a special task force investigating the disappearance of approximately fifty civilians and police officers in Jasper County over the past year," he said. "And, as I understand the situation, I'm still the only investigator assigned to the task force. But I filed a memo through Sergeant Bauer, asking for twelve additional CSI officers to—"

"Your request was denied, Sergeant," Major Hightower interjected from across the room.

Cellars turned to face Hightower.

"May I ask why, ma'am?" he said evenly.

"Given the current budget situation, the OSP lacks the resources to transfer twelve officers to any region of the state right now," Hightower replied in a cold, hard voice. "Especially for a task force that's just starting up . . . and hasn't run into any significant problems yet."

"Hasn't—what?" Cellars blinked, uncertain that he'd heard Hightower's words correctly. "Did you say 'hasn't run into any significant problems yet'?"

"That's right."

"Are you shitting me?" Cellars almost screamed before he managed to catch himself and speak in a reasonably normal tone of voice.

Hightower's steady cold gaze and impassive expression provided all the answer Cellars needed.

"No, Sergeant, I am not shitting you. I am describing the tactical and administrative situation as I see it." If possible, her voice seemed to have dropped another five degrees on the centigrade scale.

"Pardon me, ma'am, but did anybody up there in Salem even bother to read my incident report?" Cellars asked in as slow, calm, and controlled a voice as he could muster.

"Not that I'm aware of."

"May I ask why the hell not?"

"It's probably because your report on the Dawson Incident doesn't exist," Tom Bauer interjected.

Cellars spun around and stared at Region 9's acting watch commander.

"What do you mean 'doesn't exist'?" he demanded.

"What Sergeant Bauer means," Hightower went on in a glacial voice, as if dealing with outraged subordinate officers was an everyday part of her job—which, it occurred to Cellars, was probably the case— "is that last Monday, I asked him to pull the entire case file on the so-called Dawson Incident and place it on my desk. I believe that was OSP case file nine, double zero, six-six-six-six. Am I correct?"

Cellars nodded mutely. He had no idea if he should be frustrated, numbed, or enraged by the impassive expression on Hightower's face.

"There's the file I found," Bauer said, pointing to a seemingly empty manila folder on the table next to Talbert's bed. "See for yourself."

Feeling disoriented, Cellars reached over and picked up the labeled file folder. Inside, he found four pieces of paper. He glanced though the typed report forms and then looked up at Bauer.

"What the hell is this?"

"Exactly what it looks like." Bauer shrugged. "A routine DUI report. Only in this case, it's not so routine because the case file number happens to be nine, double zero, six-six-six-six, and the report has what looks to me like your signature at the bottom."

"What?"

"Even more interesting," Bauer went on, meeting Cellars's glare with the calm, unwavering demeanor of a veteran patrol sergeant who was also very accustomed to dealing with upset people, "the file also includes a complaint lodged against you by the subject of your DUI stop. A complaint that was subsequently dropped, later that afternoon, after the subject learned about the personal problems you were trying to deal with at the time."

"My . . . what?" Cellars only half heard Bauer's comments. His eyebrows were furrowed in confusion as he quickly confirmed the case number at the upper right-hand corner of the form, and then flipped to the second page . . . and found himself staring incredulously at what appeared to be his signature at the bottom of the page. Then he scanned the attached complaint report, noting the duplicate signatures initiating and dropping all charges at the bottom of the form. Finally, he looked back up at Bauer.

"I don't understand this at all," he said in a hoarse whisper. "Where's my initial CSI report on the Dawson Incident, and my follow-up report?"

"I don't know," Bauer replied calmly. "I don't even know if they exist anymore. But I can assure you of one thing: If they do exist, they're not anywhere in the Region Nine file system. I know that for a fact because I turned the entire station inside out looking for those reports . . . and that specifically included my calling in both record clerks and having them go through every folder in the central files on the chance that they might have been misfiled."

"And while Sergeant Bauer was doing that," Hightower added in her icy voice, "I contacted the other regions to see if whoever was functioning as acting watch commander for Region Nine during the Dawson Incident might have forwarded the reports to a station with an on-duty watch commander."

"However, since that acting watch commander was apparently me, although I didn't know it at the time"—Bauer shrugged ruefully—"the answer is no, I didn't. I do recall that you and I discussed the nature of the report you were going to write over a cup of coffee that evening. But I never saw the finished report, and I certainly didn't forward it anywhere."

"I don't understand any of this," Cellars muttered. "Regardless of whether or not I was drugged at the time, I definitely remember writing that summary report. I remember signing it. And I absolutely remember placing it in the watch commander's in-box for review at approximately twenty thirty hours that evening . . . right after I discussed the nature of what I intended to write with Sergeant Bauer . . . which was right after Bobby Dawson and I had our confrontation with Allesandra out in the meadow near his cabin."

"Allesandra being this extraterrestrial creature who supposedly seduced you and your friend Dawson, and who was capable of changing her shape at will? That's what you told Sergeant Bauer after the incident, correct?" Hightower asked in a voice that lacked any human warmth whatsoever.

"That's what I told Sergeant Bauer and that's . . . what I wrote in the report," Cellars replied evasively.

"You plan on sticking to that story, Sergeant?"

"Until I have good reason to think otherwise, yes, ma'am, I do."

"All right," Hightower said agreeably, even though her dark gray eyes were still chilled.

"I'm not sure I know where to start," Cellars replied. "Setting aside all the truly crazy parts, most of which make sense only if I really was drugged, it ended up as a kidnap and hostage-exchange situation. Allesandra and her shadowy friends—the ones I was shooting at that night—had Jody, and we had what she wanted . . . which were the other two stones."

"By stones, you mean the stabilized aliens? The evidence that she'd lost . . . and wanted back?"

"That's right." Cellars nodded, wondering if Hightower was simply amusing herself before asking for his badge, or if she was actually listening. The trouble was, he didn't know what he would have done in Hightower's position.

Probably ask for the badge and gun, then signal for the paramedics to move in with the nets, he thought ruefully.

"Go on," Hightower said.

"I realize I should have contacted headquarters and the FBI immediately," Cellars acknowledged. "But given the time factor, and my . . . perception . . . of what Allesandra was, or might be, and the immediate threat that she represented to Jody, I didn't feel like I had any choice. So we rigged a deal."

"We?"

"Bobby and I. It was supposed to be a simple exchange, Jody for the stones. But we knew the bitch would cheat, so we rigged a trap . . . a way to get Jody clear before the shit hit the fan. It was a long shot all the way around, and a lot of things went wrong that we'd never even thought about, to tell you the truth. But, ultimately, we caught her off guard, and Bobby managed to put her down with a single shot to the head, and she . . . died, or converted, or whatever it was that she did. In any case, her body disappeared. I don't know how or why, it just did. And in its place we found another stone, just like the others."

To Cellars's absolute amazement, the glacially calm expression in Hightower's eyes never so much as flickered.

"We were still trying to make sense of what had happened," he continued, "and watching out for more of Allesandra's shadowy friends, when Jody suddenly collapsed and went into shock. Bobby and I tried to bring her around, but she wasn't responding, so I left Bobby at the scene to watch over the evidence, and transported her here to the emergency ward. I stayed here for about an hour, until the doctors assured me she was stable. In the meantime, I was trying to contact Bobby by cell phone, but couldn't connect. So, finally, knowing that Captain Hawkins and Lieutenant Talbert were still missing, and realizing that I hadn't reported in to anyone at that point, I got on the radio and asked Sergeant Bauer to meet me for coffee. We met at the local McDonald's, at First and Lightstone, at approximately eighteen hundred hours. We sat and drank coffee while I walked him through the elements of my report. I'd say we talked for about an hour."

"What did you talk about?" Hightower asked.

Cellars shrugged. "The entire investigation in general, as I recall. But mostly about the fact that I was getting ready to write an official police report in which I would have to state that I had engaged in lethal combat with an extraterrestrial being."

"And what was Sergeant Bauer's opinion about that?"

"I don't recall his exact words," Cellars said. "But he definitely made it clear that he thought I was out of my mind to put something like that in an official report, even if I honestly believed it to be true."

Hightower glanced over at Bauer, who nodded in agreement.

"I didn't necessarily disagree with Tom's assessment," Cellars continued, "but with all the shit that happened out at that cabin, and at the station, I knew I had to write something in the way of a report. And I figured it was kind of late in my career to start perjuring myself, even if I actually thought I could make up a story that would fit all the facts . . . which I really didn't think I could do in the first place."

"That is how the clever liars usually get caught," Bauer commented. "Tripping up on all those unexpected loose threads."

Major Alice Hightower nodded slowly, her cold eyes never moving from Cellars's face.

"Exactly," Cellars agreed. "I tried one more time to contact Bobby, but if he still had his cell phone on, he wasn't answering. So, finally, I gave up, drove back to the station, wrote my incident report exactly the way it happened—or at least exactly the way I remembered it happening—dropped the report off in the watch commander's office, then drove over to the Windmill Inn and checked into a room."

"That's it?"

"Until the next day, when Sergeant Bauer gave me the standard notification that I was being put on administrative leave, yes, that's it." Cellars met Hightower's gaze directly as he slowly nodded. "No DUI

stop, no drunk black male subject . . . and absolutely no signed DUI report. Which, among many other things, means this piece-of-shit report
is a forgery, and that somebody at the station had to have been involved
in the switch," he added as he tossed the DUI report file onto Talbert's
bed in disgust.

"Oh, and by the way, in case you're wondering," Cellars went on before Hightower could respond, "the answer is yes. I'll be happy to take a
polygraph. At any time, and on any subject . . . your choice."

"You realize, of course, that the issue of drugs found in your blood
makes any such test a moot issue," Hightower replied.

"Yeah, I know," Cellars acknowledged. "But I'll take it anyway . . .
just to see what it shows."

Hightower seemed to consider this offer for a moment before suddenly switching topics. "Why were you trying so hard to contact this
friend of yours . . . Bobby Dawson?" she asked instead.

"We had some unfinished business."

"Regarding Jody Catlin?"

"Among other things," Cellars replied evasively.

Hightower appeared to catch the shift in Cellars's voice, and seemed
about ready to focus her questions accordingly when a quick pair of
beeps echoed through the hospital room.

Bauer immediately pulled a small handset radio out of his jacket
pocket, held it up to his ear, and whispered "Bauer," and then "Yes, he's
here. Why?" He listened again for about fifteen seconds, and then
turned to Cellars.

"Were you expecting a package?"

Cellars's eyebrows furrowed in confusion. "Delivered here? No,
why?"

"Shit," Bauer muttered, then quickly yelled into the radio mike,
"Get it out of the hospital building, now!" as he reached for the SIG-
Sauer in his shoulder holster.

CHAPTER EIGHTEEN

"WHAT'S THEIR ETA?" HIGHTOWER DEMANDED.

They were standing in the parking lot opposite the emergency-room entrance and staring through the slowly falling snow at the four scout cars that were now parked in a protective square formation around the small brown-paper-wrapped package. The idea was that if something in the package did go off, the cars would absorb most of the blast. It was the best they could do until the bomb squad arrived.

In the meantime, three uniformed officers were stringing bright yellow lengths of crime scene tape to keep all of the hospital staff and visitors away from the parking lot . . . and two other officers had moved Talbert to another room, where they were now on high alert.

Only Hightower, Bauer, Cellars, and the hospital administrator were standing inside the taped-off perimeter.

Bauer shook his head in frustration. "At least an hour. Maybe a lot more. They had to pull the engine on the bomb truck yesterday afternoon, and the mechanics are still working on it. Josephine County's supposed to be covering, but there's a jackknifed tractor-trailer up at the pass that's got them blocked in, and it looks like it's going to be a while before they can get clear."

"I really can't leave our emergency-room entrance blocked off for an hour . . . unless, of course, we absolutely have to," the hospital administrator quickly amended when he saw the expression in Hightower's eyes.

"Do we know anything about the person who delivered the package?" Cellars asked the group at large.

"Yes, I believe it was dropped off at the receiving desk by a delivery service," the hospital administrator responded.

"But there wasn't any delivery label on the package," Cellars reminded. "Just my name and the hospital."

"Hold on, let me confirm that." The hospital administrator quickly pulled a cell phone from his belt, punched in a number, spoke briefly, then listened for about thirty seconds.

"It was a young man, slender build, brown eyes, about a hundred and sixty pounds, from the Reliable Messenger Services," he said as he put away the cell phone. "The receptionist saw the name on the van. She said she's sure about the description. Definitely remembers him because she was surprised when he didn't ask her to sign a receipt log. Apparently he just dropped it off, ran back to his van, and drove away."

"Reliable Messenger Services. A brown van?" Cellars pressed.

"Oh, yes, she did say it was brown," the hospital administrator acknowledged.

"What time was it dropped off?"

"It was a while ago. We don't have an exact time right now, but we can certainly—"

"That's all right." Cellars shook his head as he pulled a folding knife out of his pocket, knelt beside the package, then looked back up at Hightower, Bauer, and the hospital administrator. "You all might want to back off a ways," he said, "just in case I'm wrong about this."

Twenty minutes later, Hightower, Bauer, and Cellars were back in Talbert's room, staring at the object on the adjacent bed that Cellars had removed from the brown-paper-wrapped package.

It was an Elmer Fudd doll . . . with a ten-penny construction nail sticking out of the center of its forehead. The attached note read:

THE WASCALS STRIKE BACK

ONE DOWN, AT LEAST THREE, MAYBE FOUR TO GO

BUT THESE NEW ONES ARE SERIOUSLY HARDHEADED,

PARTNER. TIME TO WATCH YOUR ASS.

PS: SORRY ABOUT RUINING YOUR DOLL. THE RECEIPT'S

INSIDE THE BOX. FEEL FREE TO TRADE IT IN FOR A NEW

ONE. YOU'RE PROBABLY GOING TO NEED IT TO SOLVE THE

PUZZLE.

"Do you have any explanation for this?" Hightower demanded, turning to glare at Cellars.

"I got a phone call from Bobby this morning," Cellars replied. "He warned me to be careful . . . something to the effect that I was going to be the rabbit in a new game."

"The rabbit?"

"That's what he said."

"So what's this game he's talking about . . . and this puzzle?"

"I have no idea," Cellars confessed. "Bobby tends to find things amusing that most other people wouldn't . . . like the idea of the entire DEA trying to hunt him down. On the other hand, I think it's safe to assume that somebody—or something—just got nailed."

"You mean killed?"

"To tell you the truth, Major"—Cellars sighed as he stared down at the plastic doll—"I really don't know what I mean."

"But you're sure the package came from your friend Dawson?"

"Sure enough." Cellars nodded. "He used a thick marker on the outside wrapper, and it looks like he deliberately disguised his printing style . . . which is why I didn't notice anything when I first saw the package. But the note is classic Dawson. No doubt about it."

"Are you suggesting that nobody could fake his printing style?" Hightower looked decidedly skeptical.

"No, not at all. He uses an open block style, easy to forge. But his offbeat sense of humor . . . that might be a bit more difficult problem for someone who's basically sane."

"When was the last time you talked with him . . . before this morning?"

"Other than this morning, I haven't seen or talked with Bobby since our confrontation with Allesandra up by his cabin . . . two months ago . . . and the recent incident with Dr. Pleausant," Cellars said. "Far as I know, he's disappeared again. Probably because the DEA's still looking for him."

"Because of his helicopter crash?"

"And because of their missing agents."

"I can see why the DEA might be gunning for him," Hightower muttered. "I'm just about inclined to give them a hand myself."

She started to say something else, then shook her head. "We'll deal with this later, Sergeant. Let's get back to that missing report of yours. The evening you dropped it off in the watch commander's office, did you talk with anyone at the station?"

Cellars hesitated, trying to think back. "No, ma'am, I don't believe so."

"Did anyone see you in the report-writing room, or see you drop off the report?"

"Not as far as I know. As I recall, the station was mostly empty. If anyone was around, and saw me, I didn't see them."

Hightower frowned, then stared down at the floor for several seconds before bringing her gaze back up to Cellars. "That is really unfortunate," she said.

"Oh? Why's that?" Cellars asked. He had the sense of being slowly dissected by the laserlike intensity of Alice Hightower's eyes.

"According to that questionable DUI report," Hightower answered, "you made the stop in the early-morning hours immediately following your investigation at the Dawson cabin, approximately three blocks from the station, on a black male—six-one, one-ninety-five—who passed a sobriety test . . . and was subsequently released with a warning to drive more carefully. You indicated that you filed a report because the subject was argumentative and threatened to sue both you and the state of Oregon. Early-morning hours would be on or about the time you were supposedly at the station composing your initial CSI report on the death investigation of your friend, Robert or Bobby Dawson, who, as far as we know, turns out not to be dead after all."

"Yeah, of course Bobby's alive. Like I said, I talked with him this morning . . . and there's the living proof, more or less," he said, pointing down at the sprawled doll. "And besides, I explained all that to Tom. But I never—"

"Bear with me a moment, Sergeant." Hightower held up her right hand. "You indicated to Sergeant Bauer, during your conversation at the coffee shop right before you supposedly wrote your missing summary report, that you fired approximately twenty-four shots at several unidentified shadowy suspects, at a relatively short range, but apparently failed to disable or kill any one of them. This in spite of the fact that your training records indicate you're a good shot with a .40-caliber SIG-Sauer at medium ranges, and under unexpected or stressful situations. You also indicated that many of these shots hit your own vehicle. Unfortunately, we're not in a position to confirm that part of your statement, either, because your vehicle was destroyed in a fire at the station parking lot that evening."

"Which was started by Captain Hawkins's cigar, and observed by Watch Commander Talbert," Cellars reminded.

"So you say," Hightower acknowledged, "but as I understand the situation, the only eyewitnesses were Captain Hawkins and Watch Commander Talbert. Captain Talbert's memories of the events of the past two months are now hazy at best, and Captain Hawkins is still missing and presumed dead, seeing as how an estimated seven pints of his blood were found splattered across your kitchen walls and floor. We'll ignore, for the moment, the fact that you and Captain Hawkins apparently had a series of disagreements that day which led, according to several police officers and sheriff's deputies who happened to be in Captain Hawkins's vicinity at the time, to his being thoroughly pissed at you. And I understand that's putting it very mildly," she added in her glacial voice.

"Yes, but—"

"You claim to have delivered the body of your friend Dawson to the county morgue that morning," Hightower went on, ignoring Cellars's objection, "but there is no record of that delivery. The individual who you claim took possession of the body—a young man named Randy Granstrom—is apparently still missing. All of the evidence you collected at Mr. Dawson's cabin has disappeared, subsequent to being checked out of the OSP and Fish and Wildlife Service crime labs by a federal wildlife geneticist named Jody Catlin, a woman who—according to you—both you and your friend Dawson were in love with."

"She—" Cellars started to interrupt, and then stopped as Hightower shook her head and continued her recital.

"Interestingly enough, Miss Catlin also stated that she had been abducted by some kind of shape-changing alien, who killed and dismembered Captain Hawkins when he followed her to your home, and then made off with all of your evidence. Or at least that was her initial statement when she regained consciousness at the hospital, which I'm told she now denies ever making. I was also advised that Miss Catlin initially agreed to seek counseling with you before she checked out of the county observation clinic, but she left in the middle of her first session with Dr. Pleasant and apparently hasn't returned since."

"I've been trying to get her to go with me to my session," Cellars offered, "but I haven't been very successful so far."

"I suggest you keep on trying, for your own sake as well as hers. In the meantime," Hightower went on, "there's the issue of your next assigned vehicle, a new Ford Expedition, which you also shot full of holes—according to your conversation with Sergeant Bauer—because you were shooting at shadows again, but which is now also missing. And the fact that the four Jasper County deputies who responded to the Dawson crime scene before you arrived are still missing.

"Which brings us to a relatively minor, but equally disturbing matter. The fact that, for whatever reason, you apparently gave a lecture to a bunch of local fruitcakes on how to collect evidence at alien-abduction crime scenes . . . on the very same evening this entire incident started."

Hightower paused, and looked at Cellars with her inquisitor's eyes.

"What can I say?" Cellars shrugged. "Guilty and stupid as charged."

"As it turns out, there's no need for you to say anything at all," Hightower said, "because we have an abundance of witnesses—about sixty in all, as I recall—who are perfectly willing to verify the nature of your talk. Unfortunately, a goodly number of them also claim to be in contact with—or abducted by—extraterrestrials on a fairly regular basis, several apparently for breeding purposes, so I don't think they're going to be of much use in helping us resolve your situation, do you, Sergeant?"

"No, I suppose not," Cellars conceded.

"Which brings us back to your DUI report . . . and the follow-up complaint. A complaint in which the suspect admits to drinking and driving, and being belligerent, but claims you incited his inappropriate behavior by making derogatory statements about his racial background and using unnecessary force to effect the arrest. However, as a result of your apology, and your subsequent explanation that you and your girl-friend had been fighting and you were still upset when you made the stop, he apparently decided to drop all charges."

"My . . . apology?" Cellars stood there and stared at Hightower in stunned disbelief.

"Before we go any further, is there anything you'd like to offer on your behalf with respect to these reports?" Hightower asked.

"Nothing occurs to me at the moment," Cellars replied, his head still reeling from the accumulated impact of Hightower's chilling recital. "Or at least nothing polite."

"Really?" Hightower cocked her head and smiled in a manner that made Cellars want to take a step backward. "Why is that, Sergeant?"

"Several reasons, ma'am," Cellars replied, trying to regain his composure. "Probably the best is the simple fact that I haven't made a stop on a DUI in something like twelve years. And that was up in Salem, on a state senator, who was a great many things—including stinking drunk and driving on the wrong side of the road—but he was definitely not six-foot-one . . . or one hundred and ninety-five pounds . . . or black. I would have remembered if he was."

"That was Senator Chambers, I believe."

"Yes, ma'am, it was."

"So, I take it, Sergeant Cellars, that you'd be very surprised if, at some future competency hearing where your ability to perform as a police officer was being assessed, a completely sober, six-foot-one, hundred-and-ninety-five-pound African-American showed up—along with the other three DEA Special Agent occupants of that car—to testify that your memory isn't any better than your shooting or reporting skills?" Hightower suggested.

Cellars started to say something, hesitated, quickly scanned down the face page of the complaint form to the list of witnesses, and then muttered "Oh, shit."

"To quote many a famed attorney, I rest my case," Hightower said in a voice that, if anything, sounded more chilling in its gentleness. "So I suppose there's just one more thing you need to know, Sergeant." Hightower fixed her glacial eyes on Cellars. "Hightower is my ex-husband's family name. My maiden name is Hawkins. Captain Hawkins is—or was, as the case may be—my brother."

Cellars stood there, dumbstruck.

"And in case you were wondering, the answer is yes, my brother is—or was—a complete asshole. I've had no use for the son of a bitch over the past forty-five years, and I have no use for him now . . . dead or alive. But the man was a captain in the Oregon State Patrol, and I do care about that. Do you understand me, Sergeant?"

For a numbing moment, Cellars wasn't sure he could get the words out. "Yes, ma'am."

"So when I assure you that I'm a worse son of a bitch to cross than my wimp-dick brother ever thought about being, you'll perhaps understand why the OSP and the state of Oregon see no conflict of interest in my conducting this investigation. Do you have any questions, Sergeant?"

"No, ma'am."

"Good."

With that, Hightower turned and walked out the door.

For a good fifteen seconds, the hospital room was deadly silent.

"Tom, I think our detective-sergeant here is finally starting to get a sense of the bigger picture," Talbert rasped from his bed. "And it's about time, because I'm starting to get tired of all this bullshit. So why don't you take him downstairs, show him his new ride . . . and tell him to be careful with the damned thing or I'll personally see to it that he's assigned to Internal Affairs for the rest of his goddamned career, however long that may be," Talbert added, his voice drifting off as his eyes started to close.

———

"Was she serious?" Cellars asked Bauer when they were alone in the elevator.

"You didn't know?"

Cellars shook his head.

"I don't think the word 'serious' even begins to do that woman justice," Bauer said honestly.

"I heard she was a hard-ass, but Jesus . . . her own brother?"

"You saying you disagree with her assessment of the self-righteous prick?"

"Well, no, but—"

"Then I suggest you take her at her word—that she's a whole lot worse than her wimp-dick brother ever thought of being—and stay the hell away from her whenever you can," Bauer suggested.

"Amen to that." Cellars nodded in agreement.

"So who are we dealing with?" he asked as he and Bauer walked out into the hospital parking lot. "Or maybe I should ask, who's dealing with us?"

"In other words, who are these people who seem to have access to our files, and seem to be screwing with the OSP in general and you and your friends in particular?" Bauer asked. "Not to mention very possibly being involved in kidnapping or killing about fifty other Oregon law enforcement officers and private citizens?"

"Yeah, something like that."

"I don't know who they are, or maybe even what they are," Bauer said as he stopped and turned to face Cellars. "And to tell you the truth, I'm not sure anybody does . . . except maybe you . . . and your friends . . . and maybe Talbert. And if Talbert does know, he isn't saying."

"Which leaves me. And my friends."

"At best, eyewitnesses complete with officially questionable medical conditions, or reputations." Bauer smiled sympathetically at Cellars. "Or, at worst, obvious targets if the bad guys decide to start clearing away witnesses . . . which may be what your buddy Dawson was talking about in his note—about watching your ass."

"I assume that's why you've got all the security on Talbert?"

"Exactly."

"So what do I do?"

"You mean about you and your friends?"

"Uh-huh."

Bauer was silent for a long moment.

"I get the impression," he finally said, "that, apart from his warped sense of humor, your buddy Dawson is perfectly capable of taking care of himself if these creatures of yours start to pick on him . . . at least up to a point. But that your mutual girlfriend may be a lot more vulnerable."

"Actually, I'm hoping that these . . . creatures . . . won't focus on her at all. Or, at least, not right away," Cellars said.

"Devil's advocate . . . why wouldn't they?" Bauer asked. "You said she was present and witnessed whatever happened between you and Dawson and this mysterious woman named Allesandra. And, as I recall, you also said she was the one who made the initial DNA extractions."

"But she was basically a kidnap victim," Cellars argued. "Bobby and I are the ones they ought to be pissed at. And besides, she has other witnesses to the DNA results: Melissa Washington, her coworker at the Fish and Wildlife lab, and Jack Wilson from the OSP lab. They were present during the reexaminations of the DNA, and all three of them worked together to dig the bits of tissue out of my expended hollowpoints."

"That might help if these creatures of yours follow the same logic," Bauer agreed. "And, in any case, she's a federal law enforcement employee, so I assume she'll have at least a couple of federal agents looking out after her welfare. But even so—"

"You think whoever's doing all this might decide to go after her anyway, just to be sure?"

"Which may be what your buddy Dawson is doing," Bauer suggested. "Drawing their attention away from her, and on to him . . . and you," he pointed out. "Does that sound like something he might do?"

"Oh yeah, that's definitely a Bobby Dawson approach to problem solving." Cellars nodded slowly, lost in thought. Then he looked up at Bauer. "So, I repeat my question. What do I do?"

"Well, based on my conversations with Hightower and Talbert—or, I should say, my listening and their talking—and my own limited perspective," Bauer said as he started walking through the hospital parking lot again, "I'd say the situation all boils down to a couple of very simple issues."

"And those are?" Cellars asked as the two police officers came to a stop next to a very large and militaristic-looking off-road vehicle.

"First of all, I think it's fair to say that these creatures, as you described them, either exist or they don't. No real middle ground as far as I can tell. Hightower claims to be keeping an open mind, and Talbert's definitely backing you up, even though he won't explain why. Personally, I'm still pretty skeptical . . . but then, I don't know you that well."

"Fair enough. And the second?"

"Secondly," Bauer went on easily, "if these creatures do exist, then they may or may not be responsible for something in the neighborhood of fifty missing civilians and law enforcement officers. I don't even want to start telling you what I think about all of that. But in any case," he added, "we definitely need to find whoever—or whatever—is responsible, and take them down before we lose any more Jasper County citizens or officers. And to do that, Major Hightower and Talbert and I are all in agreement that we need some hard evidence. Which means, among other things, that we need to get you back on the job."

"As a CSI officer . . . not a desk job?"

"Unless you'd like to be an acting watch commander instead," Bauer offered hopefully. "I can pretty much guarantee you an opening within the next fifteen minutes if you're interested."

"That's okay, I like being a field sergeant just fine," Cellars said hurriedly. "But what about my reports?"

"Which reports are you talking about?"

"The ones on the Dawson Incident. Whoever made off with them—or destroyed them—just wasted their time because I can always rewrite the damned things. I assume that's what you and Major Hightower want me to do first, before I go back to the investigations?"

"No, actually, we don't," Bauer replied.

Cellars's eyebrows furrowed in surprise. "Why not?"

"Think about it. At the moment, given the discussion she and I just had with Pleasant before you got here, there's no official reason why we can't put you back on the street immediately . . . and there's every good reason why we should. But if you were to write and sign an official report in which you claim to have killed a shape-changing extraterrestrial who immediately morphed into a small rock—"

"Ah."

"Talbert's in a whole lot better shape than he looks," Bauer added, "but he can't do much to help you without the evidence. Which brings us right back to the basic premise: that we need to get you back out in the field so you can do your job. And to do that, you're going to need some wheels."

Cellars suddenly became aware of his surroundings.

"What the hell's that?" he demanded as he stared past Bauer's right shoulder.

"That"—the acting watch commander of OSP Region 9 smiled pleasantly—"is your new ride."

CHAPTER NINETEEN

THE CAT, VERY MUCH AWARE THAT HER HINTS WERE BEING IG-
nored, reacted in true cat fashion by slashing at the offending leg.

Jody Catlin yelped in pain.

"You rotten little—" Catlin started to yell, then wisely decided to
save her breath when she realized that the coal-black Manx had already
turned away and was now sitting patiently in front of her empty food
and milk bowls.

"What? You think I've got nothing better to do than feed you
twenty times a day?" Jody demanded.

The Manx ignored what was, at best, a rhetorical question, and continued to stare into the empty bowl.

"Just because you're fixed and couldn't care less about males in general, you think everybody else . . . ah, to hell with it," Jody Catlin snarled as she opened the refrigerator, realized she was out of whole milk, pulled out a container of skim milk, and poured a couple of ounces into the smaller of the two bowls.

"There, is that better?"

The Manx continued to ignore the possibly meaningless words as she stood up, stepped forward to the bowl, sniffed the offering briefly, then turned and walked away. There was, from Jody Catlin's irritated point of view, little doubt as to the significance of the upraised tail stub.

Catlin was in the process of muttering something equally impolite while putting the skim milk container back into the refrigerator when the phone rang. She reached for the handset before the second ring.

"Hello?"

"Jody?"

"Melissa?" The encrypted phone that Malcolm Byzor had installed in Jody Catlin's rented apartment was a definite improvement over the old models, but even so, the digital scrambling techniques produced oddly flat vocal tones. As such, it was often difficult for Catlin to tell who was on the other end of the line.

"In the flesh. All hundred and fifty-two pounds of it," the federal wildlife crime lab geneticist grumbled. "How you doin', girl?"

"Other than being very lonely and very pissed, I'm fine."

"Let me guess, you're lonely because neither of those two idiot boyfriends of yours ever bothers to call . . . and you're pissed because you called one of them, and whoever it was is just as stubborn as always. Am I close?"

"Dead-on."

"So who was it this time?"

"Colin."

"Would that be Colin, the thickheaded idiot, who's so in love with this alien Aphrodite that he can't get it up with a genuine human flesh-and-blood girlfriend anymore . . . or Colin, the thickheaded idiot, who finally came to his senses?" Washington inquired.

Jody Catlin rolled her eyes skyward.

"Melissa, why do I even bother to talk with you?"

"Because at least I talk, whereas the menfolk in your life wouldn't even know how to start," Washington pointed out. "And besides, girl, you know I won't gossip about you behind your back."

"How do I know that?"

"Because all I've been doing with my spare time, the past eight weeks, is tearing my hair out trying to reconstruct that damned DNA data with Jack Wilson. And I never spill the beans without getting something back in return. And we both know that man's just about hopeless when it comes to gossiping about anybody."

"Good for Jack. So how are the two of you coming?"

"That's the reason I called. I think we're getting close."

"Really?"

"Well, maybe not all that close," Melissa Washington corrected, "but we're pretty sure we've got at least one of the extra two base pairs worked out. Jack had some notes from that first session of ours that really helped, but the silicon substitution still isn't working right when you try to bring it up as a three-dimensional model on the computer."

"Are you sure you're working on the right carbon substitution?"

"We've asked ourselves that about a hundred times," Washington said, "and both of us are convinced that the answer's yes, but we really need you in on this deal. Jack has this idea that you kinda have to finesse the substitution . . . almost like sliding that big old silicon ion in when the rest of the molecule isn't looking. Tell you the truth, I don't think he knows what he's talking about. But I also figured your organic chemistry is a lot fresher than mine, which means we definitely need to get you back in on the teamwork."

"I'm not sure that's a good idea," Jody said hesitantly.

"I know what you said . . . that your friend Malcolm has you hidden away. But the thing is, we're so close now. And Jack's got this really spacy idea about how we can replicate that first DNA run based on the Polaroid photo he took of the monitor screen right after the data started dropping out."

"But that photo only shows the first couple hundred base pairs," Jody Catlin protested. "We're going to need a lot more than that if we're going to get anyone at NIH to pay attention."

"I know, but Jack has this idea . . . listen, we've got to meet somewhere and talk. What about at a neutral spot where we can be at the same place without anyone else ever knowing we were together?"

"Like where . . . keeping in mind that we don't want to be real descriptive over the phone," Catlin reminded her.

"Remember me telling you about that really adorable salesman I met a few months ago?"

"I vaguely remember some unlikely story about a brief but torrid romance in a back warehouse or stockroom, something like that."

"Without mentioning any names over the phone, do you remember where?"

Jody Catlin thought for a moment. "Yes, I believe I do . . . and I'm still skeptical. Nobody's that adorable."

"Well, then, maybe it's about time the three of us got together so you can see the truth for yourself."

CHAPTER TWENTY

AT A POINT ALMOST EQUIDISTANT BETWEEN OSP'S REGION 9 STA-
tion and Cascadia Rain-Song's apartment, the team leader watched with
growing interest as Colin Cellars stepped down out of his new, Army-
green-painted crime scene vehicle, locked the door, then slowly turned
in place to examine the surrounding parking lot.

He's alert, she thought. *As if he's expecting some kind of surveillance.*

The prospect caused her to smile in anticipation.

She'd been following Cellars for several hours now, alternately intrigued by his stops and his new vehicle, and frustrated by his new wari-
ness. The key to a successful search and retrieval operation was the
ability to deal immediately with all related elements at the time the
pickup was made, which meant that all such elements had to be located
and monitored. Which was a definite problem in this case, because at

least two of those critical elements were still on the loose. But if Cellars was worried about surveillance, that could mean he was about to make contact with one of those elements—ideally, from her biased point of view, Bobby Dawson.

Exactly what they'd been waiting for.

She smiled again, then whispered softly:

"Units Two, Three, and Five, this is One. Be advised, subject Cellars is now driving a camouflage green, off-road vehicle of unknown model, but appears to be a civilian version of a General Motors Humvee with a sports-utility-like grill, tires, and wheels. Vehicle has e-plates, interior emergency lights, and OSP-type radio antennas, but no exterior emergency light bar, or other identifying OSP markings. He's now parked in the Rogue Valley Mall parking lot, east side, and has exited his vehicle. All units, acknowledge transmission and report in."

The replies came back immediately.

"Two, transmission acknowledged, status unchanged."

"Three, transmission acknowledged, status unchanged."

There was a pause, then:

"Five, transmission acknowledged. Be advised, subjects Washington and Wilson are in a ninety-eight blue Dodge Minivan, Oregon plates, last three numbers one-five-three, heading north on I-Five, just past exit twenty-one."

The team leader came alert immediately. Exit twenty-one was nine miles south of exit thirty, which was the off-ramp for the Rogue Valley Mall.

"One to Five, summarize their current activities."

"Five to One, subjects Washington and Wilson have been working on computerized DNA structural analysis for the past fifteen days. According to agents monitoring our bug, they just requested a meeting with Catlin a few minutes ago."

"Did they give a location for the meet?"

"No, they were evasive over the phone, and we only heard one side of the conversation. Something about a stockroom or warehouse."

The team leader frowned.

"We have to assume that Washington and Wilson are en route to meet with subject Catlin, which would certainly be helpful to our primary mission. But it's also possible they could be trying to reestablish a physical link with Cellars or perhaps even Dawson directly."

"Sounds good to me . . . but is Cellars going to be a problem?"

"Possibly. He's been watching for surveillance all day, like he's expecting us to be there. But switching vehicles out in the open like that doesn't make much sense."

"Unless he's planning on going off-road all of a sudden where we can't follow. Maybe we should have a chopper up on standby, just in case?"

"Good idea. I'll take care of it. In the meantime, stay alert. If any of them spot us now, Dawson's going to rabbit in a heartbeat . . . and we'll never find him."

A sudden movement caught the team leader's attention.

"One to all units, be advised, Cellars is walking away from his vehicle now, toward the central east side entrance to the Rogue Valley Mall."

"Where they have all kinds of warehouses and stockrooms," Two commented.

"That's right, so maintain a tight surveillance on that van," she whispered, "and stand by for further instructions. One out."

CHAPTER TWENTY-ONE

THE ROGUE VALLEY MALL, LOCATED IN ALMOST THE EXACT CENTER of neighboring Jackson County, had the distinction of being the only covered two-story shopping complex in the entire bicounty district. Purposefully designed to meet the shopping needs of the seventy-five thousand middle-income families residing in both Jackson and Jasper counties, the mall was anchored by a JCPenney store at one end, a Mervyn's at the other end, and a somewhat more "upscale" Meier & Frank at the center atrium position.

But "upscale" is always a relative measure.

Rogue Valley shoppers unwilling to settle for anything less than a Neiman Marcus or a Saks Fifth Avenue found it necessary to endure a four-hundred-mile trek north to Seattle, or an equally daunting journey south to San Francisco. Either that, or learn to live without.

But those with less sophisticated shopping concerns—such as finding a replacement for an Elmer Fudd doll with a construction nail sticking out of its forehead, and linking up with a reclusive buddy who liked to thumb his nose at the DEA—it was theoretically possible to find pretty much everything you wanted on the second level of the Rogue Valley Mall . . . at a spot where the sign said TOYS in bright bold letters.

Or at least that was the theory.

But Colin Cellars had spent too many years in law enforcement to have much faith in theories. In his experience, solutions came about through perspiration and persistence. Which was why he'd been browsing the aisles in the rear portion of the mall toy store for the last fifteen minutes, trying to figure out why Bobby Dawson had so clearly directed him to this particular store. Ideally, from Cellars's point of view, to make a face-to-face connection and provide some interesting explanations . . . such as why Dawson had disappeared right after the Allesandra shooting. And what *wascals and rabbits* had to do with extraterrestrial beings, not to mention the mysterious disappearance of at least fifty Jasper County citizens.

If anything at all.

But, so far, the only interesting people he'd found were several frazzled mothers trying very hard to keep track of one or more toy-crazed toddlers, and a couple of teenage boys trying equally hard to avoid the steely gaze of the gray-haired clerk at the register.

The teenagers were the immediate concern, because every move they made read "snatch and run," and that was the last thing that Cellars wanted to have happen just then. But there wasn't much he could do about it. If he confronted the youths, showed them his badge, and suggested that they find another place to commit their petty thievery, they'd probably take off running anyway . . . and thereby immediately attract the kind of attention that he and Dawson were, presumably, both trying to avoid.

He'd been watching carefully for any sign of surveillance from the moment he'd pulled into the mall parking lot, and he hadn't spotted anything yet. But even so, he couldn't shake the feeling that he was being watched. Probably by some DEA Internal Affairs team, but there were other possibilities that he really didn't want to think about at the moment.

Come on, Bobby, where are you? We need to link up and get away from here, right now.

The situation was so obvious now that the stock boy—a lean and very fit-looking young man attired in loose-fitting pants, a faded white shirt that read JASPER HIGH TRACK AND FIELD, and a pair of well-worn running shoes—had already come out of the back storeroom. He was now positioned at the front of the store, making a pretense of rearranging the display of stuffed animals while he kept both his targets in clear sight. And the register clerk was tapping her fingers so loudly on the handset of the phone that Cellars could hear the rattling some thirty feet away.

But, in spite of all these red-flag warnings, the two teenage boys continued their survey of the toy store shelves as though they were invisible to anyone other than themselves.

It was all that Colin Cellars could do to keep from dragging the two youths into the back storeroom and handcuffing them to a drainpipe, just for being stupid in public.

Come on, Bobby, where are you?

Distracted by his search for the familiar face or figure of Bobby Dawson, and the furtive movements of the two boys, Cellars never saw the flickering movement of a dark shadowy figure as it sought a better vantage point within the towering, three-story tree-house display. The one that rose up through a cut-out portion of the second mall level about fifty feet from the toy store.

———

Melissa Washington and Jack Wilson were still driving north on I-5 in Washington's blue Dodge Minivan, but the rapidly falling snow and a pair of slow-moving log trucks had effectively reduced their speed to something less than 40 mph. As such, they had only just passed exit twenty-seven, and were still three miles south of the Rogue Valley Mall exit when Jody Catlin cautiously stepped onto the JCPenney escalator leading up to the store's second-floor level.

It had been a stressful and nerve-wracking trip.

Damned cat, she muttered to herself.

She'd tried to keep the Manx locked in the apartment, but the wily animal seemed to sense that a car trip was in the offing . . . and had managed not only to escape out the front door, but also to lunge past Catlin's flailing arms and work herself under the front passenger seat, where she refused to be dislodged.

Finally, giving up in exasperation, she'd taken a series of back roads to the Rogue Valley Mall parking lot, thinking that such a route would make her less vulnerable to being spotted. But the darkened sky, the slick asphalt, and the rapidly falling snow made every alley and street corner seem more ominous and threatening. She'd almost turned back several times, but the need to talk with someone she could trust, face-to-face—who wasn't a damned cat—was almost visceral.

She knew she was terribly vulnerable . . . and she knew that Malcolm and Colin would be extremely upset if they found out what she was doing. But she'd made it to the mall parking lot. And the Manx had shown no interest in leaving her cozy hideaway. And now that Catlin was actually in the mall, in one of the stores, and among dozens of other shoppers, her fear began to subside.

They won't come after me with so many people around, she reasoned as she scanned the unfamiliar faces. *They wouldn't dare. Too many witnesses. And besides, they don't even know I'm here.*

As she moved through the crowded aisles, working her way toward the central mall walkway, she remembered Malcolm Byzor's last words of advice when he'd dropped her off at what he'd described as her new safe house.

If you absolutely have to go outside, try to look and act normal, use the car switches we've set up, and blend in with the people around you wherever you go. If the people around you are scraping the snow off their windshields, or shopping for clothes, you should be doing the same thing, too. No sudden movements. No furtive looks. Wherever you go, just act like you've got all of the time in the world, and no other place that you have to be in the next hour or so, and you'll be fine. Trust me on this one.

Accordingly, she paused several times to examine items on display . . . until, finally, she found herself at the wide entrance to the store and staring out into the central mall walkway where she could see, out in the middle of the walkway, a three-story tree house. She paused there, feeling her heart start to pound as she stared out across the long irregular walkway.

What if they're out there, waiting for me?

Then she shook her head.

No, don't think about it, she admonished herself. *Just go.*

Feeling somewhat bolstered, she stepped out of the protective surroundings of the store and into the far more exposed walkway.

At that moment, all the lights in the mall went out.

CHAPTER TWENTY-TWO

FOR A BRIEF MOMENT, THE ENTIRE MALL WAS DARK AND SILENT.
Then the walkway erupted into an echoing chorus of gasps and
screams, and the high-pitched sound of shattering glass, all of which
were immediately drowned out by the pulsed shriek of fire alarms
mounted throughout the shopping complex.

An instant later, the distinctive crack of a partially suppressed rifle
shot, and a chilling, high-pitched scream immediately thereafter—both
barely audible in the momentary flash of silence between the first and
second pulsed shrieks—sent Detective-Sergeant Colin Cellars diving to
the floor and grabbing for his shoulder-holstered pistol.

Cellars heard a yell of anger somewhere off to his right as a display
case crashed to the floor, and rubber-soled shoes slipped frantically
against fragments of broken glass. But it was too dark to see anything,

in spite of the eerie red glow of the emergency lighting being activated all along the walkway. And Cellars was too busy trying to stay low and away from any incoming bullets, and getting his SIG-Sauer clear of his holster and jacket, to pay much attention to what sounded like a pair of panicked teenagers trying to escape.

Fifteen seconds later, Cellars was still crouched, trying to decide if the muffled crack he'd heard really could have been a suppressed rifle shot, and ready to fire at the first sight of an armed aggressor, when the ear-piercing fire alarms suddenly shut off and the main mall lights came back on.

Cellars took advantage of the moment to scramble to his feet and lunge out into the walkway with the SIG-Sauer extended out in both hands.

As he did so, his eyes were immediately drawn to the sight of two teenagers running desperately for the mall exit in front of the JCPenney entrance, with the young stock boy in hot pursuit about thirty yards back.

"Ladies and gentlemen, please stay calm and don't be alarmed," a voice over the mall speakers boomed out. "We seem to have had a momentary disruption of power, which tripped the main circuit breaker for our lights, and set off our fire alarms. But there is no fire. I repeat. There is no fire."

———

Jody Catlin had reacted instantly to the sudden darkness, and the subsequent high-pitched screeching of the fire alarms—one of which was right over her head—by stumbling back into the relative security of JCPenney, crouching against a wooden floor display of sheets and pillowcases, and covering her ears.

It occurred to her, then, that she was in a very vulnerable position.

Thus, by the time the fire alarms shut off and the lights came back on, she was already up on her feet and ready to run. Which put her in a perfect position to see the two young teenagers with some small cardboard boxes in their hands running toward her with another older youth in pursuit.

Then, as the two desperately running teenagers cut toward the mall exit to her right, her eyes caught another movement. She turned her head and saw a very familiar figure lunge out of a nearby toy store with a semiautomatic pistol extended in both hands—which caused her eyes to go wide with shock.

Colin?

Had she stopped to think about it for even a brief moment, Jody Catlin might have remembered that her childhood friend and erstwhile lover was also an Oregon State Patrol officer; and, therefore, might have a perfectly good reason for pursuing two teenagers running out of a mall store with electronic game boxes in their hands . . . even if the threat of lethal force seemed a bit extreme for the crime of petty theft.

But in her heightened state of paranoia, Jody could only think of one reason why her friend would suddenly appear with a gun in his hand . . . right after all the lights had gone out for no apparent reason . . . and right where she was going to meet in secret with two forensic scientist friends who just might hold the key to her lost evidence.

They were back . . . and Colin, true to his word, was going to confront them.

Jody Catlin's instinct-driven survival mechanisms reacted by sending a burst of adrenaline molecules surging through her bloodstream, giving her but two immediate choices: fight or flight.

And having nothing to fight with except her bare hands, she turned and ran for her life.

The team leader took one look at the stunned figure standing in the store entranceway next to the exit where the two desperately running teenagers had disappeared, and cursed as she reached for her radio.

"One to all units," she whispered, "Cellars is inside the mall . . . and so is Catlin. She just showed up."

The reply came back immediately.

"Two to One, be advised, Washington and Wilson are signaling to turn off at exit thirty. Five'll get you ten they're heading for a meet at the mall . . . and that Dawson is with them. Probably hiding in the back of the van."

———————

As she listened to the transmitted information, the sudden, all-too-familiar feeling of measurable and significant emptiness once again caused the expression in the dominant one's eyes to fill with disbelief . . . and then rage.

Even though she'd been thoroughly briefed, and thus warned, she still found the arrogance and aggressiveness of these frail creatures to be beyond all comprehension.

The death of one retriever was difficult to accept in the best of circumstances.

The death of two—on one mission—was unthinkable.

Especially when the evidence on the road suggested the first retriever had been set up—almost certainly by the aggressive and elusive human who had caused so much grief to Allesandra and her assistants.

Dawson.

How does he dare to be so defiant? she asked herself, jarred by the awareness that she had to remain alert and elusive herself as she fought to bring her own desire for vengeance under tight control.

Moments later, having regained her sense of focused purpose, she issued the order.

Intercept and destroy them.
Now.

CHAPTER TWENTY-THREE

BY THE TIME COLIN CELLARS WALKED BACK INTO THE TOY STORE, the salesclerk had already returned the broken display case to its previous upright position and was starting to sweep up the broken glass.

She looked up to see Cellars reholstering the SIG-Sauer, blinked in shock, and then flashed a relaxed smile when she saw the OSP badge on his belt.

"This has to be one of the fastest police responses in the history of the mall," she joked as she set aside the broom and walked over to where Cellars was examining the broken display case. "I wish our own security people would respond so quickly."

"Actually, I was here to do some shopping of my own," Cellars responded as he continued to examine the display case. "Is this what they were after?" He motioned with his hand at the brightly colored sign.

The salesclerk nodded. "Looks like it. The brand new five-hundred-and-twelve-bit game machines, complete with Alien Attack V—The Good Guys Fight Back. How's that for a title?"

"A title?"

"The latest and greatest in video gaming, hot off the presses," the salesclerk explained. "Superfast three-D graphics, infinitely adaptable bad guys, interactive joystick, voice recognition, and a sound system to die for. Or so they tell me." The elderly clerk grinned. "Just got them in yesterday, and we sold out before noon . . . except for the display model, which I kept telling everybody I'm not supposed to sell."

"Which is why a couple of your disappointed customers came back and stole it," Cellars guessed.

"Three, most likely," the salesclerk corrected. "I remember them from yesterday. The third one probably tripped the circuit breakers. He talked like the type who might know how to do something like that without getting himself killed."

Which might explain the loud noise . . . and the scream, Cellars thought. He wondered if he was going to find the smoldering corpse of a young would-be electronics expert crumpled on the floor beneath the mall's main breaker switch.

"Do you want me to give you his description?" the clerk asked, jarring Cellars out of his musing.

"Uh . . . sure, go ahead."

Cellars took out his field notebook and spent a few minutes dutifully recording the clerk's description of the likely third suspect.

"That's about the best I can do," the clerk said after Cellars finished writing. "But perhaps the ones Jimmy brings back will be more helpful."

"You really think he'll catch them?" Cellars asked. "I only got a quick look, but it looked to me like those two had a pretty decent head start."

"Oh, they might outrun Jimmy the first mile or two, if they really put their hearts into it," the woman allowed. "But I don't think sitting in front of a computer all day is the best way to train for a marathon."

"Jimmy the marathoner, huh?"

The clerk nodded proudly. "My son. He placed second in the state finals last year."

"In that case"—Cellars smiled as he put his notebook back into his jacket pocket—"I think your security will be here in plenty of time to take them into custody, but you might give them a call anyway."

The clerk did so, hung up the phone, then stared at Cellars as if she was trying to remember something.

"Oh . . . that's right." She nodded in satisfaction. "You said you came here to do some shopping. Is there anything I can help you find?"

"Actually, I stopped by to see if I can get a replacement for this doll," Cellars said as he placed the doll box on the counter.

"A replacement for an Elmer Fudd doll?" The clerk scrutinized the box. "Was it purchased at this store?"

"Yes, I believe so." Cellars handed her the sales receipt.

"Oh yes, definitely one of ours." She set the receipt aside and reached for the box. "Is there something wrong with it?"

"Well, not exactly. It's just that—"

Before Cellars could react or say something, she opened the lid . . . and recoiled in surprise.

"Oh, dear."

"It had an accident," Cellars finished lamely.

"An accident?" The clerk was still staring into the box with a look of dismay on her face.

"Uh, actually, it was more like a teenage prank."

Cellars had been so focused on the idea of finally making contact with Dawson again that it never occurred to him that someone might wonder why he was carrying around an Elmer Fudd doll with a ten-penny construction nail embedded in its forehead.

So much for planning ahead, he thought glumly.

The clerk shook her head. "Whatever happened to toilet-papering houses and knocking mailboxes off their poles? Oh, well, I guess I shouldn't be so judgmental." She continued to stare at the damaged doll. "And I hate to tell you this, since you've been so helpful, but I really don't think I'd be allowed to give you a replacement—"

"Oh, no, of course not, I certainly realize that," Cellars said quickly. "I just brought this one with me so that I can buy a new one—the same exact doll—for my nephew. His mother is a little upset about . . . the way this one looks now," he added as he gingerly retrieved the doll from the clerk's hands.

"I should imagine so," the clerk said with what looked like a forced smile. "Just a moment, let me see what we have in the back."

———

Ten minutes later, having given up any hope of finding Bobby Dawson in or around this particular mall toy store, Colin Cellars walked out of the store with two Elmer Fudd doll boxes under his arm . . . and almost knocked a slender young woman off her feet. As it was, the two doll boxes and the young woman's purse tumbled to the tile floor.

"I'm sorry," Cellars started to apologize as he instinctively grabbed at her backpack to keep her from falling, then quickly knelt to retrieve his packages and the purse, "I wasn't watching—"

"That's all right, Sergeant," the young woman whispered as she knelt beside him. "I was."

CHAPTER TWENTY-FOUR

DON'T GO ANYWHERE THAT YOU'VE EVER BEEN BEFORE . . . OR where anyone might know you.

Don't use your credit cards.

Don't call anyone.

And, most important of all, don't panic.

Malcolm Byzor's instructions, repeated over and over again until she knew them by rote.

The idea is to disappear completely, without a trace. Pick a large and fairly expensive hotel you've never been to before. Register for three nights with a fake name and home address, preferably from out of state. Give them a cash deposit, however much they want—you'll have plenty—and pay cash for everything else you buy. Go to your room immediately, dial 1-800 and your mother's seven-digit phone number, wait for the beep, punch in the

*three or four digits of your room number, and then hang up. After you've
done that, order room service. Watch a movie. Read a book. Work out in the
exercise room. Whatever you want to do, just don't go outside the hotel. It
may take a while, but the message will get to me, eventually, and someone
will come for you.*

Frightened by the confused scene at the Rogue Valley Mall, Jody
Catlin had run back out into the parking lot, jumped into the new four-
wheel-drive Isuzu Byzor had made available to her, buckled herself in—
ignoring the complaining Manx, who had been jarred awake by her
frenzied efforts—and headed toward the north exit, intending to get
onto I-5 south, and head back to Ashland . . . and her hideaway home
up in the western slopes of the Cascade Mountain Range.

But the southbound traffic on I-5 was already starting to back up as
drivers merged into the right-hand lane to avoid a big chunk of concrete
center divider that had been driven into the southbound fast lane by an
overturned log truck . . . and slowed down to gawk at the dozens of
crumpled and blazing vehicles. Several of the southbound truckers and
drivers quickly pulled off to the side of the highway, grabbed fire extinguishers, and ran toward the fires, thereby adding to the confusion.

Knowing that she was far too shaken and frightened to be of any
help at the accident, Jody Catlin had been moving forward at something less than five miles per hour when, out of the corner of her eye,
she caught sight of the uniformed OSP officer emptying a fire extinguisher at a blue Dodge Minivan.

Having no idea how or why, she knew instantly that the van was
Melissa Washington's.

For a brief moment, her mind froze.

Then, as she instinctively braked and swerved to avoid hitting the
slow-moving car in front of her, Malcolm Byzor's warning words flashed
through her mind.

*If, all of a sudden, things are going crazy all around you, and you don't
know why, get the hell out of there. Don't hesitate, don't look around, don't
call for help, don't go home. Just go.*

So, instead of continuing to head south on I-5, she took the next
off-ramp, ignoring her trembling hands and the still-complaining Manx

as she made two more right-hand turns, then finally pulled into a multi-story parking garage. She found an empty space, grabbed her purse and the cat, got out, shut and locked the car, then walked up a flight of stairs to the third level, where she found the brand-new Toyota 4-Runner with the Tango-Alpha-Golf license plate waiting.

There were twelve sets of car keys in her purse, one set of which was marked "Toyota 4-Runner, TAG." She dropped the keys to the Isuzu in a nearby trash can, used the new set to open the 4-Runner, tossed the cat into the backseat—ignoring her indignant howls—got in, hit the door lock, then set her purse within easy reach on the front passenger seat.

Think of them as disposable Kleenexes, Malcolm Byzor had suggested. Use them once and then throw them away.

His words hadn't made much sense at the time, but they did now.

Thank you, Malcolm. Thank you. Thank you. Thank you.

She wasn't thinking about Melissa Washington now. She'd do that later, once she was locked inside a hotel room, dialing her 800 number and trying not to cry.

There was a shopping bag behind the rear passenger seat that contained a dark green sweatshirt, a thick, sheepskin-lined denim jacket, and a black baseball cap. After looking around to make sure that no one else was in the immediate area, she quickly changed into the sweatshirt and jacket, tied her shoulder-length hair back into a ponytail, and put on the cap. Then she reached over to reaffirm that her purse was still within easy reach.

It contained everything that she was going to need to disappear for a while. Five thousand dollars in hundreds, fifties, and twenties; an Oregon driver's license in the name of Jody Baumgaertel; a canister of pepper spray; a loaded .38-caliber Smith & Wesson revolver; a permit and thirty extra rounds of ammunition for the pistol; a new toothbrush; and a few other toiletry items in a small makeup kit.

She could feel the rage coming on now, starting to overtake and counteract the gut-wrenching sense of fear that had nearly overcome her during the past half hour of her life. Her hands were still trembling, which made it difficult to get the key into the ignition, and tears were starting to run down her face, but she didn't care. All she was thinking about, right now, was the ever-so-remote possibility that the engine might not start.

She turned the key, and the 4-Runner's powerful engine roared into life.

Yes.

Now, all she had to do was drive.

CHAPTER TWENTY-FIVE

THE TASK OF DOCUMENTING THE SEQUENCE OF EVENTS OF WHAT would later prove to be a seventy-two-car and four-truck pileup, with twelve fatalities and forty-nine other drivers and passengers injured seriously enough to require a medivac response and hospitalization, fell to the first Oregon State Patrol trooper at the scene.

Patrol Sergeant Dick Waldrip had been off the side of the freeway about a half mile back from the I-5 off-ramp to the Rogue Valley Mall, issuing an expensive ticket to a speeding and careless lane-changer with California plates and a poorly timed case of "bad attitude," when the accident began. The sounds of screeching tires, crunching sheet-metal impacts, and shattering safety glass were still echoing through the chilled evening air as Waldrip shook the snow off his jacket and hat, pulled himself back into his scout car, and flipped on his lights and sirens.

But the first thing he did—while trying to work his way to the initial impact point through rapidly falling snow, navigating a confused array of stunned survivors pulling each other out of their disabled vehicles and good Samaritans running across the roadway with fire extinguishers in their hands—was to call for help. Every fire truck and paramedic team available within a ten-mile radius . . . and any available state, county, and city patrol units to set flares and divert northbound traffic around the pileup.

"Anybody you can find, but get them here now," he told the OMARR-9 dispatcher as he inched his way forward. Then he saw the woman sprawled back in her seat with blood pouring down the side of her face.

"And get some medivac choppers in the air, right now! Traffic's stopped in both directions, and we've got a bunch of people in serious trouble out here," he added as a few feet away, a white-haired man ran across the road and carefully began to pull the injured driver out of her vehicle. As Waldrip completed his transmission, the man laid the injured driver out on the wet pavement, pulled off his coat, used his pocketknife to cut some material out of the lining, then pressed the material against her bleeding head.

Twenty-four years of experience and training sent Waldrip's left hand down to the release lever to pop his trunk. In the next instant, he threw his driver's side door open, scrambled out of the scout car, and ran around to get his first-aid kit. He was just about to release the securing latches when, about twenty feet away, a blue Dodge Minivan that looked like it had been twisted and folded by a pair of giant hands suddenly burst into flames. The veteran trooper immediately forgot about the first-aid kit, unlatched a pair of fire extinguishers instead, and ran toward the blazing vehicle.

By the time he got there, the Minivan was completely engulfed in flames. Which, in turn, were threatening three other vehicles locked together, less than ten feet away, in a twisted mass of multicolored sheet metal between two dislodged concrete center dividers. Waldrip could smell the distinctive odor of rusted steam boiling up into the sky from three nearby ruptured radiators, along with the far more frightening odor of gasoline vapors.

Waldrip was immediately aware that he was standing right in the middle of a potential fireball. But he ignored that possibility and proceeded to spray the contents of the first extinguisher in through the burst-open sliding door of the Minivan . . . praying, as he did so, that the gas tank wouldn't ignite and send flaming debris in all directions.

The distinctive high-pitched screams of the first arriving fire engines and paramedic units shut off abruptly about fifty yards behind Waldrip's scout car just as his first extinguisher spurted empty. His years of experience working traffic accidents told him that he really ought to back off now, because there was nothing he could do for anyone who might still be in the Minivan, and the van's gas tank was probably going to go at any moment anyway. But two frantically working rescuers were still trying to extract the drivers and passengers of the three crumpled vehicles a few feet away, and the arriving fire trucks were still too far away to be of any immediate help. So, without really thinking about it, Waldrip threw the empty extinguisher aside, grabbed the full one, and sent another billowing stream of white powder under the rear wheels of the crumpled Minivan in a last desperate effort to protect the gas tank from the raging flames. As he did so, two other men—a pair of burly truckers in bib overalls and boots—came running up with their own extinguishers.

The next instant, the blazing van disappeared in a cloud of white powder as the three men directed the contents of their extinguishers directly into the flames from three different directions.

Overwhelmed by the smothering powder, the flames retreated back into the Minivan's engine compartment where they had ignited . . . and then died out under a final suffocating burst from all three extinguishers.

It was only then that the trooper actually looked inside the whitened interior of the folded, crumpled, and blackened Minivan, and saw the two white-powder-covered charred bodies twisted around each other on the floor beneath the dislocated front seat.

Sickened by the all-too-familiar sight, Waldrip tossed the second extinguisher aside and turned back toward his scout car, intent on gathering up his first-aid kit and trying to help someone who was still alive. At that moment, a young woman with intense hazel eyes, short-cropped brown hair, wearing a mud-and-blood-splattered navy business suit, a black leather purse with a wide shoulder strap, torn and muddy stockings, and soft-soled black leather shoes, suddenly appeared in his field of view. As he turned in her direction, she staggered to a stop in front of the white-powder-covered wreckage of the Minivan, looking as if she'd just run a quarter mile in that outfit . . . which, in fact, she had.

She ignored Waldrip completely as she walked around to the back of the van—where she discovered, to her visible dismay, that the rear license plate was long gone—and then moved forward to examine the remaining fragments of the front license plate of the Minivan. Then, before the veteran trooper could say or do anything, she quickly moved over to the exposed side doorway, braced her hands on her knees, and stared inside the charred and powder-coated interior. Finally, she turned to Waldrip with a thoroughly disbelieving look on her face.

"Sergeant, the other occupant of this van—where did he go?" she demanded.

"What other—?" Waldrip started to say, then shook his head and stepped forward, remembering that one of his primary jobs was to preserve the scene. "I'm sorry, ma'am," he said firmly, "but you're going to have to step back out of the way so we can—"

He hesitated when he saw the gold badge and black credentials case dangling from the black leather purse.

"I'm Special Agent Elizabeth Mardeaux, Sergeant, from the DEA," she said, her eyes looking glazed and shell-shocked. "And I'm not stepping back anywhere until I find the third occupant of this vehicle. We were tailing these people, god damn it!"

Waldrip blinked in confusion.

"Listen to me, Agent Mardeaux," he said emphatically, "I don't know anything about any other occupants of that van. If there was anyone else in there, then he must have gotten out and taken off before I arrived . . . but from what I can see, that doesn't seem very likely."

The young woman's entire body seemed to sag for a moment. She looked around at the still-smoking and -steaming carnage that littered the highway as far back as they both could see through the falling snow, muttered a fervent curse, and then seemed to regain at least some measure of her determination.

"Then do me a favor, Sergeant, and get some more ambulances out here, right now," she said in a hoarse voice. "I've got one dead agent back here, and three more who need medical attention right away."

Then, before Waldrip could respond, she turned and disappeared in the direction of the flashing emergency vehicle lights.

As Waldrip was relaying this new information to the dispatcher, it occurred to him that the process of documenting this particular traffic accident was going to be a nightmare at best.

"One more thing," he added. "If we have any CSI officers available, you'd better send them out here, too."

CHAPTER TWENTY-SIX

CELLARS HEARD THE MUTED SOUNDS OF SIRENS IN THE DISTANCE, somewhere outside the mall, but there was no reason to think they might involve him, so he turned his attention back to his lunch companion.

"So, tell me, how is it that you know Bobby?" he asked after the waiter had finished setting the sandwich plates on the table.

She was tall, slender, about twenty-seven or twenty-eight years old, Cellars estimated, with fine, shoulder-length, tightly curled blond hair and gold-brown eyes that looked completely out of place in the middle of an Oregon winter. A striking young woman by any definition—especially in the tight blue jeans and snug flannel shirt—but not necessarily built to Dawson's somewhat more demanding specs, as Yvie Byzor had once put it.

"We have a mutual friend. A Mrs. Eleanor Patterson. I believe you know her?"

"The president of the Alliance of Believers." Cellars tried not to let the dismay show on his face. "Yes, we met a few weeks ago."

"She speaks very highly of you . . . and of Bobby, too, of course."

Cellars had already determined that Ms. Claire-Anne Leduc didn't know where Bobby Dawson was at the moment. Only that he'd promised to be "out on the perimeter, keeping an eye on things," whatever that meant.

Cellars had no idea what that meant either. But the mental image of Bobby Dawson lurking in the shadows somewhere nearby was definitely comforting. Cellars hadn't expected to be in the presence of an attractive young woman who claimed some link to what Dawson described as "the big question marks" . . . and it made him nervous, for one very good reason. If Allesandra had been capable of turning herself into a sensuous and fully functional human female, then what were the more advanced models capable of . . . assuming that they actually existed?

Or, more to the point, what weren't they capable of?

Probably not much, Cellars decided, feeling a familiar numbness in the pit of his stomach.

"I had a very interesting time at one of their meetings, a few months ago," Cellars said, "but I'm not sure how that relates to why Bobby wanted us to get together. He wasn't very specific, but I got the impression that you might have some information that could assist us in one of our investigations."

"Actually," the young woman said hesitantly, "I was hoping you might be able to assist me . . . to locate a friend of mine. A man named Patrick Bergéone."

"Who?"

"Patrick Bergéone, my . . . associate, and close friend," she said quickly. "He's an investigative journalist, and I'm trying to locate him."

"I'm sorry, but I don't believe I know anyone by that name."

"That's strange. He said he left you several messages."

"Probably at the station. I've been on administrative leave for a while, and I guess I've gotten out of the habit of calling in and checking for messages."

"Then perhaps you've heard about Patrick from one of your friends," the young woman suggested. "Bobby Dawson. I gave him a photograph—"

Cellars came immediately alert.

"An out-of-focus, black-and-white photo, of a man leaning against some kind of stone carving?"

"Yes, that's it. Did you see it?"

Cellars nodded slowly as he tried to remember exactly what Dawson had said. "I have it—or, at least, a copy of it—and the negative. Bobby had them delivered to my house this morning. Apparently by the same fellow who left one of these Elmer Fudd dolls for me at the local hospital, presumably so that you'd be able to identify me in the store." Cellars hesitated. "But I still don't understand what this photograph of your friend has to do with the Alliance of Believers . . . or me . . . or the problems that Bobby and I are trying to deal with right now."

"I don't know either," the young woman confessed. "All I know is that Patrick was supposed to meet me at the Alliance headquarters last Monday, a week ago, at noon."

"Did he say why he wanted to meet you there, as opposed to anywhere else?"

"No, he was on assignment in Oregon, and I was supposed to meet him here, in Jasper County, a week ago. He left me a voice-mail message saying that he'd met some fascinating people, and that he might have a lead on a really good story about extraterrestrial visitors killing and kidnapping people in your Northwest . . . and that he'd probably need some help."

"The lead being Bobby?" Cellars guessed.

She nodded. "We were going to meet at the Alliance headquarters, and then, sometime later, Mrs. Patterson was going to connect us with Mr. Dawson . . . and you, too, I believe. Or at least that was the way he explained it."

"But I take it your friend didn't show?"

Her voice caught. "No, he didn't."

"Is that something unusual . . . that he wouldn't show up somewhere when he said he would?"

"Not necessarily. Patrick moves about very freely—he's a very experienced international traveler—and you never know where a story is going to take you or when you're going to trip across a more interesting one, so it's not unusual for him to miss an appointment. But even so, he always remembers to leave a message . . . either on my pager, my cell phone, or at the place we are to meet."

"But this time he didn't?"

"No."

"Have you seen him since?"

She shook her head again, this time in silence.

"What did you do then?"

"I—I waited for him at the Alliance headquarters all afternoon. Then, finally, when I didn't get a message, I decided to see if I could find him with his new locator system."

"Locator system?"

"Yes. Last year, as an appreciation of one of his stories, the French government gave Patrick a set of GPS-based transmitters that can be remotely activated. He uses them to keep track of his camera equipment. Patrick buys very expensive cameras and lenses, you see, and he's always concerned that someone will steal them."

"So he conceals a transmitter in, what, the equipment case? And then activates it remotely if the case is stolen?"

"Yes, exactly. And, of course, if I ever need to find him, I can do the same thing. Just send an activation signal out over the satellites, or with the tracking device, depending on how he has the transmitters programmed, and then find the location of the transmitter signal."

"How accurate is it?"

She shrugged. "Not very. There are reasons why that I don't understand. Something to do with the antenna size, energy, frequency of the signal, penetrations, and reflections. Patrick tried to explain it to me, but I'm not very technical. He also said that the French modified the system they gave him so that he wouldn't get into trouble for possessing it. As I said, I don't understand the details, but I do know that you get a general location, and then you can use a separate receiver system to—how do you say it, triangle on?"

"Triangulate," Cellars corrected.

"Yes, triangulate on the signal. This is the tracking device Patrick gave me." She reached into her purse and took out a remote-control-like device. Cellars examined it briefly and set it on the table. "Only, it turns out that isn't so easy to do either," she went on, "especially if you are in places with high mountains or tall buildings."

"You get dead zones . . . I mean, areas where the signals don't travel well, or they get very confused," Cellars explained hurriedly when he saw the look of alarm in her eyes.

"Yes, I think that's exactly what must have happened. It was so frustrating because I would pick up the signal . . . sometimes weak . . . and other times strong. Then I would lose it completely . . . and then find it again, but from a different direction," she whispered, the strain visible on her face.

"But you finally located it?" Cellars guessed.

"Yes, in a store in Grants Pass that sells used camera equipment." She reached down for the backpack lying beside her chair, zipped it open, and handed Cellars a padded nylon camera case. "The transmitter is in the film pouch. It looks very much like a small light meter. In fact, I believe it functions as one as well."

"The camera case was probably in the window," Cellars replied absentmindedly. "You were only picking up a strong signal when you were within the arc formed by the transmitter and the window frame. Otherwise, you were probably getting a bounced signal . . . especially if there were other solid-wall structures in the immediate area."

"Yes, I think that is right." She paused. "I know this probably sounds foolish—to be concerned about a professional journalist who travels all over the world, just because he hasn't checked in for a few days . . . and because he was working on a story about extraterrestrials and people who have disappeared. And there are many reasons why he might not have been able to leave me a message. But I can assure you that Patrick would not have willingly parted with that camera . . . not even if he needed money very badly."

"How can you be so sure?"

"Because I gave it to him, as a special gift."

Cellars started to say something, thought better of it, and took another tack. "And you're certain this is the same camera?" he asked as he unzipped the main compartment and removed what he immediately recognized as a very expensive, professional-quality camera with a top-of-the-line lens. He whistled appreciatively.

"Yes, I am certain it is the one. I had his initials etched in the base, see?" She turned the camera over and pointed out the fine etching. "It is a good camera, yes?"

"A very good camera," Cellars agreed. "Just about the best you can buy. Which is why I'm even more confused."

"I don't understand."

"First, let me make sure I understand the sequence of events," Cellars said. "After you finally located the transmitter in Grants Pass, confirmed that the case held Patrick's camera, and bought it back, you examined the camera, discovered that there was a partially exposed roll of black-and-white film inside, and had it processed. Which is how you ended up with a blurry picture of Patrick leaning against some kind of stone . . . the first and only exposure on the roll . . . that you subsequently gave to Bobby Dawson."

"Yes, it happened exactly like that," Claire-Anne Leduc said.

"So, explain to me, please, how a professional photojournalist like Patrick manages to take a blurry photograph of himself—just himself—with everything else around him in perfect focus?"

"I—don't understand what you are saying," she said. "Are you sure he took the picture himself . . . that someone else didn't take it?"

"Pretty sure." Cellars nodded thoughtfully. "The photo was taken at night, and you could tell he didn't use a flash. If nothing else, you'd have been able to see the reflections. Which means a fairly long time exposure . . . probably at least thirty or forty seconds. Which, in turn, means the camera was mounted on a tripod. All he would have had to do was set the auto-timer for the desired exposure, then add in a five- or ten-second shutter delay to give himself enough time to get into the picture."

Claire-Anne Leduc looked crestfallen.

"I—I was hoping that something about the picture would tell you who Patrick might have been with." She looked up at Cellars. "Are you absolutely certain that someone else couldn't have taken the picture?"

"I'm absolutely certain that no one could handhold a camera for a thirty- or forty-second time exposure, and end up with the surrounding details that sharp," Cellars replied. "It's just not possible."

"But then why is Patrick blurry in the picture?"

"Either he had to have been moving—which is probably the best explanation, except that the resulting image wouldn't get progressively smaller, like he's disappearing into the wall, as it was in the photo—or he deliberately created a double-exposed negative. I'd bet on the double exposure myself, but that's something we can determine by examining the negative."

"Could you do that?"

"Yes, of course." Cellars glanced down at his watch. "I can't do it right now, though, because I have to go meet someone this evening, but I'll be happy to take it down to our crime lab tomorrow morning and see what they can tell us. Would that be okay?"

"That would be wonderful."

"So how do I find you?"

"Here is my card," she said. "It has my pager and cell phone numbers on it, and I'm staying at the Doubletree Inn in Jasper Springs. And you gave me your cell phone number, so we should be able to find each other, yes?"

"Yes," Cellars agreed, "but the thing is—I'm still a little bit confused."

"About what?"

"About why Dawson would think that the disappearance of your friend might have something to do with our puzzle."

"I don't know . . . he didn't say why." Claire-Anne Leduc stared down at her hands for a long moment. Then, suddenly, her head came up. "But I do remember something else."

"What's that?"

"I remember he got very interested when I showed him the receipt I

got from the pawnshop. Here"—she fumbled around in her purse—
"does this tell you anything?" She handed Cellars the receipt.

The name in the block titled "item received from" caught Cellars's
attention immediately . . . but even then it took him a few moments to
make the connection.

"Lonecoos Sun-Chaser," Cellars whispered. "I'll be damned."

"Does that name mean something to you?"

"I think so." Cellars nodded slowly. "He's a Bancoo."

CHAPTER TWENTY-SEVEN

DR. ERIC MARSTON WAS ONLY VAGUELY AWARE THAT THE INTERIOR of his car was freezing and that his entire body had begun to tremble uncontrollably.

He forced his eyes away from the street to look down at his watch once again, and was horrified to discover that it was already a little after five-thirty in the evening.

My God. Where is she?

He'd been sitting in his car for nearly two hours, across the street from a small trailer-home located at the far end of the temporary base housing less than a mile from the Waycross Research Center. Worse, he was forced to go outside and scrape the rapidly falling snow off the front windshield every few minutes because he was almost out of gas and didn't dare run the battery down. He was waiting with increasing desperation for a young laboratory technician named Valerie Sandersohn to return from wherever she was . . . because it had never occurred to him that she might not be home.

She was always home, watching TV, or knitting, or whatever else the poorly paid technicians did when they weren't on duty.

Where could she possibly be?

He'd been asking himself those questions over and over, numbed by the realization that all of his intricately designed plans could fall apart at the last minute. And all because a single person had decided, for some incomprehensible reason, to alter her routine and drive somewhere before her shift.

Then, in a terrifying flash, it occurred to Marston:

Oh my God, what if she goes straight to work from wherever she's at?

The thought caused Marston's right hand to lunge for the ignition and his right foot to stamp on the accelerator in a mindless panic.

She can't go straight to work! She can't—because she won't be able to get in, and then they'll know . . .

The engine started up, stuttered as Marston pounded his right foot on the accelerator, and then died under a sudden surge of raw gasoline.

Oh God, no!

The starter whined furiously—but to no avail—as he jammed the key forward again and again.

No, no . . . !

Marston started to reach for the door handle, determined to run all the way to the employees' entrance if necessary, because he *had* to stop her . . . *had* to . . . when he saw the small car make the turn onto the narrow street.

For a brief moment, he wasn't sure. But then he saw the bright yellow ribbon dangling from the antenna, and a sense of relief flooded his panicked mind.

It was all he could do to wait in his car until she turned into her narrow, crushed-rock driveway, and came to a stop beside her trailer door. Then he lunged out of his car and almost ran toward her.

"Valerie!"

The young woman whirled around, her eyes widening in panic. The packages she'd been removing from the backseat of her small sedan fell to the driveway as she jammed her right hand into her purse. She was starting to bring the small canister of pepper spray to bear on the dark, oncoming figure, when she suddenly recognized the familiar face.

"Dr. Marston?"

Marston's smooth-soled shoes slipped on the snow- and ice-covered gravel, and he barely caught himself as he staggered to a stop in front of the still visibly unnerved lab technician.

"I thought . . . I thought I missed you," he stammered.

"But why—?"

"I wanted to give you"—he fumbled in his coat pockets—"these." He handed her the pair of tickets, trying to make his hands stop shaking.

Valerie Sandersohn stared at the colorful strips of glossy cardboard in disbelief.

"Tickets to Foo Fighters," she whispered. "For me?"

"I . . . I remembered you told me you liked their music—" Marston said, trying to catch his breath.

"Like them? I love them! They absolutely rock. But, Dr. Marston, I . . . I really can't afford—"

"No, there's no charge," Marston said hurriedly. "One of my, uh, associates bought them for his daughter as a surprise for her birthday, but she came down with the flu, so he gave them to me . . . but I don't really care for their style of music, so I was going to throw them away. But then I remembered you saying last week that this was probably the only performance they'd ever give in southern Oregon, and that you'd probably never get to see them in concert, so I thought . . ."

"Oh my God, that's right, these are for tonight." As the young woman stared down at the tickets, the delight in her eyes suddenly changed to anguish. "I work tonight. I have to be at my station at seven. That's"—she pulled at her coat sleeve to expose her wristwatch—"less than an hour and a half from now."

"Can't you get a replacement . . . someone to cover your shift?" Marston could feel his mind starting to go numb again.

"Sure, usually that's no problem. I mean, Mary and I trade shifts all the time. But she's on vacation this week, and Michelle's already filling in for someone in records." If anything, the look on Valerie Sandersohn's face was even more anguished as she stared up at the research scientist. "Here," she whispered as she held up the tickets, "give them to someone else. I'll never be able to find someone to cover for me this late."

"But . . . but couldn't you just call in sick?" Marston suggested.

The young woman shook her head. "No, I can't do that. I've already been off the last two days with a cold. This would be the third day in a row, which means I'd need to see the doctor to get a written excuse. But it's after office hours now, and even if I could reach him, he'd know right away that I'm not sick anymore. And he'd want to know why I didn't try to call in earlier, and—"

"Listen, Valerie," Marston interrupted the young woman's discourse, "it's okay, I have to work this evening anyway. I'll cover for you."

"You? But . . . Dr. Marston, you're an important research scientist, and I'm just a technician. I can't expect you to—"

"To what, walk around the containment laboratory, monitor a few gauges, adjust a flow valve or two if the automated systems fail to compensate for shifting conditions, which they never do? Things like that?" Marston forced a chuckle. He felt like he was going to throw up. Why was she making this so difficult?

"Well, I guess it really is pretty boring most nights," the young woman conceded. "But, even so, like Dr. Byzor says, it's really important that us techs maintain manual backups for all the containment systems, just in case—"

"Which I'm perfectly capable of doing while I'm waiting for my experiments to cycle," Marston said, offering the young technician what he hoped was a reassuring smile, considering that his lips felt like they were frozen to his teeth.

"Would you really do that . . . for me?"

The young woman glanced down at the treasured tickets again, wondering as she did so if Marston was trying to hit on her in some agonizingly inept manner.

"Yes, of course I would. I'd be happy to."

Marston spoke the words with such sincerity that tears welled up in Valerie Sandersohn's eyes.

"Dr. Marston, I could absolutely hug you."

"No, you'd better not." Marston held up his hands, looking flustered. "You wouldn't want to give me your cold. And besides," he said, looking down at his own wristwatch with sudden alarm, "it really is getting late—"

CHAPTER TWENTY-EIGHT

THERE WAS A FOOT OF SNOW IN THE ROGUE VALLEY MALL PARKING lot, and more still falling as Cellars and Claire-Anne Leduc walked to his vehicle.

"This is your police car?" she asked, staring in confusion at the squat, camouflage-painted Humvee.

"My employer's idea of a sense of humor," Cellars said as he un-locked and opened the driver's side door. "Something along the line of if it's hard to see and armor-plated, then I might not be able to put as many bullet holes in it."

"What?"

"Never mind." Cellars looked around at the falling snow. "Are you sure you don't want a ride to your car?"

"No, thank you. I want to stay here and shop some more. I need to take my mind off of Patrick. You understand?"

"Yes, of course."

"But, here." She handed Cellars the camera bag and the tracking device. "Please take these with you. Perhaps they will help you locate him?" She looked at him with pleading eyes.

"I'll try, as best I can," he assured her as he slipped the tracking device in his jacket pocket and placed the camera bag behind the front seat of the Humvee.

"I . . . I know you will. Thank you." Claire-Anne Leduc hesitated, then stepped forward and gave Cellars a quick kiss on the cheek.

As she started to turn away, they both noticed—for the first time—the glowing and flashing lights in the distance . . . about a quarter mile away.

"Another accident?" Leduc asked. She blinked the snowflakes out of her eyes.

Cellars took in the details of the distant scene immediately. It was on I-5, and the glow of the flare patterns and the sweeping red-and-blue scout-car lights appeared to be spread out over a couple-hundred-yard section of freeway.

"I'm afraid so. Hold on just a second."

Cellars quickly reached in through the driver's side door of the Humvee, turned on his police radio, listened for about thirty seconds to the radio traffic, then keyed his mike when there was a pause in the transmissions.

"Oregon-Nine-Echo-One to OMARR-Nine, I'm ten-ninety-seven at the Rogue Valley Mall. Do you want me to respond to the accident on I-Five?"

The dispatcher came back immediately.

"Nine-Echo-One, that's a negative. Nine-Ida-Seven is coming in early right now. Be advised, we have standing orders from Oregon-Nine-Adam-One not to assign you to routine CSI calls for the next four weeks, if at all possible."

"Ten-four, appreciate the advisory. I'll be available if you need me."

CSI Officer Michael Lee is going to have himself a busy night, Cellars thought as he replaced the mike and stepped back away from the vehicle. It occurred to him to wonder if the financially ambitious young officer had ever managed to get back out to his supposed homicide scene. Probably not, as bad as the weather had been all morning.

"It's a pretty serious one," he said to Leduc. "A van apparently lost control at the northbound off-ramp from the freeway. Easy thing to happen with all this ice and snow. In doing so, they managed to jackknife a loaded log truck that took out three concrete center dividers trying to avoid the collision . . . and apparently set off a series of secondary collisions on the north- and southbound lanes. Sounds like at least five confirmed fatals, a whole bunch of other injuries, forty to fifty disabled vehicles, logs all over the freeway, and traffic stopped completely on the northbound side and down to one lane on the southbound side. Which means we should both take the back roads out."

"Isn't there anything we can do to help?" The young woman looked stricken as she continued to stare through the falling snow in the direction of the flashing lights.

Cellars shook his head.

"There are at least nine or ten emergency vehicles at the scene right now, and, according to the radio traffic, they seem to have things more or less under control. At this point, if we tried to get close enough to help, all we'd be doing is adding to the congestion. And, I can assure you, that's the last thing they need right now."

Claire-Anne Leduc held out her slender hand. "Then I will hear from you sometime tomorrow, about the picture?"

"Yes, sometime tomorrow," Cellars agreed.

"It was good to meet you, Colin Cellars." She smiled solemnly before releasing his hand. "Perhaps, by working together, we can figure out this puzzle."

"Yes," Cellars whispered as he watched her walk slowly through the falling snow to the mall entrance. "I hope so."

CHAPTER TWENTY-NINE

SHE WAS BEAUTIFUL. THERE WAS NO OTHER WORD FOR IT.

Dr. Eric Marston stood on Cascadia Rain-Song's darkened porch and basked in the glow of her brightly shining eyes and wide dimpled smile. Waiting with barely controlled anticipation for her to do the one thing that would send his heart into orbit.

She came forward, consciously molding her body up against his, and kissed him with moist, yielding lips. A kiss that pressed, and lingered, and promised more. Much more.

For a brief moment, the images of those incredibly vivid—and impossibly lifelike—dreams flashed though his mind, and it was all he could do to keep from throwing himself upon her, right there on her front porch. But he was still waiting for her to do something even more arousing.

"Eric," she whispered in that achingly familiar voice, "I'm so happy you're here."

Perfect pitch.

Absolutely perfect.

"Say it again," he pleaded.

"What?" Her lips widened into an impish grin. "That I love you?"

He nodded, unable to speak, as his finely tuned senses savored each melodious note.

"I do," she said as her dark eyes locked on to his. "I really do love you. Isn't that crazy?"

"More than you can possibly know," he rasped, forcing the words through a larynx that felt so constricted he was amazed that he could still breathe. He was trying, once again, to imagine what it would be like to be soothed and caressed by that wondrous voice every day for the rest of his life.

It was a concept almost beyond his ability to imagine.

"You're trembling," she whispered, her eyebrows suddenly furrowing in concern. "Are you all right?"

"I'm fine. It's just that I can hardly wait."

"I can't either," she confessed. "It was all I could think about all day. Can we do it now?"

His eyes widened . . . with lust and hope. "What?"

"Can we do it now . . . go see your work?"

"Oh—"

She saw the flash of disappointment in his eyes and reacted immediately. "I know I'm making this very difficult for you, Eric, and I'm so sorry. I really am," she whispered into his ear as she pressed her body tightly against him. "But I promised my grandmother I would never give myself to anyone until I really knew him . . . knew everything about him . . . and made sure he was absolutely perfect for me."

"But—"

"I know it's an old-fashioned way of thinking," she added as she put the fingers of her right hand against his lips, "but that's the way she raised me. And she was so wonderful, taking care of me after my mother disappeared, that I had to promise I'd wait. But it's been so frustrating, because none of the others have been perfect . . . not even close. And I want to make love to someone I care about . . . so bad that I ache inside . . . but I made a promise, and now that she's dead, too, I can't even ask her to break it—"

"I know, it's okay, really," Marston said quickly, numbed by the terrifying idea that he might have scared her off. "I didn't mean—"

"I know you didn't. You're a wonderful, kind, and patient man," she whispered. "But don't you see, when I met you and found out that you're so special—that everything I know about you is perfect—I knew she was right . . . even if you are a white man. I know the work you do is secret, and I don't want to ever get you into trouble. But if you can just show me where you work . . . let me see for myself that the rest of your life is perfect for me, too, then I'll always know that I did the right thing . . . tonight."

"Tonight?" he whispered in disbelief.

"Yes, tonight. But first, please, take me to see what you do, tell me you love me . . . and then take me home."

Stunned and in shock, Dr. Eric Marston could do nothing more than nod in fevered agreement.

CHAPTER THIRTY

"OMARR-NINE TO OREGON-NINE-IDA-SEVEN, ADVISE YOUR TEN-twenty." A five-second pause, then: "Oregon-Nine-Ida-Seven, do you copy?"

It was the third time the OMARR-9 dispatcher had repeated that message in as many minutes. She stared at her console, watching the signal-strength meters for any sign of movement as she listened intently to the faint hiss coming through her headset earphones. Then, after another twenty seconds, she turned to her supervisor and shook her head.

"How long has it been since he acknowledged the call?" the supervisor asked.

The dispatcher glanced at the log entries on her monitor.

"Twenty-three minutes," she replied.

"Did he give a location?"

The dispatcher shook her head.

"But you're sure he was in his OSP scout car . . . not on his portable?"

"Definitely in his scout car. It was a broken signal, like he was near one of the dead zones, but no relay pause. You know how you can always tell when one of the portable radio signals is being relayed through a scout-car transmitter . . . like there's an echo in the background that's just slightly out of sync."

The supervisor nodded in agreement.

"Anybody else on the board qualified to handle CSI at a major T/C?" he asked after a moment.

"Don't think so. We're really short on CSI officers right now." The dispatcher quickly rechecked her monitor to reconfirm the data she already knew by heart. "Ida-One's on vacation. Ida-Two called in sick this morning. Ida-Three's been handling all of the calls since eleven hundred hours."

"Anybody else available on-call?"

"Nope." The dispatcher continued down the list of CSI officers displayed on her monitor. "Ida-Four and Ida-Five are in court on the Klegghorn homicide, and we held Ida-Six over from the graveyard shift until eleven hundred hours. He's probably fast asleep by now."

"Or out of town, if he's smart," the supervisor commented.

"Which leaves us Ida-Seven and Echo-One."

"You mean Detective-Sergeant Cellars?"

"Right. He checked in a little while ago, said he was available if we needed him to come in."

The supervisor shook his head. "Major Hightower was real specific about Cellars. No routine CSI calls unless it's an absolute emergency. She wouldn't even let me pass on those messages from that foreign reporter, Patrick something-or-another."

"—or we could hold Ida-Three over," the dispatcher suggested. "He should be finishing up his last burg call at any time now." She glanced over at her map locator monitor. "That puts him about ten miles from the accident."

The supervisor hesitated, then nodded in agreement. "Tell him to expedite his response . . . and keep trying to contact Lee. We don't need any more missing officers in this region. Not on my shift anyway."

———

High over the entrance to the Rogue Valley Mall toy store, a muscular man in a pair of tan overalls and a light jacket bearing the familiar dark brown MALL MAINTENANCE CREW shoulder and rear panel patches slowly climbed a segmented, thirty-foot aluminum ladder to the top of a colorful tree-house display.

If the man was concerned—or even aware—that the ladder was bowing ominously under his weight, it wasn't apparent in his steady pace or the calm expression in his eyes.

For most of the mall shoppers desperately intent on scratching as many items as possible off their holiday shopping lists before the crowds got worse, the "accidental" blackout and fire alarm had been little more than an irritating disruption of their focused shopping efforts. But, even so, the towering height of the three-story display, and the fact that the ladder was extended over a wide opening in the second-floor walkway caused several shoppers to pause and gawk.

"Hey, shouldn't he be wearing some kind of safety harness?" someone in the growing crowd asked loudly to no one in particular.

"You bet he should," another shopper commented. "Makes you wonder if his supervisor or the union steward knows what he's doing?"

"Two to one, his supervisor told him to do it, then snuck off to the break room for a cup of coffee so it won't be his fault if something goes wrong," the first man replied knowingly.

The muscular man ignored both and continued climbing until he was finally able to pull himself into the wobbly tree-house structure.

It took him less than thirty seconds to find what he was after.

Then, after carefully securing the items in the front pocket of his overalls, quickly scanning the surrounding walkway, and making sure his .44 Smith & Wesson was tightly secured in its shoulder holster, Bob Dawson reached out, grasped the seemingly fragile ladder, and stepped out onto the rung.

It was going to be a long night.

CHAPTER THIRTY-ONE

IT WASN'T AS IF THEY WERE TRYING TO BE SUBTLE, CELLARS DE-
cided, as he stared across the parking lot at the bright orange sign that
stood out plainly against the off-white concrete. It read:

WAYCROSS
LASER RESEARCH CENTER

"Can I help you?"

The voice that emanated from a pair of small speakers beneath the
kitchen-table-size chunk of armored glass was all bass and no treble. A
deep, dark, and foreboding sound, which turned out to be a perfect
match for a cold, snowy, and deathly quiet Jasper County evening.

Must be the electronics, Cellars decided, thinking that the uniformed guard behind the thick glass looked much too young and energetic to have a voice like that.

"Detective-Sergeant Colin Cellars, Oregon State Patrol. I'm here to pick up a Dr. Malcolm Byzor."

The guard looked momentarily confused as he leaned forward, as far as he could, to examine the short, squat military-like truck that looked much too small, fancy, and "tricked-out" to be an actual military vehicle.

What's the matter, Cellars thought sarcastically, *haven't you ever seen an unmarked police vehicle before?*

"Uh, is there anyone else with you in the vehicle, sir?" The Humvee's smoked glass made it impossible for the guard to see anywhere inside the vehicle except through Cellars's open side window.

"No, just me."

"Do you have some identification with you?"

Cellars reached into his inside coat pocket and came up with his black leather badge and credentials case, which he dropped into the extended metal tray.

The guard slid the tray back into the confines of the solid concrete-and-armored-glass guard shack, picked up the leather case, examined the credentials briefly, then turned to stare at Cellars again. He seemed to hesitate.

"It will be just a moment, sir," the guard said as he reached for the phone.

But it wasn't.

Thirty seconds passed.

Then another thirty.

As Cellars remained vaguely focused on the very solid looking, welded-pipe gate blocking his way into the visitors' parking lot, the guard continued to talk in an animated manner with whoever was at the other end of the connection.

Come on, Malcolm, where are you?

The sound of air brakes behind the Humvee snapped Cellars out of his daydreaming. He was turning his head to look when the sudden movement of a dark, shadowy figure at the far opposite end of the parking lot caught his attention.

Cellars could feel his body starting to react—eyes dilating, respiration rate increasing, blood shifting down to the arms and legs—even as his stunned mind went numb. But before he could react in any other way to the sudden, gut-wrenching sight, another movement out of the corner of his left eye caused Cellars to snap his head back around.

Another one! At the edge of the trees, barely visible against the backdrop of the dark building, but definitely moving toward his vehicle. Cellars's heart rose in his throat.

Oh God, no.

The terrifying memories flooded his mind as his survival instincts screamed for attention.

Get away from here . . . right now!

The heavy welded-pipe gate and the steel post it was bolted to looked much too solid for even the heavy-duty aluminum grill and transmission of the Humvee. So Cellars reached for the gearshift knob, intending to send the heavy vehicle screeching backward in a cloud of burning rubber. But as he did so, he instinctively glanced up at the rearview mirror . . . and saw the bright chrome grill of the delivery van that had come to a stop a few feet behind his rear window.

Trapped.

His first instinct—which he forced himself to ignore—was to reach for his gun.

No, wait, something's not right.

The heavy .40-caliber SIG-Sauer semiautomatic stayed in its shoulder holster, but Cellars couldn't do anything to stop the chilling sensations traveling up his spine and down his arms. Not while the nightmarish memories—of dark, flickering figures suddenly reaching for antique revolvers or metamorphosing into creatures of irresistible beauty and unfathomable terror—still lingered in the confused recesses of his mind. Images that, with every passing day, had finally started to seem more and more fanciful, or, at least, not quite as real.

He could feel his hands start to tremble as he watched them move in.

The traumatized mind reaching out, seeking comfort and solid ground . . . it's a healthy process, Sergeant. You really shouldn't fight it.

The supposedly soothing words of Dr. H. Milhaus Pleausant.

Only Cellars wasn't convinced . . . then or now.

She was real. I know she was real. I held her in my arms. Felt the heat from her body . . . like nothing I'd ever felt before. Felt her . . . felt us . . . merge into some kind of oneness that I can't even begin to describe, much less explain. And then saw her change back . . . into one of them . . . and then change again when she died. Only she didn't die. Or did she?

Allesandra and the shadow creatures. Wondrously erotic—and absolutely terrifying. Memories that would not go away, no matter what he did, or said, or thought. And it had been that way for almost two months now.

Are you sure that's what you saw . . . and felt? the psychiatrist had pressed ever so gently. *Are you absolutely certain that at least some of it wasn't a hallucination . . . or a very bad dream?*

Progressively . . . incrementally . . . and perhaps even rationally . . . the answer was becoming no. The traumatized mind reaching out, seeking comfort and solid ground. Over the weeks and months, that one troubling phrase had become an increasingly easy and acceptable explanation.

Until right now.

As Cellars watched in wide-eyed horror, his right hand now tightly wrapped around the rubberized grip of the shoulder-holstered SIG-Sauer, the number of dark shadowy figures grew to five.

Run or fight, his subconscious was screaming. Either one, but do it now!

But either way, he had to get out of the Humvee.

His left hand was reaching for the door handle when he saw the flare of the match . . . and in the span of that moment, his perception of the scene shifted.

The first two shadowy figures were standing by the far side of the parking lot, seemingly intent on tossing some small boxes into the Dumpster, but in no apparent hurry to finish the job. The second pair had positioned themselves just outside the dimly lit visitors' entrance located right below the faintly glowing Waycross Center sign, as if they'd come outside for a quick smoke but were in no real hurry to light up.

Human, he reassured himself. Definitely human. Have to be. What other possibility is there?

As if he really wanted an answer to that mind-numbing question . . . which he most certainly did not on this particularly cold and gloomy Friday evening.

But it was the fifth very tall, shadowy figure that caused Cellars to experience the sudden perception shift. That individual was standing in the middle of the empty parking lot, drawing in on his lit cigarette and glaring in the direction of the civilianized Humvee. As if seriously displeased by the realization that some visitor was about to mess up the freshly painted bright yellow lines on the newly paved visitors' parking lot.

Cellars could actually feel his pulse and respiration rate begin to recede as his cop instincts kicked in.

Jesus, who are these guys?

It was a blatant display of raw power and arrogance. Five clean-cut, athletic, confident, and undoubtedly armed men, clearly available to respond—at a moment's notice—at six o'clock on a Friday evening to what was presumably a minor, unexpected-visitor incident at a facility that, two months ago, had been a rarely-if-ever-used university computer training center. Five very professional looking men, all uniformly dressed in light slacks and dark parkas, whose collective body language clearly suggested that not one of them would have recognized a sophisticated laser research device if they'd tripped over one in the parking lot.

Unless, of course, it happened to be mounted on an assault rifle, Cellars told himself.

Which, in the context of Detective-Sergeant Colin Cellars's mercifully adjusted view of reality, made them five very dangerous men indeed.

But Cellars was far more intrigued by his first look at the mysterious research facility than in the professional qualifications of the people who were presumably hired to keep it that way.

There had been reports of numerous late-night deliveries by huge flatbeds and vans, and late-night helicopter flights into a hundred-square-mile sector that was clearly designated as a federal no-fly zone on freshly printed flight charts. And unconfirmed rumors that at least one curious and adventuresome local pilot had been warned off with a terri-fying burst of 30mm tracer rounds streaking past his thin Plexiglas windshield, courtesy of a suddenly appearing and completely blacked-out Apache attack helicopter.

But no one at the Jasper County airport would admit to being that chastened pilot. And no local construction crew had ever even set foot on the site, much less seen a set of construction blueprints. And no one on the local planning commission professed to have any idea—or interest—in the status of such niceties as approved building permits and inspection records for a mysterious facility named, for whatever reason, Waycross.

How can you possibly change a university computer center into a state-of-the-art laser research facility in something like six weeks, Malcolm? Even with all of the resources of the federal government at your disposal?

Cellars watched with narrowed eyes as the darkened figures contin-ued to maintain their positions around the dimly illuminated parking lot. Like this was a part of their daily chores, an idea that Cellars consid-ered highly unlikely. He found it difficult to believe that the Waycross Center had many visitors.

Or at least many repeat visitors.

Especially if they're overly sensitive, or afraid of the dark, he thought as he surveyed the surrounding gloom that was cut only by the faint glow of the foot-high orange letters over the distant doorway. *Lousy way to run a visitors' reception area. You'd think a state-of-the-art laser research fa-cility could at least afford to kick in for a few argon lamps.*

Then it occurred to him.

They probably like it this way. Lot easier to put an intruder in the crosshairs of a night sight when he's busy stumbling over things in the dark.

"I'm sorry, sir, but your party still isn't answering his phone. Perhaps, if you came back later—"

The guard left the rest of his suggestion unspoken as he dropped the black leather badge case into the mechanical tray, then extended the thick, stainless-steel box back to within a few inches of Cellars's left elbow.

It was a polite way of saying "The person you want to see, who may or may not work for us, isn't here right now, but don't quote me on that.

And we really don't like police officers—or anyone else, for that matter—nosing around in our brand-new visitors' parking lot anyway, so please go away. Now. Sir."

"Maybe that's because he's on his way down here right now," Cellars suggested as he retrieved his badge case.

If the young guard thought such an event was even remotely possible, it wasn't evident in his shrugged response.

"This is the visitors' entrance to the Waycross Laser Research Center, correct?" Cellars pressed as he slipped the leather case back into his inside jacket pocket.

"Yes, sir, it is."

"And this is the place where all authorized visitors are required to check in, correct?"

"Yes, sir, but—"

"And the correct time is about"—Cellars made a show of looking at his wristwatch—"eighteen-oh-six hours?"

"Yes, sir, it is, but—"

"Then this is definitely where I'm supposed to be." Cellars smiled. "Where would you like for me to park?"

The reflected light from the few high-mounted and widely spaced sodium arc lamps made the guard shack's armored glass appear slightly translucent in the surrounding darkness, and the subtle inflections of the guard's voice were almost completely masked by the hollow-sounding speaker. But even so, Cellars could sense the young guard's growing irritation. He'd been blocking the visitors' gate for a good eight minutes now, and the two drivers in the commercial delivery trucks lined up behind him were probably starting to get very irritated and impatient also.

Which wasn't a problem at all, as far as Detective-Sergeant Colin Cellars was concerned. Nineteen years with the Oregon State Patrol had given Cellars a great deal of experience in dealing with people who were easily irritated and impatient. In fact, the technique really wasn't all that difficult. All you had to do was set yourself in a balanced and protective stance, and then remain as calm, polite, and flexible as possible while firmly probing and pressing your adversary for a useful opening.

It was a technique especially effective against aggressive and assertive individuals who tended to be easily irritated and impatient when crossed.

Especially the suspiciously young, fit, and intelligent ones who looked very much out of place in a security-guard uniform checking people in and out of the visitors' parking lot of a presumably minimum-security university research center at six o'clock on a Friday evening.

Very suspicious indeed, because working a guard shack was the kind of job that retired police officers with creaky bones and a great deal of experience in dealing with persistent individuals took on as a part-time job. Usually because they missed the authority and comradery that came with a sworn law enforcement officer's badge and credentials. You didn't waste highly trained and physically fit young officers on such normally routine and boring work, even at a presumably high-tech facility like this, unless you had a very good reason to do so. Among many other good reasons, the young, fit, and intelligent ones tended to get very impatient and easily irritated by professionally polite and aggressive visitors who knew exactly how to mess with people in charge of things.

Such as cops.

To Cellars's amusement, this young guard—who gave the distinct impression of being accustomed to dealing with people in a much more direct and forceful manner—was visibly red in the face now.

"Sir, I need you to drive forward and turn around—"

The hollow-sounding voice echoed loudly in the cold night air, and then cut off in mid-sentence as the guard hesitated, apparently listening to something being said in his earphone.

In the span of five seconds, the young guard's demeanor changed dramatically as the heavy welded-pipe gate began to rise.

"I'm sorry, sir, would you mind parking over there"—the uniformed figure gestured at a single isolated parking space about thirty feet to the right and past the guard station—"until we can locate your party?"

"Sure, no problem."

Cellars swung the heavy Humvee over to the designated parking slot, shut off the engine, and focused his attention on the surrounding environment.

As expected, he didn't have to wait long.

"Can I help you?"

A cold and very calm voice. It was the tall, darkened figure who'd been standing in the middle of the parking lot and glaring at the Humvee. Up close, the lights from the guard shack revealed a very muscular man in his mid- to late forties with broad shoulders, clean Slavic features, close-cropped gray hair, and dark, penetrating eyes. The beam from his flashlight briefly scanned across Cellars's face, then moved over enough to illuminate—at least to some degree—the squat Humvee's darkened interior.

At least six-eight, and maybe two-thirty, Cellars guessed, noting that the man had to bend over at almost a forty-five-degree angle to see inside the vehicle.

Cellars handed over his credentials case. "My name is Cellars. Detective-Sergeant Colin Cellars from the Oregon State Patrol."

To Cellars's amazement, the man seemed to ignore his answer . . . as if he already knew and didn't care.

The guard in the shack, of course. But if he already told you my name, then why are you so worried about the inside of my vehicle?

"And you're here to see who?"

"Dr. Byzor."

"Who is Dr. Byzor?"

Very nice, Cellars thought approvingly. *Don't admit you even know the name. Force me to divulge more information.*

One of the other shadowy figures had walked around to the passenger side of the Humvee and began sweeping a high-intensity flashlight beam across the front seats, across the front-floor area, and around Cellars's lap.

Looking for a gun. But you both already know I'm a cop, so why are you concerned?

"Dr. Malcolm Byzor. B-Y-Z-O-R," Cellars repeated calmly, keeping his left hand resting on the open driver's side window frame, and his right on the steering wheel. Both well away from the .40-caliber SIG-Sauer semiautomatic pistol hanging within easy reach under his left armpit. "He works here. One of your electronic wizards."

Unlike the uniformed guard, the tall man didn't seem to be inclined to argue the point.

"Is he expecting you?"

Firm, polite, calm, and probably very flexible, Cellars decided, even more alert now that he could detect a definite edge to the man's voice.

Like you're expecting me to do something. What the hell is going on here?

"He gave me the outer gate code and asked me to pick him up at the guard shack by the visitors' entrance." Cellars gestured with his head in the direction of the shack which, he suddenly realized, didn't seem to have an external door. "I assume that's the guard shack he was talking about?"

The man's eyes remained fixed on Cellars's face, as if searching for an answer to a question that he hadn't asked yet.

"We don't have you listed for a visitor's pass this evening," the tall man replied in a cold and humorless voice as he handed the black leather case back to Cellars.

"That's perfectly understandable, because I don't have any business inside the Center this evening," Cellars replied with just the slightest emphasis on the words "this evening." "Like I said, I'm just here—"

But the tall man wasn't listening any longer. He'd already turned to face another darkened figure—a short, heavyset man in his mid-thirties with short, curly black hair and an unruly dark beard—striding across the parking lot toward the squat vehicle.

"To pick me up," Malcolm Byzor finished as he flashed the laminated red-and-gold-striped ID card hanging around his neck at the tall man, walked around to the passenger side of the Humvee, opened the side door, and pulled himself into the cab.

Cellars noticed that the presence of his longtime friend seemed to cause the demeanor of the security officer to shift into something vaguely resembling deference.

Fascinating, he thought, as Byzor pulled himself into the front passenger seat of the Humvee and pull the heavy door shut. *Since when does a hotshot electronics and computer genius with a flair for bureaucratic irreverence rate the respect of a paranoid security goon?*

Cellars was tempted to press the issue, but figured he'd probably get the same old runaround that he and Bobby and Jody had been getting from Malcolm Byzor for the last fifteen years. So instead, he just grumbled: "It's about time you got here."

"Greetings, sorry I'm late . . . and where the hell did you get this thing?" Byzor demanded.

CHAPTER THIRTY-TWO

"WHAT'S THE MATTER, YOU DON'T RECOGNIZE AN OFFICIAL OSP crime scene vehicle when you see one?" Cellars said as he reached down to the floor-mounted shift and smoothly dropped the transmission into drive. Apart from the squat shape and wide chassis, he was beginning to like the Humvee. A lot.

"Apparently not," Byzor admitted. "I guess I thought you police types were into the more customer-friendly stuff." He looked around at the bare interior of the vehicle. "You know, plain old aerodynamically sleek sedans, bubble-gum lights, full pursuit package, friendly white exterior, that sort of thing."

"I think the brass were getting tired of me shooting holes in their aerodynamically sleek pursuit vehicles," Cellars said.

"An understandable concern. But if they were going to hit up the

National Guard on your behalf, why didn't they just ask for an APC instead of an H-Two?"

"A what?"

"H-Two. Civilianized version of the good old military standard Humvee. Six-liter V-eight, four hundred horses, very heavy duty auto tranny and suspension, couple of extra low gears for off-road work, some extra armor plating on the underside, chrome lug wheels, oversize mud tires, high-impact grill and fenders, fancified interior, green diodes on the instrument panel, inclinometer, altimeter, CD changer, the whole package." Byzor nodded approvingly. "Should get about fifteen or sixteen on the highway, and more like eight to ten off-road, depending on how you drive, and probably set the OSP back about forty-five big ones."

"The National Guard buys forty-five-thousand-dollar trucks?" Cellars's eyebrows furrowed in disbelief.

"Only for the generals and the governor." Byzor smiled. "Colonels like the luxury seats and suspension, too; but they tend to get shot at every now and then, so the Kevlar-armor lining's usually a little light for their taste."

"This thing's lined with Kevlar?"

"You bet. In the panels, roof, floor, in between the honeycombing. Which will probably stand up just fine against your SIG," he added, "but if you start shooting anything a little more serious, you might reconsider that APC."

"Which is—?"

"Armored personnel carrier," Byzor translated. "Also known as a Bradley Fighting Vehicle. Nowhere near as luxurious as this thing, and the gas mileage really sucks. But you do get a significant upgrade on the armor plating, not to mention a twenty-five-millimeter cannon, external flare tubes, smoke generator, and a couple of M-Sixties for shooting at shadows. Which, now that I think of it, probably explains why you got the H-Two instead. Much more neighborhood-friendly." Byzor smiled cheerfully.

"You know, it always amazes me that you know all that stuff. Not the sort of thing you'd expect the average computer geek bureaucrat to be current on, even if he does work for the NSA."

"Just goes to show you never wasted much of your life playing computer games," Byzor replied with practiced evasion. He and Cellars had had many such conversations in the past, and Cellars had no real expectation that Byzor would ever admit to what he actually did—now or in his past.

Probably just as well, Cellars thought. *Not sure I really want to know.*

"Hey, listen, not that I'm going to allow myself to be impressed or anything," Cellars went on as he carefully negotiated the dark, narrow, and snow-covered road, "but tell me, just out of pure curiosity, what does it say on that ID badge you're wearing? Minor deity?"

"Deputy project director. Pretty much the same thing, I suppose. Why?"

"I was just wondering what it took to get a character like that to back off." Cellars gestured back in the direction of the now-almost-invisible guard shack.

"You mean Gregor? Why, was he giving you a bad time?"

"Gregor?"

"Arkaminus Gregorias. Special Agent in Charge of our security section. Lithuanian. Parents emigrated from the old country when he was a kid, and then were killed in a car wreck a couple of years later. No other relatives in the US, so he stayed in a New York orphanage until he was fifteen, and then used some very authentic looking—and thus probably very expensive—papers that said he was eighteen to join the Army. Interesting history thereafter, if you're a fan of lethal weaponry, night raid teams, interrogation techniques, and the CIA. We call him Gregor for short . . . among a few other things."

"Nice fellow."

"No, he's not," Byzor corrected as he cocked his head to stare at his longtime friend. "Not even remotely so. Which reminds me, what were you doing back there? Trying to piss him off?"

"We were discussing the fact that I wasn't on his visitor-pass list when you showed up, and he suddenly got polite and almost respectful-like. On the basis of that, am I correct in assuming that a deputy project director in the National Security Agency is significantly higher up the old bureaucratic ladder than a Special Agent in Charge?"

"Only one notch, as the rungs go. As it happens, I'm his direct supervisor, but I wouldn't suggest you go out of your way to remind him of that," Byzor replied. "Gregor tends to be pretty sensitive about perceived slights to his authority."

"You mean like having to say 'yes, sir' to pathologically irreverent bureaucrats such as yourself?"

"An unfortunate flaw in what I can only assume is otherwise a very logical and well-organized life." Byzor smiled briefly.

Cellars remained silent for a few moments as he concentrated on negotiating the narrow, dark road that, amazingly, curved through five miles of old-growth forest to connect the research center to the outside world. As he did so, the truck's headlights briefly illuminated another dark road branching off to the left, then disappearing into the darkness.

"Hey, where does that road go?" he asked.

Byzor hesitated. "That's the access road to the employees' entrance at the back of the building."

Cellars's eyebrows furrowed. "Yeah, but it looks like it loops around through that grove of trees first."

"So?"

"You make your employees drive . . . what is it, an extra two or three miles every day . . . just to get in to work? They must love that."

"Actually, it's not quite as bad as it sounds. We're building a real nice apartment complex out there for the staff. In the meantime, we set up some temporary housing on the other side of those trees for our support and security employees, as well as the younger researchers—about a hundred single- and double-wide trailers, a gas station, laundromat, video store, bakery, rec center, post office, and a pretty well stocked PX. That way they're only a half mile or so from work, and they save a bundle on rent."

"So, what you're saying is, you really don't want your employees mingling with the general public?"

"I guess it probably looks that way," Byzor conceded, "but we really don't restrict anyone to the base perimeter. In fact, most of the managers and senior scientists live off base. On the other hand, security concerns are a lot less complicated if our scientists and techs keep outside social contacts to a minimum. From that perspective, providing a financial incentive for them to stay on base just makes good sense."

"Especially if it puts less stress on Gregor and his goons?"

"Always an important consideration." Byzor smiled. "But, the thing is, everybody's pretty busy at this stage of the project—twelve-hour shifts, lot of overtime assignments—so it works out a lot better if they all live close by. And then, too, it makes them a lot more available for emergency situations."

"Emergencies?"

"Sure, you know, power failures, instrument glitches, security alerts, that sort of thing."

"Ah."

Cellars remained silent for several seconds as he considered some of the things his longtime buddy probably wasn't telling him.

"Speaking of security, what do you have set up at the employees' entrance? Same friendly greeting?"

Byzor smiled. "A similar system, but a little less stringent. We tend to be a lot nicer to our own employees than we are to the general public."

"I would hope so."

"The techs and clerical staff have to check in and out on a pretty strict schedule," Byzor went on, ignoring the comment. "But, as long as the work gets done, and their ID cards and other personal characteristics match the data in the computers, the scientific staff can pretty much come and go as they please. Or at least within their assigned security areas," he amended.

"Gregor must love that."

"No, not really. Given the opportunity, I'm sure he'd love to add vampire gauges to the door locks—programmed to suck blood out of our fingertips for a routine DNA match—and make everyone check in with a security agent at every floor. So far, we've been able to hold him to code locks, thumbprints, keypad codes, retina scans, and random verification checks, but that's mostly because we have relatively few people working at this facility at the moment."

"Code locks, thumbprints, keypad codes, retina scans, and random verification checks? Are you serious?"

"Very."

"So what's next on the Gregor inquisition wish list? Anal probes?"

"Christ, don't even suggest something like that to the bastard." A brief worried frown appeared on Byzor's face. "Listen, I would have had you meet me at the employees' entrance," he added, "but you would have needed a top secret security clearance ID card just to get past the first interior gate . . . and getting you that kind of clearance might have been a problem."

"Really? Why is that? I don't use drugs, commit felonies, or advocate the overthrow of the federal government. Or at least not all of it," he added meaningfully.

"They know you."

"They know me? What the hell's that supposed to mean?"

As he said that, Cellars suddenly remembered the look of recognition on the tall security chief's face.

"Nothing." Malcolm Byzor shook his head in irritation. "Members of our external security review team would like to talk with you and Jody some more—and Bobby, too, of course, if he ever shows up again—but I understand you haven't been all that cooperative."

"Cooperative? With whom? I haven't even talked with anybody from—" Then it occurred to him. "Wait a minute, that damned shrink—?"

"Dr. Herbert Milhaus Pleausant." Byzor nodded.

"That skinny little weasel works for you?"

"He doesn't exactly 'work' for us in a true, bureaucratic sense," Byzor corrected. "We like to think of him as more of a useful resource. And I'll thank you not to talk that way about a man with four degrees, a seven-figure income, and a hundred and eighty IQ."

"You're kidding."

"About what?"

"The seven-figure income."

"No, actually, I'm not."

Cellars shook his head in disgust. "I always wondered where all of my federal tax dollars went. No way we could be buying all that many Kevlar-lined toilet seats."

"Colin—"

"And besides, I'm being polite. You want to know what Bobby said—and did—to him at that first session of mine?"

Byzor shook his head grimly. "I read Pleausant's report, in all its gory detail."

"And?"

"All things considered, I thought you could have done a better job of keeping him under control."

"Control Bobby, all by myself, without a stun gun and a net? Yeah, right." Cellars snorted. "First of all, I didn't even know he was going to show up that night. It was my appointment, and I hadn't seen Bobby since I left him with what remained of Allesandra when I took Jody to the hospital. One minute I'm sitting there in Pleausant's office, talking about my whacko childhood friends, and the next thing we both know, the number one whacko is standing there in the doorway."

"Must have been an unnerving experience."

"I'm pretty sure Pleausant wet his pants—if not then, definitely later—and it sure as hell jarred me," Cellars said. "Especially since it'd only been a couple of days earlier that I was dragging what I thought was Bobby's dead body all over the damned mountain . . . and then worrying that the live version might turn out to be a human-shredding alien in disguise."

"Definitely an unnerving possibility," Byzor agreed.

"Which reminds me," Cellars went on, "just out of curiosity, and seeing as how the Agency apparently has the good doctor on one hell of a retainer, why didn't you guys give him better protection?"

"I believe we were under the impression that we had," Byzor muttered.

"But you hadn't counted on someone like Bobby stopping by for a chat, which must have really tweaked old Gregor's chain a bit." Cellars smiled pleasantly as he kept his eyes on the slush-filled road.

"I think it's safe to say that our security chief wasn't especially pleased to find three of his crack Special Agents trussed up in the back of their vehicles like a bunch of Christmas turkeys," Malcolm said. "And yes, I suppose if Bobby was going to pop up anywhere, a psychiatrist's office would have been about the last place in the world any of us would have thought to look." Malcolm Byzor stared out into the headlight-illuminated darkness for a few moments before turning his attention back to his longtime friend. "But even so, that doesn't excuse his behavior."

"Hey, that was Pleasant's own damn fault," Cellars retorted. "He never should have reached into his desk drawer for that gun. And besides," he added, "a man that smart—and especially a man who makes a living trying to probe under other people's skins—really ought to know better than to let somebody like Bobby get anywhere near him with a deadly instrument."

"According to the report, Bobby indicated—at least at first—that he'd only stopped by for a moment to talk. And besides, I would hardly classify an unsharpened pencil as a deadly instrument."

"Depends on your perspective. Try having a couple of them pressed against your eardrums someday," Cellars suggested.

"Bobby's a hardcase, at best," Byzor conceded. "But what about you?"

"If Pleasant filed an honest report, then you know I managed to get Bobby out of there before anybody got hurt," Cellars replied. "Whereupon our whacko buddy disappeared again . . . and, no, I haven't seen him since, in case you were wondering."

Byzor shook his head. "No, I meant what about your interview?"

"What about it?"

"According to Pleasant, you weren't all that cooperative either."

"Hey, before we were so rudely interrupted, the good doctor and I were getting along just fine . . . up until the point when he tried to convince me I was delusional."

"Oh really? About what?"

"Allesandra, the shadows . . . the whole mess in general."

"Suggesting that you could be making the whole thing up, just to get back at Bobby and Jody?"

"That's right."

"Well, you have to admit—"

Cellars brought the Humvee to a sudden stop in the middle of the road. Then he turned to face his longtime friend.

"I have to admit what?" he asked in a slow, soft, dangerous voice.

Byzor hesitated, then went on. "That your story lacks . . . what would you call it?"

"Supportive evidence?"

"Exactly."

"That's because that bitch, Allesandra, stole all the evidence I collected . . . and hid all the bodies," Cellars said.

"None of which you've managed to recover in—what's it been?—two months now?"

"It's a little difficult to conduct an official investigation when you're on mandated administrative leave, and told to stay away from the station," Cellars muttered. "And besides, that evidence is probably long gone. But I am going to find those bodies. It's just a matter of time."

"But in the meantime," Byzor persisted, "even you have to admit you're starting to sound like Bobby . . . not to mention all those other Alliance of Believers characters. The people, I might add, that you yourself once described as fruitcakes with interesting delusions, but not a shred of evidence to back them up."

"The difference being that I've got witnesses," Cellars retorted. "Jody and Bobby, for two, not to mention a straight-arrow police watch commander with some very interesting wounds, who's supposedly going to be released from the hospital in a few days. And if Pleausant thinks Bobby and I are hardcases, just wait until he spends a couple hours with Talbert." Cellars smiled at the thought.

"Ah," Byzor said uneasily.

"And then there's the matter of seven very interesting little stones that seem to move all by themselves when they get warmed up with one of your blue-green lasers. You remember them, don't you? The stones that Bobby was supposed to have turned over to you after you helped us put the bitch down . . . or was that one of my delusions, too?"

"What, that Bobby really shot her?" A puzzled look flashed across Byzor's face.

"No, that you were on our side."

Byzor sighed.

"Look, Colin," he tried again, "I know this interview business with Pleausant is frustrating, but it's not as sinister as it sounds. All our review team wants to do is talk with you and Bobby. Preferably together."

Cellars's eyebrows came up. "Together? Why is that?"

"Probably because they think you're the only one who might be able to control Bobby without having to resort to lethal threats."

"That's not the way to approach him," Cellars warned. "You know that."

"Look, trust me, they're not trying to put you two away somewhere, or even shut you up. All they want to do is talk. Try to get you to see things from their point of view. After all, Pleausant did manage to convince Jody."

"He scared her half to death, you mean."

"He convinced her that government officials—people like you, for example—who start spreading stories about the homicidal intentions of extraterrestrial visitors, without any evidence at all to support their claim, can easily cause a nationwide panic. And if you focus that kind of attention on us—"

"So that's what you're worried about? That the three of us are going to expose your little—"

Then he stopped as realization suddenly took hold. "Oh Christ, that's what this is all about, isn't it?"

"Colin—"

"The Waycross Laser Research Center. That's where you're keeping the stones, isn't it?"

"I tried to tell you—"

"Isn't it?" Cellars demanded.

Malcolm Byzor stared at his friend for several seconds. "Yes."

"Jesus, Malcolm, you promised us—"

"That we'd move them to a completely secure underground location in Arizona," Byzor said calmly. "And not conduct any direct laser experiments on them until we worked out the containment issue."

"Yeah, so—?"

"We worked it out."

"What do you mean by that?" Cellars's voice had grown soft and dangerous again.

"You know I can't—"

"If you want my help with Bobby," Cellars interrupted, "not to mention my cooperation in general, you'd better start talking . . . right now."

Byzor sighed deeply again, and closed his eyes for a moment.

"Look, Colin, in general terms, when I say we worked it out, I mean we're convinced we know enough about their . . . physical capabilities to keep them contained in the unlikely event that we're ever able to restore one of them to its—what?—previous capacity with one of our lasers."

"Why unlikely?"

"It's an energy-state issue. Some pretty complicated math," Byzor said evasively.

"But you said 'we're convinced' . . . which means you haven't tried any direct experiments yet, right?"

"Look, I'm not supposed to be discussing this, even in general terms, with anyone who—"

"Who what? Doesn't have a top secret security clearance?"

Byzor remained silent.

"And I suppose it goes without saying that my chances of getting a top secret security clearance from the NSA are essentially nil, right?"

"Colin, given what they know about you and Bobby and Jody right now, I'm honestly amazed they allow the three of you to walk around without a full-time set of baby-sitters. Or to walk around at all, for that matter."

Instead of answering, Colin Cellars started the Humvee up again and kept his attention on the dark, winding road while he considered the implications of Byzor's comment.

"What exactly did you mean by, 'allow'?" he finally asked.

"Exactly what you think I meant," Byzor replied evenly. "This is a serious issue, with perfectly legitimate national-security concerns, and these are very serious people, Colin. You need to understand that. And if you're under the impression that Gregor and his playmates were anything other than mildly annoyed by Bobby's little intimidation games with Dr. Pleausant, then you don't even begin to understand the situation. They're letting you three walk around without baby-sitters because it happens to be convenient for them to do so."

"Convenient?"

"Yes, convenient. The fact that you happen to be a state police officer, or Jody happens to be a federal government criminalist—or, for that matter, that I happen to be a NSA deputy project director—means nothing to them. Nothing at all. And don't you ever forget that."

Cellars was silent for a long moment.

"So how do you know all this?" he finally asked in a less threatening voice.

"Because I'm the one who managed to convince them that the baby-sitters weren't necessary," Byzor said.

"Oh."

Then, after another few moments of silent contemplation: "So who is this Gregor guy, anyway? One of your robot creations? Thinks in straight lines? No deviations allowed?"

"That's an interesting premise," Byzor replied. "Tell you the truth, I've always wondered how personnel managed to shake him loose from our sister agency. I'll have to ask someday."

"Think they'll tell you?"

"No."

"Well, whoever he is, you ought to have him designing your roads instead of monitoring your parking lots," Cellars muttered as he slowed to ten miles per hour to negotiate a particularly sharp turn.

"Believe it or not, we had them built like this on purpose," Byzor replied. "Makes it a lot easier to spot—hey, look out!"

Cellars tried to swerve away, but the completely blacked-out vehicle that suddenly appeared in his headlights was already in the middle of the narrow road and coming too fast.

The sounds of crunching and tearing aluminum were punctuated by the sharp tinkling explosion of headlight glass as Cellars fought the wheel to bring the Humvee to a controlled stop at the side of the road.

"Shit!" he yelled in frustration as he realized that the Humvee's left headlight was out.

"You okay?" Byzor queried.

"Yes, I'm fine, but my truck isn't."

Cellars turned his head to stare back at the darkened vehicle . . . now off the road and barely visible in the Humvee's glowing red taillights.

"Is that really a problem? I mean, surely the state of Oregon carries accident insurance on their police vehicles . . . especially on the ones you drive."

"And you'd think they'd put more impact-resistant headlights in trucks designed to accompany major ground assaults," Cellars muttered as he continued to stare at the darkened vehicle, a puzzled frown appearing on his face. "Normally, no, it's not a problem. But I promised Bauer and Talbert I'd be a lot more— Hey, the bastard's trying to rabbit on us!"

"That's okay, let him, I'll—" Byzor started to say, but Cellars was already out the door and running down the road with a flashlight clenched in his hand.

———

Approximately ten minutes later, Cellars returned to the Humvee, got in, and pulled the door closed.

"The H-Two's fine," Byzor said as he watched his buddy silently secure the seat belt. "Outside of a little paint transfer, you can barely see where we hit. And I replaced your headlight," he added. "Spares are under the rear seat. They gave you the standard cheap civilian version, and you've only got one left, so try not to hit too many more vehicles until I can get you supplied with the military version."

"Thank you."

Byzor stared quizzically at Cellars.

"So what's the deal with your rabbiting driver? No felony arrest, suspect spread-eagled across the hood of his car, that sort of thing?"

"I don't want to talk about it."

"Oh really? Why not?"

"Because she was drop-dead gorgeous, and I'm trying very hard not to think about her, if you don't mind."

"Who, the driver?"

"No, the skirt that one of your goddamned eggheads had his mind on instead of the road."

"Ah." A pause. "Do I dare ask what they were doing?"

"Nothing, apparently. Or at least they were both fully dressed when I got to the car. The shithead claimed he just forgot to turn his lights on."

"And given the apparently spectacular physical characteristics of his companion, or the length of her skirt, you were suddenly sympathetic. In spite of the fact that he—or you, depending on how you want to look at it—just damaged yet another brand-new OSP vehicle. Is that what you're trying to tell me?"

"I told you, I'm trying not to think about it," Cellars muttered darkly.

"I'm truly impressed," Byzor said. "I really am. So who is this lucky fellow? Did you at least get his name?"

"Yeah, some guy named Marston."

"Marston? You mean Dr. Eric Marston?"

Cellars thought for a moment, then nodded. "That's right. Why, do you know him?"

"I know him well," Byzor replied. "Which is why I'm suddenly worried about your eyesight. Are you sure this young woman really was attractive . . . or even a female?" he added as an afterthought.

"I didn't say 'attractive.' I said 'drop-dead gorgeous,' " Cellars corrected. "And if she wasn't a one hundred percent, estrogen-soaked female, then I'm giving up on women—and sex—for good."

"Seriously?"

"Oh, yeah." Cellars nodded as he started up the Humvee, turned the headlights back on, then pulled back into the narrow road. "Very, very seriously."

CHAPTER THIRTY-THREE

LESS THAN A QUARTER MILE FROM THE FIRST EMPLOYEE ENTRANCE gate, Dr. Eric Marston pulled his badly crumpled car over to the side of the road and turned off his one functional headlight.

Outside, the winding road and surrounding forest instantly disappeared . . . leaving them alone in a cloud-covered blackness.

For a long moment, they sat there in a deep, dark silence broken only by occasional faint clicks from the rapidly cooling engine, and the even quieter sounds of their hushed breathing.

Then Cascadia Rain-Song turned to him with widened eyes.

"Is something wrong?" she whispered. "The car? Is it okay? I mean, I can hear the tire scraping."

"No, nothing's wrong . . . the car's fine. Just some scrapes and dents, and a broken headlight. No big deal," Marston said.

"Then why are we—?"

"I—I need you to do something for me," Marston blurted.

"I . . . don't understand."

Marston swallowed nervously, took in a deep breath, and removed a small flashlight from his jacket pocket. Then he opened his door, got out of the car, pulled open the left-rear passenger-side door, and stuck his head through the opening.

"Cascadia, please," he whispered, grateful that, in the almost complete darkness, he couldn't see her face, "I need you to get into the backseat with me."

"But, you said—" Her melodious voice caught in her throat.

"No, please, you don't understand," he whispered as he turned on the tiny flashlight. "I need you to lie down right here."

"What are you talking about?" she demanded as she stared down into a hollowed-out space underneath the rear seat that, barely visible in the very faint, filtered reddish light, appeared to be lined with thin pillows and blankets. He could sense her growing anger . . . although it might have been fear as well. He couldn't tell. "Why do I have to lie down in there?"

"Because if you don't, the guards will see you . . . and if they do, they won't let me bring you into the building."

"Why not?"

"Because they don't know you." He couldn't look at her face, knowing the hurt he'd see in her eyes.

"But you know me."

He shrugged helplessly. "It doesn't matter. They don't care."

"Do you really expect me to lie in there with the seat down, all the way to your lab?" She looked stricken. "I—I can't do that. I'll suffocate."

"No, you won't. It's not that far—only three-tenths of a mile. Ten minutes at the most by the time I get us into the underground garage. There's plenty of air, and no engine fumes. I checked myself to make sure," he added. "And I made it as comfortable as I could."

She continued to stare in disbelief at the narrow space that looked, more than anything else, like a shallow coffin.

"But—"

"Please, I really want to show you what I do." Like a shy young boy, desperate to impress a pretty young girl with his collection of monster comic books. "Please."

———

One of the two guards at the employees' entrance stepped out of the concrete blockhouse and focused his flashlight first on Marston's face, and then on the brightly colored badge hanging around his neck.

"Working late again, Dr. Marston?" the guard inquired as he swept the powerful beam across the front and back seats.

"I'm afraid so. We seem to be getting further behind every day," Marston replied, concentrating on keeping his voice calm.

"Would you step outside your car and open your trunk, please?" the guard directed.

"Yes, certainly."

As Marston complied, the guard stepped back out of the way, then placed his right hand on the grip of his holstered semiautomatic pistol.

Marston held his breath as the trunk lid popped open. Everyone at Waycross knew the rules of engagement. The guards were authorized to shoot any intruder on sight, with very few questions asked. And no one had any doubt about the willingness of anyone on Gregor's security teams to do just that.

Marston felt his knees go weak.

Please, don't sneeze . . . or cough . . . or even so much as move, he prayed as the guard swept the bright flashlight beam through the trunk.

"Had a little accident?"

"What?" Marston's head snapped up, and he realized that a second guard had stepped out of the concrete blockhouse and was examining the remains of the Camry's left-front headlight and the surrounding sheet-metal and fender damage. "Oh, yes, it was my fault. The road was slippery and I didn't see—"

"Okay, professor, you're clear." The second guard motioned for Marston to get back into the car, then opened the blocking gate.

———

"Aren't you glad you aren't one?" the first guard said to the second as they watched the Camry disappear around the far side of the building.

"One what?"

"A scientist."

"I don't know, why not?" the second guard asked.

"Because then you wouldn't have anything better to do on a Friday night except go to work, either."

Both men laughed at the absurdity of such a notion.

CHAPTER THIRTY-FOUR

MALCOLM BYZOR HELD THE ELMER FUDD DOLL IN HIS HANDS AND examined it from all sides for a good two minutes. Then, apparently finding nothing of interest—aside from the ten-penny construction nail sticking out of the doll's forehead—he set it aside, picked up the note, and began to read:

"The wascals strike back. One down, at least three—maybe four—to go, but these new ones are seriously hardheaded, partner. Time to watch your ass. PS: Sorry about ruining your doll. The receipt's inside the box. Feel free to trade it in for a new one. You're probably going to need it to solve the puzzle."

Byzor looked up at Colin Cellars.

"And you're sure this came from Bobby?"

"Reasonably sure. The block printing on the note, and the address markings on the package definitely look like his work," Cellars pointed out. "And the receipt took me to a toy store in the Rogue Valley Mall, where a very attractive young woman named Claire-Anne Leduc was waiting for me thanks to Bobby. And when Bobby called this morning, he said he wanted me to meet, and I quote: 'a very interesting new friend of mine.' So it all fits, more or less."

"Claire-Anne being the presumed girlfriend of Patrick Bergéone, a missing French journalist who turns out to be the blurry guy in this photo that Bobby sent?" Byzor gestured at the black-and-white photo lying on the coffee table between their chairs.

"Right."

"And Bobby got the photo from Claire-Anne, who found the film—with one exposed frame—in one of Bergéone's very expensive cameras, which had found its way to a Jasper County pawnshop, thanks to a local Native American Indian named Lonecoos Sun-Chaser?"

"A very dangerous Native American Bancoo Indian named Lonecoos Sun-Chaser, who likes to cut up people with sharp knives when he's on a drinking binge, which seems to happen on a fairly regular basis," Cellars corrected. "And which may also explain why Bergéone is missing, not to mention Bobby's comment about a possible Bancoo connection."

"I can understand Bergéone running afoul of one of the locals," Byzor said, "but what does that have to do with Bobby . . . or the rest of us? And what the hell's a Bancoo connection?"

"I haven't the slightest idea," Cellars confessed. "All I know is Claire-Anne's trying to find Bergéone, who, according to her, had a lead on a really good story about extraterrestrial visitors killing and kidnapping people in the Northwest. Bergéone wanted her to meet him here in Jasper County, but he never showed up. Claire-Anne triangulated on a transmitter hidden in his camera bag to locate the camera at the pawnshop. She finds the film in the camera, has it processed, and then ends up showing the photo to Bobby, whom she says she met through a woman named Eleanor Patterson."

"The president of the Alliance of Believers? The people Bobby conned you into lecturing to . . . on how to collect evidence of extraterrestrial contact?"

"You know her?"

Byzor shrugged. "We've met. Yvie and I attended one of their meetings a few weeks ago."

"Why would you do something like that?"

"Well, aside from a perfectly normal desire to meet a cross section of our new Oregonian neighbors, I thought it might be helpful to try to figure out why a lecture you gave to a bunch of poor, misguided souls on the collection of extraterrestrial evidence set so many interesting things into motion."

"By misguided, you're referring to their naive belief in the existence of extraterrestrial beings—the kind that Bobby and I were busy making love to then killing a few weeks ago—and the likelihood that their government's been spying on them?"

"Exactly."

"So you—which is to say, the government—went out and spied on them."

"In a manner of speaking."

"And what did you find out?"

"Nothing much that we didn't already know."

"Which means, by now, you know pretty much everything about them . . . except, perhaps, the names of their first boyfriend or girlfriend in grade school?"

"Those details usually take a little longer to track down," Byzor agreed.

"But you do care . . . about all those details, I mean?"

"Oh, absolutely." Malcolm Byzor nodded slowly. "Those details often turn out to be the most important part of the entire background check." Byzor stared at Cellars for a long moment before continuing in a softer voice. "Colin, listen to me. This is exactly the kind of situation where you pull out all the stops, because there's too much at stake. We don't dare run these checks in a half-assed manner, because, if we do, we're liable to overlook a crucial piece of the puzzle."

"Funny, that's exactly what Bobby said," Cellars commented.

"What, that the details are critically important?"

"No, that the photo he sent me might be a significant piece of the puzzle."

"Ah."

Malcolm Byzor leaned forward, picked the black-and-white photo in question off the coffee table, and reexamined it for a few moments before tossing it back onto the table.

"Oddly enough, he just might be right," Byzor went on, "but I have to admit I have no idea why. What else did Bobby have to say this morning?"

"He mentioned something about not wanting to be the only one running around with a cottontail pinned to his ass, and then made a few disparaging comments about my 'Alamo mentality.' "

"Referring to some of those tricks, traps, and wires we rigged out at your new cabin, I suppose," Byzor said. "Bobby's never been a real big fan of static defenses. He always said that was where Custer made his big mistake."

"Custer's big mistake was in pissing off a couple thousand Indian warriors with a handful of overconfident troopers," Cellars replied. "Which, when you stop to think about it, might not be a whole lot different from what we're doing."

"I can see how Bobby makes the cottontail, Elmer Fudd, and 'wascal wabbit' connection," Byzor said, ignoring his friend's morose comment. "But, other than that, I have no idea what he's talking about. Do you?"

"Not a clue . . . other than the part that scares the shit out of me every time I think about it."

"You mean the 'hardheaded' part?"

"Uh-huh."

"Yeah, that is a little unsettling," Byzor agreed. "You really think he"—Byzor gestured with his hand down at the Elmer Fudd doll—"nailed one?"

"If more of those creatures are back, and he did get one, don't you think he would have contacted at least one of us by now to let us know?" Cellars countered reasonably. "Kind of a relevant piece of information, no matter how you look at it."

"Yeah, you'd think so." Byzor nodded slowly. "Which is why I tend to think the nail might refer to something a little more cryptic. On the other hand, when was the last time Bobby did anything in a cryptic manner?"

"Not usually his strong suit," Cellars agreed. He stared down at the carpet for a few seconds, then suddenly brought his head up. "Which reminds me, what about you and Yvie?"

"What about us?"

"Are you guys okay . . . I mean safe . . . if these creatures really are out there?"

"Don't worry; we're fine," Byzor said reassuringly. "What's the matter, you starting to get jumpy?"

"I don't know; I guess it's more a lot of little things. Jody, Bobby . . . and even that guy Marston."

"You mean Dr. Eric Marston?" Malcolm Byzor's right eyebrow came up slowly. "What about him?"

"I don't know. I guess it probably has something to do with the way you reacted when I described that girl in the car. Like it was something you hadn't really expected . . . for a guy like Marston to be dating a girl like that."

"I suppose that's true. You don't usually expect a truly dedicated scientist to get lucky like that on a routine basis. But it's not entirely unheard of, either," Byzor added with an amused smile. "Take me and Yvie for example."

"Okay, good point." Cellars hesitated. "But you did check on her, didn't you? I mean, when you went back into your den for a few minutes . . . right after we got here?"

Malcolm Byzor smiled and nodded.

"And?"

"Gregor knows about her. Turns out she's a grad student in physics from the local university. Kind of a shy kid, according to her undergraduate professors, but I guess she really blossomed out when she got to grad school. Decent grades, but nothing spectacular. Barely made it into the grad program. She's registered for a class Marston's been teaching. Started seeing him a few weeks ago, which is what triggered our security team's interest."

"So she didn't just appear out of nowhere like Allesandra?"

"No, she has a very clear history. Gregor's team verified the details, talked to a couple of her professors and an old roommate, checked her birth certificate, then went on to other things. Didn't think she rated a directorate report. A perfectly reasonable decision, given the number of people we're constantly running background checks on."

"If you say so," Cellars replied.

A look of concern appeared in Byzor's eyes. "If it makes you feel better, I'll put a call in to Gregor, have him check her out a little more."

"It would make me feel better," Cellars conceded.

"Okay, stay put. I'll be right back."

Three minutes later, Byzor dropped back into his chair with a sigh. "Okay, all taken care of. Starting tomorrow morning, thanks to your paranoia, the young lady and her family, friends, and neighbors will get the full Gregor treatment."

"Thank you."

"You're most welcome."

For perhaps fifteen or twenty seconds, the two longtime friends allowed themselves to enjoy a period of comfortable silence.

"You know, Colin," Byzor finally said, "I get the impression this Marston deal really has you bugged. You're not starting to flip out on me, are you?"

Like Jody, Cellars thought but didn't say. For a long moment, he just sat back in the comfortable chair and savored the smell of freshly baked bread that filled the Byzor household. He could hear the sizzling sounds of dinner—some kind of exotic stir-fry that Yvie had found in one of her many cookbooks—being prepared in the kitchen.

Nice, he told himself. *I could get used to living like this. I really could.*

"I don't know, sometimes I wonder myself," Cellars replied, staring off into the distance. "Thing is, though, after all the craziness I went through with Allesandra, one look at a beautiful woman and I want to go find a bank vault to hide in."

"And you worry about me playing with my computers instead of Yvie?" Malcolm Byzor shook his head. "You know, I'm beginning to understand why you don't get out much. And speaking of your half-hearted excuse for a sex life"—he glanced down at his wristwatch—"I wonder what's taking Jody so long. She should have been here a half hour ago." He turned in his chair, looking in the direction of the nearby kitchen. "Hey, Yvie—?"

A visibly pregnant Yvie Byzor stuck her head around the corner. "What is it?"

"Did Jody call this afternoon . . . say anything about being late?"

Yvie Byzor hesitated. "No. Last time I talked with her was yesterday evening. She was grumbling about having to make those car switches, and not sure if she was coming anyway because Colin was going to be here. What time is it now?"

Malcolm Byzor glanced up at the living-room wall clock. "Six-fifty-five."

"Well, it looks like we're a threesome tonight." Yvie Byzor sighed as she wiped her hands on her apron. "You two had better wash up, or wipe your hands on your jeans, or whatever it is guys do before they eat. And you'd better hurry up," she added. "Dinner will be on the table in five minutes, and when it comes to food, this kid and I wait for no one."

———

"We have to hurry," Marston whispered. "We've only got five minutes."

They were in the tightly secured, underground parking garage of the Waycross Laser Research Center, walking quickly toward the still-distant bank of elevators. Marston was trying as best he could—without being too obvious about it—to keep his head and shoulders between Cascadia Rain-Song's face and the randomly sweeping array of security cameras.

He had intended to explain the basic elements of his meticulously crafted plan to Cascadia during the last few minutes of the drive in, so she wouldn't have time to ask too many difficult-to-answer questions. But the sudden and unexpected collision with the strange police vehicle—and the subsequent interrogation by the casually dressed OSP officer—had completely unnerved him. As a result, he'd forgotten about the need to instruct Cascadia in the critical sequences of the research center's security systems until he was actually approaching the garage entrance. Which, by then, was much too late, because she couldn't hear anything at all from her concealed position under the rear seat of the Camry.

So he'd been forced to try to explain the entire plan while they were getting out of his car and walking from his assigned parking spot to the bank of elevators about fifty yards away.

He wanted to take his time, because the sequences were extremely important. But he knew he had to get Cascadia checked into the building before 1900 hours. Absolutely had to because the lab technicians at Waycross worked under far tighter scrutiny than did Marston and his fellow research scientists. Valerie Sandersohn was expected to check in for her evening shift no later than 1900 hours sharp. A failure to make that check-in time—by even one or two minutes—would almost certainly attract the attention of the shift supervisor . . . which might not be too bad, because he was new. Or, worse, much worse, the evening shift watch commander who'd been with the facility from the onset and knew every employee by name, face, and family history.

That, Marston knew, would be an absolute disaster. Regardless of anything else, they had to make check-in.

"Your name is Valerie Sandersohn. S-A-N-D-E-R-S-O-H-N. You have to remember that in case you're paged by one of the security officers."

Cascadia's dark eyes widened. "What do I do if that happens?"

"First of all, it's highly unlikely that you'll be paged," Marston said. "Most of the random personnel checks are selected by the central computer, but I reprogrammed it for minimum odds on Valerie tonight. And there'll be at least forty people working the evening shift, so the odds are very much against your being singled out by one of the night supervisors."

"Good," Cascadia said softly.

"But if you do hear your name called, you have to respond immediately . . . and do whatever it is they ask you to," Marston went on.

"That's why it's so important for you remember and respond to your assumed name."

"Valerie Sandersohn," Cascadia repeated.

"Yes, that's right. But it's really not a big deal, even if her name is called, because they'll probably just want her to place her right thumb on one of the wall sensors and then punch her security code into the adjacent keypad . . . just like we're going to do at the elevators up here."

"But what happens if I do put my thumb on the sensor? Won't they know right away that I'm not Valerie?"

They were less than twenty feet away from the elevators now, Marston realized. No time left.

"Don't worry about it. I've got everything covered. For the next few hours, the computer is going to believe that you are Valerie Sandersohn, and your security code is a very simple five-digit sequence. One-two-three-four-five. Repeat, one-two-three-four-five. So all you're going to have to do is put your right thumb on the pressure pad, wait for it to turn from red to green, then punch in your security code, followed by the ENTER key."

"But—"

"It'll be okay," he whispered under his breath. "Just trust me."

CHAPTER THIRTY-FIVE

THE SILENCED CELL PHONE VIBRATED AGAINST COLIN CELLARS'S hip just as he settled back into Malcolm and Yvie Byzor's living-room couch with a steaming mug of freshly poured coffee in his hands.

He was tempted to ignore the demanding phone. Malcolm was in the middle of describing his progress on one of his latest inventions, and it had been a long time since he'd felt this comfortable. But he was back on duty, which meant he was supposed to be available on a twenty-four-hour-a-day basis. And, in any case, the locator beacon on his new crime scene vehicle would have long since told the OMARR-9 dispatcher where and how he could be found.

Gotta get you guys relocated to one of the dead zones around here, so I'll have a sanctuary where they can't find me, Cellars thought to himself. He held up his right hand in apology as he reached for the phone.

"Cellars," he grumbled into the mouthpiece, then listened for almost two minutes before acknowledging: "Okay, let him know I'm on my way. ETA about fifteen."

"Duty calls?" Malcolm Byzor raised a curious eyebrow.

"Afraid so." Cellars reluctantly set the aromatic brew on the coffee table. "Any chance I can get a rain check on the coffee?"

"Better yet, you can take some with you," Yvie Byzor replied from her rocking chair, long accustomed to her husband getting such calls during and after the dinner hour. "Traveling mugs are in the cupboard over the stove. I'd get up and fix it for you, but—"

"You stay right where you are," Cellars said as he levered himself out of the comfortable couch. "You and the kid need your rest."

"Amen to that." Yvie Byzor grinned cheerfully.

Cellars gave her an affectionate good-bye kiss on the cheek, repeated his heartfelt thanks for the home-cooked meal, walked into the kitchen, quickly transferred the hot coffee to a lidded plastic cup, then joined Malcolm Byzor, who was waiting at the front door with a pair of heavy winter coats and Cellars's pistol.

"Everything okay?" Malcolm Byzor queried as they walked through the foot or so of new snow that had fallen since Cellars had parked the cammo-painted Humvee in front of the Byzors' newly rented home. "You had kind of an odd expression on your face when you got that call."

"Probably a reflection of how much I was enjoying myself with you and Yvie," Cellars said evasively as he pulled himself into the Humvee. "There was a pretty serious T/C out by the Rogue Valley Mall earlier this evening, and I guess the requests for service are starting to back up, because they're calling people in to deal with the overload."

Byzor looked around at the falling snow, glanced briefly across the street, then shook his head sadly. "I don't know, Colin. Some days I think we both picked a lousy way to make a living."

Yeah, tell me about it, Cellars thought morosely as he waved good-bye, then slowly backed the Humvee out of the driveway . . . noticing for the first time, as he did so, the pair of dark SUVs with smoked windows parked across the street, each of which contained two darkened figures in the front seats. As he turned the corner, he saw a third and virtually identical SUV parked where it had a clear view of Byzor's backyard, and discovered that he was being slowly followed out of the neighborhood by a fourth.

It occurred to Cellars to wonder, then, if he was relieved—or more worried than ever—to learn that a team of federal government agents was, in fact, keeping a very close watch on the home of Malcolm and Yvie Byzor.

All things considered, it seemed like an ominous sign.

CHAPTER THIRTY-SIX

"AND THAT'S THE CENTRAL CONTAINMENT LABORATORY," MARSTON whispered as he stood next to the young woman who had completely captured his heart and mind.

He could feel the heat of her body through the white lab coat, and it was all he could do to keep from dragging her into his nearby office and taking her right there on his desk.

My God, he thought, *what's the matter with me? What am I turning into? Some kind of primitive animal?*

"This is all so incredible. I had no idea you were involved in something this exciting," Cascadia Rain-Song whispered as she stared through the armored picture window. "Can we go inside?"

Her words, and the perfect pitch of her voice, seemed to flow through his mind like honey. But even the melodious sound of her voice couldn't completely distract Marston from his fears. They were too visceral . . . too overwhelming. It was only the mind-boggling promise of the evening—and days—to come that kept his knees from buckling as he stood at the airlock of the main access chamber.

"Yes, but only in certain instrument bays where Valerie would normally be working," he whispered, knowing all too well that the infrared scanners had been automatically tracking their movements from the time they'd first penetrated the outer security door, and comparing that information against the data in the central memory banks. In the outer work areas, it was a more casual process. But in the central containment laboratory, the personnel flow checks were run on a far more rigorous basis. Any significant deviations from the established protocols and routine work patterns of Valerie Sandersohn would be noted immediately, triggering an emergency alert sequence in the central computers that would override his temporary blocks.

This was the point at which he and Cascadia would have to be extremely careful.

Which seemed ludicrous, Marston thought. Considering all the illegal acts he'd already committed to get Cascadia inside the facility, one more transgression hardly seemed to matter.

But that was dangerous thinking, Marston reminded himself as he paused at the airlock. Assisting an unauthorized individual to enter the central containment laboratory of the Waycross Laser Research Center was the one violation that could earn him a life sentence without the slightest possibility of parole. Assuming, of course, that one of Arkaminus Gregorias's security goons didn't just shoot them both on the spot, which—as Gregor and Dr. Malcolm Byzor constantly reminded the research teams—they were authorized to do.

Marston wondered, briefly, what it would feel like to have bullets tearing through his body, and quickly discovered that the mere thought of such an event placed a tremendous amount of pressure on his bladder. Deeply shaken, Marston forced himself to concentrate on the task at hand.

Her name is not Cascadia Rain-Song. It's Valerie Sandersohn, he told himself as he placed his right thumb on the pressure pad and waited for it to turn green. *Valerie Sandersohn is authorized to enter the central containment laboratory to make monitoring checks of specific instruments. But only if and when a senior scientist like myself is present. Tonight, the computers believe that Cascadia is Valerie Sandersohn, and I am present, so everything will be okay.*

"Well, Valerie," he said in what he hoped was his normal voice as the pressure pad shifted to a bright green, "I think it's about time you and I finished our rounds in the central containment laboratory. Are you ready?"

Cascadia Rain-Song looked up at him and smiled . . . a wide, dazzling smile.

"Yes, I am, Dr. Marston," she replied. And then, in a much softer voice, "I can hardly wait."

CHAPTER THIRTY-SEVEN

OSP PATROL SERGEANT DICK WALDRIP'S EYEBROWS FURROWED AS he watched the strange vehicle drive into the tow yard and park alongside the other three OSP scout cars, the two unmarked units, and the two morgue wagons. But his grizzled face broke into a wide grin when he recognized the man who stepped out of the truck with a CSI kit in one hand.

"Man, I sure am glad to see you here . . . and I like your new wheels. Just what you need for a night like this," Waldrip said as he stepped forward through the drifts of snow and compressed slush and extended a welcoming hand.

"Hi, Dick, good to see you again . . . I think," Detective-Sergeant Colin Cellars added as he shook Waldrip's hand, then shielded his eyes from the glary overhead lights as he looked around in dismay. The entire front half of the Oregon State Patrol tow yard was filled with twisted and blackened vehicles, three of which had been placed in a center position about twenty feet past the front chain-link gate. A tow truck was in the process of dropping a fourth vehicle at the end of the center group. Four blue-overall-and-down-jacket-clad members of the morgue recovery team were standing next to a pair of uniformed OSP officers, watching the placement of the fourth vehicle, and two more men dressed in identical tan Macintoshes stood near the entrance with their hands buried deep in their pockets. "What happened to Lee? I thought he was supposed to be helping you out."

"Beats me." Waldrip shrugged. "The guy never showed up."

"Did he call in?"

"Yeah, he did. According to dispatch, he told them he'd meet me out at the freeway, ETA about twenty minutes." Waldrip glanced down at his wristwatch. "That was a little over two hours ago."

"No other contact?"

"Not a word. Like he dropped off the face of the earth."

Cellars's eyebrows furrowed in concern. "Anybody go check on him?"

"Not that I know of. OMARR-Nine's been trying to raise him every ten minutes or so, and they put an areawide alert out for his scout car. But everybody's pretty busy right now . . . either with following up on the T/C or trying to handle all the backed-up calls. And besides, I guess you probably know this isn't the first time he's been hard to locate."

"You mean his Bigfoot patrols?"

Waldrip nodded. "Pisses me off, because, in every other respect, the kid's a damned good officer. But he's really got a bug in his ear about wanting to be the first person to come up with a photo of a real Sasquatch, and I don't know how to snap him out of it before he gets himself in deep shit."

"Fifty thousand dollars can be a pretty big incentive, especially for a young guy trying to live on a rookie salary," Cellars replied, thinking: *Yeah, but Mike knows better than to risk his career by failing to check in.* He made a mental note to check on Lee once he got clear from helping Waldrip.

"Yeah, that's a fact. But, to tell you the truth, I really don't think it's the money. I think it's just the pure excitement of the chase. I mean, it's not like he's just sitting out there on his butt waiting for something to show. Hell, the guy puts more miles on his scout car every month than anyone else at the station. Thing is, though, I've had to warn him twice about staying in his patrol area. One time, I even caught him prowling around in Area Eight, on the other side of the Cascades."

"Isn't that reservation land?" Cellars asked. He vaguely remembered seeing the color designation for Indian reservations and other restricted areas on the northeast corner of the Region 9 area map.

"Yeah, exactly," Waldrip said. "Can you imagine the kind of shit he'd be in if Hawkins or Talbert found out about that? Anyway, he was probably running around in the mountains before coming on shift, slid off the road in one of the dead zones, and doesn't want to set off his transponder to call for help."

"Which means he'd better have a major felony suspect in custody, or one hell of an interesting photograph, when he finally manages to dig himself out and report in," Cellars commented dryly.

"If not both," Waldrip said in a disgusted voice. "Anyway, sorry they had to yank you away from dinner. I really thought Toby and I could handle it when there were only the three bodies. But then we started checking cars, found two more crispy critters, and decided we need a couple more sets of experienced hands or we'd be out here the whole night working these damned cars . . . not to mention the bodies." The veteran patrol officer shook his head sadly.

"So how many did you end up with?"

Waldrip pulled a field notebook out of his back pocket and flipped through the pages. "Not done yet. But at last count, we were up to eight DOAs, approximately forty-nine medivacs to local hospitals, and a total of fifty-one passenger vehicles, a moving van, two semis, and a log truck. Several of the victims were barely hanging on when they were being medivacked out, so I figure the fatality count is probably a lot higher than that by now. At least half the vehicles are completely totaled, and the log truck did some pretty serious damage to one of the overpass support columns. Last I heard, the state engineers were talking about closing the bridge for a couple of months, and rerouting all traffic through the downtown area to the north and south Medford on-ramps."

"Jesus," Cellars whispered.

Waldrip nodded in agreement. "Worst one I've ever been on. The first twenty or so cars, the log truck, and one of the semis all looked like they went from seventy to zero in about two seconds flat, like a brick wall suddenly popped up in the middle of the freeway. From what I could see, most of them didn't even have time to brake before they hit another car, a truck, a log, or a bridge embankment. After that, the fog and the ice sucked in the rest. You could hear the locked brakes, breaking glass, and metal impacts a couple miles back. Then, once everybody finally got stopped, the quick thinkers started making a dash for an off-ramp, or trying to cross the center divider to get turned around, and ended up smacking into each other or getting stuck in the mud. We ended up arresting seven people for fighting, and I almost had to shoot one guy who was whacking on some poor bastard with a tire iron. And that was after everybody hit the ground when ammo in the trunk of one of the burning vehicles started cooking off and damn near gave me a heart attack."

Cellars shook his head in silent amazement.

"Hell, at one point," Waldrip went on, "we had every northbound off-ramp from Mount Ashland to Medford closed down, and traffic backed up to the California border. The paramedics got so busy making runs with the injured, we decided just to leave the confirmed DOAs in the cars, seal everything as best we could, then truck them to the tow yard and deal with them here. Last I heard, traffic was moving again, but I guess there's still at least another fifteen to twenty cars out there waiting to be towed."

"What's with the two guys over there?" Cellars asked. He gestured in the direction of the two plainclothesmen standing near the tow yard entrance with their hands in their pockets and glum expressions on their faces.

"A couple of local DEA agents, assigned to the Medford office," Waldrip replied. "One of the fatals is theirs. The Plymouth sedan—or

what's left of it—second from the left." He pointed to the center grouping of twisted and burned vehicles.

"DEA?" Cellars exclaimed.

"Interesting thing is," Waldrip went on, "one of their units might
have been involved in the initial collision. A female agent who contacted me at the scene and identified herself as"—Waldrip checked his
notebook again—"Supervisory Special Agent Elizabeth Mardeaux. She
claimed she had two unmarked cars and six agents tailing the subjects in
the blue Dodge Minivan, that first one on the left." Waldrip nodded in
the direction of the center grouping of twisted and burned vehicles
again. "Oh, yeah, and she was real concerned about a third subject that
she thought was in the Minivan before the crash and might have escaped on foot."

"A third subject who survived that crash?" Cellars looked at the
crumpled vehicle in disbelief.

"That's what she said, but I told her I didn't see how that was possible. She got pretty upset during our first conversation, but I managed to
talk with her a second time before she took off in a huff again. Haven't
seen her since. Best I could tell from our preliminary measurements,
and some of the initial witness statements, the Dodge Minivan probably
started the whole furball when it suddenly crossed over three lanes of
traffic, right to left, no signal, no brake lights, nothing."

"You think one of the DEA units tried to run it off the road?"

Waldrip shrugged. "Hard to say, but I wouldn't rule it out as a possibility. Either that, or the subjects might have tried to break away from
the tail the hard way, and misjudged distances. In any case, our local
DEA buddies aren't being all that helpful. They said they'd just been detailed to Mardeaux's special task force team earlier this afternoon, with
orders to stand by if needed . . . which they did, until they got a radio
call to respond here and assist as needed."

"Which is kind of difficult if they don't know who or what
Mardeaux and her team were working," Cellars commented sarcastically.

"That's what they claim," Waldrip said. "Which leaves us kind of
hanging, right now, as far as any DEA involvement's concerned. Before

she took off on me, Agent Mardeaux claimed she wasn't directly involved in the surveillance, and had no idea what had happened. And
none of her surviving agents was in any condition to be interviewed."

"Which leaves us with one thoroughly smashed and burned Minivan,
and no idea how it got that way, other than the mechanics of the impact."

"That's about it. From what I could see, it looked like one of those
big logs came loose from the log truck and caught the Minivan square
in the driver's door. Tore the door loose from the lower hinge, ripped
the driver's seat right off the floor mounts, snapped the safety belt
buckle on the front passenger's seat, and basically folded the van around
like an aluminum taco shell. I tried to make some sense of the interior
after I got the fire out; but, honest to God, I couldn't even figure out
which one of the victims had been driving."

"Great." Cellars closed his eyes momentarily and sighed, then knelt,
opened up his CSI kit, and came up with an electronic camera, flash,
and a pair of heavy-duty rubber gloves. "Well, are you ready to get this
started?"

"Ready as I'll ever be," Waldrip said.

———

They started with the vehicle on the far right in the center group.

While Waldrip played a flashlight beam across the torn metal surfaces to provide a visible focus point, Cellars took a quick series of overall and close-up photographs at right angles to the primary areas of
interest. Then he and Waldrip helped the morgue attendants carefully
transfer the burned corpse of a woman who might have been in her
early forties into a dark, zippered body bag. The remains of the victim's
purse and the contents of the glove compartment went into Ziploc plastic bags for processing at the morgue, while Waldrip made careful notes
of the vehicle make, model, license plate, VIN number, and the obvious
points of impact . . . and Cellars collected paint transfers from those impact points.

Odds were that the insurance companies would sort the whole thing
out and pay off on their respective policies without argument, which

meant none of the transfer evidence would ever be needed in court. But Cellars had learned, long ago, that it never paid to be lazy—or to make too many assumptions—when it came to collecting evidence at a crime scene. It was always the failures to collect that ended up causing the most trouble.

The occupant of the second vehicle, a late-model pickup, was a male in his late sixties, according to the Oregon driver's license in his wallet—which turned out to be one of the very few things in the truck's interior that hadn't been burned to a crisp. The transfer of the corpse into the body bag was made more difficult by the fact that the body was nearly cremated, and no longer intact in any meaningful sense. Less experienced officers would have probably found it necessary to step away at some point in the process to throw up. Waldrip, Cellars, and the four morgue attendants simply muttered to themselves and continued their gruesome task in a careful and methodical manner.

The body of the DEA agent wasn't as badly burned as the second victim, but the problem of transferring him into a body bag was made more difficult by the fact that his duty weapon—an old-fashioned Colt .45 semiautomatic with a seven-round magazine—was wedged under the body in a cocked and hopefully still locked condition . . . and there were a pair of pump shotguns, ammunition, and stun grenades stored in the trunk. Most of the shotgun ammunition and some of the pistol rounds had "cooked off" during the fire, which made the task of cautiously removing the remaining live ammo and stun grenades to a remote portion of the tow yard a number-one priority.

As one of the morgue attendants held the upper portion of the body away from the exposed seat springs and Waldrip kept his flashlight beam steady, Cellars managed to work his left thumb between the hammer and frame of the .45, and then ease the hammer down into a much safer position before pulling the weapon out from under the body. They found the distinctive DEA badge down in the seat springs, under a patch of charred seat stuffing, and placed it in one of the Ziploc bags along with the agent's wallet and the glove compartment contents.

There was a brief discussion with the two DEA agents, who had come forward and wanted to take possession of documents, badge, and armaments. But Cellars took the two agents aside and reminded them that the possible impact of DEA surveillance activities on the initial collision made the entire situation a potential federal/state Internal Affairs matter—which, at this point, could either be handled by the OSP or the FBI. Cellars professed indifference on his part, and offered to call in the FBI with his cell phone right now, if that was their preference. The offer caused the two DEA agents to confer, then quickly agree that the situation—and the related evidence—was probably best handled by the OSP.

"You starting to get diplomatic in your old age?" Waldrip inquired, nodding in the direction of the two Macintosh-clad agents who had quickly retreated to their previous positions next to the front gate.

"Not particularly," Cellars replied as he began taking a series of overall photos of the crumpled and blackened Dodge Minivan. "I just thought it'd be interesting to see if an FBI agent could find a way to tweak a sister agency, while, at the same time, avoid responsibility for investigating a sixty-seven vehicle T/C with eight fatalities and counting."

"Might be a real educational experience at that," Waldrip agreed.

"We'd end up having to do most of the dirty work anyway," Cellars predicted as he methodically worked his way around the blackened Minivan, paying little attention to the routine process of taking right-angled photographs. "But, what the hell, you gotta go for whatever amusements you can find in this kind of work."

"Speaking of which—" Waldrip held up two pairs of thick, soot-covered rubber gloves and a heavy-duty pry bar.

"Yeah, right, back to the never-ending fun part."

Working together with a six-foot length of two-by-four, a hammer, and a pair of pry bars, Waldrip and Cellars and one of the other OSP officers managed to pry and pull the smashed and twisted left-side sliding door of the Minivan back and away to the point that they finally ended up with an open gap in the doorway about thirty inches wide. Leaning in through this gap, Cellars took a quick series of overall flash photos, slipped the electronic camera back into his jacket pocket, then turned to Waldrip, who was busy writing in his field notebook.

"Any IDs on this one?" he asked.

"Nothing so far. Rear license plate's completely gone, and only the first letter's readable on what's left of the front plate."

"What about the VIN?"

"I emptied a couple of fire extinguishers into the interior, so it was kind of hard to see much of anything; but it looked like the primary plate was burned away, and I'm guessing we'll have to cut through the cross-frame to get the driver's side door untangled," Waldrip said. "Also, from what I could see out there on the freeway, any wallets or purses are probably going to be ashes and fragments. So, unless there's something to work with in the glove compartment, or our DEA buddies decide to be a little more forthcoming with the identity of their surveillance targets, I figured we're going to have to go for the numbers in the engine compartment after we get the bodies out."

"Sounds good to me," Cellars said agreeably as he picked up a pair of the rubber gloves and a flashlight. "Let me take a quick look in there—see if I can see anything else—before we start moving things around too much."

After working his hands into the gloves and setting the flashlight beam to a close focus, Cellars pulled himself in through the doorway, carefully placed his feet in the mixed layers of black ash and white extinguisher powder next to the two intertwined and charred corpses, then slowly knelt . . . trying to avoid the sharp edges of torn metal sticking out in all directions around his head, shoulders, and arms.

"Looks like we've got an African-American female, probably the driver, and a Caucasian male, both in the thirty- to forty-year range, but that's just a rough guess," Cellars called out over his shoulder, reflexively noting the closed eyelids and relaxed hands of the two victims. "Based on the morphology, I'd say both of them were probably dead or unconscious before the fire started, but it'll be interesting to see what the medical examiner finds in their lungs."

"Impact like that, you'd have to figure the deaths were pretty much instantaneous," Waldrip agreed as he continued to write in his notebook.

"Clothing's almost entirely burned away on both bodies," Cellars went on in a neutral voice. "No visible signs of gunshots. No firearms, ammunition, radios, drugs, or related paraphernalia that I can see. I'm going to try to move the male a little bit to see if . . . oh shit!"

"What's the matter?" Waldrip leaned forward into the doorway gap with his flashlight.

"Get those two DEA agents over here, right now," Cellars said in a crisp voice as he held a partially scorched OSP badge up in one gloved hand. "Tell them somebody's got some serious explaining to do about that surveillance, right now, or I'm calling in the FBI."

———

Fifteen minutes later, feeling numbed and confused and sick to his stomach, Detective-Sergeant Colin Cellars started up the engine of his civilianized Humvee, then followed the coroner's wagon out through the chain-link gate of the tow yard . . . leaving an equally numbed and disheartened Patrol Sergeant Dick Waldrip and the other two OSP officers to continue their gruesome task.

It was definitely going to be a long night.

CHAPTER THIRTY-EIGHT

THE SECURITY BREACH ALARMS AT THE WAYCROSS LASER RE-
search Center began to sound at precisely 19:16:22 hours PST.

Moments later, the overhead lights in the hallways leading to the
underground containment laboratory started flashing red, and thick steel
doors began to drop down from their ceiling mounts in a pneumatically
smooth cadence.

Jarred awake by the screeching alarms and flashing emergency lights,
on-site security team members lunged up from their bunks and chairs,
grabbed their gear from nearby hooks, hangers, and lockers, and ran for
their posts.

As these men and women entered the hallways, strapping on their
individually marked body armor and chambering live rounds into their
weapons with professional ease, wall- and ceiling-mounted scanners

began to register and tally hits. The primary function of these scanners was to detect the unique—and supposedly impossible to duplicate—mottled code-patches permanently woven into the front, back, and upper sleeve portions of the security and entry teams' uniforms and body armor . . . as well as on the more casual shirts, jackets, and lab coats of the scientific staff. In doing so, the scanners effectively monitored, on a second-by-second basis, the precise location of every individual authorized to be in the Waycross hallways, and work and off-duty areas. Which, in turn, enabled the security teams to locate specific individuals or respond to problems in a timely and efficient manner.

The point being that any attempt to breach one of the research facility's security perimeters—or move through these hallways without the proper identifying patches—wouldn't just be illegal and foolhardy. It would be suicidal.

And, in keeping with that unwritten policy, it was Special Agent in Charge Arkaminus Gregorias's job to see that every member of the Waycross Center staff understood the seriousness—and the almost certain consequences—of violating that protocol. Which was why the sudden, jarring sounds of the security breach alarms caused everyone in the Center to stop what they were doing and run for their emergency response stations with pounding hearts and widened eyes.

If the alarms were for real, and they certainly sounded that way, then somebody—or, God forbid, something—was about to die.

As the heavily armed entry and security team members, scientists, and support staff reached their assigned stations, they immediately confirmed their arrival by pressing their right thumbs against small, wall-mounted, pressure-sensitive surfaces and entering their security codes into adjacently mounted keypads . . . thereby verifying that no one was moving around in the facility with stolen ID patches. As they did so, the muffled sounds of the thick-armored doors locking themselves into place against deeply recessed floor jambs echoed through the ultra-high-security facility.

In effect, the Waycross Laser Research Center was coming alive . . . for the very purpose it had been built almost ten years earlier.

A facility watch commander and two deputies monitored this

awakening, visibly and electronically, from one of the two armored "battle cabs." These hardened control stations hung from the central containment laboratory's ceiling like huge, gray, windowed polyps, well above and on either side of the stainless-steel and armored-glass central containment laboratory, which represented the facility's primary reason for being.

At 19:23:45 hours, the centralized computer security system declared the research center completely locked down and secure. In response, the bright overhead hallway and laboratory lights automatically switched from flashing red to a much-slower-pulsed yellow.

The watch commander paused to make his own visual and electronic checks, looked for and received nodded verifications from his two deputies, then reached for the battle cab's red phone.

At 19:24:20 hours, from inside his isolated and secured command and control office, Security Chief Gregorias acknowledged the watch commander's status report. He quickly communicated with the project director, Bernard Lackman, who was the manager on call for this particular evening, and already en route from his home some fifteen miles away.

Then, having received the necessary authorization, Gregorias directed the Center's entry team commander to breach the outermost of the three security walls that surrounded the central containment laboratory—and the main containment chamber itself—like three progressively larger steel-and-armored-glass eggs.

A hush fell over the entire research center as the black-garbed entry team moved into position.

As specified in the Center's security plan, and approved by the White House, the entry team was made up of six Delta Forces NCOs and a lieutenant team leader who had worked and trained together for the past three years, wore Kevlar-and-titanium-armored space suits, carried their own breathing air, and were armed with assault rifles and semiautomatic pistols loaded with extremely lethal but non-wall-penetrating, liquid-Teflon-tipped ammunition. They were also armed with—and thoroughly trained in the use of—an interesting array of weaponry designed to stun or entangle rather than kill.

Contrary to the Waycross Laser Research Center's widely—albeit internally—discussed policy of shooting first and asking questions later, the primary directive of the Center's entry and security teams was actually far less malicious but far more chilling in nature. It read as follows:

UNLESS ESCAPE IS IMMINENT, ALL POSSIBLE EFFORTS SHALL BE MADE
TO CAPTURE ANY INTRUDERS OR ESCAPEES ALIVE . . . REPEAT, ALIVE . . .
EVEN IF THESE EFFORTS ARE EXPECTED TO RESULT IN THE LOSS OF
ONE OR MORE MEMBERS OF THE RESPONDING ENTRY OR SECURITY
TEAM.

In other words, the entry and security teams should consider themselves expendable.

This was nothing new for the Delta Forces veterans; but, as might be expected, the directive made for some interesting late-night discussions among the lesser-trained and lesser-experienced security team agents and guards, most of whom had been recruited from police and sheriff's academies throughout the US. But not a single one of these young agents or guards had ever resigned or requested a reassignment, which said a great deal about their aggressiveness and self-confidence . . . not to mention the indoctrination capabilities of security chief Arkaminus Gregorias.

Following his own often-practiced protocol, the entry team leader first checked the overhead monitors for any sign of unauthorized movement on the other side of the door, then lifted the plate in front of the small armored-glass view port to make a personal verification that the hallway was empty. Only when he was satisfied did the team leader reach for the external door lock release mechanisms. As he did so, the watch commander and his two deputies placed their hands on joysticks and arrays of locked switches on the left-hand side of their consoles.

From their secure—and virtually impregnable—positions within the battle cab, the watch commander and his deputies could operate a wide array of remotely mounted weaponry, or fill any of the video-monitored hallways in Waycross with clouds of pepper spray or cyanide gas. Or, as a last resort, they could trigger a lethal barrage of thousands of tissue- and Kevlar-armor-shredding steel fléchettes down every one of those same hallways from either direction . . . thereby guaranteeing that no unauthorized individual—be it an entry or security team member, intruder, or potential escapee—would ever pass through the outer perimeter alive.

Working under carefully established protocols that were personally approved by Project Director Lackman, and his deputy, Dr. Malcolm Byzor, these three senior security officers would remain in their self-contained battle cab for a full twelve-hour shift, leaving only when their relief shift was properly checked in and locked down in the second battle cab. As such, their actual primary directive was much more in line with the publicized version:

IT IS IMPERATIVE THAT NO INDIVIDUALS OR CREATURES *EVER* BE ALLOWED, UNDER ANY CIRCUMSTANCES, TO ENTER OR LEAVE THE MAIN CONTAINMENT LABORATORY WITHOUT PROPER AUTHORIZATION. THIS POLICY IS EFFECTIVE IMMEDIATELY, AND SHALL BE ENFORCED BY ANY MEANS NECESSARY, SPECIFICALLY INCLUDING LETHAL FORCE.

And if following that directive meant the sanctioned execution of a brilliant scientist, an entire entry team—or even the entire staff of the Waycross Center, for that matter—then that was the way it would be, because the alternative was simply not acceptable.

In the final analysis, successful containment was the only thing that mattered.

At 19:25:42 hours, the seven members of the entry team entered the first hallway, closing and securing the armored door behind them.

At 19:26:28 hours, the team opened, passed through, and then resecured the second door.

At 19:27:11 hours, and after reflexively rechecking their weapons to verify that the safety catches were in the OFF positions, the seven men breached airlock access to the central containment laboratory.

Immediately thereafter, five of them fanned out into a protective fire wall while the last two resecured the airlock, sealing themselves in.

For almost thirty seconds—while Security Chief Gregorias in his command and control office, and the watch commander team in the battle cab observed the search on their monitors—the only noise coming through the speakers was the slow, rhythmic sounds of seven men breathing in their airtight helmets as they began their methodical search.

Then, in a moment of numbing finality, the distinctively gruff voice of the entry team leader came across the console speakers:

"Jesus H. Christ."

Security Chief Gregorias took one look at the overhead monitor playing back the images captured by the entry team leader's helmet camera, then immediately spoke into his own helmet-mounted microphone.

"Dr. Byzor," he said in a deep, cold voice. "Get him out here, right now."

CHAPTER THIRTY-NINE

ON HIS SECOND ATTEMPT WITH THE SECOND NUMBER, CELLARS LET the phone at the other end ring eight times before he finally snapped his cell phone shut in frustration. Then, after a moment of silent contemplation, he tried another familiar number. This time, he got an answer on the second ring.

"Hello?"

"Hi, Yvie, it's Colin," Cellars whispered into the mouthpiece, not trusting his voice. "Sorry to drag you out of that comfortable chair, but I need to talk with Malcolm."

"No problem. I need to move around every now and then, or this kid's going to drive me crazy with all her kicking. But you just missed Malcolm. He left a few minutes ago."

Cellars glanced down at his wristwatch. It was a little past seven-thirty in the evening.

What the hell's he doing wandering around at this time of night?

"Uh . . . do you know when he's going to be back?"

"Not for a couple of hours, at least," Yvie replied. "Sounds like another one of those damned unannounced security exercises. Told him it was his own damned fault. He's the one who set up the program." She started to say something else, then seemed to hesitate, as if she'd suddenly detected the solemn tone in Cellars's voice. "Is something wrong?"

"No, not really. I'm just trying to get hold of Bobby and Jody, but neither of them are answering their phones."

"Nothing new as far as Bobby's concerned," Yvie Byzor commented.

"I figure he's either lost Malcolm's cell phone, or thrown it away by now," Cellars agreed. "Jody's usually a little better about answering; but I'm guessing she's still ticked off at me from our conversation this morning, and probably screening her calls. Perfectly reasonable thing to do, but I really need to talk with her, and I thought Malcolm might have a way of getting a message to her."

"If it makes you feel any better, it's not just you," Yvie replied. "I've been trying to get hold of her for the last half hour, too. Nothing new there either. She's always hard to track down. Probably out Christmas shopping, or maybe at a movie theater. In fact, come to think of it, the last time I talked with her, she mentioned that she and Melissa Washington have been going out to movies together the past couple of months."

The words of Sergeant Dick Waldrip, describing his encounter with DEA Special Agent in Charge Elizabeth Mardeaux, immediately echoed in the back of Cellars's mind.

Oh yeah, and she was real concerned about a third subject that she thought was in the Minivan before the crash, and might have escaped on foot.

Mardeaux and her surveillance team had almost certainly been following Melissa Washington and Jack Wilson in an attempt to locate Bob Dawson and their missing agents, Cellars figured. But there was a big twelve-screen theater with stadium seating on the other side of I-5 from the Rogue Valley Mall, and the ever-so-remote possibility that Jody Catlin might have been the supposed third missing occupant of the blue Dodge Minivan—going to see a movie with a couple of friends—sent chills down his spine.

"But, in any case, you're right," Yvie Byzor went on. "I know Malcolm always seems to be able to get in touch with both of them when he needs to. Do you want me to leave a message at the Center to have him call you?"

Cellars started to say "Yes, please," then hesitated.

Accidents happen all the time, he reminded himself for perhaps the tenth time that evening. A simple blown tire, or a driver swerves to avoid something in the road . . . and all of a sudden you've got eight dead bodies, forty-nine medivacs, and a tow yard full of junk cars. No conspiracy, no suspicious links to moving stones or shape-shifting extraterrestrials.

Just an accident.

But the trouble was, the "just an accident" theory didn't even begin to explain a DEA surveillance on a pair of state and federal criminal-ists . . . or the apparent disappearance of Bobby, Jody, and CSI officer Michael Lee on the very same evening . . . much less the fact that the federal government—in the form of the National Security Agency and his trusted friend, Malcolm Byzor—was definitely up to something with those damned stones.

The questions were "what?" . . . and "why?"

"No, that's all right," Cellars finally replied. "He's probably got a lot of other things to deal with right now. Just have him call me whenever he gets in. Doesn't matter what time, I'll be up all night anyway." Cellars hesitated again. "But, in the meantime, if Jody or Bobby happen to call you—"

"I'll make sure they call you back, on your cell phone, right away, no matter what," Yvie promised.

"Yvie, you're an absolute doll," Cellars said. "Malcolm doesn't de-serve you."

"I remind him of that all the time. Especially when he leaves me here alone with all the dirty dishes and a kid that's doing her damnedest to kick her way out long before she's due."

"Sounds like you've got yourself a little female version of Malcolm in the making," Cellars teased, grateful for even a couple minutes of distraction from the two bodies lying on a pair of stainless-steel autopsy tables about ten feet from the lab stool he was sitting on.

"Oh no, you don't," Yvie warned. "Don't you even suggest something like that—"

Cellars listened to Yvie's mildly profane rant on what was, apparently, an unthinkable idea from her point of view, said "bye" when she paused to take a breath, quickly snapped the cell phone shut, then looked up as the double door to the main autopsy room burst open.

"Sergeant Cellars, I presume?" a familiar voice growled.

"Hello, Doctor," Colin Cellars replied. "Good to see you again . . . I guess."

Dr. Elliott Sutta glanced briefly at the two body bags waiting in the middle of the large green-tiled room, then immediately turned his attention back to Cellars. The expression on his craggy face might have been described as glowering.

"I don't suppose I even have to ask who requested an immediate autopsy on these two victims . . . as opposed to waiting until the morning when all of us might be a little more awake and in a much better frame of mind?"

"I'm the one who made the request," Cellars acknowledged.

"Any particular reason why?"

There was a very distinct edge to Sutta's voice now. An edge that, under normal circumstances, would have caused Cellars to immediately respond in a polite—or at least reasonably respectful—manner. The fact that he didn't even make the attempt had little or nothing to do with his regard for the veteran medical examiner. Cellars was still lost in his thoughts, trying to make sense out of what was becoming a huge amount of conflicting information . . . while, at the same time, trying to understand how or why two people very directly related to the alien stones had suddenly ended up in body bags. On a night when Malcolm Byzor was responding to some kind of surprise security exercise in a facility supposedly devoted to figuring out how to safely reactivate these stones. And on the same night that CSI officer Michael Lee, Jody Catlin, and Bobby Dawson were suddenly no longer answering their radio or phone calls.

Too many unexplained links to shrug off as mere coincidence. And that was a problem, because Cellars didn't like the conclusions that kept popping up in the back of his mind. Didn't like them at all.

The silence hung heavy in the cold, glistening room until Cellars finally forced himself to set aside his morose thoughts and concentrate on Sutta's question.

"I requested an immediate autopsy," he replied, "because I have reason to believe that one of the victims in those bags is probably a federal wildlife crime lab scientist by the name of Melissa Washington, and the other is almost certainly an OSP criminalist named Jack Wilson."

"Washington . . . and Wilson?" To Cellars's amazement, the pathologist actually looked shocked. "Are you . . . I mean, what makes you think that?"

Cellars stood up, reached into his jacket pocket, pulled out a plastic bag, then walked slowly across the green-tiled floor. He handed the bag to Sutta.

"That's Jack Wilson's OSP badge. I found it under one of the bodies. And the car these two bodies were removed from turns out to be registered to a Melissa Washington, who has a home address in Ashland, Oregon."

Dr. Elliott Sutta started to say something, then apparently thought better of it. He just stood there for several seconds, staring at the scorched OSP star badge, before he finally spoke.

"What happened?"

To Colin Cellars's amazement, the supervising pathologist—who, Cellars guessed, had probably conducted several thousand autopsies over the span of his career as a medical examiner—was acting as if he was hesitant even to approach the waist-high tables.

"In theory, it was a simple traffic accident," Cellars replied, staring down at the glistening tile floor. "According to witnesses, a blue Dodge Minivan—the vehicle registered to Melissa Washington—suddenly crossed three lanes of traffic on I-Five, from left to right, without warning, and at an extremely high rate of speed. That, in turn, resulted in a series of crashes that ultimately involved at least eight fatalities, forty-nine medivacs, and sixty-seven totaled vehicles." Cellars looked up at Sutta. "At best, you and your staff are going to have a busy day tomorrow, Doctor."

"I'm sorry, I didn't mean—" Sutta started to say.

"No, I realize you didn't mean it that way, Doctor," Cellars interrupted, "and, believe me, I wouldn't have called you in on this tonight if it hadn't been for the fact that Jack and Melissa were apparently the subjects of a moving surveillance by a special task force from the DEA."

"What?" Sutta exclaimed, his bushy eyebrows furrowing in confusion.

"A highly unlikely situation at best . . . which is further complicated by the fact that both Jack and Melissa were deeply involved in the analysis of evidence from a very confused case that we call the Dawson Incident," Cellars added. "And may have been en route to meet with another individual, who was also involved in that case, when they suddenly . . . died."

"Dawson?" Sutta blinked, a flicker of recognition appearing in his dark eyes.

"That's right. Robert Dawson, also known as Bobby. As you may recall, that was the name on the toe tag of the body I delivered to this facility and placed in drawer twenty-eight, a couple of months ago. Or, at least, the name on the body I thought I put in drawer twenty-eight . . . in spite of the fact that, the next day, all of your facility records indicated otherwise in a very convincing manner . . . and in spite of the equally interesting fact that Bobby Dawson is still very much alive. Or, at least, he was as of this morning, when I talked with him," Cellars corrected.

"I . . . don't think I understand any of this," Sutta said.

"I don't either, Doctor. And I wish I did. If nothing else, it would probably make it a lot easier for me to sleep at night. Which is one of the reasons why I need you to verify the identity of these victims . . . and tell me how they died."

Sutta continued to stare at the dark green body bags for almost thirty seconds.

"I . . . may have a disqualifying conflict of interest in this case," he finally said. "Melissa Washington and Jack Wilson are—or perhaps were—good friends."

Cellars met Sutta's gaze. "I have precisely the same problem, Doctor. But, the way I see it, I don't have much of a choice about being here. And I really hope, when you think about it, that you'll feel the same way."

"Why is that?" Sutta asked in a much softer voice as he continued to stare morosely at the dark green bags. The odor of burned flesh had already begun to seep through the supposedly airtight seals, something that Cellars was trying very hard to ignore.

"First of all, I don't think the people in these two body bags died because of an accident. I think they were targeted by . . . individuals who lost some things and want them back . . . and don't seem to care what they have to do, or even who they have to kill, to do so." The words, even as he spoke them, wrenched at Cellars's uneasy sense of reality.

What's the matter with me? Whoever they are—whatever they are— they're all dead. They have to be. And there's no other aliens or shape changers coming to retrieve the stones. That was all bullshit. Allesandra was just trying to scare me. Trying to scare all of us.

And she did a hell of a good job of it, too, he thought ruefully.

"So what does this have to do with a special task force from the DEA, and what you described as a moving surveillance on two people who I personally know to be absolutely honest and forthright forensic scientists . . . and who were about as likely to have been involved in illicit drug dealing as you or I?" Sutta demanded, finally switching his gaze back to Cellars.

"I don't know, Doctor. Fact is, I'm not sure of anything anymore, except for one thing: I think I can trust you. Or at least I hope I can. Which is why I'm here . . . hoping you can give me some idea as to what's going on, give me some kind of lead on whoever these assholes are who are doing this, before any more of my friends and associates end up on one of your tables."

Dr. Elliott Sutta looked thoughtful for a few moments. Then he walked over to the sink, put a heavy rubber apron on over his white lab coat, reached into a box for a fresh set of plastic gloves, and walked back over to the nearest autopsy table bearing a dark green body bag. He placed his gloved hands on the bag, then looked up at Cellars.

"Are you sure you're ready for this, Sergeant?" he asked in a soft, professional voice.

"No, I'm not sure at all," Cellars replied as he stepped away from the sink. He opened up an adjoining stainless-steel clothes closet, pulled off his field jacket, and removed his electronic camera from one of the pockets. He hung the jacket and his shoulder-holstered SIG-Sauer on a pair of hooks on the left side of the closet, unclipped his cell phone from his belt and reclipped it to one of the shoulder holster straps, then reached for one of the clean blue lab coats hanging from hooks on the opposite side of the closet. There was an additional supply of clean blue lab coats in folded stacks on the closet floor.

"But I'm not leaving either," he added as he shut and secured the closet door, then tied the long strings of the wraparound lab coat behind his back. "Not until I find out what's going on. And if that means I start heaving my guts out when you make that first Y-cut, then you're just going to have to ignore me and keep on cutting."

"The sink to your right is all yours, and you wouldn't be the first case-hardened crime scene investigator to make use of it," Sutta replied, his craggy face settling into an expression of calm and professional indifference as he reached for the zipper. "Are you ready?"

"Ready as I'm ever going to be."

"Then let's get this over with," he said as he slowly drew the zipper down to the bottom of the bag.

CHAPTER FORTY

THE PHONE RANG ONCE, TWICE . . . AND THEN A THIRD TIME BE-fore Jody Catlin finally picked it up.

"Hello?" she whispered.

"Hi, how are you doing?"

"Malcolm?" The relief in her voice was tinged with a sense of un-certainty. She'd been sitting in her locked hotel room for almost three hours, alternately scratching or ignoring the Manx, the Smith & Wesson pistol at her side, afraid to go out . . . or even to order room ser-vice. Thinking about Melissa Washington and the burning blue Dodge Minivan . . . and all those other terrible images she'd been trying to purge from her memories for so long now.

And what she would do if the person who called turned out not to be Malcolm, after all.

"You remember how you're supposed to verify who you're talking to?"

"Yes, I'm supposed to come up with a question about something out of our past," Jody answered, her voice tense. "Something you probably haven't thought about for a long time, and something that requires you to think about your emotions . . . about how you felt."

"Well?"

"This is back in high school. Our sophomore year. I set you up on a blind date with one of my girlfriends, but you chickened out and never showed."

"I was scared. She was too wild of a woman for me when I was sixteen," Byzor replied. "Probably still is, for that matter. You knew that, of course. But, eight years later, when I had a much better perspective on the whole situation, I tracked her down and talked her into getting married . . . and finally managed to get her pregnant, which ought to count for something."

"Yes, you did . . . and it does," Jody replied, almost sagging with relief.

"Okay, so who led us across on that final pitch of the Windshear?"

"What?"

"We're not finished with the verification process," Byzor said.

"But you—" Catlin started to say, then stopped. "Oh."

"Exactly," Byzor said. "It's very important for both of us to be absolutely sure . . . especially right now."

"Why now?"

"Things are happening."

"What things?"

"When we made the final assault on Gravestone Peak," Byzor said, ignoring her question, "after deciding at the last minute to take that goddamned Windshear route—mostly because we were young and stupid, and nobody we knew had ever taken that route before, but also because the winds started out so mild that day that we thought we might have an easy shot at it—which one of us took the lead to the summit?"

"It was a confusing situation," she whispered. "Not to mention absolutely terrifying at times."

"Yes, it was," Byzor agreed.

"Technically, you were the best climber, the one who could always figure out the best routes," she went on, continuing to whisper softly into the phone, "so you were the logical one to lead and set the pitons. You put Bobby in an anchoring position, because you knew he was the only one who could hold all three of us on the wall if you fell. You got about halfway there when the winds started up, and then you got trapped when that little ledge you were working your way across suddenly crumbled. And then you discovered your rope was almost sliced through, where it had got wedged into that deep crack, so you had to cut yourself loose . . . which left you stranded and exposed on that outcropping while the winds got so bad that all you could do was hammer in a couple of pitons, tie in, and hunker down. Colin tried to rappel his way down to you with another rope . . . but he only got about twenty feet when the wind suddenly shifted and ripped him right off the rock. I screamed, because he fell so fast, and so far . . . but Bobby caught him, and held him, and pulled him back up. And then Colin tried a second time, and almost got to you, but he extended out too far at the last second, and the wind ripped him loose again . . . only this time he bounced off another outcropping before Bobby could get him stopped . . . and that's when he got the cracked ribs and concussion and broke his nose and hand . . . only we didn't know that until he came to a few minutes later. I thought he was dead."

"We all did," Byzor said. "Go on."

"Do I have to?"

"Yes, you do."

"You started trying to climb your way back up, but that whole section of the face turned out to be rotten, and every place you tried came apart. And Bobby couldn't move either because he had to hold Colin, and be in position to pull you up. So I tried to get to you with the rope, but I couldn't even make those first few feet, because the wind was so strong down where you were. So you . . ."

"Yes?" Malcolm pressed.

"You saw another route, almost straight up and then across to an old piton that someone had set from a previous attempt. It looked so damned scary from where I was, but it was protected from the wind, and you told me I could make it if I stayed in close to the rock . . . because I was a lot smaller and lighter, and the handholds were there if I took it slow. But there was a section where I'd have to untie myself from Bobby's rope, and work off my own safety line, because Bobby couldn't shift his position. And that's when Bobby and Colin starting yelling at you . . . and me . . . because they were afraid I'd fall and my anchor wouldn't hold in all that shit-for-granite, and they wouldn't be able to do anything to save me."

"But you didn't."

"No. I was gut-scared, but you talked me though it . . . showed me where to hammer in my anchor in a better spot, then directed me to each foothold and handhold . . . inch by inch . . . convinced me I could do it. And you made them stop yelling because you said it was distracting me. I finally reached that damned piton . . . clipped on . . . dropped the rope down to you . . . and then started crying when you pulled yourself back up to where I was and helped Bobby with Colin. That was when you kissed me, told me I was a wuss, and made me hang the rest of the pitons, all the way across the face, so I was the first one on the summit."

"In the lead," Byzor whispered. "Exactly where you deserved to be."

"Yeah . . . I guess I never thought of it that way."

"We did," Byzor said. "So what happened to dinner?"

"Dinner?"

"You were supposed to eat dinner with us this evening. You didn't show, and you didn't call. We were getting concerned."

Jody Catlin quickly described her conversation with Melissa Washington, her arrival at the Rogue Valley Mall, and the terrifying events that followed.

"Are you sure it was her van you saw?" Malcolm Byzor asked when she finally stopped.

Jody hesitated. "No," she finally said, "I'm not absolutely sure. But I knew Melissa and Jack Wilson were on their way to meet me at Meier & Frank . . . but then the lights went out in the mall, and the fire alarms started up . . . and I thought I heard a gunshot."

"A gunshot?"

"I don't know; maybe. I thought it sounded like one, right when the fire alarms started going off. But then the emergency lights came back on, and I saw Colin come out of that toy store with a gun in his hand, and I just panicked and ran."

"You thought he was engaged in a gunfight with someone?"

"Or some *thing*."

"But you didn't see anyone . . . or anything?"

"No, nothing, just some kids running away. Probably shoplifters. But it couldn't have been them he was going after. I mean, when you stop to think about it, can you even imagine Colin drawing his gun against a couple of harmless kids?"

"No, of course not. So you thought our . . . visitors . . . were back?"

"I guess . . . or I just didn't know what to think. I just ran back to the parking lot, jumped in my car, and headed out to the freeway. All I was thinking about was trying to get away from there, as quickly as I could, and back to the safe house you set up. I was just getting onto the freeway when I saw the blue Dodge Minivan, on fire, in the northbound lane, along with a bunch of other wrecked cars and trucks . . . and something just told me it was Melissa's. I don't know why. It was just one of those gut feelings. That's when I remembered what you told me. If things suddenly start going crazy all around you, and you don't know why, get the hell out of there. Don't hesitate, don't look around, don't call for help, don't go home. Just go. So that's what I did. I switched cars, changed clothes, found a hotel I'd never been to before, dialed the eight hundred number you gave me, and then waited for you to call. Seemed like it took forever."

"There are two human cutouts in the communication chain," Byzor explained. "It adds an unfortunate delay factor, depending on their availability, but it also prevents an electronic track-back on the call. The important thing is you're safe and secure."

"Amen to that."

"And you didn't try to check on Melissa from your location?"

"No, I was afraid to."

"Good." Malcolm Byzor was silent for several seconds.

"You said things were starting to happen. What things?" Jody repeated.

"We may have had an attempt to get at the stones."

Jody sucked in her breath. "By . . . them?"

"We don't know. It may have been an unrelated internal matter. We're trying to sort that out right now."

"Then what do you know?" Catlin demanded.

"I know I need to get you out of that hotel and to a new location as quickly as I can," Byzor replied.

"Why? Do they know I'm here?" Byzor could hear the panic in her voice.

"No, I'm absolutely certain no one knows where you're at, except for me. But the thing is, I really need you to do something extremely important. Something that perhaps only you can do."

"What's that?"

"I'll tell you when you get there. But the problem is, I can't be there to pick you up. It's impossible for me to leave right now, and I don't have anyone I can send whom you could trust in terms of verification."

"What about Bobby or Colin?"

"I've been trying to get hold of them for the last ten minutes, but neither of them are answering their cell phones, and we may be running out of time. So I'm going to have to ask you to do something that you may not want to do. Something that you may be afraid to do."

"What's that?"

"Cut yourself loose from this safety net we've established, and get there on your own."

CHAPTER FORTY-ONE

"SO HOW DID HE DO IT?" SPECIAL AGENT IN CHARGE ARKAMINUS Gregorias demanded.

"I don't know yet," Dr. Malcolm Byzor replied, his eyes cold with anger as he sat back down in his chair.

Byzor was aware of the conversations going on around him, but his attention was focused on a pair of flat-screen monitors. The first displayed paired blocks of machine code—the first block from the station's extensive backup files, and the second from the currently running system programs—that his jury-rigged search program was busy comparing and posting on the flat monitor screen in one-second increments. Any discrepancies would be highlighted in a bright yellow font. The program was set to halt automatically at every discrepancy, which left Byzor free to dig at the root directory codes being displayed on the second monitor. He'd already discovered that the primary security programs built into the research center's mainframe software had been compromised in a very clever looped-mirror fashion.

He hit the ENTER key and sent the programs running again. It had taken him a lot longer than he'd expected to talk Jody Catlin into coming, but the effort had been necessary. Though he didn't want to think about what Colin Cellars and Bobby Dawson would say . . . or do . . . when they found out.

Sorry guys. I know you're going to be pissed. But if Washington and Wilson are dead, and they probably are, then there isn't anything else I can do. Sending someone out to pick her up would just put her in the crosshairs, and we can't afford to risk that now. We may be completely out of our league on this, but we can't give up. We have to try.

And besides, he told himself for perhaps the tenth time in the past twenty minutes, *we can't sell her short. She's tough. Maybe even tougher than the rest of us combined, when it gets right down to it . . . and she may have to be.*

"I thought you told me this sort of thing wasn't possible," Bernard Lackman, the Center's project director said accusingly, interrupting Malcolm Byzor's train of thought.

"No, I told you this sort of thing was virtually impossible, because only three people—you, me, and Jason—have root access to the system," Byzor corrected.

"Are you accusing me?" Lackman's face turned beet red.

"No, I'm not accusing you of anything," Byzor said absentmindedly, his eyes shifting back and forth between the blocks of so-far-identical code and the amazingly complex directory tree. "Everyone in this room knows full well you don't have the technical skills to pull off something clever like this." Byzor shifted the mouse to drop his root directory search down into a folder designed to hold temporary files. "And, in case you're even wondering," he added, "I didn't do it either."

"What are you saying then? That Eric found a way to compromise Jason?" Lackman whispered, glaring over at the far end of the isolated computer room where Dr. Jason Cohan, the Waycross Center's chief computer programmer, was working feverishly at another terminal.

Lackman, a professional bureaucrat who had rapidly moved up the NSA ladder on the basis of his family's political connections, and his own considerable backroom and backstabbing skills, was very much aware that his deputy had just deliberately insulted him in front of two of his subordinate supervisors, but he really didn't care.

The main reason he didn't care was the fact that none of his subordinate supervisors, with the possible exception of Malcolm Byzor, was actually capable of impacting his career in any significant manner. To do something like that would require a considerable amount of political pull . . . far more, in fact, than Gregorias and Cohan would ever be able to garner, even if they worked together, which they never would. And he really wasn't worried about Byzor, either, because he knew his technically brilliant deputy had absolutely no interest in advancing up the bureaucratic ladder to a nontechnical position. So an internal threat to his job really wasn't an issue.

And the stones were all safe and secure in their containment chambers. Nothing appeared to have been taken from the cyberlocked desks, safes, and file cabinets.

And even better—apart from the stomach-churning gore that still covered a goodly part of the primary laser research laboratory, an improbably huge spike in the power usage for the laser lab approximately eight minutes prior to the alarms going off, and the equally inexplicable failure of the infrared-scanner surveillance system to track and record the movements of a lab technician who had clearly entered the building with Marston and then effectively disappeared off the radar screen—there was nothing to indicate that a major security violation had occurred.

Other than the obvious fact that something out of the ordinary had occurred. But that, in and of itself, wasn't necessarily a problem. The obvious could always be ignored if it became politically expedient to do so. That was the way things worked at the highest levels of government.

In point of fact, the theory that Dr. Eric Marston might have accidentally killed himself in some incredibly bizarre and violent manner while conducting an off-hours, undocumented, and completely unauthorized laser experiment was becoming an increasingly tantalizing and perhaps even viable option.

All of which suggested—from Lackman's self-serving point of view—that his meteoric career could still be saved . . . and possibly even advanced . . . if everyone involved continued to cooperate. And if Malcolm Byzor, the Center's chief scientist, and the acknowledged technical genius behind the Waycross Project, could figure out what had happened and correct the problem before the gruesome story managed to work its way back to the DC office in some unsanitized form.

Which could turn out to be a very bad thing, indeed.

Which also meant he definitely needed to identify a fall guy, quickly, before things did get worse, Lackman realized. Marston was the ideal candidate, of course, if it could be demonstrated that the young scientist had gained access to the security system in spite of the most rigorous efforts on the part of the Center's management team. But, in a pinch, Cohan or Gregorias—or even Byzor, himself—would do just as well. It was just a question of having the proper evidence fall into place before people from the Washington office started nosing around.

"Jason wasn't involved either," Byzor replied. "He's not the type."

Lackman cursed under his breath.

"So how did Marston do it?" Security Chief Gregorias demanded. Like Byzor, he really didn't care about bureaucratic career ladders or ass-covering accountability either. What he cared about was the reliability and functionality of his security system, and the eventual arrest—or, preferably, the eventual dismemberment—of the person or persons who had, somehow, managed to compromise its effectiveness. If forced, Gregorias would have probably even admitted a grudging admiration for the cold logic that Dr. Malcolm Byzor was capable of applying to problem solving . . . like he was doing right now, in spite of Lackman's nervous and incessant harping. Because that was what Gregorias was waiting for with growing impatience: for Byzor to find and evaluate the break in the system. Then he would go out and deal with the individuals responsible for causing that break.

"Most likely with a Trojan Horse."

"A what?" The security chief blinked in confusion.

"Brush up on your Greek history, Gregor," Byzor said, continuing to watch both monitors as his hands worked the mouse and keyboard, progressively allowing his jury-rigged check program to gain access to the tightly protected machine code of the main security programs. "And, in the meantime, tell me . . . if a Lithuanian army general wanted to get into a fortified castle, he'd just tear down a wall, no matter how many days or soldiers it took, right?"

"Yes, of course."

"Well, I guess that's one of the big differences between the Lithuanians and the Greeks," Byzor continued on in a casually distracted manner. "From what I've read, the Greeks seemed to prefer the sneaky approach. They were pretty tough soldiers in their own right; but if things weren't going well, they were just as likely to pull back and leave their opponents an offering—in the historical sense, a very large and impressive wooden horse. Which, of course, made it appear as if they were giving up, or, at the very least, withdrawing for a while. But, after the Trojans dragged their gift horse inside the gate and were celebrating with a few barrels of wine, they discovered—to their dismay—that the horse was hollow and filled with Greek soldiers. You're familiar with that story, right?"

The security chief grunted what might have been an affirmative.

"Well, in a modern computer sense," Byzor went on, "a Trojan Horse virus is very much like that: a small computer program specifically designed to enter a host computer in some sneaky manner, hide away in the middle of a program or a database, monitor the system entry points, make exact copies of any secret codes the owner uses to accomplish routine entry, and then send those accumulated entry codes to an outside computer by embedding them in a routine piece of e-mail."

"So how can something like that impact us?" Lackman demanded, still anxious to make certain that all of his bureaucratic flanks were covered . . . especially from computer-virus attacks. "I thought you told me our system isn't connected to the outside world?"

"We're not. Our local area network is completely isolated. But we do use it to connect all of our internal security systems," Byzor explained.

"Which means the LAN could have given Marston a pipeline connection to the mainframe from his laser research lab. Which, in turn, means—if he did create and set a Trojan Horse virus into motion—he could have had the accumulated access codes sent covertly to his own office computer."

"Is that what you're saying then, that Marston—or one of his associates—was able to break into and compromise our security systems?" Gregorias's gray eyes still simmered with controlled fury. Trojan Horse virus or not, the security chief still viewed Dr. Eric Marston's misfortune as a direct affront to his honor. It was an affront that Gregorias had every intention of avenging, in person, if it turned out that Marston had involved any other insider or outsider in his foolish games.

"Marston was a very skilled programmer, which means he was perfectly capable of creating and implanting such a virus into one of our security systems, and possibly capable of spotting the traps Jason and I rigged into the system," Byzor said as his eyes continued to scan the flat-screen monitors with methodical patience, waiting for his automated virus search program or his personally controlled root directory search to reveal a suspicious section of code. "But in order for him to do so, he would still have had to either create or find a vulnerable access point— what programmers often call a 'back door'—through our fire walls. And that's what Jason and I are looking for right now. A machine code version of a hidden back door."

"How long will it take you to find it?" Gregorias asked.

"I don't know. If it still exists, maybe a few minutes, or maybe a few hours."

"Hours?" A look of horror spread across Lackman's face. "We don't have that much time, Malcolm. I have to report to Washington within the hour. What am I supposed to tell them?"

"Tell them that one of our employees had an unfortunate accident, and that it's all been taken care of," Gregorias suggested.

Malcolm Byzor clicked the PAUSE button to halt his automated virus search program, then looked up at the security chief.

"What do you mean by that?" he demanded.

"I mean that I've taken care of the problem," Gregorias replied.

"Don't give me that evasive bullshit, Gregor," Byzor said, meeting and matching the security chief's cold gaze. "I want to know what you did, specifically, to resolve the problem."

For a long moment, neither man spoke.

Then, finally spurred to act by the unyielding look in his deputy's cold eyes, Lackman interrupted, "It's okay, Malcolm, I authorized the removal and cleanup, and told Gregorias not to discuss it any further. I didn't mean for him not to talk to you, of course, but—"

"You . . . what?" Byzor shifted his incredulous gaze to his bureaucratic superior.

"Look, Malcolm, we're a black project. You know that gives us a great deal of latitude to deal with unforeseeable events," Lackman said defensively. He could feel his risk-adverse digestive system begin to rumble ominously . . . and with good reason. Less than an hour ago, he had given the Center's security chief authorization to resolve a problem in a manner that he knew, with absolute certainty, his deputy would have refused to even consider . . . and might have even reported. Malcolm Byzor was like that.

"We do have a great deal of latitude as a black project," Byzor agreed. "And with that comes a comparable amount of responsibility. We're not supposed to be running amok here."

"The security of the project remains our highest concern, and always will," the project director retorted, far more comfortable when he was able to parrot Agency dogma. "An opportunity presented itself, time was of the essence, you were busy working with Jason, and Gregor assured me that the issue of Dr. Marston could be resolved in a safe and expeditious manner, so I issued the authorization. End of story."

"And the matter was resolved," Gregorias added. "Marston had an accident. The authorities will deal with it in a predictable manner, and nothing more will be said. You should forget about him now, and worry about finding that back door."

"What about the girls?" Byzor demanded. He knew how the Gregors of this world liked to solve problems. For one thing, by making sure there were no loose ends.

"We are looking into that right now."

"Meaning?"

"We're attempting to locate both the lab technician and Marston's young girlfriend," the security chief responded, his eyes glacial. "Once we find them, we'll determine what involvement—if any—they had in Marston's activities. After that, if they prove to be innocent or were simply pawns, we'll find a way to relocate both of them out of Oregon in a manner that doesn't arouse any suspicion. It shouldn't be all that difficult. Both of them are ambitious with respect to their educations, and neither has the means to attend an expensive university. The solution is obvious, and easy to arrange."

"Be careful, Gregor," Byzor warned. "You may be treading on very dangerous ground with those two. As far as I'm concerned, we still have no clear idea what Marston was attempting to do here this evening. Which is a problem, because now, with Marston dead, we may never know."

"Dangerous?" The security chief snorted in apparent amusement. "Do you think I would allow myself to be worried by the foolish antics of two insignificant women? Or, perhaps, even by your persistent police officer friend?"

"No, I don't think that, at all," Malcolm Byzor replied, favoring the security chief with one final glare before he hit the PAUSE key again and returned his attention to the paired monitors. "But what I'm saying is, until Jason and I figure this out, maybe you should be."

CHAPTER FORTY-TWO

THE ODOR OF BURNED, DEAD FLESH AND EXPOSED HUMAN WASTE permeated the entire autopsy room, but neither of the two men noticed. Their olfactory senses had long since stopped responding to the smells.

But the visual images were far more difficult to ignore.

Colin Cellars, in particular, was finding it increasingly difficult to block out the realization that the charred corpse on the stainless-steel table had once been a gregarious and vibrant young woman with a love for life and a wicked sense of humor . . . not to mention Jody Catlin's closest friend at the National Fish and Wildlife Forensics Lab.

"Are you sure?" he asked, for no particular purpose.

"The tattoo of four macaws—three hyacinth and one scarlet—on her right ankle," Dr. Elliott Sutta replied in a dulled voice. "She showed it to me a couple of years ago. Said she got it on a trip to New Orleans with her three brothers. I've seen a lot of parrot tattoos in my time, but never one quite like hers. You want to see it again?"

"No, that's all right."

Nodding as if to say "I don't blame you," Sutta gently draped a white sheet over the charred and now thoroughly dissected corpse of Melissa Washington. The skilled pathologist had worked fast—almost in a frenzy of practiced motions—to complete the two autopsies in just under two hours. Like Cellars, he had no intention of spending any more time than absolutely necessary over the corpses of his two friends.

"So what are we talking about?" Cellars asked, willing himself to continue functioning in a professional manner as he watched Sutta walk over to the deep stainless-steel sink with his bloodied tray of dissecting tools.

"We'll run the basic toxicology screens for alcohol and drugs, but I doubt that we're going to find anything relevant. Death was instantaneous—and the cause virtually identical—in both cases," Sutta said as he turned the warm-water faucet on with his elbow and began rinsing off the pair of extremely sharp carbon-steel knives that he preferred over the more conventional dissecting scalpel with the disposable blades. "Broken necks, severed spinal cords, and massive subdural hematomas, all of which were almost certainly caused by a sudden and violent impact originating from their right, which in turn . . ."

"You mean from their left, don't you, Doctor?" Cellars corrected, looking up from his notebook. In spite of having attended several hundred equally gruesome autopsies in his career, the familiar process of taking meticulous notes and going through the mechanical process of photographing the two autopsies had been Cellars's source of mental sanity during the past two hours. Wilson had been a longtime friend, and Washington had been Washington . . . and it was extremely difficult to think of them now as burned and dissected corpses. Images that he knew, to his dismay, would stay with him the rest of his life.

"No." Sutta shook his head slowly. "I meant right."

"But that's . . . impossible," Cellars said.

"Oh really?" Sutta kept his bloodied hands in the sink as he turned to Cellars. "Why do you say that?"

"According to the witness statements, and the sketch Sergeant Waldrip made at the scene, it's very clear that their Minivan suddenly crossed three lanes of traffic in a right-to-left direction, which took them right into the path of an oncoming log truck," Cellars said. "Based on the sketch, and the transfer evidence on the vehicles I've seen so far, that action almost certainly triggered all the rest of the impacts. And that being the case," he went on, "as Melissa and Jack crossed over those lanes, the cars to their right—the cars which would have been ahead of them on the freeway—all had to have been traveling away from them, not at them. Therefore, logically, the first impact should have come from the left-hand side of the vehicle . . . where, in fact, we know a two-foot-diameter log damn near penetrated the driver's side door."

Sutta was silent for a long moment.

"I have to agree that what you just said makes sense, in terms of traffic flows," the pathologist finally said. "But I can also assure you, with absolute certainty, that Jack and Melissa were both dead long before that log hit the driver's side of their van."

"How can that be?"

"I don't know," Sutta confessed. "But what I do know is that the evidence of the directional forces that caused both fatal injuries is absolutely clear, and, in my view, irrefutable."

"But—"

"Come over here and take a look," Sutta said as he returned to the second table and lifted the sheet.

Cellars joined him, only vaguely aware now that the burned, gutted, and dissected carcass lying before him had once been a friend. In some curious and indefinable manner, he had slipped smoothly back into the mind-set of a professional crime scene investigator working an autopsy. The bodies were just articulated pieces of bone and meat now. Things to be examined and assessed for their evidentiary content and value.

Exactly the way they were supposed to be.

"The sequence of events is a little more obvious on Jack," Sutta said, sensing with some relief that Cellars had finally snapped out of his traumatized state, as he pointed with his gloved and bloodied finger. "You can see hemorrhaging right there, in the dura mater, the interior skull lining, right temporal, parietal, and occipital sides . . . which corresponds, as you would expect, with the massive hemorrhaging in the right temporal, parietal, and occipital lobes of the brain here—" Sutta pointed to a small tray bearing purpled slices of brain in his other gloved hand. "And here"—he shifted the pointing finger to the segment of exposed and dissected neck vertebrae—"you can see where the right transverse and articular processes of the first, second, third, and fourth cervical vertebrae were smashed together before being wrenched in a lateral direction. There's a lot of other evidence to that effect—ruptured spleen, ruptured lobes of the liver, ruptured bladder—but you get the point."

"Okay, I see all that," Cellars acknowledged. "But—"

"What we're talking about here," Sutta interrupted, "is nothing more than basic physics. Pool-ball mechanics. In essence, the conservation of momentum, and the fact that every physical action imparted to an object is going to create an equal and opposite reaction. In this case, a very heavy object moving very fast strikes in a lateral direction from the right—relative to the direction our victim was facing—thereby causing his strapped-in body to be driven in the lateral direction of the force. That is, from right to left. The force was severe enough to have ripped the pulmonary vein away from his heart and the pulmonary artery from his right lung, which, I can assure you, represents a very significant lateral force."

"Incredible," Cellars whispered.

"But the impact also sends the relatively heavy head," Sutta went on, "balanced, as it is, on top of a relatively long and thin column of cervical vertebrae, in the opposite lateral direction, from left to right, causing the right cervical processes to crush against each other before the lateral forces literally tore them apart from each other, thereby severing the spinal cord and tearing capillaries—which proceeded to pump blood into the surrounding dura, connective, and spinal tissues—and, at the same time, sending the essentially floating brain smashing into the right temporal, parietal, and frontal interior surfaces of the skull. A few hundredths of a second later, having reached the full extension that the connective tissues of the neck allow, the head snaps back in the opposite lateral direction, from right to left, but with somewhat less force, causing a much lesser degree of hemorrhaging in the dura and brain lobes of the left hemisphere—understandable, because the pulmonary vein and artery have already been severed—which is exactly what we see here," Sutta pointed out.

"But none of that really mattered, in this case, in terms of survival, because the fatal damage had already been done to the heart and spinal cord, not to mention the spleen and liver . . . and probably the brain. With the spinal cord completely severed, the heart and lungs shut off, blood flow stops, and Jack, mercifully, dies."

"Right then," Cellars whispered.

"Yes, precisely then," Sutta replied. "Which explains why, when the mass of that two-foot-diameter log struck the driver's side of the van, as you say it did, it certainly caused a significant breaking of bones and crushing of tissue, not to mention a wide range of systemic pressure effects of various bodily fluids being driven outward from the force of the second impact. But there was no more focused hemorrhaging from the capillaries into the torn tissues, because Jack's heart was no longer pumping blood into those capillaries. Are you following, so far?"

Cellars nodded slowly.

Sutta walked over to the second table, but didn't bother to lift the sheet. Instead, he simply stared at Cellars with a sympathetic look on his craggy face.

"Melissa's brain, dural lining, cervical vertebrae, heart, lungs, spleen, liver, and spinal cord all showed essentially the same pattern of damage, the lethal impact occurring in a lateral direction from the right-hand side relative to the direction she was facing at that moment. The damage was somewhat less in magnitude, which is what you'd expect if she were driving the vehicle, which would have put her a few feet farther away from the right-side impact.

"So," Sutta finished, "unless she and Jack were sitting backward at the time of the first impact—which seems highly unlikely, because I don't believe any of the seats in a Dodge Minivan face that way—and someone else was driving, the fatal impact had to have come from the right-hand side of their vehicle . . . not the left. As I said earlier, the pathology is very clear in terms of what happened . . . but, given the circumstances you described, it doesn't even begin to explain how or why."

"No," Cellars whispered, "it doesn't."

For a long moment, Colin Cellars simply stared down at the gruesome evidence laid out before his eyes. Then, without saying a word, he turned away from the autopsy table, walked over to the sink, took off the lab coat, tossed it into a nearby open hamper, washed his hands, pulled open the stainless-steel closet, then yanked his jacket and shoulder-holstered SIG-Sauer off the interior hooks. All the while working hard to control the fear . . . and rage . . . churning in the back of his mind.

"Where are you going?" Sutta asked.

"Back to the tow yard," Cellars said as he quickly slipped into the shoulder-holster rig, pulled on his heavy field jacket, then dropped the electronic camera back into its customary jacket pocket. "I need to take a closer look at that van."

CHAPTER FORTY-THREE

PATROL SERGEANT DICK WALDRIP, A PAIR OF CORONER'S ASSIS-
tants, and the other two OSP officers were still working when Detective-
Sergeant Colin Cellars pulled into the OSP tow yard at precisely 10:55
that evening, the heavy snow tires crunching into the layers of snow and
ice that now covered the asphalt surface.

The five men looked up with exhausted expressions as Cellars
parked the cammo-painted Humvee by the other state and county vehicles, cautiously worked his way to the back doors of the Humvee, rummaged around in the back compartment of the vehicle, then slowly
stomped his way toward them with a CSI kit in one hand and a large
brown paper bag in the other.

"I thought you guys would be long gone by now," Cellars commented, as he handed the bag over to Waldrip—who took it with visibly trembling hands and immediately began distributing the hot chicken sandwiches, bags of fries, and large cups of coffee to the two coroner's assistants and two OSP officers. In spite of their hats, gloves, and down jackets, all four men were shivering and appeared numb from the cold.

"We would have been if the damned tow trucks would stop dragging in every abandoned junker they can find on the freeway. Probably working their way up to Grants Pass by now," Waldrip groused as he looked down into the still-half-full bag and came up with another chicken sandwich. "Looks like you bought enough to feed the whole shift. You want one?"

"No, thanks, I saved a couple for myself. They're in the truck. I'll get to them eventually, but I've got something to do first. Which reminds me, Dr. Sutta sends his greetings."

"Oh, yeah? How's that grumpy old fart doing these days?" Waldrip had spent two years as a homicide detective before promoting up to patrol sergeant, and had spent many unpleasant hours in the autopsy room with Sutta.

"A little more grumpy than usual," Cellars said. "I think he'd like us to stop sending him depressing cases to work on in the middle of the night."

"So it really was Jack and Melissa?" Waldrip asked, wincing as he sipped at the hot coffee.

"Yeah."

"Shit."

The other four men mumbled similar expressions of regret. None of them knew Melissa Washington personally, but they shared a sense of law enforcement kinship enhanced by Dick Waldrip's description of the gregarious forensic scientist. They all knew Jack Wilson, and knowing they wouldn't see him at any more OSP crime scenes was numbing as well as sobering.

Cellars remained silent as he set the CSI kit down on the snow-and-ice-covered asphalt, opened it, and began pulling out selected items of equipment—which included a powerful flashlight, a sketchbook, a steel measuring tape, some stick-on location tags, and his electronic camera and flash. Then he looked around the tow yard, observing that the two-acre, chain-link-fenced yard was now almost filled with crumpled, smashed, and burned vehicles.

"Looks like things have been busy around here. What are you up to now?"

"Seventy-three cars and four trucks of varying sizes and shapes, and another goddamned body that nobody apparently noticed when they were pushing cars off to the side of the freeway, so they could get traffic moving again," Waldrip replied. "Which makes a total of thirteen fatals, counting the three that were DOA when they arrived at the hospitals."

"I take it that's why you guys are still hanging around?" Cellars looked over at the two coroner's assistants.

"Waiting for one of those tow trucks to come back and haul a couple of cars out of the way," the senior assistant said through a mouthful of chicken sandwich. "They've got the damned things crammed in so close together, we can't even get the door open."

Cellars stood up cautiously and stared across the lot. "Where's it at?"

"It's the burned-out Camry, third row back, second from the fence," Waldrip said, pointing in the direction of the fence line near the entrance gate.

"Tell you what," Cellars said, "I need to take another look at that blue Dodge Minivan—the one we pulled Melissa Washington and Jack Wilson out of a couple hours ago. But while I'm doing that, you guys can use my truck to pull those wrecks out of the way. There's a heavy-duty electric winch mounted on the front bumper. You might tear up some asphalt in the process, but—"

"That's a problem for some number cruncher, sitting in a warm office with his feet up on the desk, to deal with tomorrow morning," the senior coroner's assistant muttered through a mouthful of french fries as he crumbled up the empty cardboard container and tossed it back into the bag. "Right now, all I want to do is get that body transported, then go home before my nuts freeze off. So how do you operate that winch?"

Cellars shrugged. "Beats me. I never had one before this afternoon."

The coroner's assistant looked over at the two OSP officers. "Either of you guys know how to operate one of those things, or am I going to have to just tie the cable around the bumper and back up?"

Ten minutes later, the two OSP officers and two coroner's assistants were in the process of figuring out the mechanics of the new electrical winch and dragging the first of several blocking wrecks out of the way as Cellars and Waldrip carefully worked their way around to the right side of the blue Dodge Minivan.

"What are we looking for?" Waldrip asked as Cellars slowly swept the beam of the flashlight across the twisted and crumpled metal panels.

"I don't know. Some kind of impact point," Cellars replied. "Something to explain why Melissa Washington would suddenly—"

Then he stopped, blinked, moved forward with the flashlight beam centered on the right sliding-door panel, and knelt. Like the sliding panel door on the driver's side, this one was also buckled and off track. But the impact of the two-foot-diameter log on the driver's side had caused the entire chassis and frame of the van to bow inward . . . and, in doing so, had almost folded the right-side panel door in half.

"Look at that," Cellars whispered, as he painted the bright beam of his flashlight across the scorched and twisted exterior panel-door surface.

"Look at what?" Waldrip demanded.

"The spherical indentation . . . right there," Cellars said. He used his flashlight to trace the hemispherical impressions on each side of the fold in the door panel. "See how it's curved inward at the edges . . . like a big cannonball hit the side door sometime before the impact of the log basically folded the chassis and the frame . . . which caused the big dent in the outer door panel to fold back out, too. You can hardly tell it's there, except at the edges, where the metal's been stretched out and the paint's popped off; but I bet if you look inside—"

Cellars stood up and leaned in through the broken-out side-door window.

"Yeah, look, right there, see how the interior door panel's been dented inward too . . . same spherical impression . . . and then stayed that way, even when the chassis and frame folded under the impact of that log."

"Yeah, I think I see what you're talking about," Waldrip said dubiously. "But what the hell kind of impact would create a dent like that in the side of a moving vehicle? I mean, maybe it happened the day before . . . you know, like a flatbed with some kind of rounded pipe load backed into the side of the van?"

"Center of impact's what, three feet off the ground? Awfully low to be a flatbed truck," Cellars pointed out. "And besides, who'd drive a Minivan around with a side door sprung like that?"

"My brother-in-law, for one," Waldrip said, but Cellars wasn't listening. He was already back down on his knees in the ice and snow, stretching the tape measure across the two segments of the bent exterior door panel.

"Indentation's a little over ten inches in diameter, edge to edge . . . and I'm guessing a depth of maybe five inches, based on the thickness of the sliding door and the distension of the interior door panel. Assume a uniformly spherical impact surface, which gives you a five-by-three right angle," Cellars muttered to himself, as he pulled out his field notebook and pen, and made a series of quick calculations. "Three squared plus five squared is thirty-four. Square root is almost six . . . times two . . . makes it a diameter of twelve inches, more or less."

"A cannonball twelve inches in diameter?" Waldrip chuckled. "You're talking about a pretty serious projectile there, partner, not to mention one hell of a big cannon to spit it out. Seems to me I ought to have seen one or the other when I was running around out there on I-Five. Be kinda hard to miss."

But Cellars still wasn't listening. Instead, he was remembering back to the day, almost two months ago, when he'd been driving Lieutenant Talbert's new Search and Rescue Expedition en route to the National Fish and Wildlife Forensics Lab . . . and had suddenly found himself sliding sideways when something very heavy struck the left side of the Expedition, almost sending him off the road . . . and then into the opposite lane of traffic when a seemingly identical object slammed into the heavy SUV from the right side. Somehow, he'd managed to get the Expedition back under control without ending up in a head-on collision with an oncoming car or immobile tree. But when he went back to search the surrounding area, after finding two bowling-ball-size dents in the left and right sides of his vehicle, he hadn't been able to find any bowling balls or cannonballs or any other similar projectiles. Just a pair of shadows that screamed and bled when wounded . . . then disappeared.

Which hadn't made much sense then . . . and only a little more now.

"Like something you might expect from the concussion wave of a tightly focused explosion, only that doesn't make sense, because the charge would have had to go off right next to the vehicle, and I didn't hear a thing," Cellars said, more to himself than Waldrip.

"What?"

"Either that or some kind of force field. No mass. No propellant. Just the symmetrical distribution of energy. Only thing that makes sense."

"A force field?" Dick Waldrip stared at Cellars as if he expected his fellow OSP sergeant to start babbling in tongues at any moment.

Cellars blinked, then suddenly became aware of his surroundings again.

"I want to impound this car," he said as he stood up and looked around the tow yard.

"But it's already impounded," Waldrip pointed out. "That's why it's here."

"No, I mean I want to have it seized as evidence and locked up where nobody can get at it until we have it examined by a forensic engineer who can figure out stress responses of sheet metal," Cellars said. "Can we do that?"

"I guess so." Waldrip hesitated. "We don't have any inside storage facilities around here, but we've got a secured garage with a pneumatic hoist at the OSP Lab in Medford, where they examine vehicles used in drug shipments or major crimes."

"Perfect. How soon can we get a tow truck to take this thing out there?"

"Well, it won't take all that long, once they get here; but, don't forget, we've still got one more body in that Camry."

"Oh yeah, right." Cellars nodded sleepily as he reached down and picked up his flashlight, tape measure, and sketchbook. "Let's go see if we can give them a hand."

By the time Cellars and Waldrip collected all their gear and walked over to the twisted and burned wreckage of the Camry, the two OSP officers had finished clearing a path to the driver's side door, and the two coroner's assistants were moving in with a gurney.

"Hey, hold up," Waldrip yelled as one of the coroner's assistants reached for the door handle. "We still need to take a quick look inside and get some pictures first."

"Not much to see," the senior coroner's assistant replied as Cellars and Waldrip came up alongside the Camry. "Other than the fact that this guy's got to be a classic poster boy for convincing people to wear their seat belts."

"What do you think, Colin?" Waldrip asked as he played his flashlight beam in through the broken-out side window and into the backseat floor area where a white-powder-and-foam-covered arm and leg were barely visible under a powder-and-foam-covered mass of books, papers, journals, miscellaneous items of clothing, and a broken-open suitcase.

"Looks like somebody—or probably a lot of somebodies—went nuts with the fire extinguishers, and no, the victim probably wasn't wearing a seat belt," Cellars agreed. He shined his own flashlight beam at the relatively clean, unscorched, and undamaged harness and buckle hanging from its interior belt mount to the left of the driver's seat. "Let me get a quick picture of that."

Cellars pulled the electronic camera out of his jacket pocket, turned it on, observed the picture count on the display screen, then muttered: "Hold it a second. I've got to switch memory cards."

As Cellars knelt and reopened his CSI kit, Waldrip stuck his flashlight under his arm, then reached into his jacket for his field notebook and pen.

"Whoever was working the extinguishers, they definitely got the fire out pretty quick, so everything isn't burned to a crisp, which is definitely an improvement over some of the other ones," Waldrip commented as he flipped to a blank page. "Major impact point on the driver's side door, and a minor one on the left front bumper and wheel well; but from the damage to the roof, I'd say the car rolled at least once, which probably explains how the poor bastard ended up in the backseat covered with all of his junk and about ten extinguishers' worth of powder and foam. No front plate. Looks like it might have been torn loose. You want to read me off the number from the rear plate?" he said to the OSP officer standing beside the Camry.

"Yeah, sure, just a second." The uniformed officer gingerly walked around to the rear of the Camry and switched on his flashlight. "Okay, looks like we've got an Oregon plate, current registration, November-Uniform-Victor-two-seven-five."

Cellars's head snapped up. "What did you say?" he demanded.

"Oregon plate, November-Uniform-Victor-two-seven-five," the officer repeated.

Cellars fumbled in his jacket pocket, drew out his field notebook, flipped back several pages, and then stared at the familiar block-printed letters and numbers. "I'll be a son of a bitch," he whispered.

"What's the matter?" Waldrip demanded.

"The name of the driver is probably going to turn out to be a Dr. Eric Marston, who worked out at the Waycross Laser Research Center," Cellars said as he stood up, stepped forward, and shined his flashlight into the rear compartment of the Camry again. "Which means you get some good news for a change: He wasn't involved in your pileup."

"Oh yeah? How do you know that?"

"Because I ran into this guy going east on Sensabaugh Road . . . or he ran into me . . . about twenty minutes after six this evening—at least an hour and twenty minutes after your accident—when he was paying a whole lot more attention to the absolutely gorgeous young woman sitting next to him than to which side of the road he was driving on," Cellars replied as he stepped back and swept the beam of his flashlight across the left front bumper. "See there? That's where we connected. You can even see some light and dark green transfer paint."

Waldrip leaned forward and examined the damaged area with his flashlight beam. "Dark green, light green, gray, and black," he confirmed. "You don't run into too many cars on the road with an ugly paint combination like that. Good thing, too," the patrol sergeant added, "because that armor-plated beast you call a CSI vehicle sure tore the hell out of his wheel well. Surprised he was able to make a full left-hand turn, the way that fender's bent in. In fact, you can see where the metal edge of the fender was cutting into the steel belt. About one more turn would have probably done it."

"Poor schmuck. Should have stayed home with his girlfriend," Cellars said, shaking his head. "What the hell was he thinking, driving on the freeway, at night, and in a snowstorm, with a broken headlight and a tire about to come apart?"

"Maybe he was taking her home, going too fast because he was thinking about a doubleheader instead of the tire, lost control trying to avoid one of the wrecks still on the freeway—that he couldn't see with only one headlight until it was too late—and rolled?" the patrol sergeant suggested. "She could have been wearing her seat belt, and ended up being medivacked—which could explain how the emergency crews managed to miss him. There was still a lot of action going on out there at six-thirty, seven o'clock."

"Getting her back into bed is exactly what he should have been doing, if he had any brains at all," Cellars said, barely listening to Waldrip. He was remembering the frightened look on the girl's face, and also the fact that she'd been wearing her seat belt. And, now that he thought about it, Cellars realized, so had Marston. "Thing is, though, a buddy of mine who works at the Waycross Research Center, and was with me when we hit this guy, acted really surprised to learn that Marston was even dating. I got the impression he was one of those seriously dedicated, all work, no play types."

"Unlike most of the forensic scientists we know," Waldrip commented.

"Yeah, probably true," Cellars agreed.

"Like you said, poor schmuck. On the other hand, since this car is definitely not part of my accident, I don't have to include it in my report." Waldrip smiled and closed his notebook.

"Except that he's definitely part of somebody's accident, not to mention dead, which means somebody's got to write a report. The question is, who? Do we know which tow truck dropped him off?"

Waldrip looked up at the two uniformed OSP officers, who looked at each other, then shrugged. "You said we could let the tow drivers hold on to their paperwork, Sarge, and that we'd all sit down and work out the receipts and transfers after they got all the cars off the freeway," one of them replied.

"Ah, shit," Waldrip muttered as he opened up his field notebook again.

"Look at it this way," Cellars suggested. "You now have two accident reports to write instead of one. But the second one isn't going to be anywhere near as complicated as the first."

"It will be if we can't figure out where this guy came from," Waldrip pointed out.

"Had to have been from the freeway," Cellars reasoned. "Even Jasper County tow truck drivers know better than to commingle separate accidents from completely different locations . . . especially if they're not filling out the release forms and getting receipt signatures with each tow. That's a good way to lose your county contact, end up in court, and not get paid to boot."

Waldrip sighed. "Okay, let's walk ourselves through it. You ran into him—or he ran into you—at twenty after six, while you were heading east on Sensabaugh Road, at which time you observed a gorgeous young woman in the front passenger seat and a broken headlight . . . left or right?"

"Left."

"Okay, left," Waldrip muttered as he began jotting notes. "Also, the damage to his left front bumper and wheel well . . . but no damage to the driver's side door or roof, correct?"

"Correct."

"So, sometime between six-twenty and, let's say, roughly nine-thirty this evening, our victim, who, at this point, may or may not be Dr. Eric Marston, leaves the—what was the name of that place again? Waycross something?"

"Waycross Laser Research Center," Cellars said.

"Right, Laser Research Center"—Waldrip nodded as he continued to write—"with or without the gorgeous young woman. He gets onto I-Five, and then—somewhere around exit thirty, where the traffic is moving about ten miles an hour in order to avoid burned-out wrecks, broken glass, car parts, and flares—he loses control, rolls his car—at least once—which flings him into the backseat. The car catches on fire, whereupon a half dozen good Samaritans come running with fire extinguishers, fill the whole damned compartment with foam and powder, but somehow manage not to see the poor schmuck driver who's managed to get himself wedged in on the floor between the front and back seats of a car that's not all that big to begin with, and buried under a library full of papers and journals, not to mention a suitcase full of clothes. All of which suggests our good Samaritans were distracted by the passenger who was probably flung out of the car when it rolled, or they would have looked for the driver. That about the way you see it?" Waldrip asked.

"Yeah, except we've got a couple other minor problems," Cellars said. He'd been taking pictures around the exterior of the Camry, and was now kneeling by the front bumper.

"And just what would those be?" Waldrip asked, his pen poised over his field notebook.

"Take a look at that left front tire again. Like you said before, no way the guy could make a full, left-hand turn, the way that wheel well's bent in. So, tell me, how would someone get from the Waycross Research Center on Sensabaugh Road to I-Five, and presumably end up in an accident somewhere around exit thirty, without making at least one full, ninety-degree left turn?"

"They don't," Waldrip said after a moment. "You can turn right out of Sensabaugh Road, which would put you south on Winchester, and then make a box series of right turns to end up going east on Causegrove, but you're still going to have to make a left at Grail or Weatherly to get over to the I-Five on-ramp."

"Both of which are sharp lefts, with not much room to make any kind of sweeping left turn, even if there isn't any traffic, which there usually is." Cellars nodded. "Which brings us to the question of headlights."

"What about them?"

"Not them, it . . . as in singular," Cellars corrected. "When Marston ran into me out on Sensabaugh Road, he definitely broke his left headlight, but the right one was still working just fine."

"Yeah, so?"

"So now the right one's broken too, which is perfectly understand-able . . . except that it wasn't on at the time he rolled the car. You can tell that pretty easily because there aren't any broken glass fragments fused to the filament . . . just like the left one, which I know was off when I broke it."

"But you definitely saw him drive away with his right headlight on?"

"Correct."

Waldrip walked over to the front of the Camry, knelt beside Cellars, and focused his flashlight beam first on the clean filament in the center of the broken right headlight . . . and then the one on the left.

"Well, I'll be damned," the patrol sergeant whispered.

"Which makes for kind of an interesting scenario . . . our victim here supposedly driving on the freeway, and in a snowstorm, without any headlights, but not being able to make any left-hand turns to get there in the first place," Cellars added.

"Might explain how he lost control," Waldrip suggested, but there was very little conviction in his voice.

"Yes, it might," Cellars agreed as he stood up. "But that still leaves the unanswered questions of how and why this particular car ended up in this OSP tow yard, at this time of night, supposedly part of a seventy-three-vehicle accident . . . when we know, for a fact, that it couldn't pos-sibly have been involved in that accident."

"But if you hadn't run into it at six-twenty, we wouldn't know that . . . and no one else would either," Waldrip pointed out.

"Precisely."

"Is all this making sense to you?" Waldrip inquired.

"I wouldn't say it's making sense," Cellars said. "Let's just say that the coincidences are starting to pile up just a little too deep in some places."

"Meaning?"

"Meaning it's about time I started figuring out how a whole bunch of seemingly unrelated people and events all fit together."

"And how do you plan on doing that?"

"I'm going to start with a body," Cellars replied. "The one we've got right here. First thing I'm going to do is make sure I know who he is. Then I'm going to find out what he's got to say for himself."

CHAPTER FORTY-FOUR

LAB TECHNICIAN KATHY BUCKHOUSE, AKA BUCKY, COVERED THE
mouthpiece of the phone with her hand as she looked up at Cellars.

"He said, and I quote: 'Tell Detective-Sergeant Cellars that if he
brought me another body to cut on tonight, then it had damn well better be his.' "

"Why don't you let me talk with him?" Cellars suggested as he held
out his hand.

"I'm not real sure that's a good idea," the morgue attendant said dubiously.

"I'm not sure, either, but we might as well find out while he's still in
a good mood," Cellars said as he brought the reluctantly relinquished
phone up to his ear. "Dr. Sutta?"

"Who the hell said I was in a good mood?" Dr. Elliott Sutta demanded.

"Pure guess. The way I have it pictured, you're all tucked in with a double nightcap, probably watching an old movie so you don't have to work so hard to block out the images of Jack and Melissa, and getting yourself mentally and physically prepared for the six autopsies you've got scheduled for tomorrow."

Dead silence on the other end of the line.

"For your information, Sergeant Cellars," the supervisory pathologist finally said in a cold voice, "I like old movies. I have no trouble falling asleep at night, with or without a nightcap. And I only have five autopsies scheduled for tomorrow, not six."

"You had five," Cellars corrected. "I found another body for you. That makes a total of six."

"Are you really making an effort to try to piss me off?"

"No, not especially. Although, the way my day's been going so far, I guess I could use some company. But, in any case," Cellars went on before Sutta could respond, "I thought you might be interested to know I might have a line on who or what killed Jack and Melissa."

"Might?"

"Make it a strong 'maybe,' " Cellars amended.

There was another long pause.

Then, finally, Sutta sighed, and said in a vaguely resigned voice: "You're not going to go away or give up on this, are you?"

"No, I'm not."

"And what if I just hang up, turn off the TV, and go to sleep like I most certainly intend to do?"

"Oh, I'll still be here in the morning, waiting for you," Cellars replied. "But I'd rather not wait that long because I've got a lot of other things to do this evening . . . which includes catching up with some people who aren't going to be the least bit happy to see me."

"I sympathize with their point of view."

"And besides, if you wait until morning, a guy named Gregor will have probably peeled the doors off this place and torn everything apart by then . . . if I don't manage to shoot him first."

"Shoot . . . who?" Sutta sounded like he couldn't believe his ears. "What are you talking about, Cellars? Who the hell's Gregor?"

"Special Agent in Charge Arkaminus Gregorias. Very large and fore-boding type. Kinda looks like Lurch on *The Addams Family*, only with mean eyes and a lot more muscles around the arms and shoulders. You'd shoot him too, if you saw him coming after you or Bucky. Works for the National Security Agency as one of their security chiefs. I take it you know who they are?"

Another long pause.

"Cellars, are you drunk?"

"No, I'm completely sober, I'm sorry to say. But I'll be happy to bring you something. What do you drink?"

"Expensive red wine."

"Twenty bucks expensive enough?"

"It'll do for a start."

"Deal. I'll be here," Cellars said.

The phone clicked dead in his hand.

"See," Cellars said as he handed the phone back to Kathy Buck-house, who stared back at him with an open mouth and widened eyes, "I told you he was in a good mood."

———

Twenty minutes later, the double door to the main autopsy room of the Jasper County Coroner's Office burst open, and Dr. Elliott Sutta strode in. Kathy Buckhouse took one look at the furious expression on the pa-thologist's face and immediately retreated to the far back corner of the room.

"You've got your entrance down pat, Doctor," Detective-Sergeant Colin Cellars commented from his seated position on a lab stool about ten feet from the closest of two stainless-steel autopsy tables. His jacket was hanging back up on the wall rack again, and he'd already garbed himself in one of the wraparound blue lab coats . . . but, this time, he'd put the shoulder holster rig with the lethal .40-caliber SIG-Sauer semi-automatic pistol and the two spare ten-round magazines back on over the lab coat.

A zipped body bag and a bottle of red wine lay on the stainless-steel table nearest Cellars's stool.

Sutta ignored Cellars, walked over to the table, and picked up the bottle.

"I thought you said twenty dollars."

Cellars shrugged. "I was feeling generous."

"And you're expecting me to share this with you?" Sutta held the bottle in both hands, the furious look on his face softening into what might have passed for awe . . . or even reverence.

"Not unless it goes good with a couple of cold chicken sandwiches and greasy fries."

"Don't be sacrilegious. Bucky'll get you a Coke out of the vending machine," Sutta replied as he gently placed the bottle into a nearby cabinet, then turned back to the body bag.

"Am I going to know this one, too?" he asked accusingly.

"My guess is no," Cellars said as he got up from the stool and stood on the opposite side of the stainless-steel autopsy table. "If the wallet in his back pocket matches the body, his name is Dr. Eric Marston, and he's employed at the Waycross Research Center."

"You mean that laser research facility out on Sensabaugh Road?"

"That's right."

"What happened?"

Cellars quickly summarized the circumstances under which he and Malcolm Byzor had come across Dr. Eric Marston and friend out on Sensabaugh Road earlier in the evening . . . and what he and Sergeant Dick Waldrip had discovered when he went back to the OSP tow yard a few hours later.

"The Waycross Laser Research Center is run by the National Security Agency? And you think they might have dumped this man's vehicle and body—one of their own research scientists—in the OSP tow yard for you to find?" Sutta whispered incredulously.

"No, actually, I'm pretty sure it never occurred to whoever did this that I might get involved with that accident out on I-Five, if they even thought about me at all," Cellars replied. "It was just a bad break, or a fluke of luck . . . depending on your point of view."

"So what you have here is a dumped body?" Sutta said.

"And, very likely, a faked crime scene, which is also a felony," Cellars added. "Not to mention a very interesting concealed compartment we found under the rear seat of the Camry, which was empty except for a few long black hairs."

"Which signifies what?"

"I don't know," Cellars confessed. "I'm guessing it means the young woman I saw at the time of my fender-bender with Marston was in that compartment . . . for whatever reason . . . either before or after our incident."

"But, when you saw her, she didn't give you the impression that she was being kidnapped . . . or was, in any way, frightened by her situation?"

"She acted like she was frightened of me," Cellars replied. "But it was dark, and I was annoyed at the time, so I guess that's more or less understandable. But, no," he added, "I had no sense she was in that car under any kind of duress. If anything, the two of them looked like they were about ready to pull off to the side of the road, jump in the backseat, tear their clothes off, and go at it. Which they probably would have if I hadn't interrupted things."

"So, thanks to you, instead of sitting around home with a pleasantly warming nightcap, and equally warming memories of getting laid by a beautiful young woman in some romantic, off-road setting, this Marston fellow—assuming that's who we have here—ends up dead on a morgue table."

"Very possibly."

"And how does that make you feel?"

"I don't know." Cellars shrugged. "Guess I really haven't thought much about it. I'll mention it to my shrink, next time I see him."

"You're seeing a psychiatrist?"

"Uh-huh."

"Mind if I ask why?"

"Departmental orders. They'd like to know why I keep shooting at shadows that I think are out to get me."

"Have you told them you're thinking of moving up to NSA security chiefs?"

Cellars smiled. "No, actually. Major Hightower, my temporary new boss, doesn't have that kind of sense of humor. Of course, she's also pissed at me because she thinks I might have been responsible for the death and dismemberment of her brother."

"Which you weren't, I trust?"

"I tried to explain to her that her brother probably got sliced, diced, and packed out by Allesandra, when she was in one of her alternate personas, but Hightower really didn't want to hear that either."

"And this Allesandra is . . . ?" Sutta raised an eyebrow as he placed a pair of carefully honed carbon-steel knives and some other surgical instruments on a tray at the far end of the stainless-steel table.

"A very sensuous woman, apparently of extraterrestrial origins, who lost some evidence and wanted it back, but ended up getting stoned when she went for the exchange," Cellars replied with a straight face. "I explained all of this to my shrink, but he cleared me for active duty anyway, so here I am."

"Your shrink and I are going to have a long talk about you in the very near future," Sutta promised. "But let's get back to some semblance of reality, if you don't mind." He gestured with his head at the body bag. "What, exactly, are you looking for here?"

"Well," Cellars said, "ideally, you're going to tell me how and why the individual in this body bag died, so that I can use that information as a twist to find out what the hell these NSA bastards are up to before they cause any more people a lot of grief . . . me and my friends in particular."

" 'These bastards' being the NSA staff at the Waycross Center, the deputy director of which happens to be one of those friends you were talking about . . . who probably isn't going to be real pleased when you accuse some members of his staff of complicity in a felony?"

"Right."

Sutta shook his head in bewilderment. "You know, Cellars, it's completely beyond me how you ever manage to sleep at night."

"Actually, that's another one of my problems," Cellars admitted.

"Tell it to your shrink; I don't want to hear about it," Sutta replied as he slipped back into the familiar rubber apron, pulled on a new pair of gloves, and reached for the body-bag zipper. "Okay, let's see if I can find something to keep you happy, so at least one of us can go home and enjoy a good night's sleep."

CHAPTER FORTY-FIVE

THEY PAUSED AT THE EDGE OF THE OUTER PERIMETER, THEN AP-
proached the cabin like three dark ghosts. They moved slowly and cautiously, because the element of danger was always present, especially
here; but also with confidence, because the dark clouds and rapidly
falling snow made a perfect cover for their movements.

No moon to reveal their position.

No fallen branches to snap or stones to rattle beneath their footsteps.

Just the soft, earthly presence of crystallized water, drifting down as
huge puffy flakes in the chilled evening air, and covering everything in
sight with blankets or mounds of white.

If they sensed they were being watched, they gave no outward sign.

The lead figure—visibly the most aggressive and threatening of the
three—was the one who discovered the Elmer Fudd dolls.

Two of them.

Mounted on the thick wooden front door.

With large framing nails punched through their foreheads.

For a long moment, she stood there on the porch, intent on trying to absorb and comprehend the incredible arrogance—and defiance—of the childish display. Then, in a series of movements that seemed more fluid than ethereal, they separated . . . the lead figure and one of the others flowing back into the surrounding forest while the other seemed to fade away into the dark shadows around the cabin.

Fifteen minutes passed, the time measured only in the number of intricate snowflakes that continued to fall unabated, and the depth of the blanketing mounds.

Then another five.

When it came, the rifle shot shattered the collective stillness of the chilled and icy night air. The rapidly expanding sound waves ripped harmlessly through the thousands of falling crystalline flakes, and then echoed off the surrounding trees and mountains with a ferocity that rivaled nature's own thunder.

And caused two very dangerous creatures to stop in their tracks, and turn their heads sharply back in the direction they had come.

As they did, the far more muted sounds of a small stone clattering on the thick, wooden boards of the cabin's front porch went unheard by all of those lesser, hidden, and quiet creatures. All save one.

The familiar sense of sudden emptiness hung in the icy air.

Minutes later, the cabin grew still again, and remained that way for fifteen minutes.

And then twenty.

And thirty.

Until, finally, the two dark, ghostly figures stepped out of the forest perimeter and approached the cabin from two different directions, very much on alert, their eyes glistening with rage.

This time it was the subordinate who approached the front door of the cabin, and observed the dolls.

There were three of them now, each fastened to the heavy wooden door with a large framing nail.

And there was something else. The front door . . . slightly open.

The subordinate stepped forward, tensed, ready to lunge forward and strike out with bared claws—at a speed faster than a human mind could react—and pushed against the door, which swung open on squeaking hinges.

The sound of the relay switch closing was nearly inaudible over the squeak of the rusty hinges. But the leader—her energies focused on analysis rather than aggression—heard it . . . and reacted instantly.

Two dark ghosts, invisible against all but the falling crystalline snowflakes, streaked away as the log-cabin walls erupted out, and then disintegrated under the force of a high-order explosion. The thunderous blast sent fragments of log and stone flying in all directions.

The ballistic impacts of those thousands of projectiles effectively obliterated the snowshoe tracks of a long-haired and muscular man for almost thirty yards. A very determined man who now possessed the advantages of Arctic military camouflage clothing, a twenty-minute head start, a .375 Magnum rifle with hollow-point ammo that could outstreak any dark ghost on the planet, and the satisfying taste of cold human vengeance in his soul.

Bobby Dawson was in his element.

But so were these creatures.

And he was exactly who—and what—they'd been looking for from the very first moment they'd arrived on this occasionally bleak and cold and all-too-inviting world.

CHAPTER FORTY-SIX

COLIN CELLARS HELPED DR. ELLIOTT SUTTA REMOVE THE PARTIALLY burned body of Dr. Eric Marston from the body bag, and watched as the pathologist conducted a quick visual examination of the white-powder-encrusted body. He took a series of anterior, posterior, lateral, ventral, and then finally dorsal photographs, as Sutta held the body on its side. And stepped back as the pathologist slowly cut away the charred fragments of clothing, then ran a stream of water over the body, washing away the crusted coating of extinguisher powder, foam, and seared bodily fluids.

"Not much to go on, in terms of facial features; they're pretty much burned away. But you've got one hand that looks pretty good for prints, and I can see a couple of interesting crowns in those molars, so coming up with a positive ID shouldn't be much of a problem," Sutta noted.

"Good, it's about time something wasn't much of a problem in this case," Cellars muttered.

"Unusual cross-checked pattern in the charred facial tissues, and that right hand," Sutta went on, talking to the overhead-mounted microphone as well as Cellars. "Looks like the cuts go right to the skull. On the other hand, I don't see any obvious bullet holes, compound fractures, broken teeth, compressions, or anything else that would make my job easier. So," he said as he reached for one of his carefully honed knives, "let's see what we find when we dig a bit."

Twenty minutes later, after repeating the words "no apparent abnormalities" about twenty times, Sutta set aside his knife. "Apart from what looks like a pretty significant loss of blood, and a curious lack of broken bones for the victim of a vehicle accident," he commented, "the lungs were clear of smoke particles, so he was almost certainly dead before the fire began, and I don't see anything else remarkable in the thoracic cavity. So, let's see what we can find in and around the cranium."

Sutta shifted over to the head of the stainless-steel autopsy table, leaned forward, and began gently to probe the charred facial tissues with his gloved fingers.

"What's this?" he muttered, mostly to himself, as he seemed to probe deeper, then reached for one of his knives.

At that moment, Cellars heard a brief, muted vibrating.

Sutta and Cellars looked up at each other, and then over at the stainless-steel coat closet.

The sound repeated itself.

Cellars stepped over to the closet, opened the door, then knelt, reached in behind one of the piles of folded blue lab coats, and came out with a cell phone.

"Who's that belong to?" Sutta asked.

"Me, I think," Cellars muttered, brushing his hand across the empty space on his belt where his cell phone should have been clipped. *Must have fallen off when I yanked my shoulder holster and jacket out of the closet,* he realized as he opened the phone and brought it up to his mouth. "Cellars."

"Thought you said you were going to start wearing that damned cell phone on a regular basis."

"Bobby?"

"Don't have much time, *compadre*. Things are getting a little intense out here. Smashed the cell phone Malcolm gave me earlier this morning, so I had to break into some poor guy's cabin to call you. Just wanted to tell you, don't go home tonight."

"Why not?"

"Well, mostly because I blew it up."

"You blew up my cabin?"

"Yeah, afraid so. Got the first two pretty easy, but it's getting a lot tougher to catch this new breed off guard. Got the third one a little while ago, but it looks like the trap didn't work out as well as I'd hoped, 'cause at least one of them's still dogging my trail . . . and she's a bitch to shake."

Cellars felt his heart start to tighten in his chest. "Bobby, what the hell are you talking about?"

"The Fudds. Seriously ornery critters, let me tell you. Make Allesandra look like a little pussycat. Real good at using trees for cover, too. Kept her at a distance with the rifle for a while, but I ran out of ammo about a quarter mile back. Still got one more load for the forty-four and my trusty fighting knife, so I'm not licked yet."

"Bobby—"

"Uh-oh, here she comes again. I'm heading over toward Little Round Top. I'll try to get you at least one more before I run dry. Meantime, watch your six, keep on working those puzzle pieces, and take care of Jody. Gotta go. *Adios.*"

"Bobby—!"

Click.

Cellars stared at the unresponsive phone, then looked up to see Sutta eyeing him curiously.

"Problems?" the pathologist inquired.

"I—I don't know."

"If you think someone just blew up your cabin, I'd say you've definitely got problems," Sutta observed. "But, hopefully, not as bad as the ones this poor bastard ran into."

"What?" Cellars stared at Sutta, vaguely aware that his mind had gone numb.

"Come here and take a look at what I found."

CHAPTER FORTY-SEVEN

THE ARGUMENTS STARTED THE MOMENT THAT STATE CIRCUIT COURT Judge David W. MacMullen signed the warrant with a tired flourish.

Supervisory Special Agent Elizabeth Mardeaux argued that the evidence suggesting Dr. Eric Marston's vehicle had not been part of the multivehicle accident on I-5—an accident that had claimed the lives of two of her agents—was inconclusive, at best . . . and, therefore, wanted the state search warrant placed on hold until a federal judge could be located. And, in any case, she wanted her DEA agents in on the search, even though she conceded that no illicit drugs had been found in any of the relevant vehicles, and that no link had been established between the suspicious death of Marston and the unknown whereabouts of ex–DEA Agent Bobby Dawson.

The FBI's senior resident agent argued that the state warrant should be placed on hold so that he could contact his supervisor in Portland before he agreed to commit his Medford-based team of FBI agents to provide backup for the search of a federal laboratory run, at least in theory, by the National Security Agency—who, as he put it, with barely restrained sarcasm, were probably going to object to the search in a manner that would cause a significant number of bureaucrats and politicians back in Washington, DC, to void their bladders.

Major Alice Hightower wanted the feds out of the picture completely, or at least standing back on the sidelines, when the warrant was served on the Waycross Center. But she also insisted that she had to contact the chief of the Oregon State Patrol in Salem before she could possibly allow a team of Oregon State troopers to forcibly search a federal laboratory supposedly protected by teams of NSA agents and Delta Forces troops thoroughly trained in counterterrorism tactics and armed to the teeth.

Captain Don Talbert, who, as Bauer had suggested, turned out to be in much better physical condition than he'd let on, was reminding Hightower—in an extremely forceful and arguably disrespectful manner—that the murder of an Oregon University employee on Oregon University property, and the possibly linked traffic death of an Oregon State trooper, were very clearly the concern of the state of Oregon, regardless of who might be leasing what. And that the state of Oregon, and the county of Jasper, had already lost too many good officers and citizens to allow the identified suspects to slip out of town in the middle of the night. And that the reason the judge had signed an extremely rare nighttime warrant was exactly because those same suspects could easily be long gone—and even out of the country—by the time everyone managed to sort out the jurisdictional complexities. And that, as of six hours earlier, the command of OSP Region 9 had been officially turned over to him by that very same OSP chief, along with the official rank of captain, which meant the good Major Hightower ought to be keeping her nose in her own business . . . which, presumably, had a lot more to do with crooked or corrupt cops than homicide suspects of questionable allegiance or origin.

Serve the warrant, take anybody who resists into custody, and let the administrators and the courts sort it all out later, Talbert argued in an amazingly forceful voice for a man whose condition, not three days earlier, had been listed as guarded. As he did so, he ignored the supportive hand of acting OSP watch commander Tom Bauer, who looked perfectly ready to arrest the first man or woman who tried to lay a hand on Talbert. And there was no real indication that Bauer considered the commander of OSP's Internal Affairs Division exempt from such an action.

US Fish and Wildlife Special Agent Wilbur Boggs, who had been invited to the meeting because of a number of wildlife issues possibly relating to the suspicious death of wildlife forensic scientist Melissa Washington, listened politely for about fifteen minutes, then motioned for Bauer to follow him out the door.

Gradually, the high-powered members of the group worked their way out to the judge's outer office, Talbert found a comfortable chair, the three additional phones were quickly put to use, and the argument continued unabated.

As a result, Colin Cellars was left sitting by himself in Judge David W. MacMullen's richly appointed office, lost in his thoughts, as the bemused judge toggled the speaker phone on his desk, directed his secretary to go home, then stood up, walked over to a solid mahogany coat tree, and retrieved his overcoat.

Cellars was still lost in his thoughts, wondering—among other things—if Bobby Dawson was still alive and how many of the Elmer Fudd creatures might have survived his heroic diversionary tactics, when he felt a hand on his shoulder.

He looked up into the elderly jurist's twinkling eyes, and realized that MacMullen was holding a thick cream-colored envelope in his other hand.

It was the warrant.

"I got up out of a warm bed to drive down here and sign this damned thing," he said in a quiet, husky voice. "Do you people want it or don't you?"

"I definitely want it," Cellars replied.

"Good. Glad to hear someone does."

Cellars started to say something, but MacMullen waved him off.

"Don't tell me anything I don't want to hear," the crusty judge advised. "Just grab your jacket and follow me."

Cellars followed MacMullen through a concealed door—located behind his ornate rosewood desk, and to the left of a beautiful matching set of bookcases and credenza—that led to the rear parking lot where Special Agent Wilbur Boggs of the US Fish and Wildlife Service and Acting Watch Commander Tom Bauer were waiting.

It was over an hour later before anyone in the outer offices realized they were gone.

CHAPTER FORTY-EIGHT

THE NIGHT-VISION CAMERAS MOUNTED ON CONCRETE POSTS, AND the sensors buried at half-mile increments along Sensabaugh Road did their job, so the muscular young man in the guardhouse wasn't the least bit surprised to see an expensively civilianized Humvee pull to a stop in front of the visitors' gate.

He was, however, very surprised to see the OSP badge . . . and the warrant.

"Tell them," Cellars said into the speakerphone, "that they've got five minutes. Then I'm coming in."

"Sir," the guard said, "you can't do that. This is federal property, and a restricted area."

"Tell them five minutes, then I'm coming in," Cellars repeated. "With the US Fish and Wildlife Service . . . and the FBI, if necessary."

That got the guard's attention.

Four minutes later, Special Agent Arkaminus Gregorias stormed out of the building and into the visitors' parking lot. There, he found Cellars, Bauer, and Boggs leaning against the camouflaged Humvee.

"What the hell is this?" Gregorias demanded as he almost charged into Cellars and ripped the warrant out of his hand.

"It's a search warrant," Cellars pointed out helpfully.

"But it's a state search warrant," the security chief spit as he quickly scanned the first page, then snapped his head back up, his dark eyes glaring. "This is federal property. You don't have jurisdiction."

"Yes, actually, we do," Wilbur Boggs interrupted.

"And who the hell are you?" Gregorias demanded, whirling around to glare at the federal wildlife agent, who was at least as tall as Gregorias, with perhaps an extra twenty-five pounds around the arms, shoulders, and gut.

"Agent Boggs is a Special Agent for the US Fish and Wildlife Service," Cellars explained calmly. "And, as I understand it, he was once a member of the Secret Service's Presidential Protection Team before finding a much more peaceful way of making a living. So I'm sure he's intimately familiar with all of the federal rules and regulations that might apply here."

"Such as the Endangered Species Act," Special Agent Wilbur Boggs said with a cheerful smile. "Which specifically prohibits the importation and/or containment of an invasive species without a federal permit. Which you folks here don't have," he added. "I checked."

Arkaminus Gregorias blinked.

"A what?"

"Invasive species. Something that doesn't belong here, has no natural enemies, and therefore may be extremely dangerous to the local environment or inhabitants therein," Boggs explained patiently.

"Which, I believe, includes eggs, larvae, cysts, and other reproductive or dormant forms of the species which could be brought to life under the proper conditions," Cellars added. "And which are specifically included, under a special rule, that allows agents of the US Fish and Wildlife Service to enter private, state, and federal land without a warrant if they have reason to believe that an invasive species is about to be accidentally or deliberately released into the local environment."

"Absolutely correct." Boggs nodded. "Which, as I understand it, is exactly what we're dealing with here."

Special Agent in Charge Arkaminus Gregorias erupted. "Listen to me, you goddamned, bunny-hugging asshole," he snarled as he grabbed Boggs by the front of his jacket collar. "You are not going to—"

Gregorias suddenly found his wrist encased in a scarred, callused, muscular hand.

"And that," Boggs replied, "is definitely assault on a federal officer while in performance of his official duties . . . which means you're under arrest. You have the right—"

The security chief attempted to wrench himself away from the wrist lock . . . then screamed in agony as the sound of his wrist bones crunching together echoed across the visitors' parking lot.

The security guard started for his holstered pistol, much too late, then hesitated when he found himself staring into the barrel of a .40-caliber SIG-Sauer pistol held in the steady hands of OSP Sergeant Tom Bauer.

"Don't," Bauer said, and the security guard complied, watching with widened eyes while Boggs finished reading the sprawled and wrist-locked Waycross security chief his rights, snapped a pair of handcuffs around his broken and unbroken wrists, and then covered his mouth with a strip of duct tape from a roll he took from his jacket pocket. Boggs then used several loops and twists of sticky tape to fashion a temporary set of leg restraints designed to restrict Gregorias's movements to short, jerky steps.

"I love this stuff," Boggs said as he slipped the tape roll back into his jacket pocket and leveraged the struggling security chief to his feet. "Makes for a more pleasant search and transport, especially when your subject starts getting mouthy *and* twitchy."

"Now," Cellars said, turning back to the young security guard, "before this entire situation gets completely out of control and somebody gets seriously hurt, I want you to open that door and let us in." He nodded his head in the direction of the visitors' entrance.

"I . . . I can't."

"Yes, you can," Cellars said reassuringly. "In fact, you have to. That's what the warrant says, in very specific terms."

"Yes, sir, I understand that," the security guard said as he continued to stare at Gregorias with an incredulous look on his face. "And I can take you in through the first door, no problem. But the entire facility's in a code-red lock-down situation right now, which means if I try to take you in through the second door without the proper badges and scanner labels, the automated security system will tag you. And there's nothing I can do to stop it."

"By 'tag,' you probably mean kill or severely injure us, and anybody else who's foolish enough to be standing in our near vicinity?" Cellars guessed.

The young security officer nodded unenthusiastically.

"In that case," Cellars suggested, "why don't you and I go back into that concrete bunker you call a guard shack and get Deputy Director Malcolm Byzor on the horn? I think he might be very interested in what I have to say."

CHAPTER FORTY-NINE

"INVASIVE SPECIES . . . AND MURDER?"

Malcolm Byzor stared down at the warrant, then back up at Cellars. They were sitting in Byzor's office, on the second floor of the Waycross Laser Research Center: Byzor, Cellars, Bauer, Boggs, and the still-secured and now nearly apoplectic Gregorias. Bernard Lackman, the Center's project director, was standing outside Byzor's office door, looking as if he was about ready to bolt for the parking lot—and the nearest airport—at any second.

"Actually, that warrant is only for murder," Cellars corrected. "We added the invasive species bit for your security chief's sake. It occurred to us that he might not be all that impressed by the signature of a state circuit court judge."

"The invasive species violation being a federal charge, which we would normally handle ourselves, and not ask to be included in a state warrant," the federal wildlife agent added helpfully.

"But which the OSP would certainly be happy to include, if he asked politely," Bauer pointed out.

"At the risk of sounding completely ignorant of state and federal laws, which I mostly am, do you guys really know where you're going with all this?" Byzor asked, directing his question at Cellars.

"I know we've got the body of an apparent murder victim," Cellars replied. "A victim who couldn't possibly have been killed in the multi-vehicle accident where he and his car were dumped, because you and I smacked into him an hour and a half later, and knocked out one of his headlights. Looked to me like somebody just rolled his car over with a forklift, stuffed him in the back, set the interior on fire with some gaso-line, let it burn a while to cover up some interesting injuries, and then put it out with a bunch of fire extinguishers. That would probably ex-plain why we found the gas tank intact, as opposed to being ruptured, like you might expect in your average car fire with accelerant residues soaked in all the little cubbyholes."

"No shit?"

"None whatsoever," Cellars replied.

For a brief moment, Malcolm Byzor actually smiled.

How can he possibly find this amusing? Cellars wondered, still amazed at the degree of control his friend was able to maintain . . . over himself and over the mix of incredibly high-tech scientists and lethal support staff wandering around the Waycross facility. A flash of pain had crossed Malcolm Byzor's eyes when Cellars briefly described the traffic-accident deaths of Jack Wilson and Melissa Washington, and the deep series of parallel grooves Sutta had found on the frontal and temporal surfaces of Eric Marston's skull. But other than that one revealing moment, the deputy director's expression remained impassive.

Who are you, Malcolm? Or, more to the point, what the hell have you become?

Byzor turned his head to stare contemplatively at his secured and still visibly infuriated security chief. "I thought we'd hired better than that."

"I take it he's also the one who came up with all this code-red nonsense?" Cellars asked.

"I'm afraid so." Byzor's cold, calm eyes were still fixed on Gregorias.

"That was probably your clue," Cellars commented dryly. "If nothing else, the man is seriously lacking when it comes to imagination."

"Point taken." Byzor broke off his silent assessment of his security chief and turned his attention back to Cellars, Bauer, and Boggs. "I assume this means he's under arrest?"

"That's right."

The security chief's eyes bulged as he struggled—with little apparent effect—against Boggs's restraining hand.

"Which, I suppose, goes for Lackman, too," Byzor said quietly as he turned in his chair to stare out his office doorway. The portly bureaucrat was hurriedly moving toward the distant elevator, his face ashen. Another brief smile crossed Byzor's face as the elevator door opened, and three members of the Waycross Center's Eighth Delta Forces Detachment stepped into the outer office area with assault rifles at the ready, causing Lackman to freeze. "As long as you're arresting people, you might as well toss him into the pile, too."

"Why would we do that?" Bauer asked.

"We had an accident here a few hours ago. One of our employees was killed. A Dr. Eric Marston. We're not sure how or why yet, but we're starting to develop some rather interesting theories on the subject. In any case, he died, probably as a result of his own clever manipulations of our security system. Our security chief and our project director both came to the brilliant conclusion that the presence of a dead scientist might be difficult to explain. So they decided to make Marston's death appear to be part of an off-site accident. Unfortunately, for everyone concerned, they seem to have chosen the wrong accident."

"Are you suggesting things might have worked out a lot better for the NSA if your security chief and project director had been more adept at committing felonies?" Cellars asked.

"Yes, as a matter of fact, I am," Malcolm Byzor said with a sigh. "In their ineptitude, Gregor and Lackman managed to make things far more complicated than they already were. And that's something we really can't afford right now."

"That's an interesting word, 'complicated,' " Boggs said quietly. His dark eyes were fixed on Byzor as he continued to assess the deputy director's relaxed demeanor. Boggs had already made a similar assessment of the three SWAT-equipped dark figures who had stopped just outside the elevator, and were now conversing with the young security guard whom Cellars, Bauer, and Boggs had earlier taken into custody and then released.

"Yes, it is," Byzor agreed.

"You're the deputy director of this place, which presumably means you're in a position of authority," Bauer said, his eyes briefly flickering toward the three black-clad figures who were still conversing with the security guard. Like Boggs, the calm, professional demeanor of Byzor and the SWAT-like assault troops was beginning to make him uneasy. "So what's your involvement in all this?"

"I became aware of the fact that Marston was dead and Gregor had done something with his body when I arrived here a few hours ago," Byzor replied evenly. "And I haven't reported that second part to my superiors in the Washington office. Or, at least, not yet. That would, I suppose, make me some kind of coconspirator. I'll be happy to make that statement in a formal deposition, if that's what you want."

"If you don't mind my saying so, Dr. Byzor, you don't seem overly concerned by your Agency's involvement in all of this, not to mention your own possible complicity," Bauer commented. "You do realize that the illegal disposition of a human body—even if you didn't actually kill the fellow—is a serious charge . . . and that your buddy, Colin, here, really can't do much to help you?"

"I understand the seriousness of the charges," Byzor acknowledged, "and I certainly don't expect Colin to misuse his authority on my behalf. In fact, I'd be very amazed—even appalled—if he did." Byzor then looked up again as the three black-garbed figures began walking toward his office with assault rifles at the ready. "Excuse me for just a moment, please."

Byzor reached for the search warrant, got up out of his chair, and walked over to the doorway.

"Everything's under control here, Mike," Byzor said as he handed the warrant to the Delta Forces Detachment commander. "These people are federal and state officers. Detective-Sergeant Colin Cellars, Sergeant Tom Bauer, and Special Agent Wilbur Boggs. They'll be serving a legitimate search warrant relating to the death of Dr. Marston, and possible illegal actions taken by Mr. Lackman and Special Agent Gregorias. Accordingly, I'm assuming full command of the Center until we can get an inspection team out from the Washington office to assess the matter fully."

"Gentlemen," Byzor briefly turned to Cellars, Bauer, and Boggs, "this is Captain Mike Montgomery, commander of the Eighth Delta Forces Detachment. He and his troops are temporarily assigned to security duties at the Waycross Center."

Montgomery's steely eyes shifted from Cellars to Bauer and Boggs . . . and seemed to pause on the federal wildlife agent for a couple additional beats. Then he turned his attention to the warrant, examined it briefly, and handed it back to Byzor with a quick, "Yes, sir."

"Once these officers begin their search," Byzor went on, shifting his attention back to the Delta Forces captain, "I want you and the entire security section to assist them in any way possible, within the scope of the warrant. But, in the meantime, I want you to place Mr. Lackman and Mr. Gregorias in protective custody before they do something even more stupid, and get themselves hurt. And, while you're doing that, I also want you to assume command of the entire security detail and make certain we're still locked down in a code-red status. Is all of that perfectly clear?"

The black-garbed figure nodded sharply. "Yes, sir. Right away, sir."

The detachment commander motioned with his gloved hand, and Byzor stepped aside to allow the other two Delta Forces troopers—a first sergeant and a staff sergeant, according to the barely visible black emblems on their collars—to come into his office and remove the handcuffed, furious, and still-struggling security chief.

" 'Yes sir? Right away, sir?' And Delta Forces troops running around as security guards?" Cellars whispered in disbelief as he and Bauer and Boggs watched the three black-garbed troopers escort the two struggling ex–NSA managers into the elevator. "Why do I get the feeling I'm drifting around in some kind of dream world?"

"A simple matter of command presence, Colin," Byzor said. "An incredibly powerful tool, once you learn to use it properly."

"Something your project director has no understanding of at all," Wilbur Boggs noted.

"No, he hasn't," Byzor agreed. "Oh, and by the way, regarding Mike's detachment, you really shouldn't call them security guards. They'd feel a bit insulted."

"Then what do they do here?" Cellars asked.

"Within this facility, Mike oversees the activities of a seven-man fire team whose primary responsibility is to make entries—searches, if you will—of our secured areas in the event of an attempted break-in. They're extremely well trained, as you might expect; which, among other things, significantly reduces the possibility of some innocent individual being hurt or killed. By the way, they're the ones who went into the main containment area and found Marston," he added helpfully.

"Ah," Cellars replied, still feeling confused.

"Which brings up a relevant question, Dr. Byzor," Boggs went on in his deceptively casual voice. "Are the people in this facility—and I'm specifically referring to these Delta Forces troopers—really under your control? I ask that only because, one, I'd really hate to see a fellow like Special Agent Gregorias regain control over those troopers and their weapons; and, two, it's been my experience that—with the exception of MPs—military men tend to be very reluctant to take a superior into custody, even if they are civilians. Yet, you just ordered that Captain Montgomery to arrest the security chief of this facility, along with the director—your boss—based on your authority alone, because neither of those individuals is named in our warrant. At the very least, I would expect Montgomery to try to contact his military superior and ask what the hell he's supposed to do in such a situation."

"A very relevant question," Byzor agreed. "First of all, let me assure you that Captain Montgomery is an extremely disciplined and professional officer. And, secondly, as unlikely as it may seem, at least to one person in this room"—Byzor glanced at Cellars and shrugged apologetically—"I am his military superior. As it happens, I hold the rank of lieutenant colonel in the United States Army."

"What?" Colin Cellars blurted, but Byzor continued on.

"Accordingly, I can assure all of you that Special Agent Gregorias and Mr. Lackman will be held in very restrictive custody until you're ready to transport them out of here. But, to answer your earlier question more directly, Agent Boggs, may I ask you if you're familiar with the terms 'black operation' or 'black project'?"

Wilbur Boggs nodded slowly.

"Then if I were to tell you that the Waycross Laser Research Center is a White House–authorized black project—?"

Boggs blinked . . . first, in shock, then in apparent understanding.

"What's he talking about?" Cellars demanded.

"The manager of a black project, and/or his deputy, is fully and completely authorized to take whatever means are necessary to maintain the security and confidential nature of the project . . . up to and specifically including the use of any and all necessary lethal force," Boggs recited as if by rote, his probing eyes still fixed on Byzor. "The authority is absolute, and does not require prior confirmation by a higher authority. The check on the system is a thorough assessment of the situation by higher authorities after everything calms down," the Special Agent added dryly.

"Can you imagine the White House giving such power—not to mention direct supervisory control over a fifteen-man Delta Forces Detachment—to an idiot like Lackman?" Byzor asked quietly.

"No, sir, I can't," Boggs replied. "But I can imagine that someone like you would be given an authorization code."

"White Knight, Charlie-Alpha-Tango," Byzor said with a half smile. "Lack of imagination seems to be endemic within our organization. And, of course, there's another code series which I may be required to provide over a secure phone, if an outside query is made," he added, almost as an afterthought.

"Do you have a phone with an outside line that I could use?" Boggs asked.

"Certainly. Any of the beige phones out there." Byzor gestured in the direction of the outer office. "Area code and number."

"Are they monitored?"

"Yes, of course."

"I'll be right back," Boggs said as he stood up and strode out the door.

Colin Cellars turned to his longtime friend. "Lieutenant colonel?"

Byzor nodded.

"Tell me it's an honorary title . . . something to wave at the guards when you're traveling around God-knows-where doing God-knows-what."

"No, actually, I went through all the requisite ticket punching," Byzor replied, looking mildly embarrassed. "Kind of a parallel-track career thing."

"Including combat?"

"In a manner of speaking. I don't actually leap over walls with sword in hand. Or at least I try not to."

"Where?"

Byzor shrugged. "Kuwait. Iraq. Somalia. Places like that."

Cellars blinked, incredulous. "Does Yvie know about all this?"

Byzor nodded his head. "One of the hazards of marrying a computer geek with delusions of grandeur. But, look at it this way, at least now you know why I have some familiarity with Humvees and Bradleys."

"If not simple arithmetic," Cellars responded. "What's with this fifteen-man Delta Forces Detachment business? I thought you said a seven-man fire team supervised by the captain?"

"Actually, the detachment is made up of two six-man fire teams, each under the command of a first lieutenant. One team guards the facility, one guards Yvie and me, and Mike—that is, Captain Montgomery—keeps a general eye on things."

"You mean those guys I saw outside your house—?"

"No. Those were Gregor's men."

"But—?"

"Sorry to play games with you, Colin, but I got the distinct impression you were starting to worry about me . . . and Yvie," Byzor said softly. "Appreciated the concern, but I really didn't want you to start snooping around my neighborhood. Too many added complications. So I had Gregor put a few of his men out there for effect. I doubt very seriously that you would have seen anyone from Mike's detachment. They tend to be a little more covert and professional about that sort of thing."

"Oh."

"Was Lackman aware of your assigned authority . . . and rank?" Bauer asked.

"Only in the vaguest sense," Byzor replied, turning his attention to the plainclothes patrol sergeant. "As far as I'm aware, it was never actually spelled out for him. Probably just as well. The added stress would have been a little much for a guy like that. Probably given him an ulcer."

"Then what, exactly, was his authority around here . . . as the project director?" Bauer pressed.

"Director Lackman's job was to deal with the university, the politicians, the media, the vendors, the personnel issues, and the Agency administrators," Byzor answered, "leaving me free to do my job . . . which was, and still is, to press forward with the project as rapidly and carefully as I can."

"Then he was just a front . . . like Gregor's men cruising around your house," Cellars said.

"In essence, yes."

"What about Gregor?"

"He was fully aware of my authority under the black-project rules," Byzor said. "That was essential, since he also functioned as the primary check on the system."

"An individual capable of surviving at least long enough to report in, if you suddenly went nuts?" Bauer suggested. "As, from his perspective, you may have done just now?"

"Yes, exactly." Byzor nodded. "As I said, added complications."

Boggs walked back into the room. "It's a legitimate code, and the

White House is aware of the general situation," he said, then sat back down in his chair.

"And they're not concerned?" Bauer asked, incredulous.

"Apparently not."

Colin Cellars just stared at his friend, shaking his head in amazement.

"So, in further response to your question, Agent Boggs," Byzor went on as if nothing of any particular importance had just happened, "yes, Mike and his men are very definitely under my control. And yes, they will carry out any lawful order I give them . . . which, as I suppose you've already surmised, could include taking the three of you into protective custody as well. But, I can assure you, I have absolutely no intention of issuing such an order, now or in the future."

"Damned good thing," Wilbur Boggs commented dryly.

"You're probably right about that, for everyone involved." Byzor nodded reflectively, then hesitated again before continuing. "But rather than dwelling on such depressing concerns, let me finish answering all of your questions." He turned back to Bauer. "You suggested that I didn't seem very concerned about the events going on around here. In point of fact, I'm very concerned; but perhaps not about the events you're thinking of."

Bauer looked like he was about to ask something else, but Byzor held up his hand. "Rather than try to explain it all, here in my office," he said as he stood up, "why don't you let me show you."

CHAPTER FIFTY

MALCOLM BYZOR LED CELLARS, BAUER, AND BOGGS THROUGH A SE-
ries of corridor turns until they found themselves in what Byzor described as the Waycross Center's VIP viewing room.

The room itself was hexagonal, each of the six sides approximately
twenty-five feet in length and height. Upon entering, the first thing a
VIP visitor saw was four opaque blue, wall-to-wall windows, three
smaller ones to the left and one to the right, which was separated from
the others by a solid wall. The left sidewall windows were each ten feet
high and twenty-five feet wide. The window to the right of the doorway
went from wall to wall and floor to ceiling—in effect, a twenty-five-
foot-square piece of opaque blue glass.

Immediately to the left of the doorway was a pair of designated-sex rest-room doors. The floor was thickly and expensively carpeted in a light blue-gray pattern. There were a dozen plush rotating chairs in the middle of the room, arranged in two semicircular rows, facing the huge right sidewall window.

Across the room to the right was a grid of sixteen thirty-six-inch monitors arranged around a central sixty-inch monitor that covered the right side portion of the solid wall. A wooden podium stood between the monitors and the huge main window.

To the left, two black-garbed men stood in a parade-rest position.

"Gentlemen, this is Lieutenant Kessler and Staff Sergeant Dombrowski," Byzor said, introducing the pair of Delta Forces commandos who stood solemnly with their backs against the wall, wearing armored vests and shoulder-holstered 9mm Beretta semiautomatic pistols, but no helmets, gloves, or assault rifles. "They are, as you have probably already guessed, members of Captain Montgomery's detachment . . . and Lieutenant Kessler is one of the fire team leaders. I've asked them to see to your needs while I excuse myself for a moment. I need to verify that everything's ready for our little demonstration."

"What are they gonna do, make sure we don't hurt ourselves taking a piss?" Boggs inquired as he eyed the young, clean-cut soldiers.

"Or burn yourselves with the coffee." Malcolm Byzor grinned, and gestured with his head at a nearby table containing a coffee urn, mugs, and plate of cookies.

"You are coming back, I assume? I mean, we're not going to have to go out looking for you, are we?" Cellars cocked his head curiously, searching for any sign of malicious amusement in the seemingly relaxed expression of his longtime friend. Malcolm Byzor had been a master of the intricately staged practical joke when they were in school together, and the memories of the ease with which he and Bobby Dawson had been sucked in, time after time, made him vaguely uneasy.

"Oh, I'll be back." Byzor smiled. "Believe me, I wouldn't miss this for anything in the world."

Cellars, Bauer, and Boggs looked at each other, shrugged, waited until Byzor closed the door, looked around the curiously designed room for a few seconds, then walked over to the coffeepot. They ignored the two black-garbed soldiers.

"I thought Talbert looked pretty frisky at the judge's office this evening," Cellars commented as he set one of the mugs under the coffee urn tap, "especially for a guy who was supposedly at death's door earlier this morning. Or was that another one of my ongoing delusions?"

"That was Talbert's idea," Bauer said. "I think he wanted to see what Major Hightower had to say before he was a little more forthcoming about his own rate of progress."

"Basically, a covert intelligence-gathering operation."

"Exactly."

"Clever man, our Captain Talbert." Cellars nodded as he stepped back out of the way to let Bauer at the coffee urn. "Which, I suppose, might also explain how my CSI reports managed to walk out of what's supposed to be a reasonably well guarded OSP records room."

"Damn," Bauer muttered as he set his mug under the coffee urn tap.

"What's the matter?"

"I bet Talbert twenty bucks you wouldn't put that last part together for at least another twenty-four hours."

"What, that he had you pull my CSI reports and put that faked DUI report and complaint in its place?"

"That's right."

"You going to tell me why?"

"Sure." Bauer shrugged agreeably. "Talbert absolutely did not want Hightower—or anyone else in Salem, for that matter—reading that original report you filed. He figured if she did, she'd have put you on administrative leave for the rest of your career . . . or at least until she got you booted on a psycho fitness evaluation. Which, I'm sure, based on the way she reacted when Dr. Pleasant gave us his evaluation of your sanity and stability, was exactly what she had in mind. And that was going to be a problem, as far as Talbert was concerned, because he wanted you back out in the field where he could keep you digging at the evidence . . . but he couldn't argue too strenuously, because then they'd probably start worrying about him, too. I might add, however, that I was the one who came up with the DEA agent discrimination-complaint twist. Figured that was the kind of thing that would really get her attention," Bauer added as he stepped back out of the way to let Boggs at the coffee.

"Like a starving bat locked on to a nice, fat, and completely oblivious bug," Cellars commented.

"Exactly."

"Wonderful." Cellars sipped at the hot coffee.

"Shit!"

Cellars and Bauer turned to stare at Boggs.

"What's the matter with you?" Bauer demanded.

"Burned myself on the fucking coffee," Boggs muttered. He held the coffee cup in his deeply scarred left hand as he shook his equally scarred right hand in the air.

Cellars glanced over at their black-garbed baby-sitters.

"Thought you guys were supposed to be watching out for that sort of thing," he commented dryly.

"Yes, sir," Kessler agreed with what Cellars thought was an amazingly straight face, all things considered. "We'll be happy to help the Special Agent—"

"First one of you touches this mug goes through a window," Boggs warned as he finished pouring his coffee.

"Yes, sir," Kessler replied cheerfully.

Cellars and Bauer had already set themselves down in nearby chairs. Boggs started to sip at the warming brew, then seemed to consider the soldiers.

"Either of you guys ever drink coffee?" Boggs inquired.

"Yes, sir," Lieutenant Kessler responded.

"Then why don't you pull those MP sticks out of your butts, pour yourselves a cup, and sit down over here so we can start pumping you for information about this place?"

Ten minutes later, Lieutenant Kessler and Staff Sergeant Dombrowski were sprawled in a pair of chairs casually explaining why they—and the rest of the Delta Forces Detachment, apparently—thought Lackman was a typically incompetent ass-kisser with shit for brains; why Gregorias was considered tough and competent, for a Special Forces type, but poorly controlled and fatally arrogant; and why Byzor was viewed as pretty damned tough, aggressive, knowledgeable, and confident . . . especially for an egghead scientist who had earned the right to wear a pair of silver oak leaves and a CIB.

"Man's definitely a tactician and a leader," Kessler said. "Don't know that I'd necessarily want him leading one of our teams in through a door, even if he did earn that Combat Infantryman's Badge the hard way. But—"

"What do you mean 'the hard way'?" Cellars interrupted.

"A purple heart and a silver star, for dragging a wounded medic away from a firefight. Definitely ain't the easy way," Kessler pointed out.

"Oh."

"Should have sent one of his grunts in instead, so he loses points as a team leader," Kessler went on. "But, hey, you give him two or three of those fire teams, an objective, and a map . . . I'm telling you, the man would kick serious ass."

"Damned straight," Staff Sergeant Dombrowski agreed.

"So, what else do you want to know?" Kessler asked.

"Whole bunch of things," Boggs said. "But before we get to all that, what about you guys? Anything you want to ask us?"

"Yes, sir." Staff Sergeant Dombrowski nodded. "What does a guy have to do to be a federal wildlife agent these days?"

CHAPTER FIFTY-ONE

WHEN MALCOLM BYZOR FINALLY CAME BACK INTO THE ROOM, LIEU-
tenant Kessler and Staff Sergeant Dombrowski lunged out of their
chairs and into a parade-rest position . . . an action that caused Byzor to
pause in the doorway and glare briefly at the two soldiers before rolling
his eyes skyward.

"I see I got back here just in time," he commented as he pulled the
door shut, causing the lock mechanisms to engage with a solid double
click.

"Actually, you're a little late," Cellars said. "We've already corrupted
them."

Byzor glanced down at his wristwatch.

"Great. Seven years to turn these guys into the ISO standard for

Kevlar-coated killing machines, and roughly seventeen minutes to find and exploit a chink in that armor. Mind if I ask how you did it?"

Wilbur Boggs reached into his shirt pocket, pulled out his badge case, and wiggled it in his thick, scarred fingers. "Turns out, with a little work, these two might make a halfway decent pair of federal wildlife agents."

A look of thoughtful and perhaps malicious amusement crossed Malcolm Byzor's face.

"You're actually proposing to turn a couple of fully trained, Delta Forces commandos loose on some extremely wealthy and influential CEO asshole who doesn't think the local hunting laws or the Endangered Species Act apply to him? A man who gets his jollies using a thirty-thousand-dollar rifle to take hundred-yard potshots at a bull elephant from the back of a Range Rover, then keeps on shooting until the poor damned critter finally keels over and bleeds to death?"

"You see something wrong with that?" Boggs inquired.

Byzor seemed to consider the question for several seconds.

"For reasons we really don't need to get into here, the idea has a certain amount of appeal at the moment," he finally said. "But what were you planning on doing to make it fair? Give Dombrowski a pocketknife and the asshole a hundred-yard head start?"

"The asshole can have two hundred yards, the Range Rover, and the rifle, and I'd be happy to pass on the knife . . . uh, sir," Staff Sergeant Dombrowski said hopefully.

For anyone in the room other than Cellars, who knew Malcolm Byzor all too well, it would have been difficult to read the expression that flickered in the deputy director's eyes. But there was no mistaking the approval of Special Agent Boggs.

"Like I said, just a little bit of work, sand down a few rough edges, and they'll do just fine," the wildlife Special Agent chuckled.

Kessler and Dombrowski smiled in agreement.

"Okay, fine." The expression in Byzor's eyes seemed to fade away, at least for the moment. "I'll let you know when I'm done with them. But, in the meantime . . ." He gestured with his head for Kessler and

Dombrowski to move to the back of the room, "we have some serious issues to discuss here . . . and a little test that we all may find instructive."

Byzor walked over to the podium between the bank of monitors and the large viewing window, flipped some switches on the podium console, and waited until all three rows of diode lights on the console glowed green. Then he looked up at Cellars, Bauer, and Boggs.

"As some of you may know by now," he began, "we've been gearing up to conduct a series of laser-based experiments on a collection of small and supposedly inert objects—rocks, if you will—that are suspected of being of extraterrestrial origin. We're doing so because we have reason to believe, thanks to Detective-Sergeant Cellars here, that certain frequencies of blue-green light may have an animating effect on these objects."

"What do you mean by 'animating'?" Boggs asked.

"Hit them with a blue-green laser, and the damned rocks move," Cellars translated.

"No shit," Boggs said. "You mean hopping around like Mexican jumping beans?"

Cellars shook his head. "No, actually, more like a smooth stone sliding on wet ice, only without a push."

"Damn."

Wilbur Boggs glanced over at Bauer, who shrugged his shoulders as if to say "Don't ask me."

"Apart from the movement issue, which, I would emphasize, we have not confirmed yet," Byzor continued, glaring at Cellars, "there are a couple of significant issues here. First, and perhaps most significant of all"—Byzor paused to look around the room—"we have reason to believe these rocks may actually be inanimate forms of extraterrestrial life. Or, to put it more accurately, inanimate states of some very aggressive forms of extraterrestrial life."

"Fucking monsters that can read your mind, and change their shape to look exactly like any one of us, anytime they want," Cellars added helpfully.

Wilbur Boggs's right eyebrow rose as he turned his head slowly to stare at Cellars.

"And if that truly is the case," Byzor went on patiently, "which I again emphasize, we haven't proven yet, then you understand why we have to be extremely careful . . . and thoughtful . . . before we make any attempt to replicate Colin's, uh, laser experiments."

"So you haven't tried any of your lasers on the stones yet?" Cellars asked.

Byzor shook his head. "We were still working on the last stages of the containment issue when Dr. Marston caused a disruption in our schedule."

"Thank God," Cellars replied.

"Why do you say that?" Wilbur Boggs asked, managing to look confused and vaguely uneasy all at the same time.

"Because the idea of these things coming alive again—especially Allesandra—scares the shit out of me, no matter how well they're contained."

"Allesandra?"

"It's a long story," Cellars replied. "Suffice it to say that Dawson and I got to know her on an intimate basis."

"*That* exact a mimic?" Both of Wilbur Boggs's eyebrows rose this time.

Cellars nodded grimly.

"Was this before or after you zapped her with a laser?" the wildlife agent asked after a long moment.

"If I told you she was—or is—a different stone than the one that moved inside the evidence envelope, then you'd probably start worrying about my sanity," Cellars suggested with a half smile.

"Not exactly," Boggs replied, his dark eyes fixed on Cellars. "I'm long past the 'start' part."

"Colin, maybe this is a good time for you to explain to everyone here exactly what happened at Dawson's cabin," Byzor suggested.

Cellars quickly described how he'd responded to a supposed homicide scene call-out at Bobby Dawson's cabin, accidentally damaged his primary and backup cameras, and then tried to use Byzor's experimental crime scene scanning system—which was based around an assembled array of blue-green scanning lasers and sensors—to create a three-dimensional image of the interior of the cabin. He went on to explain how he'd run out of battery power at the very start of the first scan, and had to abort the run after the first few seconds . . . and how the resulting full-density image from the second scan, successfully completed a few minutes later, had been virtually identical to the much-less-dense first scan . . . except for one small stone that was in a different location on the cabin floor.

"I'm a lot more interested in hearing about this Allesandra broad," Boggs said, "but I'm willing to humor you about these stones. Just so I have it clear, you're saying this stone actually moved, on its own, between the two scans? Nobody pushed it or kicked it?"

"I don't know that for a fact," Cellars conceded. "I didn't actually see it move. But I know I didn't move it, because I never entered the cabin between the two scans. And considering the fact that I sealed the doors and windows with evidence tape before going back to my truck to charge the computer batteries, I'm pretty damned sure no one else did either."

Then something occurred to Cellars. *But what about Bobby and his trapdoor?* The trapdoor Bobby Dawson had constructed under the stairs in his cabin leading down to his basement. The trapdoor that Dawson had meticulously designed and constructed to conceal the entrance to an underground cavern where he'd been able to stay hidden from the furiously searching shadows . . . and Cellars.

He could have come up after I went out to the truck, moved that stone, gone back down, and I would have never known about it, Cellars realized. *But why would he possibly want to do something like that?*

"Something wrong, Colin?" Byzor asked.

"No, I was . . . just remembering some of the gory details of the scene," Cellars said, shaking his head. He then went on to describe how—much later that evening and alone in the Region 9 OSP Station's evidence room—he'd been sealing and tagging his evidence, preparing his CSI report, when he'd accidentally triggered one of the crime scene scanner's blue-green lasers . . . and then sat in the chair, stunned and disbelieving, as a sealed manila envelope containing the same stone and some glass fragments slowly moved across the top of the desk.

"You actually saw the envelope move?" Wilbur Boggs pressed.

Cellars nodded firmly. "I can't even begin to tell you how or why, but it definitely moved."

"What about some kind of trick? Somebody playing games with you . . . maybe putting a magnet underneath the table?" Bauer suggested.

Cellars hesitated for a long moment.

"I don't know how anyone could have possibly done that," he finally said. "I was alone at the crime scene when I collected the evidence, and no one at the station knew anything about it. I returned to the station at an essentially random time; in fact, no one knew when, or even if, I was coming in that night. I chose to seal the rock in that envelope, and place it on that particular table, which was just a plain old table—four legs and a Formica top. I accidentally triggered the laser system. And, finally, I know I was alone in that evidence room the entire time all this was taking place."

The room went silent again for a good fifteen seconds, as everyone seemed to digest this new bit of information.

Byzor finally broke the silence.

"I can't verify the envelope incident," he said, "but I can tell you that I personally reviewed the crime scene scanner data. The first scan was pretty faint, but there was no question about the stone being in two different locations on the two scans . . . while everything else in the room remained in the same location."

"Would it have been possible for Colin to have manipulated the data?" Bauer asked.

"I'm a little reluctant to suggest that anything's impossible at this point," Byzor said after a moment, "but I really don't think he could have. First of all, the program was written for a Mac and not a PC . . . and I got the impression that Colin had never used a Mac computer before I loaned him that system."

"Correct," Cellars confirmed.

"Secondly," Byzor went on, "Colin's not a programmer . . . and you'd definitely have to understand the basics of Mac programming to manipulate the data set.

"And finally, as far as I'm aware, I'm the only one who knows exactly how the program compiles the data, applies the algorithms, and resets the pointers. Jason, our chief programmer, might have been able to do something like that if he had the inclination and the time to dig at the underlying code. But I really don't think Colin could have done it . . . especially with all of the other things he had going on at the time."

"Trust me, guys, it was all I could do to turn the damned thing on and recharge the batteries," Cellars said to Bauer and Boggs.

"So if we accept your assurance that Colin, here, isn't sufficiently brainy or geekish to have successfully messed with the Mac-based scanner data, where does that leave us?" Bauer asked.

"Hopefully, with this Allesandra broad. I want to hear more about her," Boggs interjected.

Byzor looked over at Cellars, who shrugged. "I'm not sure where to start with Allesandra," he said, "other than the fact that I first met her at an Alliance of Believers meeting that Dawson set up."

"You mean those fruitcakes who run around claiming they've been abducted by aliens?" Boggs asked.

"Those are the ones." Cellars quickly summarized his unplanned lecture to the Alliance audience, and his progressively confused and intimate contacts with the beautiful Allesandra, finishing with a description of how she'd changed form out in the meadow by Bobby Dawson's cabin . . . how Dawson had tricked her with the old Sharps rifle, and managed to put a .45-70 slug through her head from an improbable distance. And how her body had fallen to the ground . . . in the form of a small stone.

This time, the viewing room was completely silent for a good thirty seconds.

"On the face of things," Byzor finally said to Bauer and Boggs in a soft voice, "I would be the first to acknowledge that very little of what Colin has just told you sounds even remotely plausible. In fact, if I didn't know him as well as I do, I would be very concerned about his mental condition right about now . . . not to mention his sense of humor.

However, you should all be aware there have been other incidents in which an apparent living creature of extraterrestrial origin was hit with a presumably lethal projectile, then simply vanished into thin air, apparently leaving a stone in its place."

"Are we talking military here?" Wilbur Boggs asked.

Malcolm Byzor hesitated. "Yes."

"Which would explain why a place like this exists in the first place," Boggs noted. "You don't just set a White House–approved black project into motion, based on some wild story from three of your childhood friends, and end up with a full-on laser research laboratory like this a couple months later."

"No, you don't," Byzor agreed. "Even in the federal government. In point of fact, we've been working on this project for a little over three years now."

"In Oregon?" Cellars asked.

"Among other places," Byzor replied evasively. "We built a number of essentially identical research facility shells, with the idea that we'd quickly activate and equip the ones closest to a set of statistically interesting events. And, as it turned out—even before Colin and Bobby came into the picture—the correlations here in Jasper County were a little too compelling to ignore."

"You mean the disappearances?" Cellars pressed.

"The recent disappearances in Jasper County certainly fit the profile," Byzor acknowledged, "but there were other similar patterns that first caught our attention. Up to that point, we'd spent three years—and a goodly number of your federal government tax dollars—exploring a lot of fruitless leads and getting nowhere. Ironically, a little over two months ago—and just as we were starting to activate and equip the Waycross facility—a fairly demented DEA Special Agent/pilot buddy of mine named Bobby Dawson crash-landed a very expensive Army helicopter in a national forest, then started making a fuss about being hunted down by shadowy creatures who wanted their evidence back. To carry the irony further, Dawson draws two more of my childhood friends—Detective-Sergeant Colin Cellars and forensic scientist Jody Catlin—into the picture . . . which gets terribly confused when Colin gets called out to work the homicide crime scene at Dawson's cabin, and Jody ends up examining the resulting evidence."

"What evidence?" Patrol Sergeant Tom Bauer demanded. "These stones you've been talking about?"

"That's right. First evidence, albeit of a circumstantial and perhaps even corroborative nature that these extraterrestrial life-forms do exist. And not only exist, but are also capable of protectively deanimating themselves—shifting into some kind of extremely stable form—if taken down with a properly placed bullet."

"So the idea is that you might, somehow, be able to reanimate these stones?" Bauer asked. "Turn them back into the original extraterrestrial life-forms with some kind of laser beam?"

"That's the theory. In point of fact, we have no real idea what will happen if we—"

Wilbur Boggs raised his right hand. "Hold it just a second, Colonel, or deputy project director, or chief scientist, or whatever the hell you are—"

"Malcolm will do just fine," Byzor said calmly.

"Okay, then, Malcolm. Apart from Colin's descriptions of these shadow creatures, and this Allesandra broad—both of which, I suppose, we have to take at face value—and some scanner data that may or may not prove a little stone moved from 'A' to 'B' on its own volition, exactly what proof do you have that any part of what you and Colin have been saying is remotely true?"

"At this point? Nothing at all. In fact, if we were to accept a certain toxicology lab report at face value—a report suggesting that Detective-Sergeant Cellars had a very potent hallucinogenic drug in his bloodstream during the time that all of these events supposedly happened—then none of us would be sitting in this room right now. Fortunately for Colin's reputation, and his story, the chain of custody on his blood sample is more than a little suspect."

"Then what the hell—?"

"—is the federal government doing spending approximately one-point-two billion dollars on this project, you might ask?" Byzor finished.

"One-point-two . . . billion?" Boggs could barely get the word out.

"Yes."

"A billion's serious money," Boggs muttered to Bauer and Cellars. "Even for the fucking federal government."

"Yes, it is," Byzor agreed. "And far too much to spend on some drugged or demented fantasy. But perhaps not nearly enough if the evidence for extraterrestrial life-forms is, in fact, in our custody. Which, we believe, it is."

"The stones?" Boggs persisted.

"Yes."

The room went quiet again.

"What we have in our possession," Byzor went on, "are seven stones . . . which may prove to be inanimate forms of the rather frightening extraterrestrial creatures Colin just described. In fact, we have ample reason to believe that will be the case. But just as significant, or perhaps even more so, we also have reason to believe that a very innovative and aggressive attempt was made, earlier this evening, to steal—or, perhaps, retrieve—these stones."

Cellars felt his blood turn cold.

"By who? Other . . . similar creatures?" Bauer asked in a soft voice.

"Possibly," Byzor replied. "We don't know that for sure . . . yet."

"But—"

Byzor held up his hand. "We don't know for sure because the burglar, if you will, seems to have either escaped or found a hiding place within this facility, and the only person who actually saw him—or her, or it, I suppose—was Dr. Marston."

"Were any of the stones taken?" Cellars whispered.

"No, they're all present, as you can see on the monitors to your left."

Byzor reached over to the podium control panel and pressed one of the raised buttons. Seven of the sixteen smaller monitors on the solid wall to Byzor's right immediately came to life, each displaying what looked like an irregular stone lying on top of a black resinous block.

"And, in case you're wondering," Byzor said as he shifted his index finger over to another button, "this is where we keep them."

The huge twenty-five-foot-by-twenty-five-foot opaque blue window to his left—the window that the two rows of chairs were facing—suddenly turned transparent, revealing a large open laboratory area . . . the floor of which dropped down approximately three feet from the level of the VIP viewing room, and extended out approximately a hundred feet in all directions. The ceiling looked to be at least ten feet higher than that of the viewing room.

The visual effect, Cellars thought, was very much like suddenly finding yourself dangling out the open door of a low-hovering helicopter.

"What you are looking at is our main containment laboratory," Byzor explained. "As you can see, it's filled with a large number of fairly sophisticated scientific instruments, most of which are directly related to our laser research. In the center of the laboratory, you can see a glassed-in stainless-steel cage that is approximately twenty-five feet square and twelve feet high, containing fifteen glassed-in containment jars arrayed in groups of five along the three nonentry walls. Seven of the jars are currently in use. Inside each one of these jars is a small, irregular stone. The size and shape of these stones vary, but each one could easily fit into a box one inch by one inch by three-quarters of an inch deep. With the exception of one stone that's chipped, the weights do not vary significantly."

Byzor paused. "You'll notice that each stone is sitting on what appears to be a black, rubberized resin cube that is four inches on a side and weighs approximately three ounces. The glass itself is a new, very transparent and extremely resilient cross-linked polycarbonate capable of containing a small explosion."

"What do you mean by small?" Cellars asked.

"I'll explain in just a moment," Byzor said. "The containment jars are actually made of two cast pieces, the walls of which are approximately two inches thick. The base has only one access point—a self-sealing, screw-open, stainless-steel nozzle with a maximum opening of a quarter inch—that we can connect to tanks of air, gas, or water as needed."

"In the event you ever do reanimate these things and they need more air?" Cellars guessed.

"That's the idea. The top piece, which is about seven feet tall and four feet in diameter, screws into the base, and compresses against a recessed gasket made of similar but much more flexible material. It requires twelve complete turns to effect an airtight seal. Once sealed, we've determined that the containment jars and the base nozzle can contain the radio detonation of a two-ounce chunk of C-Four without so much as even cracking."

"No shit?" Boggs whispered.

"Which, I assume, explains the three-ounce resinous cubes the stones are mounted on," Cellars said. "What are we talking about, two ounces of C-Four and one ounce of remote-controlled detonator?"

"Exactly." Byzor nodded approvingly. "You'll notice there's a small remote Velcroed to the outside of each containment jar. The remotes are individually programmed for their specific detonators, and require the resetting of three separate safety switches before the recessed button will set off the charge."

"In the event all else fails . . . ?" Cellars raised an eyebrow.

"We will blow the damned stones into so much powder," Byzor said emphatically.

"On your authority?"

"That's right."

"I'm glad to hear that."

"And," Byzor continued on, "we've also made a transport version of the containment jars—each of which is roughly sixteen inches long and six inches in diameter, with one-inch-thick walls, but no external nozzle in the base—which has been successfully tested with a radio-detonated one-ounce charge. The only problems being that, one, the base gaskets and nozzles on the large jars do leak slightly, which is a little bit unnerving; and two, if you conduct such an experiment with a one- or two-ounce charge, you end up with a polycarbonate tank of extremely compressed gas that you really don't want to have sitting around a laboratory."

"So how do you open it, then, after you've detonated the charge?" Cellars asked. "I take it you don't just screw open the nozzle?"

"Not unless you want to set loose one hell of a fast and uncontrolled missile," Byzor agreed.

"So?"

"We conducted the explosive testing at Fort Irwin, from inside a Bradley . . . and used the twenty-five-millimeter cannon for the 'disarming' process," Byzor said. "The effects were interesting. For example, you definitely don't want to be standing outside the Bradley when the jar ruptures. They had to repaint the one we were using."

"Ah."

"The polycarbonate walls of the larger containment chamber are approximately three inches thick, and are mounted in a stainless-steel box frame, the walls of which are six inches thick," Byzor went on. "The polycarbonate wall seals, and the seal on the one entrance door, are made with a similar gasketing material. In essence, we feel extremely confident that we can contain any 'reanimation' of the stones . . . either inside the smaller chambers, or, if necessary, inside the larger chamber."

Byzor paused for a moment, then pointed through the large window at the containment lab's ceiling.

"The two pods hanging out of the ceiling are called battle cabs. They're mounted overhead and on opposite sides of the room to provide a total monitoring and control system for the main containment laboratory. The pods are comprised of three-inch-thick armored steel— same specs as for our main battle tanks—and three-inch-thick poly-carbonate glass panes. Entry and exit are through the armored steel tubes leading up to the ceiling. And, for obvious reasons, we've made certain there's no possible access to the battle cabs from inside the containment laboratory.

"You will also note a pair of twenty-five-millimeter cannons and a seven-point-six-five-millimeter machine gun mounted to the underside of each of the two battle cabs," Byzor went on when no one responded. "One cannon of each pair and the machine gun are loaded with thin-lead-walled, liquid-Teflon-filled rounds of sufficient mass and velocity to turn a steer carcass into so much hamburger within a couple of seconds, but leaving surrounding stainless-steel and polycarbonate structures completely intact. The other cannon of each pair is armed with armor-piercing and explosive rounds in alternating sequence, that are perfectly capable of penetrating the polycarbonate panes and the individual chambers."

Byzor paused for effect.

"There are other protective systems in place as well; but the important point is, in essence and if necessary, we have the capability to reach out and kill—or destroy, depending on your definition—any and all living creatures attempting to enter or leave any of those containment chambers."

Byzor was staring directly at Cellars now. "And if it's ever necessary, we will do exactly that . . . without hesitation . . . and without regard to whoever else is in that chamber at the time. Which could certainly include Lieutenant Kessler and Staff Sergeant Dombrowski, as well as any of us. For whatever it's worth, you all have my word on that."

Cellars turned around and stared at Kessler and Dombrowski. "Were you guys aware of all this?" he asked.

"Most of it, sir," Kessler answered in a hoarse whisper.

From Cellars's perspective, the faces of the two Delta Forces troopers had taken on a slightly pale sheen.

"The entire security force, including the Delta Forces Detachment, were told as much as they needed to know in order to perform their mission," Byzor said. "In essence, that someone might attempt to steal some rocks that might be of extraterrestrial origin, and that any such attempt was likely to be well financed and well organized. Anything more than that would have risked leaking information to the public, and possibly causing a panic."

Cellars, Bauer, and Boggs nodded agreeably.

"That was this morning," Byzor went on. "But, this evening, as you are all aware, the situation changed. A few minutes ago, all of the security and Delta Forces personnel—with the exception of Kessler and Dombrowski—were fully briefed on the current situation. That's why Kessler and Dombrowski are hearing some of this information for the first time."

"Did Marston gain access to the larger chamber?" Cellars asked.

"We think so."

"What do you mean, you 'think so'?" Cellars sat upright in the chair. "What were your people doing up in those monitoring pods, playing cards?"

"Two people in white lab coats were definitely in the larger containment chamber for a short period of time," Byzor said. "Marston was probably one of them, but we don't know for sure."

"But . . . how is that possible? What about this fancy scanning security system you've been describing? And all those video cameras?" Bauer asked.

"It appears that someone, possibly Dr. Marston, was able to gain root access to our security system, and reprogram our computers to ignore two sets of cloth-embedded ID codes—that of Marston and a young technician named Valerie Sandersohn," Byzor replied. "In effect, the cameras ignored the two figures wearing Marston's and Sandersohn's lab coats. As a result, their faces never showed up in any of our internal monitoring tapes, and their names were never selected by our watch commander's random checks."

"So anyone could put on your coat and walk around the lab like Deputy Director Malcolm Byzor?" Bauer asked.

"No, that's why we have our photographs embedded into the cloth ID badges sewn and glued onto our coats, jackets, overalls, and lab coat pockets," Byzor said, motioning with his hand down at the embedded badge photo of himself on his own lab coat. "People are supposed to look at the badges, and react when they see the wrong face on the badge . . . but it's easy to get complacent, and the badges aren't easy to see at a distance."

"So Marston could have just put Sandersohn's lab coat on his girlfriend?" Bauer asked.

"Perhaps. But if he broke into the security system, it's also possible that he could have faked a badge photo, too. We haven't resolved that issue . . . yet," the deputy director added with a look of frustration in his eyes.

"But your entry team did find Marston's body in the main containment lab," Cellars pointed out.

"That's right," Byzor acknowledged, "so it seems reasonable to assume that Marston was one of the two white-coated figures the watch commander observed from the battle cab when he glanced up from the exercise he was running. We have no idea about the whereabouts of the second figure, because he or she has effectively disappeared."

"You mean . . . escaped from the building?" Cellars demanded.

Byzor shrugged again. "It's theoretically possible."

"But . . . what about the guys up in that battle cab? What about their monitors? Didn't they see someone leave?"

Byzor sighed. "The watch commander and his two assistants were busy running what turned out to be an unauthorized but very complex mock exercise that someone—presumably Marston—had set into motion just before he entered the building at seven. We will do that on occasion, so it wasn't an event the watch commander found suspicious. The exercise required all three members of the watch shift to focus on specific exercise components, which forced all three of them to depend on the computer/scanner system to maintain an automatic watch on things. So it's possible that Marston could have come up with some way for him and his assistant to exit the building in some location where he wouldn't have shown up on the external monitors. I don't know. In fact, I'm guessing about a lot of this," he admitted, "because whoever subverted the system also arranged to have their Trojan Horse virus automatically erase itself at the end of the sequence. I only know about that erasure—and a few other things—because the actions showed up on an activity log I maintain on a separate computer that Marston didn't know about."

"So, in essence, Marston beat you with your own security system." Cellars half smiled.

"Yes, he apparently did. But the question is, why?"

Cellars cocked his head. "I don't follow."

"There was no apparent attempt made to move or open any of the smaller chambers . . . or at least none that we could detect," Byzor amended. "So why go to all that effort? It doesn't make any sense."

"He could have been showing off the facility . . . or the stones themselves . . . to that young girl I saw."

"A definite possibility, given the infatuation issue," Byzor agreed. "Which is why I had Gregor track her down. If you'll look behind you." He reached up to the control panel and pressed another button.

The opaque blue window behind them suddenly turned transparent, revealing a smaller room that looked more like a jail than a laboratory. One of Montgomery's black-garbed troopers was standing at parade rest with his back to the window, facing a row of eight transparent-walled, stainless-steel cells. There were two young women in the first two cells, each wearing an identical pair of orange overalls, the oversize front zipper of which seemed to be secured in place with some kind of snap-lock.

As Cellars, Bauer, and Boggs turned their chairs around, Cellars immediately recognized the dark-haired young woman in the second cell.

"Is that her?" Byzor asked. "The one you saw when we ran into Marston?"

"Yeah, it is," Cellars acknowledged. He eyed the young woman warily. She didn't look as seductive and enticing as she had with Marston, but Cellars figured that probably had something to do with being in a cell and wearing a pair of orange prisoner's overalls. "Where did you find her?"

"At home, asleep. She claims she'd gone to bed early with a migraine headache."

"How did you go after her?"

"Standard Delta team entry, windows and doors, fast, hard, stun grenades, the works," Byzor said. "Literally scared the piss out of her . . . not to mention her cat and several of the neighbors, according to Mike. We've got a bunch of people out there right now, working the neighborhood, trying to calm things down."

"She didn't resist . . . or change?" Cellars asked hesitantly.

"No, she didn't. She just screamed, and cried . . . then started yelling at Mike and the rest of the team when she got over the shock. She's calmed down considerably, but she's still not very happy about being in custody."

"Is that roughly what you expected?" Cellars asked uneasily.

"Not really," Byzor confessed. "But, given everything else that's happened on this project, it's a rare day when I'm not surprised by something."

"What about the other young woman?"

"The blonde in the first cell is Valerie Sandersohn, the lab technician I mentioned previously. We found her at a Foo Fighters concert, at the Britt Center, in Jackson County, where she'd apparently been most of the evening."

"So she wasn't anywhere near the facility at the time of the break-in?" Boggs asked.

"We don't think so. As far as we know right now, Valerie was just an innocent victim of Marston's little access game . . . somebody we believe he used to help rig an entry for his companion. But that's the problem: what we know and what we don't know."

As Byzor spoke, a white-coated lab technician entered the cell-block area with a small cart containing a rack of purple-stoppered glass tubes, gauze, tape, some kind of portable scanner, and a tray of prepped Teflon syringes.

Cellars nodded slowly in understanding as the lab technician walked up to the first cell, opened a small door in the cell wall about four and a half feet up from the floor, then apparently directed Valerie Sandersohn to extend her arm through the portal.

"What if they refuse to cooperate?" Cellars asked as they watched the technician quickly and methodically draw a tube of blood from Sandersohn's arm then run the scanner over the ID tag sewn into Sandersohn's orange overalls and the tube label before securing the outer portal door.

"We have other means of obtaining the sample," Byzor replied in a neutral voice.

"Ah."

They all watched silently as the dark-haired young woman in the second cell seemed to argue with the lab technician. After approximately twenty seconds of screaming, the black-garbed soldier broke out of his parade-rest position and stepped forward with a 9mm Beretta semiautomatic pistol in his hand. After another thirty-or-so seconds of less emotional arguing, she reluctantly put her arm through the portal and cooperated with the blood-drawing process.

After drawing the blood, the lab tech ran the scanner over the dark-haired young woman's orange overalls and the tube label.

As soon as the dark-haired young woman withdrew her arm from the portal, and the small door was secured from the outside, the black-garbed soldier returned the 9mm Beretta to his shoulder holster and proceeded to roll up his right sleeve.

"What's that all about?" Boggs demanded as they watched the technician repeat the entire blood-drawing process with the young Delta Forces commando.

"Before we go any further, we need to know who's who—or what—inside this building," Byzor said as he stepped away from the podium, walked across the room, stood by a portal in the wall to the left of the opaque blue window, and waited for the lab technician to climb a set of stairs and open the portal.

"She's going to take your blood, too?" Boggs asked, looking puzzled.

"She's going to take blood from all of us, and herself while we watch," Byzor answered as he rolled up his sleeve and then stuck his arm through the portal. "That's the only way we can tell for sure."

"And if we don't cooperate?" the wildlife agent asked.

"That's what Kessler and Dombrowski are here for," Cellars guessed.

"But they didn't disarm us when we came in, and there's three of us against two of them," Boggs pointed out. "Understand, I'm not trying to be argumentative," he said to Byzor. "Just pointing out what might be a couple of flaws in your plan."

"Which I do appreciate, believe me," Byzor said as he waited for the technician to finish the scanning process before withdrawing his arm. "However, I think we've taken at least some of your concerns into account. Mike, will you demonstrate the primary backup system for our guests here?"

"Yes, sir." Mike Montgomery's voice boomed out over the overhead speakers.

An instant later, a set of bright yellow crosshairs appeared on the center of Wilbur Boggs's chest.

Boggs looked down, immediately stepped aside . . . then froze as he realized no matter how he moved or turned, the crosshairs smoothly realigned. He looked up through the large viewing window and discovered that the 25mm cannons and the 7.65mm M-60 machine gun mounted under one of the battle cabs were locked on his movements.

"Don't take this too hard, Wilbur," Patrol Sergeant Tom Bauer said in a soft voice as he began to roll up his sleeve, "but, as far as I'm concerned, you're all by yourself on this deal."

Fifteen minutes and six more blood draws later, the lab technician finished scanning Kessler's blood sample and his black overalls.

"Okay," Malcolm Byzor said from his position back at the podium, "now that our technician has collected all of the blood samples, including her own, she's going to take them over to our laboratory"—he pressed a button on the podium console, which turned the middle left wall window transparent and revealed a corridor that the lab technician stepped into with her cart of blood samples—"where, I think, we may have a surprise for Colin."

Malcolm Byzor pressed another button on the podium console. The final left-side wall window instantly turned transparent, revealing an expensively equipped, analytical chemistry laboratory filled with an impressive array of shiny analytical instruments and four white-coated scientists.

But Cellars wasn't looking at any of the impressively shiny instruments. Instead, he was staring at one of the white-coated scientists.

"Jody?"

CHAPTER FIFTY-TWO

"HOW DID SHE GET HERE?" CELLARS ASKED AS HE WATCHED THE lab technician finish drawing Jody Catlin's blood, and then help Jody transfer the rack of blood tubes into an autosampling tray sitting in front of a large multi-instrument array . . . one of which looked like some kind of mass spectrometer.

"I arranged to get her here," Malcolm Byzor said. "She was at the Rogue Valley Mall to meet Jack and Melissa when the lights went out and the fire alarms went off. She saw you come out of the toy store with the SIG in your hand, panicked, ran for the parking lot . . . then got it together and went to ground just like we taught her. She dialed the eight hundred locator number, I contacted her, worked her through the verification procedure, then talked her in."

"You didn't go get her?"

Byzor shook his head. "I couldn't get loose. I had to stay here and figure out what Marston had done before we lost control of the Center."

"But—"

"And I couldn't send anybody else to pick her up," Byzor went on, "because they wouldn't be able to work the verification procedure. But I knew where she was, and what she was driving, so I had her stay put long enough to get some of Mike's men out to her hotel so they could be in position to give her a stand-off escort. Worked just fine. Nobody tagged her from the hotel. Mike made sure of that."

Cellars gave a heartfelt sigh. "So how's she doing?" he asked hesitantly.

"Not too bad," Byzor hedged. "She wasn't exactly thrilled when she found out we've got the stones. But the analytical lab's completely isolated from the main containment lab by an airlock and two additional sealed and protected doors, so I think that helped."

"Can she see us?"

"No, it's all one-way glass in this room . . . except for a four-foot-square block around the portal, which I can make transparent or opaque on either or both sides."

"Does she know I'm here?"

Byzor shook his head. "I didn't want to distract her until we got these samples running."

"A perfectly reasonable precaution," Cellars agreed. "So what's the plan?"

"First off, we verify that everyone in this facility, including Gregor, is more or less human."

"With the blood samples?"

"Right. You see that array of instruments behind the autosampler?" Cellars nodded.

"That's a very expensive state-of-the-art automated DNA sequencer . . . basically, a robotic arm that first extracts and isolates the DNA, then pumps the resulting extract into a liquid chromatograph, mass spectrometer sequencer. The tubes are identified only by a mottled and extremely complex ID pattern, very much like the one embedded in the fabric of our lab coats and jackets, so no one can visually identify the donor source of any particular tube. Every step is automated, and the tubes are randomly mixed and scanned internally once they're inside the system, so there's no chance that anyone could use tube sequence to make a switch or alter a result."

"So why have four scientists in there?" Cellars asked.

"Mostly to work in pairs, monitor the system—and each other— and make sure everything keeps running," Byzor replied. "Goddamned robotic arms are notorious for jamming up, but I think we've got the bugs worked out of this particular unit. In any case, we've got the entire system programmed to look for that third set of base pairs Jody, Jack, and Melissa supposedly found when they were analyzing those tissue samples you collected at Bobby's cabin."

"Supposedly?"

"I'm being conservative. Until we see it for ourselves . . ."

"Fair enough," Cellars agreed. "So how long's all this going to take?"

"For seventy-eight samples, including the extraction time? Probably a little over twelve hours."

"We've got to hang around here for twelve hours before we know for sure who's what?" A pained expression crossed Cellars's face.

"No, actually, we don't," Byzor said in a softer voice as he stepped over to where Cellars, Bauer, and Boggs were standing, looking into the analytical lab, effectively cutting Kessler and Dombrowski—who were now back into their seemingly reflexive parade-rest positions on the opposite side of the room—out of the conversation. "Do you remember what else Jody said was odd about those DNA samples?" he asked Cellars.

"Sure, the silicon substitution in that third set of base pairs," Cellars replied. "Substitutions that, as I recall, a couple of Nobel Prize–winning chemists claimed were absolutely impossible."

"What do they know?" Byzor grinned. "Anyway, just to make things interesting, I had our own Nobel Prize–winning chief chemist, and one of our electronics engineers, rig a little covert analytical capability within that Rube Goldberg mess of instrumentation out there, before I sent them off to Barbados for some well-earned R & R."

"To detect silicon in the blood samples?" Boggs asked.

"Exactly. It's just a simple, yes-no, probable-cause type of analysis," Byzor replied. "No need to run the quantitations. The silicon's either there, in a reasonable concentration relative to the amount of DNA present, or it's not. We triple-washed a batch of brand-new Teflon syringes to draw the blood samples, and exhaustively confirmed the negatives, so there's only one reason I can think of why we'd find silicon in any of those blood samples."

"But everyone else—including any substituted bad guys—will be expecting a twelve-hour delay before the sequencers start kicking out the revealing data. So, if any of them are still in this facility, we just might be able to catch them off guard." Cellars smiled.

"You mean you approve?" Byzor raised one eyebrow expectantly.

"You bet," Cellars said. "Anything that gives us the slightest advantage over those bastards is definitely fine with me."

Then he realized something.

"Hey, wait a minute, you've got these Delta Forces guys in the containment lab, and the lockup, and here with us, and probably scattered throughout the facility. But what about the analytical lab?"

"Tell you the truth, I've been a whole lot more concerned about the blood-drawing process than the actual analysis," Byzor replied. "Once the blood samples are in the automated sampler system, there really isn't much anyone—or anything—can do about it . . . other than go at the sequencer . . . in which case, the guys in the battle cab start making extraterrestrial hamburger."

"Okay, that makes sense," Cellars agreed. "But what happens if one of your chemists turns out to be a ringer?"

"Same basic—" Byzor started to say, then hesitated. "Oh, I see what you're saying. What happens to Jody?"

"Yeah."

Byzor took in a breath, and then let it out with a deep sigh. "Okay, good point. I'll put one of Mike's—"

"No, wait. Let me go in there."

Byzor raised a skeptical eyebrow. "I thought we all agreed we didn't want her distracted."

"We don't, but all of the blood tubes are in the autosampler now.

The system's locked down and running. So all she's got to do—in conjunction with her paired partner—is monitor the process. I'll stay back out of the way. Just keep an eye on things. It might even make her feel a little more relaxed to know I'm there."

"Or thoroughly piss her off. As I recall, you two haven't been getting along all that well lately," Byzor rejoined.

"In which case, I'll happily come back in here and leave the overseeing to one of Mike's men," Cellars offered.

"And, in any case, if I don't let you in there, you're probably going to start pacing around this room and driving us all nuts."

"Not for very long, he's not," Boggs said.

Byzor hesitated again, then seemed to come to a decision.

"All right, I'm convinced," he said as he reached into his pocket and pulled out some change. As the other men in the room watched, he rummaged through the coins, selected a pair of quarters, then walked over to Kessler and Dombrowski and handed one of the quarters to each of the men.

"Okay, Colin, take your pick," Byzor said as he walked back to where the three men were standing. "Older or newer?"

"You're not very trusting, are you?"

"No, I'm not," Byzor agreed. "People in my business who are too trusting usually end up suffering untimely deaths, or spending the rest of their careers writing memos, trying to explain how and why things went wrong. If it's all the same to you, I'd just as soon not have to do either just yet.

"But, on the other hand," he added, "I certainly do believe in the value of tossing a few random monkey wrenches into the works every now and then. Especially at a time when devious plots might be in play, conspiracies abound, and important choices have to be made."

"In other words," Cellars translated, "if I'm a ringer, you don't want me selecting my baby-sitter . . . who just might turn out to be one of my three-base-pair buddies in drag."

"Or some equally twisted variation thereof," Byzor acknowledged. "Older or newer?"

"Older."

"That's me," Staff Sergeant Dombrowski said as he and Kessler compared coins.

"Okay," Byzor said. "You and Cellars will go into the analytical lab and keep an eye on our chemist team, and each other," he added pointedly. "The rest of us will stay here and keep our fingers crossed."

CHAPTER FIFTY-THREE

"HOW'RE YOU DOING?" CELLARS ASKED SOFTLY.

A few minutes earlier, Jody Catlin had looked up in surprise when he and Dombrowski had entered the analytical lab . . . but a flashing light and beeping alarm immediately drew her attention back to the instrument monitors. It was another five minutes before she was finally able to step away from the instrument array and walk over to where he and Dombrowski were standing by the door, her chemist partner maintaining a respectful but watchful distance.

"You know, you scared me half to death earlier this evening, when I saw you come out of that mall toy store with your gun in your hand, but I feel a whole lot better now," she said. Her all-too-familiar smile was back in place, but it was the expression in her flashing eyes that caused Cellars's heart to leap in his chest.

Like she truly cared about him again.

"Yeah. Me too."

He'd gone into the analytical lab intending to tell her about Jack Wilson and Melissa Washington, figuring he owed her at least that much. But the sight of her dimpled smile, and the warm, affectionate look in her eyes, made him hesitate.

Later, he rationalized. *I'll tell her later, when it won't affect her work.*

"You look tired," she said, her expression immediately switching to concern. "Malcolm said you haven't been sleeping well lately."

"I've been having some weird dreams. What can I tell you?"

"Her again?"

Cellars tensed for the expected outburst. But, to his amazement, the look of warmth and concern in her eyes never shifted.

Like old times, he thought hopefully, as he shook his head.

"No, I really don't dream about her anymore. Or, at least, not very often." He felt himself blush . . . then saw her cheeks dimple into another one of those familiar smiles that, many years ago, had torn at his heart on a regular basis.

"You know, you guys are absolutely hopeless when it comes to sex and relationships," she whispered.

"That's probably because we're forced to go about with a severe handicap."

"Oh, yeah? What's that?" she asked, cocking her head in amusement.

"We don't run across people like you very often. Usually about once in a lifetime, if we're lucky."

Cellars could almost feel the electricity flow between them, and it was all he could do to keep from stepping forward and taking her into his arms.

"You keep on saying nice things like that, Detective-Sergeant Colin Cellars," she whispered in that familiar husky voice, "and Malcolm's going to find us—"

At that moment, the lights in the analytical lab turned a flashing red . . . and muted alarms began to sound an urgent cadence. To his horror, Cellars saw the yellow crosshairs appear—and then center—on Jody Catlin's chest.

The horrifying realization that the Waycross Center's computerized security system had suddenly engaged and was running amok flashed through Cellars's stunned mind.

"No, stop, shut it off!" he screamed as he lunged for the woman he loved, determined to put himself between her and the weapons . . . knowing, even as he did so, that there was nothing he could do except die with her. The armor-piercing and Teflon-filled rounds would tear them both apart in the blink of an eye.

The sound of the shots—jarringly loud, but, at the same time, oddly muted—were just beginning to register when the pair of 9mm slugs streaked past Cellars's head and slammed Jody Catlin backward against the wall.

Cellars saw the bloody aftereffects of the head and heart shots . . . knew instantly the wounds were fatal . . . and whirled around to lunge at Dombrowski—who stood there with his 9mm semiautomatic pistol extended out in both hands, a stunned look in his eyes.

Then he caught himself in mid-lunge as his gunshot-ravaged eardrums somehow detected the chilling and yet all-too-familiar sound of something clattering to the floor behind his back.

He tried to say something else as he forced himself to turn around—feeling, as he did so, as if his arms and legs were surrounded by a thick, viscous liquid—but the words wouldn't come.

All he could do was stand there and stare—shocked and disbelieving—as the small stone clattered to a stop amid the splattered patterns of bright red blood spread across the shiny linoleum floor.

CHAPTER FIFTY-FOUR

"HOW COULD IT HAVE HAPPENED?" COLIN CELLARS WHISPERED
sometime later.

"We don't know," Malcolm Byzor replied. "We're still trying to figure that out."

They were back in the VIP viewing room. Byzor, Cellars, Bauer,
Boggs, Kessler, Dombrowski . . . and Captain Mike Montgomery.
Only, now, the windows were opaque blue again, and a small rectangu-
lar table had been brought in by a maintenance crew and placed in the
center of the room. On it, they'd placed a telephone, a replica of the
podium controller, and an assortment of items retrieved from a knapsack in the rear of Cellars's Humvee:

A pair of Elmer Fudd dolls, one with a nail sticking out of its forehead.

Patrick Bergéone's camera case and remote-tracking device.

A glassine envelope containing a black-and-white negative.

And the oddly blurred, black-and-white photograph of Bergéone standing next to what looked like the mouth of a cave.

Lying next to these items was a nearly transparent polycarbonate transport jar—approximately sixteen inches long and six inches in diameter, with a remote detonator Velcroed to the outside—containing a single small stone.

The maintenance crew had also taken the time to rearrange six of the chairs around the table, facing in the direction of the wall-mounted monitors. Byzor, Cellars, Bauer, Boggs, and Dombrowski were sitting in the chairs, the Delta Forces staff sergeant looking solemn and decidedly uncomfortable in his unaccustomed position. Montgomery and Kessler were standing behind and on either side of the table and chairs in parade-rest stance.

"By the way," Byzor said, "everybody else checked out negative on the silicon screening test. Jody's—or the Jody-replica's—was the only sample that came up positive. That's what set off the alarms and activated the automated security system."

Cellars blinked. "What about Marston's girlfriend?"

"Definitely negative."

"Are you sure?"

"We took a second sample from her, and that came back negative, too," Byzor replied. "They're running another panel of basic blood-typing tests—ABO, hemoglobin, that sort of thing—but so far, everything's coming up human." The deputy project director shrugged. "What can I tell you?"

"Well, so much for that theory," Wilbur Boggs muttered.

They sat in silence, lost in their thoughts. When the phone on the table rang, Byzor reached for it.

He listened for a few seconds, said "Thank you," replaced the phone in its receiver, then pressed a button on the console.

Instantly, the large center monitor came to life.

"They've isolated the tape from the security camera," Byzor said, first looking over at Cellars and then at Dombrowski. "Are you two ready to see it?"

Cellars and Dombrowski nodded glumly, and Byzor reached forward to press another button on the console.

The seven men watched in numbed silence as the video images of Colin Cellars and Jody Catlin engaged in visibly warm and affectionate conversation . . . right up to the point when the flashing lights and alarms began and the bright yellow crosshairs appeared in the center of Catlin's chest. Cellars made his futile lunge to save the woman he loved . . . only to see her flung backward and start to crumble against the nearby wall as Byzor froze the image.

Cellars cursed under his breath.

"Sorry about this, Colin, but I want to back it up a few seconds . . . to the point just before Sergeant Dombrowski began to reach for his pistol," Byzor said as he turned the dial on the console, reversing the images.

"There." Byzor stopped turning the dial, pressed it in, and the image immediately sharpened then began to move forward at one-tenth normal speed. "Talk to us, Sergeant," he said to Dombrowski. "What are you reacting to?"

"The alarms, first . . . and then the crosshairs, sir," Dombrowski spoke in a dulled voice as the seven men watched the Dombrowski-image's legs step apart into a slightly crouched position . . . and the right hand come up and grasp the shoulder-holstered 9mm Beretta semiautomatic pistol . . . pause . . . and then, in a visibly smooth and much faster series of movements, bring the pistol out and up into a two-handed, point-shoot position.

"What now, Sergeant?"

"She was going for him, sir. That's why I fired."

" 'Going for him'? Are you sure about that?"

The slow motion of the video images paused and then reversed as Byzor worked the console again, moving in on the image of Jody Catlin . . . who seemed to be reaching out in desperation for Cellars with . . .

. . . outstretched claws?

"Jesus Christ," Dombrowski and Boggs whispered almost in unison as Byzor froze, then sharpened the monitor image again, bringing the clawed fingers and the strangely glistening eyes of Jody Catlin into tight focus.

In the now-enlarged and sharply focused image, they could all see the glistening arcs of the visibly curved and pointed structures extending from the tips of Catlin's outstretched fingers . . . and the purple-violet slits of her eyes.

"Is that what you saw, Sergeant?" Byzor asked in a soft voice, edged with something Cellars couldn't quite define. Something visceral and determined.

"I . . . I guess I don't know what I saw, sir. I . . . just reacted."

"Good job, soldier," Captain Mike Montgomery said in an oddly gruff and gentle voice.

"Yes, thank you, Sergeant. Your reflexes saved my ass," Colin Cellars said in a hoarse voice as he watched the crumpled image of Jody Catlin suddenly dissolve and then disappear in a brief explosive flash of what looked like variably dense vapors.

"So that's how it works," Byzor said . . . as much to himself as the room's other occupants.

"What are you talking about?" Cellars demanded.

"The loss of mass when they dissolve into the stonelike structure. We don't know how much they weigh, and there's the underlying issue of the fast-moving, shadowy form that you described, which certainly suggests a relatively low mass-to-volume ratio. And we also know the stones are very light . . . which has always implied the loss of a significant amount of mass. The question was how. And I think what we just saw was very rapid—and perhaps even explosive—vaporization."

"You mean the loss of water?" Boggs asked.

"Water is undoubtedly the primary component of the vapor," Byzor agreed. "What are we, roughly ninety-eight percent water? No particular reason why they would have to be even that dense. I'm guessing there's a lot of other proteinaceous, connective, and probably bone material that's expendable, too, assuming that the important part of the stabilization process is to retain the critical structural blueprint as well as the memory data. Which makes sense to me, but what the hell do I know about extraterrestrial life and death?"

"Does the system work with metals, too?" Cellars asked. "I mean, even her belt buckle and hair clip disappeared."

"It must," Byzor agreed. "The question is 'how?' Unfortunately, we can't get much in the way of useful spectral information on that vapor cloud from a digital video signal . . . but at least we have a start."

"And they have Jody," Cellars whispered. "They'd have to, wouldn't they?"

This time it was Byzor's turn to nod silently.

"That's what she was terrified of, all along," Cellars continued in a soft voice. "That they'd come back and get her, and there'd be nothing we could do about it. Nothing at all."

"I tried—" Byzor started to say, then stopped.

Cellars could hear the pain in Byzor's voice, and it helped him to focus.

"We have to find her," he said. "How do we do that?"

"We've still got a crime scene," Patrol Sergeant Tom Bauer rejoined.

Cellars looked at him blankly.

"The hotel room. That's where they would have had to grab her, wouldn't they?" Bauer said. "If Montgomery and his people were outside watching when she came out of the room?"

"Of course. We need to get out there, right—" Cellars said as he started to lunge up from the chair . . . then hesitated as Byzor put a restraining hand on his shoulder.

"We've got a crew out there right now, Colin, literally taking the place apart with crowbars and tweezers," Byzor said.

"Yeah, I know, but—"

"I need you here," Byzor said. "I've got a hundred people on call who can disassemble furniture, vacuum a carpet, and scan a hotel room for latents. But you may be the only one who can help us put the pieces of this puzzle together."

"Puzzle." Cellars blinked in remembrance as he dropped back down in the cushioned chair. "That's the last thing Bobby said when he called me at the morgue earlier this evening. That I need to watch my six, keep on working those puzzle pieces, and take care of Jody."

"Puzzle pieces . . . as in plural?" Byzor asked.

"Yes, definitely plural."

"Which, presumably, includes at least one or more of the things on this table?" Byzor said, gesturing with his hand at the assortment of items spread out on the glistening wood surface.

"I guess . . ." Cellars said hesitantly. "But I—hey, wait a minute. Yesterday morning, right after I got that special delivery package from Bobby, Jody told me she got something from Bobby, too."

Malcolm Byzor came alert.

"What was it?" he demanded.

"It was a black-and-white photograph of Bobby's latest art project," Cellars said. "Something about the Pope in a seventeenth-century hockey stadium, sitting with the Stones, the Three Musketeers, the Pep Boys, a bunch of artists I can't even begin to remember, Elvis, and the Holy Trinity of Blondes."

"Sounds like one of Dawson's typical sketches," Byzor commented.

"Yeah, that's what I told her, too. But she also said there was another sketch. I'm trying to remember . . . oh, yeah, a cartoon sketch of Elmer Fudd surrounded by a bunch of gargoyles, icons, and other religious statues, one of which was labeled 'Mother of something.' "

"Mother of the Loire?" Byzor asked.

"I don't know, could be. Would that mean something?"

"It might," Byzor said as he reached for the phone and punched in a three-digit number. "This is the deputy director," he said into the mouthpiece. "Put out an immediate APB on Jody Catlin. List her as a kidnap victim, and emphasize that her kidnappers are to be considered armed and extremely dangerous. Her personal information and last point of contact is in the files. Last seen at the hotel approximately three hours ago. Yes, immediately . . . and then connect me with the search team at the hotel."

Everyone in the room remained silent as Byzor waited. Then: "This is Malcolm. What have you found so far?" He listened for a few seconds, then: "Good. Put both drawings—and the envelope they were in—on the chopper, and get them here to the VIP viewing room, ASAP.

"Okay," he said to the room at large as he hung up the phone, "they found the drawings, and they're on their way here, right now. So what else do we know?"

"I'm trying to remember everything else Bobby told me," Cellars said. "A lot of it didn't make much sense."

"You mean like 'watching your six'?" Bauer asked.

"Well . . ." Cellars hesitated.

"Nothing especially weird about 'watching your six,' " Wilbur Boggs commented. "That's just something military pilots say to each other when they part company. Basically means 'Don't forget to look behind you, every now and then, because, if you don't, somebody's going to sneak up on your ass and tear you a new one.' "

"Okay, but Colin's not a pilot. Or at least I don't think he is," Bauer added, looking over at Cellars suspiciously. "Are you?"

"No, I'm not. But—"

"But what?" Byzor pressed, his eyes focused on Cellars's face.

"I've been having these really strange dreams lately . . . like I'm a helicopter pilot, flying at night just above the tree line . . . out toward the outer perimeter, where I'm not supposed to be." Cellars allowed his mind to replay the disturbing images. "The strange thing is, the dream's so damned real, I can remember every detail . . ."

"Did you ever fly with Bobby?" Boggs interrupted, his head cocked in a curious manner as he stared at Cellars.

"Are you kidding? When we were kids, I wouldn't even ride with him . . . especially on his damned motorcycle. The guy's a maniac when it comes to pushing the edge. Can't even imagine what it would be like sitting in a plane with him at the controls, much less a helicopter."

"What were you flying?" Boggs pressed.

Cellars's eyebrows furrowed in confusion. "What—?"

"In your dreams. What kind of helicopter were you flying?"

"Oh, an Apache . . . because we—"

Cellars brought his head up suddenly, then looked around the room in confusion. "What the hell's an Apache?"

"It's an Army attack helicopter," Byzor said calmly. "Can you describe the inside of the cockpit in any detail?"

"Yeah, sure," Cellars said, searching his memory. "It's a two-seater, front and back. I'm in the back, the pilot's seat, above and behind the gunner's seat . . . which we usually fly empty, because we didn't need a gunner for the night runs," he added in the same hesitant voice, as if he wasn't quite sure what he was saying.

Cellars went on to describe the cockpit of an Apache gunship in increasing detail until Malcolm Byzor finally held up a hand.

"And you say you've never been in one of those aircraft?"

Cellars shook his head slowly. "I keep wanting to tell you I don't even know what one of these things looks like on the outside, much less the inside, but—"

"But you clearly do know. And in considerable detail . . . like you've flown one before."

"Yeah . . . but it wasn't me," Cellars said after a moment, the hesitancy in his voice shifting to something more like awareness. "It couldn't have been."

"Then who was it?"

"Bobby."

Malcolm Byzor seemed to be probing past Cellars's eyes, into his conscious thoughts. "Are you sure?"

"Yeah, has to be. Only thing that makes sense."

"Would you mind expounding on that?"

"It was Allesandra," Cellars went on. "When we made love to each other, it was like her whole mind and body was flowing into me . . . into my head . . . seeing everything I'd ever seen, knowing everything I ever knew . . ."

"You told me she knew all about Bobby's guns . . . the effective range of that Sharps carbine, as an example," Byzor encouraged him in a quiet voice.

Cellars nodded. "She recognized the weapon, and knew exactly how far away to stay from him when we made the exchange. But she didn't know that he'd hot-loaded the round to increase the range because he did that afterward."

"But that's . . . highly classified tactical equipment," Byzor said, looking stunned. "What the hell made them think they could—?"

"I understand it had something do with the new coordinator for drug enforcement," Boggs replied. "You assign a job like that to a major general, I guess he sees to it that all the latest military gadgets are made available."

"For fucking *dope* raids?" Malcolm Byzor looked apoplectic.

"Not the raids themselves, just the surveillance," Boggs said. "The way Bobby explained it, they had to use the more heavily armored Apaches for the overflights because they were taking too many ground-fire hits from the growers when they flew that low."

Byzor reached for the phone on the table.

"This is the deputy director," he said into the mouthpiece. "Get the SAC of the Portland DEA Office on the horn, right now. Yes, I know he's going to be pissed. Do it anyway, and transfer the call to Captain Montgomery's office. I'm sending him over there right now." Byzor paused. "And tell Dobres to bring one of the Mark-Twelve FOILER packs to the VIP viewing room, right now, along with a dozen sets of night-vision goggles. Thank you."

Byzor hung up the phone, then turned to stare at Captain Montgomery.

"Did you know about this?" he demanded.

"No, sir."

Malcolm Byzor closed his eyes and sighed heavily.

"Okay," he said, "go back to your office and talk to the SAC, find out if he knows anything about three ultraclassified FOILER systems being used by DEA agents in his region to look for goddamned marijuana fields. And when he tells you he doesn't know what you're talking about, advise him that a national-security review team should be landing in Portland within the next eight hours to check on the matter. That might help spur his memory."

"Yes, sir."

As Captain Montgomery disappeared through the door, Byzor turned to Cellars, Boggs, and Bauer, who were sitting at one end of the table opposite Dombrowski. Lieutenant Kessler remained by the door.

"FOILER. Field Operational Infantry Laser Enhancement Reconnaissance system," Byzor continued. "A hundred-million-dollar, ultra-classified research program to develop a field laser scanning system that locates, locks on, and tracks individual moving or fixed targets at long distances."

"You mean like infiltrating soldiers?" Cellars asked. He was trying to keep his mind focused on the discussion, knowing that Malcolm Byzor hadn't forgotten about Jody.

"Yes and no. The system was actually designed as a counterterrorist weapon, capable of scanning large areas of ground and automatically spotting, locking in on, and tracking multiple infiltrators . . . thereby giving hunter-killer teams in the area a set of focused targets. It has obvious application to military units in the field, both in terms of long- and short-range reconnaissance, and in perimeter defense."

"Which explains why you were experimenting with the blue-green lasers you put in that crime scene scanner I used out at Bobby's cabin."

"Exactly. In fact, the lasers you used were just a powered-down and single-wavelength version of the ones we installed in the FOILER systems," Byzor replied as a heavyset and slightly balding, white-coated figure rolled a lab cart into the viewing room.

"Gentlemen, this is Dr. Bill Dobres," Byzor said by way of introduction. "Bill is the primary design engineer on the FOILER program, which means he's probably going to be very surprised to learn that the DEA's been using three of his prototype systems on routine pot field surveillance flights. Presumably the ones we sent to Fort Bragg for some field tests in a swamp environment."

"What?" Bill Dobres's mouth dropped open.

"I'll tell you about it later," Byzor said. "In the meantime, I want you to show these people how a FOILER system works."

Dobres took the field pack off the cart, set up the sturdy tripod legs, aimed the two-inch-diameter lasering optic tube toward the far wall, then quickly ran through the basic mechanics of the system, pointing out the purpose and function of the knobs and buttons.

"Main thing is to watch your power and wavelength knobs," Dobres finished. "There are locks in place that can be overridden. But if you do that, and set one of these things on the wrong frequency and at maximum power, you could have a real mess on your hands."

"As you can see," Byzor said, as Dobres carefully placed the FOILER pack back on the cart, "it's a very portable system, designed to be carried into the field and operated by an individual soldier . . . much in the way that crime scene scanner I lent Colin was designed to be used by a single CSI officer. This is the nuclear-powered two A version, which kicks out about three times as much energy as the laser Bobby apparently used. Unfortunately, because of the lead shielding, this model weighs in at close to fifty pounds, but that's still well within the acceptable range for a field-packed weapon."

"Is there a point to all of this?" Cellars said impatiently. "I don't see how this military toy of yours is going to help us find Jody, and we could be running out of time."

"I don't know, for sure, either," Byzor said as he picked up the polycarbonate transport jar containing the single stone. "But we're about to find out. Each of you grab a pair of those night-vision goggles and follow me."

Cellars, Boggs, Bauer, Kessler, and Dombrowski obediently followed Byzor and Dobres—who was pushing the cart with the FOILER pack—through two airlocked doors, into the main containment lab . . . and then into a twenty-five-foot-square stainless-steel and thick polycarbonate-walled containment chamber.

"What the hell are we doing here?" Cellars asked as he looked around uneasily at the fifteen containment jars. The five jars standing in front of the left wall, and the first two jars from the left standing in front of the center wall, each contained a single mounted stone. One of the stones was attached to a small golden chain.

"We're going to conduct an experiment," Byzor said as he placed the smaller polycarbonate transport jar on a table in the center of the room, then waited for Dobres to remount the FOILER laser.

Colin Cellars's face paled. "You're going to try to reanimate these damned things?"

"The FOILER system is designed to illuminate humanoid targets," Byzor said. "Humans give off visible light at a specific wavelength when exposed to another . . . as do marijuana plants, apparently," he added sarcastically. "If these creatures fluoresce differently than humans, or pot plants, then we should be able to spot them at long distances."

"But—"

"Colin, if we want to find her before . . ." Byzor shook his head, then started over. "If we want to find her, we've got to have something better than an All Points Bulletin. You know how this sort of thing works. Once they get her hidden away, they're not going to take her out in public again."

"Not until they're ready to deal," Cellars rejoined.

"For what? These stones?" The expression in Malcolm Byzor's face shifted . . . to something that Cellars immediately interpreted as sadness. He felt his stomach sink.

"You . . . wouldn't make the trade?" he whispered.

"You know the answer to that," Byzor replied, meeting Cellars's horrified gaze. "I couldn't make the trade, even if I wanted to."

"But—"

Malcolm Byzor shook his head slowly. "Colin, if I so much as tried to move these stones to another location without highest-level NSA approvals, Montgomery would have me—and anyone else involved—in custody within five minutes. Isn't that right, Kessler?"

"Yes, sir," Lieutenant Kessler responded immediately.

"An alternate check on the system?" Cellars asked.

"That's right. So, instead of making Don Quixote–like gestures that won't help Jody, we're going to try something that might work," Byzor said as he adjusted a pair of night-vision goggles over his head. "Put on those goggles and let's see what Dobres here can do with that laser."

"Any one in particular?" Bill Dobres asked as he finished setting up the FOILER tripod.

"Take the last one over there," Byzor said, pointing to the second containment jar in front of the center wall.

Dobres walked over to the jar, peeled the Velcroed remote detonator off the side, walked back to Byzor, and handed him the device. "What settings?" he asked.

"Start at the low end of the spectrum, w the lowest power level all the way through the ⌐

"That was the power level we used on the ⌐ noon, and they didn't move an inch," Dobres said.

"I know, but that was at the lower frequencies, not the wave⌐ we used for the CSI scanner. And besides, I want to play this safe," Byzor said, ignoring Cellars's glare. "Step by step. We'll activate the motion detectors in the detonators. Once we determine the frequencies at which the stones start to move, then we can start working on the power curve . . . with us outside the containment chamber," he added emphatically. "Don't forget, we're not talking about keeping these things alive for any extended period of time. All I want to do is animate one for a couple of minutes to see if and how it fluoresces."

"And after that?" Cellars asked.

"If it stays quiet in its jar, no problem. If it causes a ruckus, and looks like it's going to get out, we either mush it with the C-Four, or we put the crosshairs on the damned thing. Fair enough?"

Cellars nodded silently.

"Okay, everybody got their goggles on?" Byzor looked around, confirmed that everyone in the chamber had their night-vision goggles in place, then nodded to Dobres. "Okay, Bill, go to it."

The sudden appearance of the two-inch-wide beam—almost a robin's-egg blue in the viewers of the goggles—startled Cellars, Boggs, and Bauer. They watched as Dobres focused the beam down to about one inch at the point it passed through the polycarbonate walls of the containment jar and hit the stone.

"Okay," the scientist said, "I'm set on low power, blue end of the spectrum, and I'm going to work my way slowly across to green. We're probably going to get a lot of random scattering off the glass surfaces, so keep your goggles on."

As the three men watched in fascination, the color of the laser beam in their goggle viewers began a barely perceptible shift . . . that progressively became less blue . . . and was approaching what Cellars thought of as a bluish teal just as Dobres said, "We're coming up on the CSI scan-

ength" . . . when the alarms in the containment chamber suddenly began to shriek.

Cellars had already dropped into an instinctive crouch, right hand
reaching for his shoulder-holstered SIG-Sauer and his eyes focused on
the unmoving stone in the jar in front of them when Boggs yelled out,
"Behind you!"

Cellars whirled around, the SIG-Sauer out in a two-handed grip,
then stood there, staring in disbelief at the stone inside the small transport containment jar resting on the table in the center of the room.

The stone in the crosshairs that was now glowing a faint orange and
moving in a small, tight circle.

CHAPTER FIFTY-FIVE

THE SEARCH HAD BEEN GOING ON FOR ALMOST TEN MINUTES WHEN
Malcolm Byzor and Bill Dobres returned to the VIP viewing room, the
latter pushing the lab cart bearing the FOILER pack and the small polycarbonate transport jar containing the single—and now immobile—
stone.

Dobres pushed the cart over to the far wall underneath the monitors,
then quickly exited the room, leaving Byzor staring thoughtfully at the
three seated men.

"Having a bad day?" Cellars inquired from the center table where he
and Boggs and Bauer had been sitting for the last ten minutes.

Byzor started to say something, then shook his head, sighed deeply,
and turned to Staff Sergeant Dombrowski, who was standing at parade
rest next to the cart. "Sergeant, do not, under any conditions, let either

of those items out of your sight," he said, pointing to the FOILER pack and the transport jar.

"Yes, sir."

Then Byzor turned back to Cellars.

"You think Bobby scammed us?"

"It's a real possibility," Cellars replied. "The guy's always been an artist with hand tools. Wouldn't have been all that hard for him to make seven replica stones, although I can't imagine what he'd do with the real ones."

"Probably mounted the damned things on little wood plaques and hung them on his wall like a bunch of trophy deer heads," Byzor muttered.

"Assuming he even has a wall—or his own head—anymore," Cellars said. "And besides, you know what Bobby was always saying. He really doesn't like to hunt animals, only people. And, as far as I know, the only thing he's ever collected are nineteenth-century guns related in some manner to the good General Custer."

"Okay . . ."

"So I can't see him keeping those damned things for himself, even if he did scam you. And besides," Cellars added, "we know he's been out there somewhere, hunting them down . . . and taking the risk that he could be captured."

"So?"

"Why would he hide the real stones somewhere, knowing the shadows—or the Fudds, as he likes to call them—could easily acquire that information just by getting back inside his head?"

"So you think he gave the stones to somebody . . . if he ever had them in the first place?" Byzor asked.

"Which he probably didn't . . . or one of us would have known about it by now. So what do we do? I mean about the FOILER tests . . . and trying to find Jody?" Cellars explained when Byzor looked puzzled. "They've still got her, remember?"

"I haven't forgotten," Byzor replied, "but I've had to put everything else on hold until we make a complete search of this damned facility. Odds are that whoever or whatever Marston brought in with him immediately recognized the stones as fakes and took off . . . which would probably explain why he ended up with the better part of his face torn off. But there's always the possibility that he might have been able to switch fake stones for the real ones during the last couple of months."

"Is that really possible?" Bauer asked. "With those motion detectors under the jars, and all the other security systems you've got up and running in this place?"

"I honestly don't know," the deputy director confessed. "I've got my computer people poring through every line of security systems data we've been accumulating over the past two months, trying to answer that very same question. And, right now, everyone else around here—the scientists, technicians, security teams, janitors, and even the clerical staff—are taking this entire facility apart, the containment lab specifically included, looking in every nook and cranny where you could possibly hide seven small stones."

"Which, from a crime scene investigator's perspective, is pretty much anywhere," Cellars pointed out.

"Right. Which means we're all going to be pretty damned busy around here for a while, so . . ."

At that moment, Lieutenant Kessler entered the room with a piece of paper in his hand.

"Sir, Captain Montgomery said to tell you that the DEA just called. They want to know if Detective-Sergeant Cellars, Sergeant Bauer, and Special Agent Boggs are in the facility. They sounded pretty upset. Something about a missing search warrant."

"Tell the DEA to—" Byzor hesitated. "No, better yet, tell them that Cellars, Bauer, and Boggs left here over an hour ago . . . then have someone move Colin's Humvee to our underground employee parking lot."

"Yes, sir, we already did that," Kessler replied. "Also, Captain Montgomery said you'd better take a look at this. It just came in on the main fax." Kessler handed the piece of paper to Byzor.

Byzor glanced at the fax . . . then his eyes widened. He read it slowly, then wadded it up into a ball, threw it across the floor, and cursed.

Colin Cellars got up from the table, picked up the wadded paper, opened it, and read it silently.

"What does it say?" Wilbur Boggs asked after several seconds.

"It seems to be a message from our shape-shifting visitors," Cellars said. " 'Colin, we have Jody and Bobby. We want the stones. All of them. Meet us at the rendezvous point. Just you. No one else. And remember, we have all the time in the world. You and your friends don't.' "

The room was silent for several seconds.

"I don't suppose there's a source fax number at the top?" Bauer asked hopefully.

There was a distant look in Cellars's eyes as he shook his head.

"Colin, even if we had the stones—" Byzor started to say, but Cellars waved him off.

"It's all right, I understand," he said. "It's out of your hands, and ours. And we can't use the fakes. They'll spot those right away. We've got to come up with something else."

"Where's this rendezvous point they're talking about?" Bauer asked.

"I have no idea."

"The thing is, they want to deal . . . and they know you're here," Bauer went on. "If you don't show, they're not going to do anything to Bobby or Jody. Not as long as they think they can make a trade."

"Which means we've got some time," Byzor said, the stress evident in his eyes. "I've got to get back to the computer room, see if I can help Jason find a trail that leads somewhere. In the meantime, I was going to suggest that you all go home and get some sleep. But in light of this latest development, you might be better off staying here . . . where you've got some protection."

"I can't just sit here," Cellars responded. "I've got to do something."

"Yeah, same here," Boggs said . . . and Bauer nodded in agreement.

"You guys want to help in the search?"

"If I thought we could be useful around here, sure," Cellars replied before Boggs and Bauer could respond. "But the truth is, we'd probably just end up getting in the way. Everybody in the building knows this place better than we do."

He looked around the room for a moment, then suddenly focused his attention on the lab cart.

"Hey, wait a minute, what about the other stones . . . the seven originals?" he asked. "Did they fluoresce a light orange too?"

Byzor cocked his head curiously. "I really don't know. We didn't test them early on, so if Bobby did scam us, that may be the only real one we've ever had." He gestured at the small transport jar. "And besides, what good would fluorescence do us if they're hidden in some cubbyhole?"

"I was just thinking that whoever snuck in here with Marston was probably in a panic to get out. If she was able to make the switch, and had the real stones with her, it's always possible she could have dropped one or more of them somewhere outside when she was scrambling around to escape. And we know, at least according to that fax, that the bad guys don't have them all. Have you guys searched the grounds around the outside of the building yet?"

"No." Byzor shook his head thoughtfully. "Given the circumstances, I really don't think that's a high-probability scenario, but—"

"If all of the real stones fluoresce, then we could use that FOILER system of yours as a mobile crime scene scanner. Probably search the entire facility perimeter in a couple of hours."

"In the snow?" Byzor said dubiously.

"Hey, it's worth a shot. What do we have to lose? And besides," Cellars added, "it might keep us out of your hair for a few hours . . . and give us something to do while we're waiting for the next message from these kidnapping bastards. Unless, of course, you'd rather have me poking around in this place?"

"I like the 'out of your hair' part," Byzor replied. "And, I suppose, as long as you don't stray too far from the building . . ."

"Trust me, any shadows start showing up, we're going to be back inside and yelling for help long before you even know you've got a problem."

"Okay." Byzor nodded. "Just watch yourselves."

"So, does that mean you're going to trust Boggs, Bauer, and me outside the Center with your precious hundred-million-dollar, nuclear-powered laser system?" Cellars asked.

Byzor's eyes flickered from the lab cart to Dombrowski . . . then back to Cellars, immediately suspicious and appraising.

"Hey, don't worry, we'll bring it back," Cellars said. "All we need to do is run a test, scan across the blue-green frequencies at low power, and see if we get a brighter fluorescence. If we do, then we leave the FOILER locked on that setting, go outside, and scan the whole perimeter using the most diffuse collimator setting while Dombrowski stays in here and keeps an eye on the stone. Or," Cellars added, "you can always send Dombrowski outside with us, and pull someone else off security duty to watch the thing."

Byzor hesitated, then nodded. "Okay, but stay inside the perimeter fence. The entire perimeter is armed with every kind of motion and intrusion sensor we could find in the inventory. You try to go over it, and you'll have dog teams on your ass in five seconds . . . and they will shoot to kill."

"Just in case we happen to trip across one of the stones out there, and decide not to share?" Cellars's eyes flickered with amusement.

"The thought did occur to me," Byzor said as he reached for the control panel on the table and pressed a button.

"This is the deputy director," he said into what was apparently a recessed microphone. "Detective-Sergeant Cellars, Sergeant Bauer, and Special Agent Boggs will be conducting a search of the grounds with one of the FOILER systems. Consider them cleared within the confines of the outer perimeter fence."

"Yes, sir," a disembodied voice responded.

"Is that going to do it for you?" Byzor asked, looking over at Cellars.

"For the moment," Cellars replied. "You just get your butt in gear and find me a path to Jody and Bobby."

"I'll do my best," Byzor said as he headed to the door.

"Yeah, I know you will," Cellars replied seriously. "I'm just giving you a bad time. Trying to take my mind off all the bullshit."

"Just be careful," Byzor said as he paused at the doorway. "You start to get tired out there, come back inside and Dombrowski will show you to the guest bunks. And you," he said to Dombrowski, "keep a sharp eye on that rock. That may be the only piece of evidence we've got left, and I don't want to lose it."

CHAPTER FIFTY-SIX

"SO, YOU KNOW HOW TO SET THAT THING UP?" CELLARS ASKED
Dombrowski after Byzor closed the door firmly behind him.

"I'm checked out, but it's been a while," the staff sergeant said uneasily. "It's not something we normally pack out in the field."

"That's okay. I think I was following Dobres pretty well during his
demo. Let me give it a shot, see if it's cop-proof."

Dombrowski grinned. "It had damned well better be. Dobres is always telling us how he designed the thing so that even a shavetail second lieutenant could use one, if things got really desperate."

"Must be talking about the Army," Cellars said as he went over to
the lab cart and tentatively hefted the heavy FOILER pack. "Our lieu-
tenants usually have a hard time reading a street map . . . hey, which

reminds me," he added, "can you guys pull a local map up on one of those monitors?"

"Yeah, sure, what area do you want?"

"How about the southern half of Oregon?"

"Yeah, no sweat. Coming right up."

Dombrowski reached for the telephone on the table, pressed a two-digit code, then said: "This is Dombrowski. You want to flash me a south sector map of Oregon on the main monitor?"

Moments later, a colored map of the southern half of Oregon appeared on the screen.

"The next question," Cellars said as Boggs came over, picked up the FOILER pack in one muscular hand, and set it down on the floor by the table, "is where do I find a place called Little Round Top?"

"You mean in Oregon?"

"Uh-huh."

Dombrowski spoke into the handset again. "Can you guys give me a set of crosshairs on a place called Little Round Top? Yeah, in southern Oregon."

He waited for a few seconds and then looked over at Cellars.

"The graphics unit says there's no such place in Oregon, period."

"Shit," Cellars muttered.

"What's the problem?" Bauer asked, as he and Boggs began to help Cellars set up the FOILER tripod.

"When Bobby called me this evening, he told me there was at least one of them on his trail, and that he was going to try to work his way back to Little Round Top. I assumed he was talking about some kind of mountain."

"Not exactly," Boggs said as he walked over to the huge monitor.

Cellars's eyebrows furrowed.

"What do you mean, 'not exactly'?" he demanded.

"Remember I told you I used to fly with Bobby on some of his night surveillance missions? Well, one of his favorite spots was right here." Boggs stabbed a thick finger at a pink-colored section of the electronic map. "Couple miles past the outer-perimeter warning markers. That was where he liked to position himself when the sun came up . . . so that the first rays bounced off this raised dome in the mountains that he liked to call Little Round Top. Hell of a sight."

The familiar dream-images began to flash through Cellars's mind, and it was all he could do to contain himself.

"Why do you keep calling it the outer perimeter?" Bauer asked.

"Because it's absolutely forbidden territory for us," Boggs said. "Federal Indian reservation."

"I don't understand. Why would a federal Indian reservation be off-limits to a federal agent?" Bauer asked reasonably.

"Because back in eighteen ninety-three, the Ah-Ree-Ban-Coo-Tak Indian tribe worked out a deal with the federal government to keep part of their land, only they must have had a lawyer hidden away in the woodwork, somewhere, because they came up with one hell of a treaty. The basic elements were simple enough. In exchange for abandoning any and all rights to a couple hundred thousand acres of prime grazing and farmland that they really didn't have much use for anyway—because none of them were farmers or ranchers, and the open lands were too hard to defend—they got to keep ten thousand acres of mountainous terrain . . . which happened to contain some of the best hunting and fishing areas in southern Oregon, as well as their holy sites, which was all they really wanted anyway."

"So why was that such a hot deal?" Dombrowski asked. "Sounds to me like they got ripped off."

"Oh, they did . . . but they were going to get ripped off anyway, and they knew it." Boggs smiled. "So what they did was get a provision put into the treaty that said, in very specific terms, that no federal or state or local agent could, under any circumstances, trespass on their land without their express permission. And that any violation of the treaty would result in the direct payment to the tribe—or its surviving members—of a fine equivalent to the prevailing cost of the land . . . in cash . . . for each transgression. Which was ultimately interpreted by the United States Supreme Court, in nineteen thirty-seven, to mean the average cost of ten thousand acres of free range Oregon land *per individual federal or state agency transgression.*"

Bauer blinked. "That was upheld?"

"Upheld in thirty-seven, and reaffirmed in fifty-three, to include agents on horseback, in motor vehicles, or in low-flying aircraft. The last transgression, by a pair of BLM agents in a Cessna looking for a missing hiker, cost the federal government a little over two million dollars . . . which was ultimately paid, in cash, out of the agency's operating budget. Needless to say, us federal types no longer trespass on the Ah-Ree-Ban-Coo-Tak reservation if we'd like to remain gainfully employed . . . which was why Bobby damn near gave me a heart attack when he flew past those outer-perimeter markers like they didn't even exist."

Cellars stood close to the monitor now, staring at the colorful map.

"You know, that's right by where one of our CSI officers disappeared this morning," he said thoughtfully.

"Who was that," Boggs asked. "Mike Lee?"

"You know him?"

"Hell, yes, I've warned him to stay out of that area at least a half dozen times in the past year," Boggs muttered. "Damned kid wouldn't listen. Bound and determined he was going to get himself a Sasquatch picture. I told him he was a lot more likely to get himself nailed by one of those big cats if he wasn't careful."

"Big cats?"

"Cougars," Boggs said. "That whole area, which includes the reservation, happens to be one of our more productive wildlife habitats. One, because we protect it, or at least the outer perimeter of it. And two, because most of the local hunters are afraid to go hunting that close to the reservation. Rumor has it that you go tramping around in those mountains, you don't always come back . . . and nobody's going in there looking for you . . . which is damn near the truth," he added.

"How do we get in there?" Cellars asked, staring intently at the pink-designated section of land.

"What, on the Ah-Ree-Ban-Coo-Tak reservation?"

"That's right."

"We don't," Boggs said flatly. "Not unless we've got ourselves a genuine Bancoo guide . . . which is damned near impossible, these days, because there aren't many of them left."

Cellars's head snapped around. "What did you say?" he whispered, glaring into Wilbur Boggs's eyes.

"I said . . . you can't go on the reservation unless you're accompanied by a Bancoo Indian guide . . . which is damned near impossible these days for most people . . . but maybe not for us," Boggs added, almost as an afterthought.

"Why's that?" Cellars demanded, his mind churning.

What was it Bobby Dawson had said?

That's not just a photograph, Colin, my man. If my guess is right, it may turn out to be a significant piece of the puzzle. Maybe even some sort of Bancoo connection.

Well, I'll be damned.

"Because we've got one of the last genuine Bancoo Indians right here in the Waycross Center," Boggs said. "Or, at least, we did."

"Where do I find him?"

"Her, you mean," Boggs replied. "Marston's supposed girlfriend. A young woman known as Cascadia Rain-Song."

CHAPTER FIFTY-SEVEN

"WHY WOULD YOU WANT TO GO THERE?" SHE ASKED IN A SHY, HESItant voice.

One of the Waycross Center's security guards, and their public affairs officer, had been getting ready to drive Cascadia Rain-Song to the best hotel in Jasper County—intent on leaving her there with a one-month prepaid room; five thousand dollars in cash for miscellaneous expenses; one more profuse apology; and a signed promise on NSA letterhead to finance a doctorate degree at any major university she could get accepted to—when Dombrowski's progressively insistent calls brought her back to the VIP room.

She was wearing a pair of short-sleeved Waycross Center–embossed blue overalls, instead of the long-sleeved orange prison garb, the supposedly "skin-toned" bandage on her inner elbow where the technician had drawn the blood sample now readily visible against her reddish brown skin. The "civilianizing" effect of the form-fitting overalls, the bandage, and the down jacket she held in her hand, made her appear far more withdrawn, vulnerable, and frightened . . . and much less like the defiant and angry young woman they had all observed during the blood-drawing process.

So what happened to the sensuous little minx that had Marston wrapped around her little finger? Cellars wondered. *Probably scared that attitude right out of her.*

"I have two friends who may be in the hands of some very dangerous . . . people," he explained as he took her jacket and hung it over one of the chairs. "They want to make an exchange at a place called Little Round Top, which Special Agent Boggs tells me is located inside the Ah-Ree-Ban-Coo-Tak Indian Reservation."

"I think I know the place you're talking about," she said, looking uneasy. "The raised dome near the top of our highest mountain. We have a more descriptive tribal name for it, but Little Round Top means roughly the same thing."

"Is there a place near there where these people could be hiding . . . with my friends?" Cellars asked.

She nodded silently, the fear evident in her eyes now.

"Would you take me there?"

"If your friends are in the hands of the Kray-Sacs, there is nothing you—or anyone else—can do for them," she said after a moment.

"The Kray-Sacs?"

"The shadow people who inhabit the mountain," she whispered.

"There are some who would say the Kray-Sacs are mythical creatures," Wilbur Boggs suggested in a quiet voice. "Created by the Bancoos to keep the local hunters and hikers from trespassing onto their mountains."

"There's probably a great deal of truth to that," she said. "Our mountains are sacred, and we do want to keep them for ourselves. But mythical creatures don't kill . . . and the Kray-Sacs most certainly do."

"How do you know that?" Cellars asked.

"I . . . just know," she whispered. She stood up and started for the door when something on the table seemed to catch her attention.

She walked over to the table, picked up the black-and-white photograph of Patrick Bergéone, stared at it for a long moment, then turned her frightened dark eyes to Cellars. Her face paled as she collapsed into the nearest chair.

"This is him, isn't it?" she whispered, her voice almost shaking with fear.

"Who?" Cellars asked.

"The Frenchman. The man my father took to the mountains."

"Did you see him?"

"No. I . . . heard about it from Lonecoos. I was calling to talk with my father, to tell him that I'm safe, and to tell him what I've been doing since I ran away from home, but Lonecoos answered the phone. He told me that . . . the Frenchman and my father and Lastcoos, his brother, were all dead . . . killed by the Kray-Sacs. Only he escaped, with the Frenchman's camera. And that now only he can save me from them."

"Do you believe that?" Cellars asked gently.

The young woman was silent for several seconds.

"I don't know what to believe." She was still whispering, mostly to herself, as she stared down at the photograph in her trembling hands.

"Do you think Lonecoos might lie to you?"

"Perhaps. He wants me to be his wife. He might tell me such things to try to make me believe I have no other choice. But how can you deny the truth of this picture? Here he is, the Frenchman, right in front of their lair."

"Their lair?"

"Where they live," she whispered. "Where our medicine men have always taken offerings."

"Have you ever been there?" Cellars asked, sensing he could lose her at any moment, but knowing also that he had to persist. She was the link. She had to be.

She nodded silently.

"Recently?"

"No. Many years ago, when I was a child, I followed my father to the cave entrance one morning. As he had done with his father before. But, later that day, when my father discovered my climbing rope, and then found me hiding in the trees, he told me very sternly that I must never go there again. And that if I did, I would die in a very horrible way."

"Could you draw me a map of how to get there?"

She shook her head again. "I only know the way in my head . . . and it was a long time ago."

"In that case, would you take us just far enough, so that we—"

"No!" She shook her head firmly as she continued to stare down at her trembling hands. "I can't take you there. I would die, like all of the others."

Cellars sensed that he was about to lose her, and he knew he couldn't risk that. Not now.

"Cascadia, you need to understand something," Cellars whispered. "Your friend, Dr. Marston . . ."

Her dark eyes snapped up.

"It's very likely—almost certain, in fact—that he was killed by the same . . . people who took my friends."

She stared at him then, her eyes filled with anguish.

"But why would they do that?"

"I don't know," Cellars confessed. Then, taking a gamble, he asked: "Were you in love with him?"

She hesitated, and then nodded slowly. "He was such a warm and gentle man, and it didn't matter to him that I am a Bancoo. Some nights, I would dream that we would be married . . . but then, the next day, he would say strange things, and I would wonder."

"Strange things? Like what?" Cellars pressed.

"Nothing specific. Just things he would say, things that didn't make any sense. As if we'd had a conversation—or gone out on a date—the day before, when we hadn't. It was as if he was confused, and couldn't keep the days, or our conversations, straight in his mind."

"Did he do that often?"

"No, only a few times. I know his work was very stressful, and I think our relationship made it worse. Sometimes we talked about how wonderful it would be if we could both just go away somewhere, and study music, and enjoy the things we both love so much."

Cellars hesitated. "Cascadia, do you remember what you said to me yesterday evening, when you were in Dr. Marston's car?"

She blinked her dark eyes in confusion. "But I didn't say anything to you yesterday. I've never seen you before, and I wasn't in Eric's car yesterday. Like I told the other people here, I had a bad headache yesterday afternoon, so I went to bed early . . . and slept until the soldiers broke into my apartment and scared us nearly to death."

"Us?"

"My cat was sleeping with me when the soldiers came. I heard her yowling outside, but the soldiers wouldn't let me catch her. That's why I was so angry."

"I'm sorry about that," Cellars said, "but I'm sure she's okay. Cats are very resilient." And then, after a moment, he asked: "Do you get these headaches often?"

"No. I used to get them when I was younger, but they only recently started up again."

Cellars glanced over at Byzor, then turned his attention back to the young woman.

"Cascadia, I don't know why Dr. Marston was killed, but we're going to find out. And we're going to find my friends . . . and see if your father is still alive."

"By going to their lair?"

"Yes."

"But you can't do that," she protested. "I told you. They'll kill you."

"My friends and I, we're not afraid of the Kray-Sacs," Cellars said. "They can be made to die, just like anyone else. We've already proven that."

"You've killed a Kray-Sac?"

"We've killed several of them. They're dangerous, without a doubt, but they're not invincible. And they must be confronted; otherwise, they will continue to kidnap and kill many others . . . and perhaps even succeed, at whatever it is they intend to do here."

She looked up at him then, with something else in her eyes. The fear was still there, but so was the other thing. Cellars thought he knew what it was.

The will to survive . . . and fight back.

"But, for you to face them," she whispered even softer now, "do I have to take you there? Is there no other way?"

"No," he said. "There is no other way. And we have to go now."

"Then I will take you," she said, her voice strengthening. "How do we leave this place?"

"We'll go very soon," Cellars said, "but not quite yet. There's something we have to do first."

"What's that?"

"We have to test one of our weapons. If you'll move back over there, by the monitors . . ."

Cellars waited until the young woman was standing against the far wall, and then stepped up to the tripod-mounted FOILER system, checked the settings, and finally looked around the room.

"Okay, everybody grab a pair of the night-vision goggles. Tom, why don't you stand over there by Cascadia and help her with the goggles," Cellars suggested. "And Wilbur, why don't you and Dombrowski stand over there by the door so we don't have anyone accidentally walk into a laser beam."

Cellars waited until everyone was in position and had their goggles on, ignoring the odd look that Wilbur Boggs gave him before slipping the goggles on over his broad, scarred forehead.

"Okay," Cellars said, "everybody ready?"

Four goggled heads nodded.

"I think I've got this thing set to the same blue-green frequency Malcolm used in his CSI scanner, and it's locked in on the lowest power setting. Get ready . . . now."

An instant later, a bright, blue-green, two-inch-diameter laser beam shot out of the lasing tube, which immediately caused the small stone in the polycarbonate transport jar to glow a bright orange . . .

. . . and sent the Elmer Fudd doll with the construction nail sticking out of its forehead gliding slowly across the table.

CHAPTER FIFTY-EIGHT

"JESUS CHRIST!"

Staff Sergeant Ed Dombrowski stared, wide-eyed, at the doll for almost two full seconds before he suddenly remembered his primary purpose for being in the room.

He lunged for the red alarm button on the wall near the podium . . . and then dropped to the floor like a 190-pound sack of grain in response to a stunning blow just below the right ear administered by Special Agent Wilbur Boggs.

Cascadia Rain-Song started to scream . . . then caught herself, wide-eyed, as Cellars quickly motioned her to silence.

"Hope that was what you had in mind," Boggs commented as he slipped the birdshot-filled blackjack back into his jacket pocket, dropped to his knees next to the unconscious Delta Forces commando, brought out a pair of handcuffs, and quickly secured the muscular young soldier's wrists behind his back. "This kid's really going to be pissed when he wakes up."

"Yes, he is . . . and I don't plan on being around here when that happens, so make sure you tuck him away where they won't find him for a while," Cellars answered.

"No problem," Boggs grunted as he reached into his jacket pocket for the roll of duct tape.

"Tom, give me a hand with this thing." Cellars gestured with his head at the tripod-mounted laser system. "And Cascadia—" He looked at the visibly confused young woman. "There's a knapsack under the table. Grab it, and fill it up with four sets of the night-vision goggles, that containment jar, and both of those Elmer Fudd dolls. And don't worry," he said when he realized she was still staring, wide-eyed, at the nail-impaled doll, "they're just stones. Nothing that can hurt you."

As Cellars and Bauer worked to reassemble the FOILER system back into its fifty-pound backpack, Wilbur Boggs wrapped lengths of tape around Dombrowski's mouth, ankles, knees, and wrists—thus making it extremely difficult for the young soldier, or anyone else, to unlock the handcuffs—then dragged him into the women's rest room.

"Ready?" Cellars asked as Boggs reemerged two minutes later with a satisfied smile on his face.

"You bet."

"Okay, you take the laser pack, I'll take the knapsack, and Tom and Cascadia will lead the way out to the parking lot."

Five minutes and two helpful sets of directions later, Colin Cellars, Tom Bauer, Wilbur Boggs, and Cascadia Rain-Song found themselves in the Waycross Center employees' parking lot, where they quickly unloaded the FOILER pack and knapsack in the back of the OSP Humvee. Two minutes after that, they were approaching the employees' guard gate in the rumbling vehicle.

"What are you planning on telling them?" Bauer inquired from the right rear passenger seat.

"As little of the actual truth as I possibly can," Cellars replied, then rolled down his side window as he brought the Humvee up alongside the armored glass window.

"Detective-Sergeant Colin Cellars, from the OSP," he said, holding up his credentials. "Special Agent Boggs, Sergeant Bauer, Miss Rain-Song, and I are going to be conducting a laser search of the grounds over the next several hours."

The young guard looked down at his clipboard.

"Yes, sir," he acknowledged. "Deputy Director Byzor notified us that you'd be searching within the inner fence perimeter. Kind of a lousy night to be working outside." He glanced out at the slowly falling snow.

"Bad timing. No doubt about it," Cellars agreed. "Do you guys have any guard teams patrolling the area?"

"Yes, sir. We have a number of dog teams that work the facility grounds and perimeter fence in random patterns."

"Okay, then you'd better let them know we're going to be working with an unshielded laser system. We'll have it set on low power, and the beam will be fully diffused; but even so, they probably should avoid staring directly at it."

"Is that really going to be a problem, sir?" the guard asked. "I mean, in terms of safety?"

"It shouldn't be," Cellars replied. "At least, as far as humans are concerned, and especially if they're all wearing their night-vision goggles. But, now that you mention it, the dogs might have a problem." Cellars turned to Boggs, who was sitting in the front passenger seat with a gently amused expression on his face. "What do you think would be a safe working distance for the canines? A hundred yards?"

"I'd make it two hundred, just to be sure," Boggs suggested.

"Yeah, makes sense." Cellars turned back to the guard. "Is there a service road around the perimeter fence?"

"Yes, sir. All the way around the inside. It's a little rough in spots, but you won't have any problem in a Hummer."

"Okay, here's what we're going to do. Tell the teams to keep the dogs at least two hundred yards from our location . . . and, ideally, facing in the opposite direction. At that distance, with the beam diffused, aimed down at the ground, and at low power, they probably won't be able to see much of anything anyway, but we'll use our headlights to keep them advised of our position. We'll start at the main gate, work a fifty-yard-radius semicircle, relative to the fence line, and then shift a hundred yards at a time in a counterclockwise direction. Once we get the equipment set up and working, it'll probably take about fifteen to twenty minutes to search each semicircle. We'll have a better idea after the first one. The patrol teams will know when we're moving, because we'll turn our headlights back on. Got all that?"

"Yes, sir." The guard nodded firmly as he reached for his pack-set radio.

"Okay, we're out of here. Better tell those guys to move away from the main gate area right now, and to keep their eyes open. We don't want to get surprised out there."

"Yes, sir, no problem."

Cellars waited for the guard to open the gate bar, drove forward, and then cruised along the main access road at a steady ten miles per hour.

"You really think they'll be hotfooting it out of there?" Boggs inquired.

"If it wasn't for the dogs, hell, no. They'd all be moving in on us, just to see what we're doing," Cellars said. "But I've never met a dog officer who'd expose his furry partner to a risk that wasn't absolutely necessary."

Sure enough, two minutes later, when they came to a stop about thirty feet from the closed gate, there was no one around as far as they could see through the falling snow. Cellars turned off the lights of the Humvee, reached down for the set of night-vision goggles and a small toolkit, got out of the vehicle, and approached the gate.

Ten minutes later, the chain-link gate was standing wide open, and Cellars was shaking the snow off his jacket and climbing back into the Humvee.

"See anybody?" he asked as he worked himself back into the seat belt. Boggs, Bauer, and Rain-Song were all wearing night-vision goggles, and maintaining a watch through the opened back and side windows of the squat vehicle.

"Not a soul," Boggs confirmed. "By the way, I saw you bypass the gate closure switches with that long run of wire, but what about the ground sensors?"

"There's a bunch of them on either side of the gate and fence line, but it looks like the signals get relayed back to the main building through a couple of concealed transmitters . . . a primary and what looked like a backup," Cellars said. "Makes sense, from a security standpoint, if you think you can keep the bad guys from finding both transmitters. A mile's a hell of a long way to run buried wire if you don't have to."

"So what did you do?"

"Just wrapped all the transmitter and sensor antennas I could find with pieces of foil."

"Is that going to work . . . assuming there's only two transmitters instead of three?"

"It should. If not, we'll probably find out pretty damned quick," Cellars replied as he started up the Humvee's engine, but left the headlights off. "Everybody ready?"

There were three quick affirmatives.

"Okay, hang on. We're out of here."

Ten minutes and several night-vision-guided turns later, Cellars turned the Humvee onto the main road, removed his night-vision goggles, and switched on the headlights.

They were back on the freeway, and heading toward the distant mountains, when Cascadia Rain-Song broke the silence.

"Can we stop at my apartment before we go up the mountain?" she asked.

"Is it absolutely necessary?" Cellars replied.

"It might be," she said. "The Kray-Sacs are used to us moving around their lair in our traditional clothing. But they might get suspicious if they see me coming in these blue overalls. They make me look like I work for the government. And besides," she added, "I want to check on my cat."

"Okay," Cellars said agreeably. "How do we get to your apartment?"

———

Fifteen minutes later, Special Agent Wilbur Boggs and Sergeant Tom Bauer approached the broken and resealed rear door of the ground-floor apartment, while Colin Cellars and Cascadia Rain-Song waited in front. All the windows in the surrounding apartments were dark, which suggested that the neighbors had finally recovered from the evening's earlier events and gone to bed.

Cellars glanced down at his watch, counted off thirty more seconds, then gestured with his head for Cascadia to stand back as he reached for the door handle.

In one smooth motion, he shoved the sealed door open with his shoulder, with his left hand flipped on the light switch by the door, and entered the small combined living room and kitchen with his SIG-Sauer out and ready to fire.

At the same instant, first Boggs then Bauer burst in through the rear kitchen door with flashlights in one hand and pistols in the other.

It took the three men another two minutes to quickly and professionally confirm that, aside from a startled and now loudly complaining calico cat—who immediately began rubbing up against Cascadia's legs while looking up questioningly at the three men—the small apartment was definitely uninhabited.

"It's okay," Cascadia whispered in a soothing voice as she scooped up the loudly meowing cat. "I'll be right out," she said to Cellars as she grabbed some traditional buckskin clothes from her closet, then disappeared into the bathroom, closing the door firmly behind her.

"Why do so many women keep cats as pets?" Bauer wondered out loud.

"Beats the hell out of me," Cellars said. "Jody's like that, too. Long as I've known her, she's always had a damned cat hanging around. You couldn't hardly get her to go anywhere without—"

Cellars blinked, then started to say something when a sudden, loud cracking noise caused all three men to snap their heads around.

The three instinctively arranged themselves in a three-pointed, back-to-back position in the middle of the small living room, and waited expectantly for some other indication that someone—or something—was moving around outside the apartment complex.

But there was no further sound.

"What do you think?" Bauer asked uneasily.

"I think I want to get out of here as soon as we possibly can," Cellars replied.

"Why? You think we've got more of those damned shadow creatures out there?" The idea clearly didn't appeal to Bauer at all.

"Not necessarily," Cellars said as he and Boggs quickly moved to the two sets of windows and peeked around the side of the curtains. "I think we're far more likely to run into them on the way up to Little Round Top. Right now, I'm a lot more worried about Malcolm. Those Delta Forces guys of his already hit this place once. As soon as Malcolm realizes we've skipped out, this'll be one of the first places he'll have them check."

"Then let's get the hell out of here," Bauer agreed as he went over and knocked gently on the bathroom door. "Cascadia, are you about ready?"

"Coming out right now," Cascadia said as she opened the door and stepped out of the bathroom wearing a long buckskin skirt over a pair of tight, black, short-sleeved leotards that did nothing at all to conceal her considerable feminine charms. Caught off guard by the sight, Cellars quickly dropped his gaze to the floor . . . an act that caused the woman to flash a dimpled smile in his direction. "I just need to get my ceremonial shirt and down jacket out of the—"

Hey, wait a minute! Where's the damned—?

Cat?

She was reaching out with her left hand to open the closet door when Cellars's eyes snapped back up . . . and suddenly focused on her bare—and unbandaged—inner arm.

"Tom, look out!"

Tom Bauer instinctively brought his nongun hand up in front of his face just as a clawed hand slashed viciously at his eyes . . . and tore through the fabric of his down jacket. The force of the impact sent the patrol sergeant sprawling backward to the floor.

Boggs and Cellars opened fire almost in the same instant. Four streaking, hollow-pointed bullets slammed into the chest and head of

"What about you?"

"I'll live."

"Don't go getting optimistic on us," Wilbur Boggs muttered from the front passenger seat as he continued to watch the side of the road for any sign of the shadowy Kray-Sacs, a black-finished Remington model 870, 12-gauge pump shotgun with an extended magazine held loosely in his left hand.

The wounds in Tom Bauer's forearm were deep, and would probably require surgery to repair nerve and tendon damage. But Boggs had quickly stopped the bleeding, and Cellars had used the gauze pads, tape, and dressings in the Humvee's first-aid kit to fashion a functional compression bandage that he and Boggs agreed would probably keep the bleeding under control for a few hours. And, in any case, Bauer had adamantly refused to be dropped off at the emergency room.

"Somebody's got to stay with the vehicle and radio to call for help when things go to shit, and keep an eye on Cascadia if she can't make the hike," he'd said. A point Cellars and Boggs hadn't been able to argue.

"What are we going to do if she stays that way?" Boggs asked.

"We know roughly where the dome is," Cellars replied. "If she can't lead us to the cave, all we have to do is start hiking in the right direction. We've got what they want. They'll find us."

"Is that a good thing?" Bauer asked.

"Probably not," Cellars conceded, "but I'm starting to run out of clever ideas."

"Screw the clever ideas," Boggs muttered. "Like you said, we've got what they want, and they've got what we want. They've got two choices: trade, or try to make a grab."

"And if you guys are outnumbered ten to one?" Bauer asked pointedly.

"Then you'd better get on that radio and call for the cavalry before we end up with another Little Round Top episode for the history books," Boggs replied.

"Dawson would absolutely love that," Cellars commented, mostly to himself.

"What?" Boggs responded, glancing over at Cellars quizzically before returning his attention to the side of the road.

"Never mind. Here we are," Cellars said as he pulled the Humvee over behind a snow-covered mound.

"Lee's scout car?" Boggs asked.

"Probably." Cellars stared out the window at the still-falling snow. "How's she doing back there?" he asked Bauer.

"Still out."

Cellars sighed heavily. "Okay," he said, "let's get this turkey shoot on the road."

For no particular reason other than to satisfy his curiosity, Cellars first walked over to the huge mound, brushed away several armloads of snow from the windshield and driver's side door, confirmed the presence of the thirty-five-millimeter camera mount on the white scout car's dashboard . . . and quickly verified there were no bodies in the front or back seats.

Then he unlocked and removed the pump shotgun from the scout car's console mount, closed the driver's side door, checked the magazine, racked a round into the chamber, and walked back to the rear of the Humvee, where he found Wilbur Boggs waiting with the FOILER backpack on his shoulders, the Humvee's pump shotgun dangling from his right hand, and a four-cell flashlight in his left. A second four-cell flashlight, the bulging knapsack, and an open box of 12-gauge buckshot rounds lay in the snow next to the open driver's side door of the Humvee.

"You going to be able to hump that thing up a mountain?" Cellars asked dubiously as he dropped a handful of extra 12-gauge rounds into his jacket pocket, then reached for the knapsack and flashlight. "We may not have much use for it once we're up there."

"May not do us much good as a laser, but it'll make one hell of a nice battering ram," Boggs replied. "Lot better than one of those hundred-thousand-dollar toilet seats the government's always buying."

"Okay. You can explain the damage to Malcolm when he catches up with us." Cellars turned to Bauer, who was now sitting in the front seat of the Humvee with his SIG-Sauer resting on his lap. "You still doing okay?"

"I'm fine," the sergeant said impatiently. "What about the goggles?"

"I think we're going to hold off on the night-vision gear, stick with the flashlights as long as we can. Gives us better peripheral vision in the forest. On the other hand, the goggles might give you an extra few seconds to react if they decide to try to peel a door on this thing."

"Makes sense," Bauer agreed.

"Also, I'm pretty sure we're in an intermittent dead zone out here. I remember Lee had trouble with his cell phone when he called me yesterday evening. So we may have difficulty maintaining radio contact," Cellars said as he slung the knapsack over his shoulder, then patted the pack-set radio mike he'd clipped to the outside collar of his down jacket. "If you hear shooting and can't reach us, activate the emergency transmitter and yell for help. Odds are, Malcolm and his chopper pilots will be monitoring all our state and local frequencies. After that, try to watch your own ass while you're watching out for hers," he added.

"We'll be fine," Bauer replied, his eyes looking slightly glassy from the pain. "Just don't get carried away and start shooting at your vehicle again. Talbert'll be pissed . . . and so will we."

"I'll keep that in mind." Cellars grinned, then glanced over at Boggs. "You ready?"

"Anytime you are," the massive wildlife agent muttered.

"Okay, let's get to it."

———

They'd gone only a hundred yards into the darkened, snow-covered forest when Boggs spotted the first body.

"In the trees, to your right, in the old black oak . . . about thirty feet up," he said in a casual voice as he quickly swept his flashlight beam across a mass of huge branches. "One, maybe two."

Colin Cellars stared up at the white-covered masses for a few seconds. Then, after taking and releasing a breath, he slid the knapsack off his shoulder and set the pump shotgun against the massive tree trunk that separated into three equally huge main branches about three feet off the ground.

"What're you planning on doing?" Boggs asked.

"I need to find out if one of my theories holds water," Cellars replied. He swept the surrounding forest with his flashlight beam, then stuck the heavy flashlight in his belt and jammed his right boot into the gap between two of the main branches, telling himself that one of the bodies up there couldn't be Jody's. They'd need her as a bargaining chip.

If they intend to bargain, he reminded himself.

"Sounds like a real bad idea to me," Boggs said.

"I'm not thrilled with it, either," Cellars agreed as he reached up for one of the slightly smaller snow-covered branches. "Why don't you see if you can keep me covered for a couple of minutes, make me feel a little better about the whole idea?"

Four minutes later, he was back on the ground.

"Well?" Boggs demanded.

"Trooper Lee and the good Dr. H. Milhaus Pleasant," Cellars replied in a neutral voice as he placed the knapsack back over his shoulders and picked up the shotgun.

"Any idea how long they've been up there?"

"In the case of Lee, I'd say a little less than twenty-four hours. But probably more like a week for Pleausant . . . which complicates the situation just a bit."

"Why's that?"

"I had a long conversation with Pleausant yesterday afternoon, about twelve hours ago, in his office. Or, at least, I thought I did."

"You sure it's him up there?"

"Unless he's got a twin brother."

"So what are we talking about? Another example of that shape-shifting crap you were telling me about?" Boggs asked after a few moments.

"Apparently. Either that, or I'm just losing my mind," Cellars said.

"You think he had a cat, too?"

"Wouldn't surprise me one bit."

"I almost hate to ask, but what did the two of you talk about in his office while the real Pleausant was out here moldering away in a tree?"

"Nothing much. Just my collection of mental problems. And, of course, my plans to hunt down all the shadowy bad guys who've been making my life miserable for the past couple of months."

"Wonderful," Boggs muttered.

"Yeah, exactly."

They continued to work their way through the falling snow for another five minutes or so . . . and then came to a stop when Cellars suddenly turned his head to stare up into the trees to their right.

As he did so, an elongated form immediately separated from the thick, dark mass of intercrossed branches . . . turned away, and disappeared.

"You know, for a moment there, I would have sworn that was a black panther," Cellars commented.

Boggs chuckled. "Yep, that's exactly what it looked like to me, too."

"What the hell's so funny about seeing a black panther in the middle of the night, in a darkened forest?" Cellars asked. The two men continued to sweep their flashlight beams across the high cross branches of the surrounding trees, but saw nothing.

"For one thing, we don't have any black panthers in Oregon," the wildlife agent replied.

"Oh."

They started forward again, moving slowly through the downed branches and deep drifts of snow . . . then came up short when a deep, husky voice suddenly echoed across the chilled darkness.

"You were told to come alone."

"I'm not that stupid," Cellars replied in the general direction of the voice.

There was a long pause, then . . .

"Show us the stones."

"After we see Jody and Bobby."

Another pause.

"They're not here."

"Then take us to them," Cellars demanded.

"No."

The wind was starting to pick up again, causing the tops of the tall trees to sway and send their accumulated drifts of snow crashing through the lower branches.

"The stones are in a containment jar . . . along with an explosive charge," Cellars said after a moment. "If you make any attempt to take the stones away from us, I'll detonate the charge."

"And destroy yourself . . . and your friends . . . in the process?"

"They tell me the jar can contain a small explosion," Cellars replied. "I have no idea if that's true or not, but I'm perfectly willing to find out."

Another pause.

"I don't believe you."

"Then try me . . . see what happens to your evidence."

"If you destroy the stones, then we no longer have to concern ourselves about missing evidence," the voice pointed out. "We will have accomplished our mission."

"Perhaps," Cellars agreed. "But I don't think that's the only issue here."

This time, the silence continued on to the count of twelve, as another dark, lithe, and stealthy form became intermittently visible, moving swiftly through the huge upper limbs of the surrounding trees.

"Fucking cats," Boggs muttered. "Give me a lazy, good-for-nothing dog any day."

Then, suddenly, Cellars and Boggs heard soft footsteps behind them.

Both men whirled in unison with shotgun barrels extended. Their flashlight beams triangulated on a small, dark-haired figure clad in blue overalls and a down jacket slowly trudging toward them in the falling snow.

"Don't pay any attention to the evil ones," Cascadia Rain-Song said, gesturing at the surrounding trees as she approached the two men. "You don't need them. I'll take you there."

A half hour—or perhaps forty minutes—later, Cellars wasn't sure, he and Boggs found themselves crouched against a huge Douglas fir, gasping for breath and trying to keep from sliding back down the narrow, slippery, clay-mud-and-rock ravine.

They were wearing the night-vision goggles now, and very much aware of the pair of long, lithe, and graceful shadow figures trailing behind . . . and every now and then, to the side. Like predators, gradually moving in on their prey.

A few feet in front of them, Cascadia Rain-Song sat crouched on a narrow ridge.

"We're almost there," she whispered. Unlike the two men, her breathing was steady and unlabored.

"Good," Wilbur Boggs muttered. "I'm about ready to trade this half-million-dollar battering ram in for a good-size rock."

They rested for another five minutes. Then, after another agonizing, fifteen-minute climb, the trail they were following suddenly narrowed down to a ledge that looked to be barely six inches wide as it curved around a huge rock and disappeared. Cellars eased forward and swept his flashlight beam into the dark void below. He saw nothing.

"It's at least three hundred feet to the bottom, maybe more," the young woman said. "We have to be careful here."

"There's no way we can make that. Not without climbing gear, and not with these packs and the shotguns," Cellars said. "We have to find another way."

"Wait here," she whispered. Then, before Cellars could do or say anything, she scampered forward along the narrow ridge and disappeared around the huge rock.

Five minutes later, as Cellars and Boggs waited with increasing uneasiness in the night-vision-enhanced darkness, the end of a long, dirt-stained rope dropped down at their feet.

Cellars went up first with one of the shotguns and the knapsack. At the top of the ledge, he retied the hundred-foot length of weathered rope around a bigger tree, and pulled up the heavy FOILER pack. Then, while he and Cascadia kept an eye out for any shadows, Cellars coaxed a much heavier, less agile, and furiously muttering Wilbur Boggs up the series of barely visible foot- and handholds with the rope secured around the agent's thick waist.

They rested at the top of the ridge long enough for Cellars to help Boggs resecure the heavy FOILER pack over his shoulders. Then both men picked up the shotguns and set themselves at Cascadia Rain-Song's right and left flanks as they moved toward a small clump of trees.

Five minutes later, they stood at the maw of the cave, where an evil-looking gargoyle grinned back at them.

Cellars immediately recognized the figure from the black-and-white photo of Patrick Bergéone.

"This is the place," he whispered as he looked around for their shadowy tags . . . who were now nowhere to be seen.

Wordlessly, Wilbur Boggs slid the heavy pack off his shoulders, unclipped the canvas covering, and pulled the FOILER laser out, leaving the base and tripod inside the pack.

"This'll do just fine," he muttered, holding the blue-green laser in his left hand and the 12-gauge pump shotgun in his right.

Cellars looked at Cascadia Rain-Song.

"You can stay outside, if you want," he said. "You might be a lot safer."

She shook her head wordlessly.

"Are you sure?"

She nodded.

"Okay." Cellars shrugged as he stepped up to the maw of the cave. "Let's go see if we can make ourselves a deal."

CHAPTER SIXTY

AS CELLARS STEPPED FORWARD INTO THE ROUGH-CARVED STONE entranceway, he experienced the unnerving sense that the tunnel had begun to narrow in response to his presence. He forced himself to ignore the sensation, and continued to move forward . . . ignoring, too, the fact that his shoulders continually brushed against the narrow, cold, confining walls. He could hear Boggs behind him, grunting from the effort as he worked his shoulders and bulk through the gradually narrowing tunnel.

He made another sharp turn . . . and then, without warning, found himself inside a cavernous place that was suddenly brightly illuminated by what seemed like thousands of lights in the high ceiling overhead.

Lights that immediately threatened to burn out the fine phosphor screens in his night-vision goggles and sear his eyes.

Cellars reacted by pulling the goggles off his face and throwing them aside—only vaguely aware of a fleeting image, burned into his retinas, of something that might have been a disklike ship in the back of the cavern.

The lights in the ceiling instantly dimmed to a barely visible glow, leaving Cellars and Boggs and Cascadia Rain-Song in almost total darkness.

Cellars immediately thumbed the switch on his four-cell flashlight; but, for some reason, the once-powerful beam was greatly weakened now, resulting in only a faintly visible circle of light on the rough, stone floor.

As Cellars slowly moved forward, the incredibly weak flashlight beam revealed a square chunk of stone roughly eight feet on a side and four feet high. It looked, to Cellars, like some kind of crude altar.

And beyond that, another dark shape about fifteen feet away.

Another altar?

No, he realized as he moved forward, it was much too tall for that.

He moved closer, and was able to make out what looked like a small mountain of clay—with hundreds of irregular stones of varying sizes embedded in hollowed-out niches—that rose high into the darkness. Surrounding the small clay mountain on all sides lay hundreds of broken and shattered gargoyles, icons, and statues.

He started to move closer when he suddenly heard the whisper of something that sounded very much like soft, padded feet moving across the stone floor to his right.

Cellars immediately stepped back to the altar, slipped the knapsack off his shoulders, and pulled out the almost-invisible containment jar, an Elmer Fudd doll, and two stone necklaces. He set the jar upright in the middle of the rough stone surface, placed the two stone necklaces next to it, set the doll and knapsack over to one side, then moved farther back in the direction of the cave entrance.

As he did so, an oddly diffuse beam of bluish green light suddenly appeared to his left—from the lasering device held in Wilbur Boggs's steady hands—and illuminated the nearly invisible jar . . . revealing the second Elmer Fudd doll with a construction nail sticking out of its forehead, and eight orange-glowing stones at its feet. One of the stones was slightly larger than the other seven, and glowed more of a reddish orange . . . as did the two stones mounted on the gold chains—one fine and delicate, the other thick and masculine.

Slowly, and barely visibly, all ten stones began to move.

Beyond the altar, the array of perhaps three hundred stones—all glowing in varying shades of orange to light brown, and seeming to hover in midair—began to move.

Cascadia Rain-Song gasped, and began to back away toward the cave entrance.

Cellars heard the scraping of her running shoes on the rough stone floor, but by the time he turned around it was too late. The barely visible movements of a large, black, pantherlike shadow warned Cellars and Boggs that the young Bancoo woman had been cut off from their protection.

"Colin! Wilbur!" Cascadia cried as she found herself forced to retreat deeper into the darkness of the cave in response to the herding movements of the shadowy creatures.

"Don't move. Stay where you are!" Cellars urged, frustrated by the awareness that he and Boggs didn't dare shoot because they could only pinpoint her location by the sound of her frightened voice. "They won't hurt you."

"Very good, you brought them all," the familiar, husky, and now-approving, voice interrupted from somewhere in the darkness.

Boggs started to shift the laser beam in the direction of the voice, but then quickly brought it back when Cellars yelled, "No, keep the beam focused on the jar . . . no matter what!"

"You're not very trusting," the voice chided.

"Of course not," Cellars replied. "Where are they?"

"Who?"

"Bobby and Jody. My friends."

"Why should I tell you?" the voice asked reasonably. "We have what we want now."

"Not yet, you don't."

"Do you really think you can stop us from taking the stones?"

Somehow, the voice managed to sound cold, threatening, and jokingly chiding all at the same time.

Like an adult talking to a stubborn and disobedient—but ultimately helpless—child, Cellars thought uneasily. *What if I'm wrong?*

He didn't want to think about that.

The source of the voice was moving now. Cellars tried to follow it with his eyes and ears, but he still couldn't see anything.

"Can you spot him?" Cellars whispered to Boggs.

"No." The wildlife agent responded in a deep, growling voice . . . giving the distinct impression of a mother grizzly prepared to defend her cub by shredding every creature in sight but frustrated by the fact that she couldn't find anything to shred.

"The others were more threatening," Cellars said, trying to taunt the creature into a response. "But you're not. Why is that?"

"It's not my job to be threatening."

"Oh, really?" Cellars cocked his head. "Then what, exactly, is your job?"

"You might say I'm a keeper of the rules," the voice replied.

"The rules?"

"Yes, as I believe Allesandra told you, we have very specific rules which govern our visits to other worlds." The deep voice echoed throughout the cave. "Specifically, we're not allowed to stay long, and we're not allowed to use our advanced technologies . . . only those that are immediately available."

"What about those invisible impacts against my vehicle that damned near knocked me off the road and left impressions the size of a bowling ball, and the even bigger ones you used against Melissa Washington's van?" Cellars demanded.

"Simple point-sources of energy that expand in a spherical manner when released, and leave no evidence of their use, other than a hemispherical impression mark that could have been caused by any number of things," the voice replied. "Which is, after all, the most crucial rule of all: the fact that, regardless of anything else, we are never allowed to leave any evidence of our visit. Much like the visitors to your wilderness areas, we are required to clean up after ourselves."

"But she did leave evidence," Cellars pointed out. "Allesandra, I mean."

"Yes . . . and she was expected to resolve that problem herself."

"And when she failed . . . ?"

"We sent a mother to retrieve her child . . . and, like her daughter, she allowed her emotions to get in the way of her duty. That was a mistake. We won't allow that to happen in future retrievals."

A big cat snarled in the darkness, and Cellars felt a chill run down his spine.

"The mother . . . of Allesandra?"

"Yes."

"Where is she?" Cellars asked. He could feel the hairs on the back of his neck starting to rise.

"Here, with us."

Cellars blinked in shock.

"In this cave?"

"Yes."

The ceiling lights flickered off to the right, revealing, for a brief moment, a huge, pantherlike creature with glaring eyes that instantly turned away and disappeared.

"Fucking cats," Wilbur Boggs muttered.

"You can understand her displeasure. You and your friends managed to destroy her entire team . . . five retrievers," the husky, disembodied voice echoed throughout the vast cavern. "It appears we should have given her six . . . but such an idea would have been unthinkable, perhaps even laughable, before now. We underestimated you humans. Another mistake that we won't repeat again."

"We killed five of them?" Cellars whispered in disbelief.

"Destroyed, not killed," the voice corrected. "Why? Do you find that difficult to believe?"

"Yes, I suppose I do."

"Good," the voice said approvingly. "That suggests humbleness on your part . . . and an awareness of your tenuous bargaining position."

There was a long pause.

"My friends?" Cellars tried again.

"They're safe, for the moment," the voice warned. "Your male friend, Bobby, continues to resist beyond all logic . . . and remains alive only because Allesandra's mother has been forbidden to exact her vengeance. You should understand, however, that I'm inclined to grant her that pleasure before we leave."

"Leave? Where are you going?" Cellars asked quickly, desperately seeking some kind of verbal "grip," something he could use to his advantage, but the voice ignored him.

"I will keep him contained . . . and alive . . . while we negotiate," the voice added meaningfully.

"You used the word 'retrievers,'" Cellars pressed on, working for time now. Time to think. And time for Malcolm and his Delta Forces commandos to triangulate on Bauer and the Humvee . . . and maybe, somehow, find their way to the cave before it was too late. It was a long shot at best, but Cellars couldn't see that they had many other options. There were at least three or four of the shadowy, pantherlike creatures moving around the cave now. He was able to spot flashes of purple when their eyes briefly turned in his direction . . . and brief, shadowy flickers of movement caused by the diffused remnants of the blue-green laser light reflecting off the slightly irregular, curved surface of the containment jar.

But there could easily be a dozen, or even more, he reminded himself. It was impossible to see beyond fifteen or twenty feet in the huge cavern.

"You sent them here . . . to retrieve all of those stones, not just Allesandra and her . . . protectors?" He gestured in the direction of the glowing and seemingly hovering array of stones with the barrel of his shotgun.

"Yes."

"But those stones must have been hidden in church artifacts— statues, icons, and gargoyles all over our world." Cellars tried to remember how Jody had described Dawson's sketch. "From a long time ago. A very long time ago, in some cases."

"Our earlier travelers had to find safe places to store the stabilized remains of their lost companions, until the retrievers could come for

chose that moment to make a whimpering sound deep in her throat . . . then made a desperate dash for the mouth of the cave.

"Don't . . . !" Cellars and Boggs yelled simultaneously as Cellars tried to bring the pump shotgun to bear on the barely visible flash of shadow that lunged out of the deeper blackness . . . but it was too dark, and much too late. They both heard her gasp . . . and then the sound of her lifeless body crumpling to the rocky floor of the cave.

For a long moment, the entire cave was silent.

Then the cell phone in Colin Cellars's jacket pocket began to ring.

CHAPTER SIXTY-ONE

CELLARS REFLEXIVELY PULLED THE CELL PHONE OUT OF HIS JACKET
pocket . . . wondering, as he did so, how the tiny antenna could possibly
be picking up a distant signal from inside a cave.

"Hello?"

"Colin?"

It was Malcolm.

"Where are you?" Cellars barked, his voice tight with rage.

"Standing in the snow outside the mouth of a cave. Presumably the
one you and Boggs are in."

Cellars blinked.

"How the hell did you find us?" he demanded, his confusion momentarily overcoming his anger.

"Patrick Bergéone left one of his light meter/transmitters out here on a rock ledge, by the trees, probably to help him find the way back in case his Bancoo guides changed their minds about being cooperative," Malcolm Byzor replied. "We found the transmitter and the tracking device he left in his camera bag, activated the missing transmitter by satellite relay, and then reprogrammed one of our K-Thirteens to look for the resulting signal. No sweat."

"You used a multibillion-dollar military satellite to look for us?" Cellars said, incredulous.

"Sure, why not? Gotta use it for something."

Cellars started to say something in reply when the disembodied voice interrupted.

"Is that your friend Malcolm?"

"Yeah, he's right outside the cave, along with a couple dozen commandos armed to the teeth," Cellars replied, the sound of the deep echoing voice causing his memory of Cascadia Rain-Song's last moments—and his own rage—to return.

"Good, I want to talk with him, too."

"You think those soldiers are going to let you anywhere near him?"

"I know only one of them can enter the cave at a time, and we can narrow or even close the tunnel at any place we choose," the voice replied. "It would be a shame to waste such courageous young men. Tell him to come in . . . alone . . . if he wishes to talk."

"Tell the shithead I'm looking forward to it."

That last was Malcolm Byzor's voice, emanating from Cellars's cell phone.

Cellars hesitated, then shook his head.

"No, not until I see Bobby and Jody, right in front of me," he said emphatically.

"If you insist."

Off to Cellars's right, a distant section of cave wall began to shimmer . . . then disappeared altogether, leaving two dark figures barely visible in the softly glowing ceiling lights.

Cellars could just make out their dark shapes as they moved toward the glowing pile of stones, one in front of the other.

The knife became faintly visible first . . . the randomly diffused wisps of blue-green laser light reflecting off the bloodied surface. Then a ripped shirtsleeve and bloodied hand and arm. And finally the clawed shirt, bloodied torso, and fierce, protective features of Bobby Dawson . . . followed by Jody Catlin, who was held tightly in the crook of Dawson's left arm, her clothes soaked a blackish red color. She seemed barely able to stand upright.

They were still about thirty feet away when the voice ordered: "Stop right there."

"Colin?" Dawson rasped, blinking his eyes against the reflective blue-green light.

"I'm over here, with Wilbur Boggs," Cellars said. "Are you two okay?"

"I've got a whole new insight in what it feels like to be a goddamned mouse," Dawson replied, "but Jody's not doing so good. Lost a lot of blood when one of these friggin' cats went for her. I got most of the bleeding stopped, but we need to get her medivacked out of here, soon as we can."

"Malcolm's outside with the cavalry. I'll see what I can work out with these assholes."

"Good, you do that," Dawson replied in a weak voice. Then: "How you doin', Wilbur?"

"Just fine," Boggs replied. "Good to see you again."

"About time you fellows got here," Dawson commented with what sounded like the last reserves of his strength. "Thought I was going to have to fight off these critters all by myself, without so much as a dead horse to hide behind."

"Actually, I think the Apaches are going to be on our side, this time around," Cellars replied.

"That a fact?" Dawson cocked his head curiously.

"Trust me," Cellars replied, his voice edged with rage.

"Are you satisfied?" the voice asked.

Cellars turned to face what seemed to be the general location of the voice.

"No, I'm not, but I doubt you really give a shit."

"Tell Malcolm to come inside."

"Let Jody go, first. She needs medical attention."

"No."

The final confirmation.

Cellars brought the cell phone up to his mouth.

"Malcolm, you're welcome to join us in here, if you want. I wouldn't recommend it, but it's your call. Oh, and don't bother with the goggles. They'll just burn out in here."

"I'm coming in right now . . . by myself."

Moments later, Malcolm Byzor came into the cave, stopped for a few moments to let his eyes adjust to the darkness, then slowly walked up to where Colin Cellars and Wilbur Boggs were standing.

"Finally, I have you all together again," the disembodied voice said with audible satisfaction.

"And it seems we have all of you together as well," Malcolm Byzor pointed out. "It works both ways."

"Does it, now?" The voice seemed to soften with amusement. "I thought you were trying to stay apart from each other, to make it more difficult for our retrievers."

"Only until we got the playing field leveled," Byzor replied.

"You think this is now what you humans call a 'fair fight'?" The voice laughed. "What's to prevent me from simply taking the stones and disposing of *all* our evidence?" The emphasis was evident to everyone in the cave.

"I imagine that laser in Wilbur's hands is giving you second thoughts," Byzor replied. "And then, too, I'm assuming you still want all your evidence back."

The disembodied voice chuckled. "Detective Cellars, would you please take the stone necklace on the altar—the one with the heavier gold chain—and place it around the young Bancoo woman's neck?"

"Why would I want to do that?" Cellars asked.

"Perhaps because she was the last living member of her tribe, and it would be a fitting gesture?" the disembodied voice suggested.

"What about Lonecoos and Lastcoos . . . and her father?"

"We left them all in a tree, very near your Dr. Pleasant and Trooper Lee, until we have further use for them."

Cellars ignored the chills traveling up his spine. "She's the last member of a tribe you people created, to preserve your sanctuary . . . and then destroyed because you didn't want us poking around in their genetic history after you were gone."

"Be that as it may, please place the necklace around her neck, as you were told," the voice ordered. "Either for her sake, or Malcolm's."

"Why Malcolm?"

"I intend to satisfy his curiosity."

"Really?"

"Yes. As you said yourself, 'trust me.' "

"I have other plans, but I'll let Malcolm speak for himself," Cellars replied, finding it easier to keep his rage tightly controlled now that he knew there was no other choice.

"Let's humor the fellow for a few more minutes, Colin," Byzor suggested with what Cellars thought was an amazing sense of serenity under the circumstances.

Shrugging, Cellars handed the shotgun and detonator to Malcolm, drew the SIG-Sauer pistol out of his shoulder holster, and walked over to the altar—holding his left hand up to protect his eyes from the intense glare of the blue-green laser. He picked up the heavy gold chain and stone necklace, then started to turn back toward the cave entrance.

"No, over here," the disembodied voice ordered.

In some manner that wasn't apparent to Cellars, the faint lights in the ceiling shifted, creating a glowing circle around the sprawled body of Cascadia Rain-Song . . . that was now lying faceup on the cave floor, halfway between the altar and the spot where Bobby Dawson and Jody Catlin were standing.

Cellars walked over to the body, alert for the first sign of a shadowy lunge, knelt, and gently placed the stone necklace around the young Bancoo woman's blood-smeared neck. He steeled himself to ignore the savage wounds across her face.

"There's a small, hemispherical device on the ground next to her head, with a button in the center," the disembodied voice pointed out.

"Place the device over the stone, depress the button, hold it in place for two seconds to allow the adhesive around the edge to set, then step back. Oh, and Mr. Dawson, you and Ms. Catlin are welcome to move in closer, so you can get the full impact of our little demonstration."

As Bobby Dawson and Jody Catlin staggered forward, Cellars did as he was told, keeping the index finger of his right hand firm against the trigger of the vaguely comforting SIG-Sauer.

After a few seconds, an intense blue-green glow became visible behind the transparent adhesive seal around the edges of the hemispherical device.

Then, as Cellars and the others watched in stunned horror, the body of Cascadia Rain-Song began to fade away—

Much like the fuzzy image of Patrick Bergéone in the black-and-white photo, he realized numbly.

—only to reappear, suddenly, in the form of an equally beautiful woman, who lay sprawled on a bed of Cascadia Rain-Song's empty and flattened clothes, completely naked, blinking her eyes in confusion.

Allesandra.

In the darkness, an invisible feline creature growled her approval.

"As you can see, my dear friends, your crude laser is completely useless, because you can't possibly reanimate the stones without a source of material for all of the varying structures and fluids."

"Patrick Bergéone," Cellars whispered. "How—?"

"That's right, you have a picture, don't you?" The voice chuckled. "Leave the laser on, press your hand against one of the older stones, and find out for yourself."

"Turn it off, Wilbur," Malcolm Byzor said quietly.

"Shit," Wilbur Boggs muttered as he turned off the laser, set it down against the altar, then quickly picked up his shotgun.

As Colin Cellars continued to stand there, unable to speak, the beautiful woman rose to her feet, stared first at Jody Catlin, and then at Bobby Dawson.

"Hello, Bobby," she whispered in apparent delight.

"Hello, bitch. Nice to see you again . . . and keep your distance, or I'll gut you like a nice, fat bass," Dawson warned, the knife in his hand up and ready.

Allesandra's lips formed another smile that Colin Cellars could only interpret as pleasant anticipation.

Then she turned to Cellars with an altogether different smile of recognition.

"Hello, Colin," she whispered. "I'll bet you're glad to see me again."

She started to place her hands on his face . . . to the point that he could actually sense the heat from her approaching fingers . . . when the disembodied voice caused her to pause.

"Not now, Allesandra. You can play with them later. First, bring the stones to the ship. Start with the elders."

Seemingly oblivious of her naked state, Allesandra walked over to the altar, picked up the discarded Elmer Fudd doll, examined it curiously, then casually ripped the doll's head off and tossed it aside. After removing the doll's stuffing, she walked over to the small mountain of glowing stones, and began to place them, one by one, into the hollowed-out doll.

As she did so, Cellars quickly moved to where Dawson and Catlin were standing, bent down to scoop up Cascadia Rain-Song's jacket and clothes, then stood up and reached for Jody's dangling free arm.

Now that he was closer, he could see that she was just barely conscious, still bleeding from the nose and mouth.

"Quick," he whispered to Dawson, "get her down behind the altar." He tossed Cascadia Rain-Song's jacket over the containment jar, and then stepped forward with the rest of the clothes. "Here," he said in a normal voice, "let's use these clothes to wrap her up . . . and stop some of that bleeding. Malcolm, Wilbur, get over here and give us a hand."

The moment they had Jody stretched out on the rough stone floor beside the altar, Malcolm whispered, "Everybody keep your heads down, in case this doesn't work." Then, at the same instant, he stuck his left hand up over the edge of the massive stone altar, pressed the remote detonator button, and sharply smacked the barrel of the shotgun against the heavy stone.

The muffled crump of the contained C-4 explosion was completely masked by the echoing noise of the clanging metal.

"Hey, watch it, you're going to shoot somebody with that damned thing," Bobby Dawson yelled, shoving the shotgun aside. He started to stagger back to his feet with the bloody fighting knife still clenched in his right hand, but Cellars pushed him back.

I'm right. I know I'm right.

"No you don't, buddy," he said firmly, meeting Dawson's fearsome glare. "Fair is fair. This time, you get the girl . . . and I get to kill the bitch."

Then, before anyone could say anything, Cellars grabbed Wilbur Boggs's massive arm. "When you hear me say the word 'one,' " he said, "you stand up with that laser on full power, step to the side so you're not lined up on that pile of stones, aim it at their ship—it's gotta be out there on the other side of the cavern, somewhere—and keep it on the damned thing until something happens. But no matter what, everybody be ready to dive back down behind this chunk of stone when I yell 'two.' Got it?"

"Not a problem," Boggs growled.

"Colin, you're right . . . but let me—" Malcolm Byzor began, but Cellars shook him off. "No, it's gotta be me. I'm the only one she'll let get close enough."

Then, before any of the men crouched down behind the altar could say anything else, Cellars stood up and scooped Cascadia's jacket and the containment jar into a wrapped bundle—feeling the intense heat already starting to burn his hand through the layers of down jacket. He yelled, "Come on, let's get this show on the road. Get those things loaded so we can all go home."

The disembodied voice chuckled somewhere in the darkness, but Cellars ignored it as he walked toward Allesandra, who was coming back from the ship for another doll-load of stones.

"What do you say, lover," he said as he stopped less than a foot away from the gorgeous—and still-naked—woman who had been an inescapable part of his dreams for the past two months. "One more kiss for old times' sake?"

At that instant, an impossibly bright, blue-green laser beam shot across the cavern and then quickly centered on a huge, flat, disk-shaped object sitting at rest near the far cavern wall.

"No—don't!" Allesandra screamed as she spun around and stared at the huge ship—that was already starting to buckle outward from the internal pressure of hundreds of tiny, compressed metal-and-stone blocks that had suddenly begun to absorb metallic atoms from the ship and expand back out to their original uncompressed shapes.

Cellars sensed, out of the corner of his eye, a huge, dark, catlike shape lunging at Wilbur Boggs, and the bloodied form of Bobby Dawson suddenly in the way, grunting under the impact as the knife in his hand flashed upward in the blue-green glow of the laser beam. He never saw Jody rise up in a futile effort to try to help her fearless childhood friend.

Instead he heard her scream—first in horror and then in pain—as another dark, streaking cat-shape suddenly appeared from the opposite direction, taking her down . . . and then lunging back up at Dawson.

And then the roar of a 12-gauge pump shotgun in the hands of Malcolm Byzor.

And the crash of bodies tumbling on the rocky cavern floor.

And savage cursing, intermixed with a much-higher-pitched scream of feline rage and agony, as Bobby Dawson fought desperately for time—and for vengeance—with the wickedly sharp blade.

But the sounds barely registered in Colin Cellars's mind. His attention was focused on the ship that was starting to split open at its outer edge like a ripe seed, disgorging swords and shields and vehicles and what looked like the twisted shape of an Apache helicopter out onto the cavern floor . . . and on the remaining pile of stones that was beginning to shimmer.

The distinct odor of aviation fuel seemed to fill the cavern as Cellars threw the still-searing-hot containment jar and jacket as far as he could in the direction of the erupting ship; ignoring, as he did so, the screaming protest of the disembodied voice that echoed loudly in the darkness.

Then, in the next instant, knowing that there was no time left, he grabbed Allesandra around her upper torso with his left arm, extended the SIG-Sauer out under her right arm, screamed "Two, two, two!" and began firing at the distant, glowing bundle.

The first three shots either missed—or failed to crack the surface of the thick-walled jar—and Cellars had the sickening sensation of feeling Allesandra's body begin to change into something far more dangerous and sinister than he could possibly control . . . just as he saw the dark shadow of an impossibly large cat appear out of the darkness and lunge for the glowing bundle.

But the fourth, high-velocity, .40-caliber projectile struck the base of the jar . . . and the entire cavern seemed to erupt in an explosive roar that sent lethal polycarbonate fragments ripping into his exposed arms and Allesandra's still-shifting body . . . flinging both of them backward, over the altar, and into the cavern wall near the cave opening.

And that was the last thing that Colin Cellars remembered.

———

Except for the odd sensation of being winched out of a torn-open, rock-faced dome that—edge-on—appeared to be incredibly thin and fragile . . . in a snug and oddly comforting wire-framed gurney—by a blackened helicopter that seemed oddly devoid of markings, circling slowly in a strangely hypnotic black sky filled with a whirling mist of gently falling snowflakes.

And of being surrounded by the gently smiling faces of Jack Wilson, Melissa Washington, Cascadia Rain-Song, and Jody Catlin, all of whom seemed to be trying to reassure him that everything was going to be all right. While the sensuously glowing eyes of Allesandra seemed to be contemplating, in an amused and curious sort of way, what might have been . . . and what still might be at some later date.

But Colin Cellars would have to wait several more days for the far more solemn faces of Malcolm Byzor, Bobby Dawson, Wilbur Boggs, Sergeant Tom Bauer, and Captain Don Talbert to suddenly appear in the middle of his wildly imaginative, will-o'-the-wisp dreams, and hover beside his hospital bed to explain—in terribly sad and gruesome and yet fascinating detail—what parts of the story had been hallucinatory . . . and what had been real.

THE END

ABOUT THE AUTHOR

A former deputy sheriff, police forensic scientist, and crime lab director, Ken Goddard is currently the director of the National Fish and Wildlife Forensics Laboratory. His previous novels include *Balefire, The Alchemist, Prey, Wildfire, Cheater, Double Blind,* and *First Evidence.* Ken and his wife live in Ashland, Oregon.